FROM BLACK TO BLUE

(Book 2 of 7 in the Nostrils series)

Author: Jonathan Cox

First published March 2013

Publisher: JJ Cox Publishing Limited

All intellectual rights belong to the author.

This is a work of fiction and whilst influenced by the experiences and recollections of the author, no characters are based upon anyone living or dead and any similarities are purely coincidental. This book is sold on the condition that it is not re-sold, copied, or otherwise circulated without my prior consent. All intellectual and property rights belong to the author. This work has been registered with the Writers' Copyright Association (www.wcauk.com Registration #C104383)

The Nostrils Series

Book 1 – From Green to Blue

Book 2 – From Black to Blue

Book 3 – From Blue to Brown

Book 4 – When You Wear the Blue

Book 5 – We Don't Call Them Raids

Book 6 – A Necessary Fiction

Book 7 – Purple Cover

Chapter 1

It wasn't an easy decision to nick the money, but it was a quick one. With half a dozen people on their way to eighty-two Roundhouse Avenue, there wasn't a lot of time for prevarication.

I examined the unopened post, which had formed a pile on a coarse haired brown mat behind the front door, for evidence to justify my action and found it. From the dates on the postmarks at the bottom of the pile, I could work out that the old woman had been dead for at least four months.

All the correspondence was addressed to Miss Edith Mansfield, which, I assumed, meant she was a spinster and therefore had no children or grandchildren to lay claim to the small fortune I had discovered.

I found her date of birth on an old bus pass, she was ninety-seven. I noticed her birthday had been in November, some two months ago, so I returned to the pile of post and looked through it to see whether anyone had sent her a birthday card. They hadn't.

No one had missed her in four months. I felt kind of sad for the old girl, I really did, but what could I do?

I wasn't stealing the money because it had no owner and anyway if I'd booked it in at the nick it would just end up going to the government as there was no one to inherit it. I knew that much about the law of probate.

I'd have been really stupid not to take it, but don't think for a minute that I didn't know what I was doing was wrong. If I was caught, I'd be in one big pile of shit and probably looking at a good four years.

The old lady obviously had a system to ensure she put aside enough money for her household bills. She rolled up about twenty assorted bank notes and secured the bundle with an elastic band. Then, under the band, she slipped a small piece of paper on which she'd scribbled the words 'gas bill', 'water rates', or some other anticipated expense. There were about eighty bundles, and I quickly undid them all. Then I sorted the notes by denomination and laid them out flat. I didn't count them, as there'd be plenty of time for that later.

The biggest problem was that the notes had been rolled up for so long they fought to curl up at every opportunity. In the end, I had to roll the bundles in the opposite way several times to persuade them to straighten out.

Then I hid the money. I put the twenty and ten pound notes in my socks beneath the soles of my feet, and did my laces up loosely, to make extra space. I must have grown at least an inch but fortunately no one noticed. The rest, the fives and the ones I hid in the two deep inside pockets of my tunic.

With the money safely tucked away, I got on dealing with, what was, a very ordinary sudden death. I searched the rest of the house and was fascinated by a photograph album which tracked the old lady's life through the first half of the twentieth century. She'd been thirty-one when the First World War ended and fifty-seven on VE day, and there were pictures recording celebrations for both significant events. There was little else of value to seize in the house, only some pieces of jewellery and a purse with seven pounds in it.

The CID came, satisfied themselves that there were no suspicious circumstances, and went. The Divisional Surgeon arrived, pronounced Miss Mansfiled's life extinct, filled in his expenses form and left. The Duty Officer showed up, briefly, established that I didn't need any help, and left me to get on with it. And finally, the Undertakers turned up and took Miss Mansfield away in a black body bag.

As I left the address, I noticed that a flurry of snow had deposited a thin layer on the roof tops and pavements. It was cold and, as some thieving bastard had stolen my gloves from the PC's writing room, I plunged my hands deep into my overcoat pockets to keep them warm.

The cash was exactly what I needed to sort out my dire finances and I simply couldn't wait to count it out and see how much I had. I felt like a child on Christmas Eve.

Chapter 2

As I walked back to the nick, I heard Paul Pollock on my radio doing a car check and his voice bought me back to reality.

The money would sort out one of my problems but not the one I had with Paul. He was one of the more mature PC's on our relief, forty-two years old, ruggedly good looking, charismatic and living with the lovely, and much younger, Sarah Starr.

Sarah had been a model before she joined the job and, within a year of her arrival at Stokey, Paul had left his missus and three kids and moved in with her.

Overwhelmed at first by feelings of guilt, he'd given everything to his wife; the house, the contents of the house, the family car, their apartment in Minorca, their savings and most of his monthly salary. Over the next year, and with increasing desperation, he unsuccessfully tried to claw some of this back. His bitterness and legal bill grew with each solicitor's letter.

Having lost everything, only one thing kept Paul from going over the edge, and that was the knowledge he had the most attractive WPC who'd ever worked at Stoke Newington nick. The problem was, he didn't.

Sarah and I had been posted together for the month of December and we'd worked really well as a team. We were posted together again for January and, within a week, we were having an affair.

That Sarah was interested in me said more about her own unhappiness than it did about my desirability, because good looking I wasn't. At first, she'd talked about Paul as if everything was hunky dory, but after a short, while she started moaning.

Her problem was, whilst she'd been happy enough having a bit of a fling with him, she'd never wanted or anticipated that he would leave his wife. Then, after only a few months and completely out of the blue, he turned up at her flat one evening with his suitcase in hand.

Sarah was presented with a fait accompli and Paul moved in. It was alright at first but six months later, she found herself trapped with a man nearly twice her age, who drank too much and constantly complained about having no money and not being able to see his kids.

All I did was listen.

Sarah was a good listener too, and sometimes I needed to talk about Dawn, about what had happened that July afternoon in 1983 when I'd been blown up in an IRA bombing and, my partner and friend, Dawn Matthews had died in my arms.

The bombing had left me with several nasty, but not life threatening, injuries. These included a four-inch gash to my head requiring thirty stitches, two badly burst ear drums, a broken right cheek, a broken jaw, and an injury to my right hand which, because it kept getting infected, took the longest of all my ailments to mend.

I was only off work for three months and people said I was mad going back so soon but I was going crazy stuck at home. Home? Home was now Stoke Newington Section House.

I'd missed Dawn's funeral because I was still in hospital. She had the full works; the Met flag over the coffin, the Met band playing Amazing Grace. It was on the news, and I briefly saw Dawn's Mum dressed in black and sobbing into a white handkerchief.

At first, I got a regular flow of visitors. The Commissioner came, and then Deputy Assistant Commissioner Denis Farrington-Smythe, which even in my battered state, made me smile. The little Chief Superintendent came several times and always stunk of booze. The Campbells popped up, always happy, cheerful, and very mischievous. As the weeks passed however my visitors faded away, it was only natural, and I didn't take it personally. There was only one guy that kept coming, who never let me down, who sorted everything out for me, like moving my stuff from Dawn's Mum's place to the Section House. That guy was Andy Welling.

After the bombing my attitude to life had changed dramatically and this manifested itself primarily in the way I spent money. Whereas before, I'd been really careful, after it, if I wanted something I just bought it.

As a consequence, I had a brand-new Ford XR2, fully loaded and colour coded; the newest TV and Dolby stereo system; a wardrobe full of designer clothing; a Tag watch and Ray-Ban sunglasses.

I also had an overdraft which was frightening, and my monthly loan repayments were only a couple of hundred less than my take home pay.

The bombing did, however, assist me in one regard, or perhaps it would be more accurate to say I used, or rather, abused it. About a month ago, Sarah and I were parked up in Golf November four five, one of the panda cars, by the River Lea, and, as usual, we were deep in conversation.

"Can I ask you a really personal question?" Sarah said.

"Of course, you can." I replied, a little surprised that she thought she had to seek permission.

"Did you and Dawn sleep together? There were rumours at the time and afterwards."

"No, no. I would have, I fancied her like mad, but she didn't fancy me and, of course, she was quite a lot older." I replied.

As soon as the words left my mouth, I realised I'd been rather tactless.

"There's nearly twenty years between Paul and me." Sarah said.

"Yeah, I know, sorry, I didn't mean …"

I didn't finish the sentence and we sat in silence for a few moments.

"I wish I had slept with Dawn." I said quietly, sensing the tiniest of opportunities.

"Do you?" Sarah asked.

"Yeah, you see ... oh it doesn't matter." I said, setting the trap.

"Go on, out with it." Sarah encouraged me.

"No, it's really embarrassing." I said.

"No secrets remember, we made a pact, we can tell each other anything." Sarah declared.

"Since the bombing, I haven't been able to have sex."

It was a complete and utter lie. Jessica Campbell had been playing with my cock under the sheets, whilst I was lying in my hospital bed, not a week after the bombing.

"Why, were you injured?" Sarah asked.

"No, it's nothing physical. It's just I've never met anyone who really understands me, you know after what happened."

"I understand you." She whispered.

And that was all it took.

Now though, on this cold February morning four weeks later, I had a serious problem. Any time now, Paul was bound to discover the woman for whom he'd given up everything, was shagging someone behind his back. To compound matters, she wasn't seeing someone of any standing, like the DCI or Superintendent, or even a DS from Special Branch. She was seeing me, a twenty-one-year-old, uniform PC, who was still in his probation, and who had little more credibility in terms of competition for your stunning girlfriend than the Garage Hand.

Chapter 3

When we came on duty, we always paraded in the Collator's office, which was on the ground floor at one end of the building, but going off duty, we gathered in the PC's writing room by the Station Office, and it was here I sat, that February afternoon, my pockets and shoes stuffed with cash.

Sarah's boyfriend Paul and several others were there too. I'd become really sensitive to every interaction with Paul, whenever we were in the same room, I carefully watched his body language and mannerisms for any clue that he suspected me. That afternoon Paul was his usually chatty self, so I assumed everything was sweet. Sarah was tucked up somewhere with an RTA.

Paul was probably the oldest officer, and certainly the strongest personality, on our relief; as far as I knew, everyone liked and respected him. His position as top dog was reinforced by two credentials, which were highly prized amongst his peers; he was an area car driver, which meant he was qualified to drive the Division's most powerful police cars, and he was an authorised firearms officer.

In some ways, he was like a Sergeant without stripes and influenced those around him, but not always for the good. He was sound old bill and still took his fair share of bodies, but he was a bit punchy, and prisoners didn't have to say much to get a slap.

He'd raised a few eyebrows when he walked out on his wife and three kids, not because anyone had any moral issues about his actions, but because, financially, the decision would destroy him.

When I joined the relief from Street Duties, unlike most of the others, Paul had been friendly and given me a few of his bodies to help me settle in. It was a nice gesture, particularly as he was under no obligation to do it. I liked Paul, I really did, but I liked his girlfriend more.

"Another sudden death, Nostrils? What is it about you? Every time you leave the nick, somebody in Stoke Newington drops dead." Paul said.

Lately, I'd been getting more than my fair share of sudden deaths to deal with.

"This one died in the summer, Paul; she was practically a skeleton."

"No mouth to mouth, then? I bet you were disappointed." Paul said, with typical police humour.

"Gutted." I replied, and a few people laughed.

"Didn't you take that sudden death, yesterday?" Matt asked, a tall thin ginger haired PC, a few years older than me.

"Yeah, seventy-year-old Greek lady who dropped dead outside the big furniture store just down the road. I had to do mouth to mouth for ages." I replied.

"Did you slip her the tongue, Nostrils?" Paul said.

"Well, she was gagging for it." I replied.

"What woman wouldn't be with you? It probably made dropping dead at ten o'clock on a Wednesday morning entirely worth her while. You sex machine, Nostrils." Paul said.

The remark made me feel really uncomfortable but fortunately Sergeant Key chose that moment to walk in, conduct a quick roll call and dismiss us. As I stood up, I collected a handful of elastic bands which I'd found in the top drawer of a vacant desk. Out of habit, I went to unbutton my jacket as I always did at the end of the day, but remembered the money stuffed in the pockets and left it fastened.

I didn't have a locker in the nick anymore because I lived in the Section House, so I made my way across the backyard to the multi-storied 1960s building that was my home.

I noticed Sarah parking her panda car and, as I walked by, she winked at me and smiled. I wanted to go over and have a chat with her, but it wouldn't be wise with Paul about to emerge any second, so I just smiled back and kept walking.

Sarah was tall, nearly six foot, blonde, slim, and stunning. Even in her uniform she could turn heads, and everywhere she went, eyes followed her. She was slightly older than me, but half Paul's age, so he was taking a real gamble leaving a happy home for her. I enjoyed our clandestine relationship, but I kept my emotions in check as I knew I really couldn't afford to fall in love. Sarah was too good for me, and deep inside, I knew that. We'd been thrown together by a combination of circumstances, and I was making the most of the situation, whilst it lasted.

As I walked into the Section House, I got collared by Sergeant Bellamy who reminded me I owed six weeks' dues. Although technically our accommodation was rent free, we paid a small service fee, which went towards the rates, cleaners and general maintenance.

Sergeant Bellamy had been in charge of my Street Duties course, but right at the end, he'd had a heart attack and, when he returned to work, he'd been given the easiest job at the nick, that of Section House Sergeant. In this role, he had about an hour's work a week, so he whiled away the days by reading the Sun newspaper, selecting his gee gees and chatting to everyone as they came and went. He was a nice chap and as part of his recovery, he'd lost about six stone, but it left him with folds of skin on his chin and upper arms. When people called him 'Skinny', he took it as a compliment and laughed, in fact, they were being a bit mean, or so I thought. I always called him Sarge. Sergeant Bellamy and I shared an unbreakable bond; both of us in our own way had loved Dawn Matthews.

"Listen Nostrils, I don't want to do this but, if I don't get it soon, I'm going to have to do a report to the Chief Super to cover myself 'cos I've got the Auditors in next week."

"Sarge, I've got it. I went to the bank this morning. I'll pop upstairs and come back with what I owe. I'll front up for a couple of months in advance too, if you like."

"Bloody hell Nostrils; you suddenly come into money? Or have you sold your XR2?"

Suddenly come into money? Sold my XR2? I realised I was going to need a cover story to explain why I was suddenly much better off.

"I got a few grand through from my Mum's estate. Because she never made a will, it's taken years to sort out." I replied, thinking quickly.

"Good for you, Nostrils; you lucky bastard."

"Yeah, really lucky, but I think I'd rather have my Mum."

"Yeah, of course you would, mate. I'll tell you what, you can have mine. She's seventy-four and completely doolally tat."

"I'll stick if you don't mind but thanks for the offer." I replied, jovially.

I was really keen to get upstairs to my room and count the money, so I cut the Sergeant off.

"I'm knackered, Sarge. I'll get an hour's kip and be down with the dues."

"Don't leave town, Nostrils." Sergeant Bellamy called after me, as I took the stairs two at a time.

Chapter 4

I lived on the third floor, opposite Rik Patel, a lovely guy who I'd first met on my selection day at Paddington Green; and next to Andy Welling, a black PC and my best friend. Rik was at Holloway and Andy at Stoke Newington, but they were both on the same shift pattern, which was different to mine.

All the women fancied Andy and Rik fancied all the women, which was ironic really because Andy was gay and Rik, as a Paki, had no chance of pulling a girl that wasn't from his own race. I know it drove him mad, and we talked about it frequently, but the fact was white women just didn't go for Asian men, not unless they were Imran Khan. No one tried harder than Rik to pull women and his chat up lines were a running joke amongst the three of us.

"Get your coat love you've pulled."

"What makes love like a tiger and winks?"

"I love that dress, but it would look better on my bedroom floor."

Rik had delivered them all and each, in its turn, had failed. He confided in us that a few months ago, out of sheer desperation to lose his virginity before his twenty-first birthday, he'd paid a classy prostitute a small fortune and spent the night with her in a fancy hotel in Kensington. I can't say I blamed him.

That Andy was gay was a secret he shared with few people because the Met was full of homophobes, a feature I attributed to the fact that so many officers were ex-military. I don't think any of them were card carrying queer bashers, but I wouldn't bet my newfound wealth on it.

The three of us were good mates and people called us the United Nations, not just because we were from different racial backgrounds but because we never actually did anything but sit around talking all the time, or so Sergeant Bellamy once told me.

My small Section House room was very ordinary with a single bed and a thin mattress, dark brown carpet tiles, which kept coming unattached, a pine desk, wardrobe, and a sink.

I'd broken my chair mucking about with Andy and one of the legs was really loose, but I fixed it, so it looked okay to avoid getting fined for the damage; though woe betide anyone who sat on it.

I knew both Andy and Rik were on night duty, so I didn't let my door slam, but I did double lock it. I took the continental quilt off the bed because I wanted to count the money on the mattress and, if anyone came to the door, which was unlikely but not impossible, I could quickly throw the quilt over the cash and my room would look perfectly normal.

When I had left at five-thirty that morning it was still dark, so I walked over and pulled the curtains back as far as they would go to let some light in. My room overlooked the back yard, which was a bit of a pain in the arse, as police cars often left the nick on blues and twos at all hours so it wasn't uncommon to be woken up several times a night. I thought I'd get used to it but never had.

When I glanced down, I saw Sarah leaving with Paul. As they walked through the open back gates, Paul took her hand. I watched them as they turned right and went down the side road towards Sarah's car. Just before she went too far, Sarah turned briefly and looked up at my window. She must have seen me standing there, but before I could wave, they'd passed out of my sight.

I dropped the selection of elastic bands on my desk and my latest Barclaycard bill caught my eye. I picked it up, opened it, checked the date, and calculated that my payment was now five weeks overdue. For the first time in ages, I read the total amount outstanding, two thousand eight hundred and something. The minimum monthly repayment, which is all I ever looked at, was two hundred and forty-four quid.

I took my boots off and placed the twenties and tens on the bed. I got undressed and, in the process, dug out the fives and ones. I counted the ones, one hundred and four, then the fives, eighty-nine, the tens, one hundred and fifty-two and, saving the best to last, the twenties, one hundred and eighty-seven. I wrote the sum on the back of the credit card bill and added it up, a grand total of five thousand eight hundred and nine pounds.

My money worries were a thing of the past. With this I could pay off my credit card, overdraft, and half of my outstanding car loan.

I experienced an enormous sense of relief, and it was only then I realised how much the debts had been playing on my mind. I slumped down on the bed and thought that, at long last, things seemed to be going my way.

But I had to be careful and clever. I couldn't just pay off everything because anyone looking at my finances would ask where I'd got the money. I could run the line that I'd inherited some from Mum but, of course, that wouldn't stand up to scrutiny if anyone checked. What's more, if I had got the money in that way, it would be paid by a solicitor directly into my bank account and not given to me in cash. My cover story would hold if I kept everything low key and no one saw the cash.

What could I do with the money, then? In the short term I had to stash it away. I couldn't keep it in my Section House room and, although keeping it in my car, was a better option, it still wasn't great. For one, my car could get stolen and two, if anyone did search my car and find it, I'd be bang to rights. I had to find somewhere neutral, where no one else would find it but just in case they did, they couldn't attribute it to me. It had to be somewhere which afforded me relatively easy access. I decided to have a punt around the nick and Section House to see if I could locate such a place, but returned half an hour later, having failed to do so.

Then I realised there wasn't a note I hadn't handled at least twice and therefore my fingerprints would be all over them. I looked around the room for my uniform gloves before remembering someone had had them off.

I decided, quite literally, to bury the money until I was absolutely certain there was no investigation into its disappearance. I removed a century and packed the rest into a carrier bag and hid it temporarily in the U bend underneath my sink.

I then went down the High Street and purchased a metal cash tin, a spade, a pair of rubber gloves, washing up liquid and a cloth.

Wearing the gloves, I thoroughly wiped both sides of each note with a damp cloth soaked in warm water and washing up liquid. Then I dried each one out using a hand towel. If anyone was going to find my fingerprints on them, they were going to be extremely lucky. The process had the additional advantages of cleaning the notes which made them look less scabby and flattening them out too. It took me nearly three hours but was worth every second.

By eight o'clock that evening, I was sipping a pint in the White Hart pub in Stoke Newington High Street and the money, like an East End grass who'd been caught whispering, was buried in Epping Forest.

Chapter 5

I really struggled to sleep that night because I was excited but there was something else tugging away at the back of my mind. When I did eventually drop off, I was dogged with dreams of the old lady and her money. In the middle of the night, I woke needing the toilet and whilst I stood there pissing in the small hand basin in my room, which we male Section House residents used as an en-suite urinal, I pictured the mud encrusted tool in the back of my car and the receipt for the money box and spade which was still in my wallet.

I'd been seriously stupid; it wouldn't take Sherlock Holmes to work out what I'd done with the money. Even though it was four in the morning, I got up and sorted both issues out.

I tore up the receipt into tiny pieces which I threw away in several different places.

Although I knew I'd need the spade again, I couldn't risk keeping it. I mean, what reason would a Section House resident have for keeping a garden spade? So, I dumped it in someone's front garden, as it was brand new, I was confident the resident or a passer-by would soon procure the item and, when I looked later, it had gone.

When I was disposing of the evidence, I realised I'd made another idiotic mistake. Why oh why had I paid off my Section House dues? An error which I then compounded by telling the lie about inheriting Mum's money. If I'd been shrewd, I would have continued going into arrears. Sergeant Bellamy's report to the Chief Superintendent would have been strong supporting evidence to suggest I hadn't stolen any money.

As it was now, if anyone made enquiries, they'd discover, not only did I pay off six months' dues, but I'd also paid three in advance. And I'd done so, only hours after the money went missing!

When questioned, Sergeant Bellamy, being the decent fellow he is, would say 'Oh Nostrils hasn't stolen any money, he told me he'd inherited it'. This lie would of course unravel as soon as I was asked to provide details of the solicitor dealing with the probate.

I'd been rash and foolish, and knew I needed to sharpen up or I'd go down for sure.

At half four I got back into bed to try to get another hour's sleep, but I was restless and wide awake and soon found myself getting up to shower.

As I walked back to my room, I bumped into Andy.

"What you doing back so early?" I asked.

"I've just looked in the nine forty, I'm in bloody court tomorrow."

"Where? When?" I asked.

"Old Street at ten-thirty. Skipper told me to get a few hours." Andy replied.

"I won't keep you then, mate." I said and went to go into my room.

"Hang on, Nostrils; I got a question. What were you doing leaving the nick an hour ago carrying a spade?"

I was certain no one had seen me, so I was completely stumped by the question. In the second I had to answer, my mind raced for a plausible explanation.

"Didn't I tell you?"

"Tell me what?"

"I had no choice. I've had to murder Paul. It's left the way clear for Sarah and me. His body's been in the back of my car for the last week but it's starting to smell so I thought I'd bury him in Epping Forest."

"I've got to be up in three hours, I haven't got time for this bullshit." Andy said, impatiently.

He slipped his key in the door and went inside his room.

"Night." I called after him.

Chapter 6

I was early turn Assistant Station Officer and took over from the night duty guy at half five. He couldn't believe his luck, getting away so early, but I was up anyway so, what the hell! I thought it was quite fortuitous that I was working at the front counter that day because, if anyone did come in to complain about some money being stolen from the old lady's house, I'd be the one to take the initial allegation, which would allow me to find out exactly what I was up against.

The first caller at the counter was a man who'd lost a Cavalier King Charles Spaniel. I had good news and bad news for him, the dog had been found and handed in the previous evening but, according to the Dog Book, it had escaped overnight whilst being fed by the Night Duty Station Officer. He didn't seem very pleased, and I can't say I blamed him. I couldn't quite understand how a dog could escape whilst being fed because there was a small hatch in the kennel door to pass the bowl through; I'd done it several times myself. I apologised repeatedly, assured him that his dog would turn up very soon, and took his telephone number so I could contact him when it did. He stormed off in a huff after writing down my shoulder number and saying he was going to complain.

I'd been at the counter for another half an hour when a young paperboy came running in.

"There's a house on fire over the road, there's an old man trapped upstairs, please hurry."

I jumped over the front counter and told him to take me there. That was my first mistake because, within seconds, I realised I should've grabbed a radio, but the young lad was stopping for no-one. He ran across the High Street, down a road opposite and then turned right. I followed only a few feet behind.

About fifty yards along on the left, smoke poured from a terraced house and, at an open upstairs window, an old white man, wearing a string vest, leaned out dangerously far in an effort to breathe clean air; he was calling for help. I noticed immediately that his eye sockets were peculiar and, when I looked more closely, saw they were hollow, the man was completely blind.

The front door was on the left and, I knew from entering similar houses, would open almost straight onto the stairs. The front room was to the right and looking through the window the seat of the fire seemed to be against the right-hand wall and bright yellow flames were clearly visible stretching up towards the ceiling.

I was annoyed that I'd come out without a radio, what was I thinking off? I told the paperboy to go back to the nick, get someone to call the fire brigade, and to get more officers. I knew I had to try to get in. When I put my hands against it, the front door felt unnaturally warm. I pushed at the top, middle and bottom trying to ascertain where it was locked and bolted. I was encouraged when it seemed only the middle was secured. There was no time for delay, so I put my shoulder to the door with considerable force. It sprung open.

It was the first time a door had opened so easily and, having not expected it to, I fell into the hallway coming to rest on my hands and knees at the foot of the stairs. I didn't think and took a breath, my lungs filled with burning smoke. I moved quickly back outside coughing and spluttering. I looked up. If the old man leant any further out of the window he'd fall. Above his head deep black smoke billowed out and up into the early morning clear blue sky.

"Help! Help!" He called, desperately.

I took several really deep breaths and then sprinted in and up the stairs taking them two at a time. On the landing I turned back on myself and ran into the front bedroom. The smoke was burning my eyes and making them run but I knew I'd be all right as long as I didn't breathe in. I put my arms around the old man's chest and lifted him up. He weighed very little but started to pull back against me in an attempt to get his head back out of the window. I wanted to tell him that I was a policeman and that I was going to get him out of the house, but that would use all the air in my lungs, and I'd have to breathe again, and then I'd be in trouble. I yanked him unceremoniously backwards, turned him round and lifted him up onto my shoulder in what I knew was called a fireman's lift. I'd never done it before, but it seemed very natural under the circumstances.

My lungs were hurting no, and I had the strongest desire to breathe. I hesitated for a moment as I considered leaning out of the window to take a few clean breaths before making my way down, but I'd just got the old man in a perfect position. I made my decision and moved as quickly as I could.

When I got to the top of the stairs and looked down, I could see flames were now reaching from underneath around the stairs and wondered momentarily whether, if the staircase was on fire, it would support our weight. Go now or go back and hope the fire brigade arrived before we're burnt to death? I went down slowly, the urge to breathe almost insuppressible and, several times the muscles in my chest and throat refluxed, as if gasping for air.

Just as I was getting tunnel vision and felt like I was about to pass out, I was out. I dropped the old man abruptly on the pavement and fell to my knees, panting rapidly to replace the missing oxygen. My lungs still felt quite sore from my initial inhalation of smoke.

When I looked back inside the house, not fifteen seconds after I'd got out, the stairs were engulfed in flames and completely impassable. Although the whole adventure had taken less than a minute, I'd literally made it out with only seconds to spare. If I'd delayed to pick up a radio before I'd left the nick, I'd now be trapped.

The old man was shaking, coughing and spluttering but otherwise seemed unhurt.

"Are you ok?" I asked.

"Yes, thank you, thank you so much. You saved my life." He stuttered, between breaths.

When I helped the old man leave the premises, as I got my breath back, and for no earthly reason that made any sense at all, a vision of the money buried in the forest came to mind. My thoughts were jolted back to the present when the old man starting speaking.

"I knocked the electric fire over; I'm blind, you see." He replied.

"Are you injured, Mr, what's your name Sir?" I asked.

I put my hand on his arm.

"Wheatley, my name's Jim, Jim Wheatley."

"Are you injured Mr Wheatley, are you burnt, at all?"

"No, no I'm not, thanks to you. Are you a fireman?" He asked.

"No Mr Wheatley, I'm a policeman."

"Well thank you, whoever you are, you saved my life." He said, his voice bursting with emotion.

I felt somehow strange, confused, like something wasn't quite right but the feeling only lasted a second. In the distance I could hear a siren.

"Stay here, Mr Wheatley. I need to warn your neighbours in case the fire spreads."

I knocked first at the house on the right, but they'd obviously already noticed because almost immediately four of them, Mum, Dad and two teenage children, appeared in dressing gowns and slippers.

From the house on the other side, I could get no reply, although I'd knocked really loudly, so I assumed the house was empty or the occupiers had already gone to work. I thought I'd better check with Mr Wheatley.

"Mr Wheatley, who lives next door at number forty-two?"

He pointed at the wrong house.

"No, the other side of you" I said.

He looked confused.

"Mr Wheatley, can you remember who lives at number forty-two, not the white family with the two teenage daughters, they live at forty-six, the other side. Please try to remember?"

"I'm sorry, I don't know. It used to be Mrs Tipler, but she moved the year of the Silver Jubilee." He replied.

Whilst I was still deciding what to do, three police officers, Sergeant Felix, Bob and the lovely Sarah, came running down the street, being led by the young paperboy.

"Are you or the gentleman injured?" Sergeant Felix asked, immediately.

"No Sarge, we're fine; the family who live there have been evacuated but I can't get any reply at forty-two and Mr Wheatley here can't remember who lives there."

"Will there be anything left of my home son?" Mr Wheatley, asked quietly.

Before I could reply, a fire engine pulled into the street with its siren screaming and I was grateful I didn't have to answer Mr Wheatley's question. I looked up at the still open window which had been Mr Wheatley's refuge, yellow and orange flames were now clearly visible where he had been standing.

Mr Wheatley and I relocated fifty yards further along the road and I watched the fire crew disembark and go about their perfectly orchestrated business. In no time at all, they had the fire under control and, a few minutes later, it was out completely.

As they were busy doing this, two other firemen broke into forty-two with an axe, making light of the thick wooden door, and saving Sarah and Bob a lot of hard work.

I chatted to Mr Wheatley, trying to keep his spirits up, but he just couldn't stop thanking me for what I'd done.

"It was a pleasure, Mr Wheatley. Is there anyone we can contact for you?" I asked.

"Yes please, my daughter." He replied.

"Where does she live?" I asked.

"Forest Hill; I can give you her telephone number." Mr Wheatley replied.

The forefinger of his right hand turned semi-circles as if he were dialing the phone number and he rattled it off quickly.

"Two nine one, four four four two."

I wrote it down in my notebook and, using Sarah's radio, called the station and asked them to do a 'please allow'.

Sergeant Felix came over and called Sarah and me to one side.

"Listen, you two. In a minute, the Fire Brigade will go into the house to see if they can ascertain the cause of the fire and I'm sure, confirm it as non-suspicious. Go with them and don't let them out of your sight; they're all thieving bastards."

Chapter 7

Sarah and I went inside the damp, smoldering ruins which, when he'd got up that morning, had been Mr Wheatley's lifelong home. We watched the firemen like hawks to make sure they didn't steal anything. If they were perturbed by our vigilance, they never let it show.

We recovered what we guessed were some of Mr Wheatley's most important possessions; his war medals, a bundle of old letters and family photographs, an old gold watch and a worn wedding ring, which were on his bedside table.

I knew he wouldn't be able to see the photographs or read the letters, but I suspected they were still important to him, so we put them into a plastic bag.

"Is there anything else we can get?" I asked, as I placed the bag into his hand.

He shook his head.

"You've got a lot of medals there." I commented.

"I fought in two wars son, but I never did anything braver than you did just then when you rescued me."

"I've told you Mr Wheatley, it was nothing. Now there's a police car here that's going to take you over to your daughter's. She's been told what's happened and is expecting you."

"Thank you, son." He said and I shook his outstretched hand.

We helped him into the panda, and he set off.

"So, what did you do that was so brave?" Asked Sarah, as we started to walk back to the nick.

"Nothing really." I said modestly.

"Go on, did you fight your way through flames to carry him out of the burning building?" She asked, half-jokingly.

Then something really strange happened, I lied.

"Don't be silly, nothing like that, at all."

It wasn't strange that I told a lie; I did that quite a lot. What was unusual was that I'd lied under those circumstances. Why didn't I want to take credit for what I'd done? It didn't make any sense, but I didn't, I *really* didn't, and such a modest attitude wasn't like me.

Sarah and I took an elongated route back to the nick, as it gave us an opportunity to chat and to plan our next clandestine meeting.

"I've got some really good news." She said.

"That's what I like to hear." I replied.

"Paul's been posted to jury protection. He's likely to be away from the relief for months and he'll be working twelve-hour shifts, six or seven days a week. It'll give me a break 'cos quite frankly he's driving me mad, and we'll have much more opportunity to see each other."

"What exactly does jury protection entail?" I asked.

I heard others refer to it and, when they did, the sentence normally started with the words 'I earned a fortune on jury protection …"

"It's a team they set up to protect members of a jury from being got at by the defendants. It's quite rare and only used when the defendants are serious criminals who have the capability to intimidate. They have to be armed which is why Paul's gone. They follow around who ever they're assigned to protect. If you get someone quite busy, with an interesting life, it can be a really good job. If he goes out for a meal in a top London restaurant, you go too. I mean you don't sit with them, that would be completely against the rules, but you sit at a nearby table and have a meal, courtesy of the Commissioner. If they go to the cinema, you go too. Of course, if you get Mr or Mrs Boring then you end up just sitting outside their house. Paul will be working twelve hours a day, it'll be heaven."

"Twelve-hour days? He'll earn loads of overtime. He must be delighted." I commented.

"You'd think so, wouldn't you? But all he can think about is that he's got to give half of any overtime he earns to the ex."

"How's the divorce settlement going?"

"Don't ask. His wife stays in the house, gets the car and he has to pay her four hundred a month. He retains a fifty percent share of the house, but it hasn't got to be sold until their youngest finishes full time education and she's only three. They've got to sell their place in Minorca and split the equity, but that'll only be a few grand, by the time the mortgage's paid off. To make matters worse, his ex is now seeing some guy who works in the city and earns a fortune, but as long as he doesn't actually move into the family home, it doesn't affect the settlement."

"So, he's completely screwed then?" I asked.

"Completely; and so am I, Chris. What the hell am I going to do? He's such a miserable bastard." Sarah said.

"He doesn't seem too bad at work. I mean he's cheerful enough and always quite chatty with me." I commented.

"He likes you Chris, but he's on the edge, really on the edge. If I finish it with him, I'm frightened it'll tip him over."

"If you're not going to be with him in a year's time, then it's best to do it now, don't you think?"

"It's complicated." She replied.

"Do you think he's got any idea about us?" I asked.

"No, I really don't. My best mate knows, you know, Brenda, but she's not in the Met. Have you told anyone?"

"No." I lied, as I had in fact told Andy, but I knew my secret was safe with him.

"Sarah?"

"Yes?"

"Are you still sleeping with Paul?" I asked.

"The odd sympathy shag and the occasional pity blow job. I don't think he's particularly bothered, Chris, and he struggles to get an erection these days because of the amount he's drinking. Sometimes, when he's had too much to drink, he tells me things that I just don't want to hear; horrible things that keep me awake at night."

"What sort of things? You mean about him and his wife?

She shook her head.

"It's a real mess, Chris, and I need out before I get sucked in."

"It can't be that bad, can it?" I asked.

"You've no idea."

"What is it?" I asked, getting a bit frustrated.

She shook her head.

"Jesus, Sarah, if it's that bad, for fuck's sake leave him." I said.

"He might kill himself." She replied.

"Bollocks, Sarah, he won't." I asserted.

"You don't know what I know."

"How can I, if you don't tell me?"

"Let it go, Chris."

We walked in awkward silence for a hundred yards. In an attempt to lighten the conversation, I joked.

"I will rescue you from the evil Sheriff of Nottingham, Maid Marion, just say the word."

"You? Robin Hood? I don't think so, Chris. You're more like..."

"Who?" I asked, curiously.

"Danger Mouse." Sarah said, breaking into a smile.

I laughed too.

"What you doing, later, Chris? Do you want to meet up?"

"Sure, but I'm going to put some flowers on Dawn's grave this afternoon and I can't be late because it's dark at five." I said.

"Oh god, Chris, you've never been there, have you?" Sarah said.

"No Sarah, never, but the time has come. It won't be easy, but you know, I want to."

"Do you want me to come with you? Where is it?" She asked.

"Her grave is at a church in Buckhurst Hill. I want to go alone, if you don't mind. If I'm being honest, I think I'll probably get a bit upset." I replied.

"You don't have to be embarrassed about being upset in front of me, Chris, not after what you've been through." She said, sympathetically.

"I know; I mean, I won't cry or anything, but, you know, I want to be alone with her. Perhaps have a chat, like say sorry for not coming, tell her there's not an hour goes by in any day when I don't think about her." I said.

"I understand. Anyway, can you give me a lift home? Paul's taken my car to a briefing at Snaresbrook."

"Only if you promise to give me a blow job." I said jokingly.

"Deal." She replied.

Chapter 8

We walked on for a few minutes and rounded a corner, only to be met by the most dreadful throbbing music, coming from a black Golf GTI, double parked in the road, about thirty yards ahead. The hazard lights, or as we called them in the job, the 'park anywhere lights' were on, and, as we got nearer, I could see no-one was in the vehicle.

Although cars could pass, a larger vehicle, like an ambulance or fire engine, would really struggle. What's more the music was so loud anyone within ten houses, in either direction, was having their quality of life seriously impaired.

It was so loud I had to walk back round the corner to do a vehicle check, otherwise I wouldn't have been able to hear the reply. What a surprise, no current keeper. It was the habit of the local community, and by that, I mean the young black community, not to register ownership of their cars with the DVLA, thereby escaping liability for most traffic offences; and it also made insuring and taxing your car just an optional extra. The punishment for failing to notify the DVLA was a non-endorsable £25 fine so, quite frankly, I couldn't blame them. If I hadn't been in the job, I suspect I'd have adopted the same approach.

When I got back to the vehicle, Sarah shouted above the racket that she'd called at all the nearby houses to trace the driver but without success. She suspected the guy in number thirty-three because the bloke who'd answered the door had a load of attitude.

"Well in that case, I fear the car might be stolen." I said, indicating to Sarah my intention to gain access to the vehicle.

"That's funny, 'cos so do I." She replied, signaling her consent for what I was about to do.

Although Sarah had six months more service than me and was therefore, in the well-defined pecking order, my senior, we'd worked together a lot and, by and large, I led the way in situations like this.

I removed my helmet because inside I kept a length of blue tape, the kind used to secure bundles of newspapers and such like. I folded it over to give it strength and slipped it through the gap where the driver's door meets the frame. After a little manipulation, I worked it inside the car and then, feeding more of the tape but from one side only, formed a loop, which I put over the little plastic catch, which you pushed down to lock the door from inside. Then I lifted the tape up at an angle. It took several attempts but, eventually, it caught the small lip and unlocked the door. I had done this plenty of times, but the newer cars were now being made with a smooth, and much shorter, catch and on these, the trick didn't work.

I reached inside, turned the music off and flicked the bonnet open.

My plan worked, as I suspected we were being watched, and, within seconds, our actions had flushed the driver out, a black man, in his early twenties with impressive dreadlocks, although I confess to missing exactly from which house he emerged.

"What you doing?" He asked, aggressively.

"Is this your car, Sir?" I said, the epitome of politeness.

"Yeah, what you doing?" He replied.

"Are you the registered keeper?" I said, knowing, of course, there was no registered keeper, so whatever he said I had him.

"It's my car." He replied, not falling into the trap.

"Did you park it here?" I asked.

He sucked his teeth, about as rude a gesture as he could make. I knew this was going to be really confrontational, but quite honestly, you couldn't let that stop you or you'd never leave the nick.

There was no love lost between the young black community and us. In fact, I'd go further than that, we hated one another, it was like we were at war. They committed ninety percent of the crime in Stoke Newington and always hid behind the racist thing. Take this incident for example, when we decided to trace the driver, we didn't do it because we thought he was black, we did it because he'd parked illegally and was thoughtlessly disturbing the local environment with his ridiculously loud music.

When I joined the Metropolitan Police, there wasn't a racist bone in my body. After eighteen months walking the streets of Stoke Newington, and even though my two best friends were black and Asian, I really hated these people. I couldn't help it, every day the same old shit, the same old 'you've only stopped me because I'm black' – no, mate, I've stopped you 'cos three black youths have just mugged an old lady!' 'You've only stopped me because I'm black' – no, mate, I've stopped you 'cos you're driving at fifty in a thirty.' 'You've only stopped me 'cos I'm black' – no, mate, I've fucking stopped you because a member of the public has just seen a BLACK man with a gun!

There was a part of me that knew I was wrong, that somehow my programming had become corrupted and that I'd have to get out of this place and become normal again, one day.

"I've done a car check, this vehicle has no current keeper, have you got any proof this is your vehicle, Sir?" I asked.

I always used the address 'Sir'; it drove them mad. If I really wanted to piss them off, I used the word kaffir which someone, probably Paul Pollock, had told me was an old African term for slave.

He sucked his teeth again.

Sarah had moved away and was calling for the van; she could see where this was going. If he didn't start to cooperate, at least a little, I'd have him off on suspected theft. It was bollocks; I knew the car was his because no one double parks a nicked car and then draws attention to it by playing music so loudly every old bill within five miles will find it.

The man opened the passenger door, opened the glove compartment, took out the logbook and handed it to me. He'd completed the new driver details section, the oldest trick in the book, fill it out but never send it off. I read the details out loud.

"Is this you?" I asked.

He nodded.

"Have you got your driving licence, insurance, MOT?"

"Producer." He replied.

As I was dealing with the driver, Sarah had opened the bonnet and I assumed she was going to check the chassis and engine numbers to see if the vehicle was a ringer. I suspected it wasn't.

I got my HORT/1 pad out and started to complete a producer.

"You got anything with your details on, Sir?"

The man reached in the glove compartment again, took out several small pieces of white paper and handed them to me; they were three almost identical producers. Repeatedly getting stopped by the old bill was something this bloke did *really* well.

Chapter 9

When I drove Sarah home, I cut down through the roads opposite the nick to bypass the one-way system. By chance we drove along the road with the black Golf GTI. It was still there; the bonnet was up, and a mechanic was staring into the engine and scratching his head.

"Spark plug leads?" I asked.

"I don't know what you're talking about." Replied Sarah, innocently.

It was an old trick.

"So, it's good news about Paul, then?" I said.

"It might be even better; Sarge just told me Paul's been given some rich bitch who's got a country cottage somewhere, so he's likely to be away weekends, too."

"Touch." I commented, but Sarah just huffed.

"What's the matter, hon?"

"Chris, he's drinking a bottle of vodka a day." She said, sounding desperate.

"That can't be good." I replied.

"It's not; and he gets so morose."

"Sarah, why don't you just finish it with him? I know it'll be hard but it's the best thing in the long run, I mean it's going to happen anyway. Do it now, and then after a few months, we can start officially seeing each other, without having to creep around everywhere."

"I can't; and besides, you know with us ..." She stopped.

I waited for her to continue but she didn't.

Should I ask?

Pulling away from traffic lights I changed through the gears; neither of us spoke.

"I can't just finish with him, Chris."

"Why? Because you think he'll kill himself?" I said.

"Well, yes, that wouldn't surprise me; but it's not that." She replied.

"What is it then?"

"Just don't judge me." She said.

"I won't."

"Promise?" She asked.

"Promise." I assured her.

"Before my modeling career took off, I made a couple of films..."

"You've never mentioned that. I'm impressed." I said.

"They weren't the sort of films you go around bragging about." Sarah said.

"Oh." I replied, realising what she meant.

"Pornographic?" I asked.

"Yes."

"How bad?" I asked.

"I'm pretty sure some of its illegal but let's just say the job wouldn't be very impressed and, more importantly, if he sells them to the papers, my parents will see them and I'll die. I'd never be able to face them again. I did it when I was eighteen and the ironic thing was, within weeks, I'd got my first proper modeling job and started to earn really good money. There was no need for me to do the films at all, if only I'd known, hey?" She said, regretfully.

"It's always easy to be smart after the event, Sarah. Don't be too hard on yourself. Where did you do it?"

"In Amsterdam." She replied.

"How much did you get paid, to get laid?" I said, deliberately rhyming the words.

"Five hundred pounds, each." She replied

"Each?"

"I made two. *Cindy Sucks* and *Cindy Fucks*."

"I think I remember them. Weren't they on Film 80 with Barry Norman?"

"Very funny." She said.

"Okay, so what's the problem? What's this got to do with Paul? It was years before you two met."

"Remember you're not judging me?" She said.

"I promise." I assured her.

"Well, when we started having an affair, as a bit of foreplay, I put one of my videos on. I'd just bought one of those new video recorders; you know state of the art with a remote control on a wire. I didn't tell him I was in it. I just told him it was a porno and how I liked to watch pornos. Anyway, of course, he sees it's me and it's like the best sex ever."

"Please don't tell me he's got the tapes." I said.

Sarah didn't reply so I glanced across at her, she was nodding her head.

"Do you know where they are?" I asked.

"No idea, Chris; but they both disappeared several weeks ago." She replied.

"Why's he done that?" I asked.

"Insurance?" Sarah replied.

"Insurance? That you don't dump him?" I asked.

"Yes and no. I think there's more to it than just me dumping him; it's so that I keep quiet."

"I don't understand Sarah, keep quiet about what?" I asked.

"Several months ago, when he was pissed and we were discussing stuff, he told me something which he should really have kept to himself. I'm guessing he's taken the tape to make sure, not only do I not end our relationship, but, more importantly, that I keep my mouth shut."

"Are you sure he's taken it and you haven't just lost it?"

"Absolutely; he even admitted as much when I challenged him." She replied.

"Are they really that bad?"

Sarah shuffled uneasily.

"I'm not proud of what I've done, Chris." She said, coyly.

"Listen, Sarah; you were young, you made a mistake. These things happen." I said.

"I know, but now I can't finish with Paul until I get those tapes back. I'm completely buggered!" She said.

"Apparently, so." I replied, with a smirk.

"I was." She replied sheepishly.

"You never let me do that!" I moaned.

"I got paid a lot of money Chris. You pay me that amount of money, you get to have anal. Fair enough?" She said.

"Fair enough." I agreed.

"But seriously, Chris, what am I going to do?"

"I don't know. Is there any chance he's got them at work? In his locker perhaps?"

"It's possible, I suppose." She replied.

"I could banjo his locker, if you like?" I suggested.

"It's an option. I'll think it over and let you know."

"So, what did he tell you that he really shouldn't have?" I asked, curious to know more.

I pulled up around the corner from her flat, just in case Paul was about, and I looked across at my passenger. From the expression on her face, Sarah was deciding whether to tell me. After a few moments, she'd made her decision and shook her head.

"I can't tell you. It's serious shit, Chris." Sarah said.

"How serious? Imprisonment?" I asked.

She nodded.

"Life?" I asked.

She shook her head.

"Ten to fifteen?" I suggested.

She nodded.

Sarah was right; ten to fifteen years imprisonment was serious shit and only left a few options.

"Corruption?" I said.

"No." She replied, but she curled her nose up suggesting I was getting warmer.

"Perverting?" I asked.

She nodded.

"Fuck, Sarah; you weren't kidding. All I know is this…" I said.

"What? She asked.

"First thing we've got to do is get those tapes back."

"I agree." Sarah replied.

Chapter 10

I bought an expensive array of orchids and made my way to St John's church in Buckhurst Hill. I didn't know exactly where the grave was, but it only took a few minutes to find. Even though it was eighteen months since my Street Duties instructor had lost her life in an IRA bombing, her grave was awash with flowers, to such an extent that one would have thought her funeral had taken place only a few days before.

As I approached, I felt really nervous and, for a few seconds, thought that I couldn't face this. I hesitated. I could make out Dawn's name engraved in gold leaf on a stunning black granite headstone and my eyes started to fill with tears.

WPC

Dawn Jayne Matthews

Born 24th February 1957

Killed in the line of duty

28th July 1983

No parents were ever prouder

Or a daughter more missed.

By the time I'd read the inscription tears were streaming down my face and my legs were turning to jelly. It took several minutes to pull myself together, wipe the tears from my face and place the flowers on the grave. When I had done so, I knelt, so the open palm of my right hand rested against her name.

"Hello, partner." I said, in no more than a whisper.

My fingers traced the carving of the letters D a w n.

"I'm so sorry, Dawn." I murmured.

The thing was, just before the bomb went off, Dawn and I had quite literally swapped places. I'd been looking to see why everyone in the shopping centre was laughing at her. I'd taken her by the elbows and turned her around. She'd tucked her denim skirt inside her knickers. I was just telling her, and she was saying something about a coded message when, at that moment, our lives, as we knew them, were blown away in a flash of brilliant white. Dawn died within fifteen minutes, my life would go on, but it would never be the same.

I was quite proud of myself though, because since that day, I'd become hard. I'd not shed a tear or thought too long or too much about what had happened. I'd moved on, determined that terrible part of my life would make me stronger.

"You're still the best old bill I've ever worked with, I miss you, partner." I said to my old friend.

"Hi, Chris." A soft voice said in my left ear, and I could have died from a heart attack.

I jumped up, and turned around simultaneously, to see Dawn's Mum standing by my side; she smiled.

"Sorry, if I made you jump." She said.

I'd moved in with Dawn and her Mum a few weeks before Dawn was killed but I hadn't seen her since the bombing. I should have visited her but just couldn't because I'd made this promise to look after Dawn, who'd then died, trying to save me. I felt too embarrassed, too ashamed to face Mrs M. Now she was here by my side and the smile on her face showed that she held no malice towards me; in that second, guilt that weighed a thousand tons lifted from my shoulders.

"Hi, Mrs M." I said.

"I've been waiting eighteen months to bump into you here, Chris. Every time there's a new bouquet, I check the tag to see if it's from you. I know how much you loved her."

I burst into tears. I completely lost control. I cried like a child. I sobbed and wailed. I don't think I'd ever felt so much pain, even when my Mum died. Eighteen months of guilt, fear, sadness, and anger came flooding out. Mrs M took me in her arms, cuddled and rocked me gently backwards and forwards, and then sat me down on a bench. Every time I thought I'd pulled myself together, it started over again. I was absolutely pathetic; after all, I wasn't the one who had lost a daughter.

A long twenty minutes later, the pain started to subside, and my sobbing became slower and more controlled.

"I'm sorry, I'm so embarrassed." I said.

"No need to be, Christopher." She replied.

"It was too hard, Mrs M. I couldn't face coming, I had to pretend everything was okay."

For the next hour we sat on a bench in the graveyard and chatted. Mrs Matthews said that she visited the grave every day and brought fresh flowers twice a week. She chatted to Dawn, and told her how much she missed her, and what was going on in her life and the world, in general.

She explained that after the bombing, a female officer was appointed to visit her every day and help her. She said that there wasn't a day that went by when she didn't ask her how I was getting on. She'd even come to the hospital to see me, but I'd been discharged that morning.

I felt touched and then guilty that I hadn't made more effort to go and see her, but I knew it wasn't a case of making the effort, I just didn't have the strength to handle it.

"I saw the funeral on telly. I've never seen so many people at a funeral." I said.

"I can't really remember it Chris, it was all just a blur. It's just such a waste of a young life, she had everything in front of her, you know marriage, children and now …"

"I don't know what to say." I replied, quietly.

"There is nothing to say, I just hope the bastards they arrested go to prison for the rest of their lives."

"Me, too."

It was lovely to see Mrs M even under these circumstances. How she managed to keep going, I'd no idea.

"How's Dawn's Dad?" I asked.

"Oh David, he's devastated of course. He comes up quite often but it's harder for him because he's living way out in Braintree or somewhere."

Mrs M paused, awkwardly, and I wondered what she was going to say.

"I've met someone, Chris."

I was really shocked. I shouldn't have been, as Mrs M was an attractive woman, but I'd only ever seen her in the context of Dawn's Mum. And especially after what had happened to Dawn, I thought she wouldn't be in the right frame of mind to meet anyone.

"Who is he?" I asked trying to conceal my surprise.

"He's a really nice fellow, Chris. His name is Donald Cole and he's a property developer, he's shown me several houses which he's done up and sold on. He's divorced and is looking for somewhere to live and wants a woman's input, so he's taking me round house hunting. Chris, I like him a lot, I really do but I'm reticent about getting too committed because …" She hesitated.

"No, I don't think Dawn would mind." I said, anticipating her next question.

"Mrs M, Dawn loved you, unconditionally. She would be happy knowing you were happy." I assured her.

"Do you really think so, Chris? You're not just saying that?"

"Absolutely not; I promise you." I said, turning to look her squarely in the eye.

I remembered the last time I'd promised Mrs Matthews something.

"Thanks Chris, it means a lot to me." She said, quietly.

I smiled and we hugged.

"Chris?" She asked.

"Yes"

"Can I ask you something?" She said

"You can ask me anything."

"You were with her at the end, weren't you? They said she died in your arms."

I nodded.

"Was she conscious, did she say anything?"

I nodded. I didn't really want to tell Mrs M what Dawn had said in case it was too upsetting, but I realised, she had a right to know.

"Her last words were …" I could barely speak but I forced the sentence out.

"…I want my Mum." I whispered.

Mrs Matthews grimaced. I held her hand and we sat there in silence. I didn't want to look at her, just in case she was upset, because I knew that would set me off again.

"She was really fond of you, Chris; you do know that?"

"I know, she didn't think much of me at first, you know. I was pretty useless." I said.

"Didn't you arrest a man for disqualified driving when he was walking to work?" She asked.

"I did." I replied.

We smiled.

"Do you know what changed her mind about you?" Mrs Matthews said.

"Of course." I replied.

"Go on then, what was it?" She asked.

"It was when I came to her rescue when she was fighting that burglar." I replied.

"No, it wasn't then. It was when you refused to take a bribe, when a guy, some dodgy factory owner, offered you a suit. That was the moment; Dawn said it was like a breath of fresh air to be working with someone with so much honesty and integrity."

I tried not to think about Mrs Mansfield's money buried in the woods, not a mile away from where we were sitting.

Chapter 11

On the shift pattern we were working, you only got one weekend off in four, so these long weekends, as they were called, were much valued. You finished work at 2pm on Thursday afternoon, and your next shift wasn't until 10pm on Monday evening.

Relief social functions were often arranged for the Saturday of the long weekend. That weekend about twenty of us were going to see the musical Cats which was on in Drury Lane. Sarah and Paul never came to these functions, so I knew I'd be able to relax a bit.

These gatherings were an important part of life on the relief and anyone who went got some credit amongst their peers.

On relief there was a social pecking order based, by and large, on length of service. It was interesting that, whenever two police officers met, inevitably one of the first questions asked was 'how long you got in?' It was like two dogs sniffing each other's backsides to establish seniority. Even if you only had a few months more service, your opinion carried more weight, your jokes were funnier, and your attractiveness greater to the opposite sex.

Some old stick once told me that you know you're getting on in service when the question 'how long you got in?' is replaced by 'how long you got to go?'

In the social pecking order, I was pretty much at the bottom. Although I was acknowledged by most to be a good thief taker, in the eighteen months I'd been on relief, only one person had joined after me and he'd left, when he discovered the job really wasn't for him.

The main disadvantage of being the most junior on the team was that I was always the one that made the tea. It drove me mad but that was about to change because a young WPC had completed her Street Duties course and was joining our relief for night duty on Monday. Her name was Kitty, and I was really looking forward to handing over the teapot to her.

That Saturday night we met in a pub, around the corner from the theatre, called the Freemasons Arms. The name prompted talk about the secret society and how many police officers were Masons. One guy, Roger Class, a PC with about twenty years' service, was quite open about his participation. He said his father had been a very senior mason, whatever that meant, and that he'd joined on his twenty first birthday.

"I'm telling you; you can't get on in this job without being on the square." He declared.

"Well, it's hardly done you much good, Roger." Observed one of the guys, making a fair point I thought.

"Really?" He replied.

"Well, you're hardly flying through the ranks are you *Constable*?" The critic explained.

"Look, it's not all about promotion, you know. There's a senior officer from Stokey in my lodge and he's junior to me. If I needed a favour, well, you know what I mean."

"Like what?" I asked, genuinely interested to know more.

"Ok. The Crime Squad boards are coming up; I've told him I'm applying; we'll see what happens." Roger replied.

"That's bollocks, Classy; you'd never get on the Crime Squad, you take less prisoners than the Gurkhas." Dave Preston said.

Dave was a Federation Rep and one of the relief's most active body takers, but he'd dipped the last two Crime Squad boards.

"We'll see." Roger said, who sounded quite confident.

"Listen, I'm going up as number one, what are you?" Dave asked.

"Don't know, mate; I don't take any notice of that bollocks." Roger replied.

"And it didn't help you when you got in that bit of bother, did it?" Another PC said, he was called Ben Bending.

"Well, that was because it was with a plonk; only men can be masons." Roger replied.

"What bit of bother was that?" Someone else asked.

"Well, I might have mentioned once or twice that I used to be at SB." Roger said.

"One or two thousand times." Dave said, and everyone nodded in agreement.

"Well, I'd spent the afternoon in the Tank…"

"A tank?" Dave asked incredulously.

"No, not a tank, the Tank you wanker. The bar at the Yard, on the ground floor behind the Back Hall Inspector. Anyway, I popped back up to the eighteenth to book off and called the lift. When it arrived, I got in and pushed ground, but the lift only went down a couple of floors and stopped again and a woman was waiting to get in. She's in plain clothes and looks quite young so I assume she's a civvy.

'Going down?' She asked and, quick as a flash, I reply 'Shouldn't we at least kiss first?' Which I thought was quite funny. She didn't. As it turns out, she's actually some carrot cruncher ACPO just transferred in. She asks to see my brief and, next thing I know, I'm bloody transferred to the shit hole that is Stoke Newington." Roger said.

"How come you're back in uniform? Did she Con Memo Four you, too?" Someone else asked.

"No; at SB you're only ever a Branch detective, so I was completely buggered. Bitch." Roger said.

"Lesbian." Someone suggested, and everyone agreed.

As the discussion moved on, I wandered off to use the toilet and, when I returned, everyone was leaving to go to the theatre.

"Can I have a word, Nostrils?" Ben Bending said.

Ben Bending was a genuinely nice guy. A PC with five years in, who'd passed the Sergeant's exam and was waiting to be promoted. Ben also lived on the third floor of the Section House, a little along the corridor from me.

Ben held me gently by the arm until everyone had left and then he turned to me; I guessed what he wanted, it was bound to be a warning about Sarah, he would tell me to be careful, I would deny anything was going on and say we were just friends.

"You're a nice fellow, Nostrils, I don't want to see you drop in the shit." He said, his voice was low.

"Ben, don't worry I'm fine, there's nothing going on." I assured him.

"What?" He said.

"What?" I replied, realising he may not be talking about Sarah and was really annoyed with myself for being so stupid and jumping straight in.

"Why am I going to drop in the shit?" I asked, trying to recover quickly.

"I've got a mate at CIB." He replied.

"CIB?"

"Complaints Investigation Bureau, the new A Ten." He said.

My heart missed a beat, fuck, did they know I'd taken the money?

"Yeah?" I said.

"Well, they're investigating a theft at Stokey."

"What's that got to do with me, Ben?" I said, trying to be casual.

"Well, you might be one of the suspects. My mate heard your name and knew of you obviously, because of the bombing thing." Ben explained.

"But I haven't stolen anything Ben. I've no idea what it could be about." I lied.

"Just thought I'd mark your cards. If you get a one six three and they ask you if you want to make a statement, say nothing, and contact the federation; they'll get you a brief, okay?"

"Okay." I said.

"Don't tell anyone we've had this conversation. I just thought pre-warned is pre-armed." Ben added, and his hand squeezed my arm to emphasis the point.

"Thanks, Ben." I said.

"No problem, Nostrils. As for that other thing, just keep denying it and you might eventually convince yourself, and everyone else, but you won't convince me."

"What other thing?" I asked, although my mind was racing, and I was only vaguely aware we were still talking.

"The affair you're having with the lovely Sarah." He said, with a wry smile.

~~~

I thought Cats was rubbish. There was no story to it at all; it was just a series of songs, and I only knew one of those, Memories. Mind you, my head was spinning with the revelation I was under investigation by CIB. I'd never had a one six three, a formal notification of allegation, served on me before, although I knew it wasn't that unusual to get one. I was amazed that my transgression had been discovered so soon. Who on earth was close enough to Edith Mansfield to know she kept all that money hidden in a bin liner in her kitchen? And I hadn't told a soul, I wasn't that stupid. I may have only been in law enforcement for two years, but I knew most people got caught because they tell someone what they've done.

After the musical, we briefed it into a casino in Tottenham Court Road. I'd never been to a casino before and was surprised at how formal it was, several of us were given jackets by the door staff, who kept some behind the counter just for that purpose.

I still had eighty pounds of my ill-gotten gains and decided playing roulette was as good a way of losing it as any other. I watched a five-pound table for a while, so as not to make a complete arse of myself. It seemed to me that the way most people played, by covering dozens of different numbers on a single spin, was a certain way to lose everything very quickly. After all, you were betting against yourself as only one number could come in; and every time you split a chip to cover more than one number, the payout percentage decreased. I decided to play one number each spin. My mind searched for a reason to play a particular number and I decided on ten, the sum total of one, six and three. I played five pounds each go, so I would have sixteen goes. When I had just four chips left, ten came in and I won one hundred and seventy-five pounds, I was really pleased. As the croupier was guiding a tall pile of chips across the green baize towards me, I looked around and saw everyone else gathering by the exit to leave. I quickly counted out eighty pounds, my original stake, put it in my pocket and placed the rest back on number ten. I stood up ready to cash out. What came in? Ten! I won three thousand eight hundred and fifty pounds. Well, fuck my old boots!

Chapter 12

I stayed in bed until after two the following day. We hadn't got in until gone three and it was a Sunday, so I wasn't in any rush to get up. I was awake at about one but lay there chewing things over. At one point, I got up to examine the evidence of my win to make sure it wasn't all a dream. Rather than carry a load of cash, when I'd had too much to drink, I'd taken my winnings in the form of a casino cheque, which I'd later pay in to the bank.

After months of not a lot happening in my life, over the last few days it felt like I'd got on a roller coaster.

I should have been really happy but the news from Ben that I was under investigation for the theft was worrying. Of course, with hindsight, I shouldn't have taken the money but, then again if I hadn't, I wouldn't have been gambling with it in the casino and therefore wouldn't have won the three grand.

I tried to put myself in the mind of the detectives investigating the case. They'd have to prove the money existed in the first place and that wouldn't be easy; no one had seen Edith Mansfield for four months and, in that time, her house was hardly secure. Her bedroom window was smashed; perhaps someone had broken in and stolen it?

If they could establish that the money existed, they'd then have to prove I'd taken it. No one had seen me; I hadn't told anyone, and no one would find it where it was buried. Save for a couple of hundred, I hadn't spent any and now with the roulette win, I had a legitimate reason to have some money, which would certainly muddy the waters of any enquiry into my finances. The more I thought about it, the more confident I became.

There was a tap at my door.

"Come in, I think it's open." I called.

It was Andy.

"Fuck me, what you doing up? You're on nights, aren't you?" I asked.

"I'm going for Sunday dinner with Mum and Dad. Listen, I've just been downstairs to get a cup of tea and bumped into Paul Pollock, he wants to see you."

"Oh, fucking hell, here we go." I said.

"What you going to do?"

"I'll go down and see him, of course. Does he look pissed off?" I asked.

"He's not ranting and raving, if that's what you mean, but it's got to be about you and Sarah, hasn't it? I didn't say you were in, I said I'd *see* if you were in. I'll tell him you're not in your room if you like?"

I shook my head.

"No, don't do that, mate. Do me a favour, go and tell him I'll be down in ten. I need to jump in the shower and do my teeth. It's been coming Andy, let's get it out of the way."

"You gonna deny it?" Andy asked.

"I'll see how it goes; I might just put my hands up. I think she's going to dump him anyway." I said, turning my options over in my mind.

"If she dumps him, the way will be clear for you two at least. That's good, isn't it?"

"I don't think she sees a future with me either, if I'm being absolutely honest, mate. I think she thinks she can do better, and I think she's probably right." I replied.

Andy smiled.

"Don't run yourself down, Nostrils; I'd marry you tomorrow."

It was a strange thing for one man to say to another, but I took it as a compliment.

"Thanks, mate." I said.

"Good luck, Nostrils, do you want me to stick around?"

"No thanks, Andy, you get off. I'll be fine."

"You seem okay, I thought you'd be shitting yourself."

"Listen, mate; live by the sword, die by the sword. I knew it was coming, let's see how it all unfolds." I replied, pragmatically.

~~~

Fifteen minutes later Paul and I were sitting opposite one another at a table in the corner of the canteen. We'd exchanged pleasantries and he'd even bought me a cup of tea. It all seemed far too civilized for what was about to come.

"I bet you're wondering why I need to see you?" He said.

I shrugged my shoulders; obviously I didn't want to say anything until I knew exactly what he knew. Paul looked awkward, and, in that moment, I felt sorry for him.

"Just say it, Paul, let's get it out into the open." I encouraged him.

"Okay, here goes..." he took a sip of his tea, to buy himself a few more seconds.

"...I gather you won a load of money last night. Someone said six grand?" Paul said, the words rushing from quickly from his mouth.

I was completely taken aback. That was not what I expected him to say.

"Sorry?" Was all I could mutter.

"You won six grand at a casino, you know last night, on the night out with the rest of the relief." He explained.

I gathered a little composure.

"I didn't win six grand, Paul. I won three. Who told you six?"

"Roger Class." He replied.

"Six grand, he said six grand?"

"It doesn't matter. So, you did win something?"

"No, yes, no, I mean I did win, yes, no it wasn't a wind up. I won three grand playing roulette."

"You lucky bastard." He said.

"My luck seems to be changing." I said.

"Can you lend us a grand, Nostrils? Please I'm desperate?" Paul was pleading.

"What?" I said.

"I owe the blood sucking solicitor. Unless he gets paid, he won't do any more work on my case, and I can't see my kids. It's killing me."

I hesitated.

"I promise you, I'll pay you back."

To say I was surprised is an understatement, but I had to think fast. Did I want to lend him the money? My chances of getting it back when he discovers I'm screwing the love of his life will be nonexistent. That said, I could see certain advantages in having Paul, metaphorically and literally, in debt to me. I definitely needed to speak to Sarah and get her take on this development before I agreed.

"Listen, Paul; give me forty-eight hours. I promise you; I'll have an answer by Tuesday. It's not as simple as you think; I want to help, I really do, but I'm up to my eyeballs in debt myself." I said.

"Oh, I didn't realise, I thought you Section House boys were rolling in it?" Paul replied.

"I should be but I'm not. After the bombing I didn't give a shit about money and spent it like there was no tomorrow, now tomorrow's arrived, I owe about as much as Mexico."

"Listen, I'm sorry to ask, I really am. Look I've just been posted to jury protection and the trial's likely to last three to six months. I'm going to be earning like over a hundred hours a month, I'll be able to pay you back, I promise." He said.

"Does Sarah know?" I said, and realised I was taking a bit of a risk bringing her name into the conversation.

"No, mate; she's really distant at the moment, I think something's on her mind."

"Listen Paul; I'll think it over. I'll pop a note in your tray. Is it a grand, exactly?"

He nodded and I stood up. Paul got to his feet and held out his hand, I shook it. What else could I do?

Chapter 13

I knew I'd have to speak to Sarah first, but decided I wanted to help Paul, and anyway, what with the money I had hidden in the forest, I could afford to be generous. I did feel sorry for the bloke, and it must be awful not being able to see your kids. What's more, he'd always been good to me.

On the Monday of nights, I drove over to Epping Forest, dug up the box and removed a thousand pounds. All the way there, I took measures to make sure I wasn't being followed. I went round roundabouts twice, turned down side roads and then stopped immediately, and even turned left on a red light just to see if anyone else did too. I didn't make my way to the box until I was certain I wasn't being followed.

When I got there, I realised I needed a spade and ended up, with considerable difficulty, managing to persuade some Asian guy in a petrol station to sell me a cheap gardening tool, which they were giving away free on some offer, in exchange for vouchers.

I eventually got the box up and open, and selected the newest looking notes, so Paul would think I'd drawn them out of the bank. I hid the thousand pounds under the carpet in the front passenger foot well of the XR2.

When I got back, I wandered into the nick to check the Duties Binder which showed me, for the first five nights, posted to Clissold Beat with five five four. There was no one on our relief with this shoulder number, so I'd assumed it must be the new plonk that was joining us from Street Duties.

I was right. That evening at parade I was posted out with Kitty, the newest member of our team. I took it as a compliment to be paired up with a brand-new probationer, as it demonstrated that Sergeant Felix had an element of trust in my abilities. It was the first time I'd ever worked with someone with less experience than me, which meant, technically, although not officially, I was in charge of her.

Kitty Young was a light skinned half-caste girl; a few years older than me. There's not a polite way to put it but she was short, dumpy, and spectacularly unattractive.

Immediately after parade, I introduced myself and informed her that my first responsibility was to show her how to make the tea. With great pleasure, it was my turn to hand over this core policing role to my successor. As it transpired, on that first night, I still ended up doing everything whilst Kitty observed proceedings down her nose.

We left the nick and spent the next hour discussing the rights and wrongs of the tradition of allocating tea making responsibilities to the newest probationer on the relief. Clearly, Kitty wasn't impressed about being appointed OIC teapot. I detected that she somehow considered the matter gender related, although I was at a loss to understand how, as me and my penis had done it for the last eighteen months. Amazingly, she also seemed to think it was relevant that she didn't drink tea or coffee herself.

Her attitude was so very different to my own. When I'd joined the relief, I would have done anything to fit in, including making tea for twenty-five officers but Kitty was, clearly, wired differently.

I think on some level I admired her because I'd never have had the strength of character to stand up for myself. In fact, it just wouldn't have crossed my mind, not even for the briefest moment, to say no.

I also thought, however, that if she wasn't careful then such an attitude could quickly lead to problems. The relief was like a family, everyone looked after each other and, when the chips were down, we would quite literally risk our life in defence of our own; but also like a family, little niggles and complaints could grow ridiculously out of proportion.

As the new sprog, there was a significant level of expectation on Kitty to behave in a certain way, keep her mouth shut and learn the ropes. If she'd have been really attractive, she might have been allowed more leeway, as the alpha males jostled to get in her knickers, but for young male probationers and plain looking plonks, it was a slow process to get accepted.

On one level I was luckier than most; having been blown up, everyone made allowances because they didn't know how badly I'd been affected. Kitty however hadn't had such an advantageous start to her probation. It must sound strange to people on the outside but, if she refused to make the tea, I could see it having a domino effect on the rest of her interactions with the relief. I tried to advise her, but she knew better. The discussion was interrupted by our first call of the night.

"Four six six, four six six, receiving Golf November?"

"Go ahead, Golf November." I responded.

"Four six six, can you attend thirty Kier Hardy House? The female occupier is at Casualty claiming to have miscarried at seven months. Only yesterday she attended the hospital demanding to have her pregnancy terminated, as the baby's father had just died. The hospital refused because the pregnancy is beyond the legal limit of twenty-eight weeks. They believe, therefore, she may have deliberately aborted. The front door should be insecure and no one else on premises."

I was a little confused, what exactly where they asking us to do?

"Golf November, do you want us to secure a possible crime scene?" I asked.

"Yes and no, Nostrils. The thing is the female has arrived at the hospital without the foetus and the hospital is asking for our assistance to locate it. Also, can you search for signs of an unlawful termination, perhaps any implements that have been used?"

"Golf November, four six six?" I said.

"Go ahead?"

"Whatever the Receiver is paying me to do this, it's not enough." I said.

There was a slight pause, I knew that Inspector Portman was a stickler for correct radio procedure, and everyone waited for him to come in and reproach me for my casual remark; right on cue he transmitted.

"Four six six, Golf November one."

"Go ahead, Sir?" I said, awaiting the rebuke.

"I agree." Inspector Portman said.

It was a nice touch.

"What have we got to do?" Kitty asked.

She'd heard the conversation, so she had as much information as I did. I ignored her thinking the question must be rhetorical.

"Chris? What have we got to do?" She asked again.

"Kitty, you must have heard. We've got to search a flat for an aborted baby." I replied.

"You have got to be kidding me?" She said, and I must admit I wished I had a camera, so I could have taken a picture of her face.

"Chris, I'm serious. That's ridiculous." Kitty said.

"What do you mean?" I said impatiently.

"Well, someone from the hospital should be doing that, you know, a doctor or a nurse or someone." Kitty said, earnestly.

"I don't think so, Kitty." I replied.

When I'd taken the call, I'd started to walk quickly but now I noticed Kitty wasn't matching my pace and had started to fall behind. I stopped and turned to her.

"Hurry up, Kitty, it's only a short walk but let's get there." I said.

She responded, but only slightly, and we walked on for about another hundred yards, then she stopped.

"Now what?" I said, really frustrated by her negative attitude.

"I've just had a thought. We don't have any power to enter the address." She declared.

"We do." I replied.

"No, we don't, we don't have a search warrant, we're not arresting anyone, and you can hardly argue that there's a breach of the peace going on."

"Kitty, we have the power." I said definitively.

"No, we don't." She argued.

This was a ridiculous conversation, so I thought I'd put an end to it once and for all.

"Listen Kitty. On the information received, we have reason to believe there may be a seven-month-old unborn child in the address."

I realised that was a slightly contradictory thing to say but I couldn't think of a better way to put it.

"Now it's possible, unlikely I know, but possible, that the baby or foetus or whatever you call it, is still alive. We are entering under the common law power to preserve life, it's as simple as that. What's more, you heard Inspector Portman on the radio, he knows what we're doing and if there was a problem, he would have stopped us wouldn't he? Now, for fuck's sake, Kitty; shape up or ship out."

"I'm not going anywhere if you're going to swear at me." She said indignantly.

I was at the end of my tether with Kitty.

"Don't be such a wanker." I replied.

Chapter 14

Kier Hardy House wasn't far away, and we arrived a few minutes after taking the call. Kitty trailed a few yards behind, like a reluctant sulking child.

Number thirty was on the fourth floor.

"I'm not using the lift." Kitty said.

"Why? Because they all smell of piss?" I replied, trying to get the conversation going.

"Nope. I don't do enclosed spaces." She replied, curtly.

"Well, at least we won't get stuck in the back of an O P van together."

"I get claustrophobic." She explained.

"Any other phobias I should know about? Making the tea, enclosed spaces, anything else?" I asked, sarcastically.

"I don't do dogs." She replied.

I hadn't anticipated that she would take my question seriously and was really tempted to make a joke about doing dogs but something inside me told me that wouldn't be appropriate.

"So, making the tea, enclosed spaces and dogs? Well let's hope you don't get trapped in a small café with a Great Dane."

"We all have things we don't like; even big tough men like you, Chris."

"I've only got one." I replied, crossing my fingers that she would walk into my trap.

She did.

"And what's yours then?" She asked.

"People who don't pull their weight." I replied.

A stony silence hung in the air as we completed the final two sets of stairs, so I guessed she'd taken my hint.

As the Reserve had said, the front door was on its latch and opened with a firm push. I entered an untidy, dirty, smelly council flat, the sort of place where you wiped your feet on the way out. I also noticed, all the lights were on, every window open, and each radiator boiling hot to touch. Whoever lived here, I thought, wasn't responsible for paying the utility bills.

"You coming in?" I asked Kitty, who seemed reluctant to cross the threshold.

She looked awkward and, although I hadn't realised at the time, it dawned on me then she'd run out of excuses not to do this. The first excuse being that medical staff should be doing this and the second, that we didn't have the power to enter.

"Kitty, we've all got to do things we don't want to do, it's part of the job." I said with as much sympathy as I could muster.

"This is really stupid. I didn't join the police to go searching for dead babies. I really, really don't want to do this, Chris." Kitty said.

I was quite taken aback; I'd never considered not doing something, which I had to do, simply because I didn't *want* to; but Kitty did look genuinely distressed.

"Wait in the hall then, while I look round." I suggested.

She nodded and whispered thanks.

For a second, just a second, I felt a tiny bit sorry for her.

The first room I went into was the bedroom and I noticed, immediately, there was an enormous amount of blood right in the middle of the unmade double bed. This suggested that whatever had happened, whether naturally or not, had happened there. The blood smelt pungent and unpleasant.

The only piece of proper furniture in the room was the bed and there were four open suitcases full of colourful clothing laid about the room. In one corner, an enormous pile of dirty laundry grew towards the ceiling.

Above the bed was a framed picture of Christ on the cross. I looked from the picture to the blood on the bed and found the whole scene somewhat disturbing.

There were a few sheets curled up on the bottom corner of the bed and I pulled these off and shook them out, searching for anything the woman might have used to trigger the miscarriage. I wasn't quite sure what I was meant to be looking for, perhaps a knitting needle and a bottle of gin? Whatever it was, I didn't find it.

Looking down, something caught my eye amongst the hideous swirling orange and brown patterns on the dated carpet, a thin trail of blood went from the side of the bed. I followed it from the bedroom, across the hall, and under a closed door, opposite.

Kitty was standing right on the blood so, with two hands holding her upper arms, I gently moved her to one side. She followed my gaze down to see why, and promptly retched several times.

"You're going to have to toughen u, Kitty. I've got a feeling this nightmare hasn't even started yet." I said.

I took my truncheon out and used it to push open the closed door. I don't know exactly why, but whenever I was going into a room which I suspected contained something horrible or unexpected, I always used my stick. Somehow it distanced events and made everything just that little bit more palatable.

The door swung slowly open from the right, as I'd expected. I saw it was the bathroom. The first thing to come into view was the bath, which was full of washing. I was constantly amazed at how many residents of Stoke Newington washed their clothes in the bath, rather than use a washing machine or the launderette. As the door opened further, I saw the sink below a window on the opposite wall, also full of washing, and then the door stopped against, what I knew from previous visits to similar premises, would be the toilet.

I took several deep breaths, stepped into the bathroom, and turned left and back on myself. To my surprise and very temporary reprieve, the toilet seat was down. Once again, using the end of my stick, I lifted up both the top and the seat, whilst leaning back as far as possible.

I don't know exactly what I expected to see, perhaps a small, fist sized, blob of flesh?

Underneath the toilet seat the woman had dropped a brown towel, which I gingerly lifted up and dropped on the floor. Lying at an angle, and slightly curled up by the round tapering of the basin, was a baby, both his eyes were open, I mean really open and his mouth too, as if he had died gasping for his first breath. He had black hair, a perfect nose and tiny delicate fingers and toes. In the middle of his stomach, a long umbilical cord hung.

Of course, I wanted to look away, in fact I wanted to run away, but I knew, in order to deal with this, I would have to overcome my natural urges, and the process to do this, began with coming to terms with what I was looking at. So, I stood there staring at the pitiful sight of this baby, for how long I've no idea, until it no longer shocked or frightened me.

When I'd mentally accepted what I was looking at, I stepped back into the hallway. I didn't notice it at the time, but there was no sign of Kitty.

"Golf November, four six six?" I transmitted into my radio.

"Go ahead, Nostrils?"

"I've located the dead baby. Can you inform the usual please; the Coroner, CID and the Duty Officer?" I said.

"Four six six, Golf November One?"

Inspector Portman was calling me.

"Go ahead, Sir." I answered.

"I've been speaking to the doctor in Casualty. She is now quite happy that the miscarriage was natural and not, I repeat not, self-induced. Are you able to confirm that there are no obvious signs of foul play?" He asked.

"Yes, I think so, Sir, there's nothing obvious." I replied.

"Have you checked the body for any signs of deliberate injury?" Inspector Portman asked.

"No, no." I replied.

"Well, please do so. If there are no signs, it is not a sudden death and there is no need to inform the Coroner."

"Received, Golf November one, but what am I to do with the body?" I asked.

"Golf November will contact undertakers but, as the baby has not lived outside its mother's womb, it cannot die in the true sense of the word." Inspector Portman replied.

"Received. Golf November did you receive regarding the undertakers?"

"Yes, yes, Nostrils, I'll get onto them."

So now I had to go back and take the baby from the toilet and examine him for any signs of injury, I would rather have done just about anything else. The thought didn't make me feel sick, it made me cringe. When you have to do something really nasty, like examine a dead baby, it's nice to have someone else with you, it just helps. It was then I realised Kitty was nowhere to be seen. I called her name several times but got no reply.

"Five five four, four six six, over?" I transmitted.

There was no response.

"Five five four, four six six, are you receiving over?" I said again.

"Four six six, you haven't lost her, have you?" The Reserve asked, unhelpfully.

I was in a bit of a dilemma here. I suspected Kitty had just buggered off of her own volition, but it was dangerous to make that assumption, just in case she was actually in trouble, somewhere nearby.

"Four six six, can you confirm you are with or know the location of five five four?" It was Golf November One.

Now the bloody Duty Officer was asking; the pressure to find her was mounting.

"All units, stand-by one, please." I replied, buying a minute or two to find my colleague.

I stepped into the hall and again called Kitty's name loudly, several times. I heard nothing, but just as I turned to walk back outside, a noise came from behind the only unchecked door, which by a process of elimination, I guessed must be the lounge. What the hell was Kitty doing in there? I took two steps across the blood-stained carpet, turned the door handle, and flung the door open impatiently.

For a moment I thought I'd caught Kitty giving some bloke a blow job. Nothing, however, could have been further from the truth.

Chapter 15

I'd arranged to meet Sarah after night duty in a little café in Dalston Lane which served the best breakfast, north of the Thames.

"I gather Kitty didn't take it too well?" Sarah said, even before I'd taken my first sip of tea.

"What, you mean being told she had to make the tea for everyone?" I replied.

"No, you idiot, you know what I mean."

"Oh, you mean when she found the late Mr Ruddock? No, she fainted bless her. She was lucky though, 'cos she fell on the settee. When my old Mum used to faint; bang, straight down on the concrete pavement, blood everywhere."

"Did your Mum faint a lot then?"

"Almost every week." I replied.

"Oh, the poor thing." Sarah said, sympathetically.

"Normally after her second bottle of vodka."

"Chris, that's your mother you're talking about." Sarah reproached me.

"I know, but it's the truth." I replied.

"Never mind that, tell me about Kitty."

"I'd found the baby, poor thing, literally down the toilet. I went looking for Kitty, who'd wandered off. I suppose, when she heard that I'd located the baby, she thought it was safe to take a look around the rest of the flat."

"And what happened?" Sarah asked.

"She saw Jeremy Ruddock, sat bolt upright, with a long crimson silk scarf around his neck, twisted countless times until, probably at about the same time his eyes popped out their sockets, his windpipe broke and killed him. It all looked rather weird, like he was playing some kind of long, wind instrument. The Coroner's Officer said it was quite a common way for Asian women to kill themselves, you know, with their long saris, but that it was the first time he'd seen a white man do it. Anyway, when Kitty realised what she'd stumbled across, she fainted, falling forward onto the settee, and her head came to rest on the corpse's lap, which is where she was when I found her, just starting to regain consciousness. The bizarre thing was, it looked like she was giving him head, it really did.

You should have seen the look on her face, I nearly pissed myself. To make matters worse our Kitty's a bit of a delicate flower."

"I think what happened to her is enough to send anyone over the edge." Sarah commented.

"Well, she shouldn't have fainted, should she?"

"Chris, she couldn't help that, you're so insensitive. Mind you, this'll make you smile; do you know what Kitty's nickname was on Street Duties?"

"Cat?" I replied.

"No, egg-shell."

"Go on?" I said, though, if I hadn't just come off nights, I'd like to think I'd have worked out the reason why, myself.

"Because working with her was like walking on egg-shells."

"Working with her tonight was more like walking on broken glass. How on earth is she going to cope when some stroppy I C 3 really lets loose?" I said.

"I've no idea. But's she's taken an instant dislike to you." Sarah said.

"How do you know? Has she been moaning?"

"Yeah, in the locker room. How do you do it? You couldn't have been out with her for more than thirty minutes."

"It's a gift."

"You're out with her for the rest of the week, aren't you?" Sarah asked.

"Yeah, 'til the weekend."

"Have fun!" Sarah said.

Our breakfast arrived. My plate contained an impressive assortment of everything you shouldn't eat and Sarah had a bacon sandwich on unbuttered brown bread.

"Anyway, you wanted to see me, you said it was important." Sarah said as she removed every trace of fat from her bacon, which she then deposited on my plate.

"Paul came to see me today, I mean, yesterday." I said.

I'd timed the news perfectly because Sarah, who had just taken a bite of her sandwich, went into a coughing fit. I slapped her several times between the shoulder blades, to persuade a piece of meat to vacate her lungs. The other customers glanced up, over their tabloids, to see what all the fuss was about.

"Glad that news went down so well." I said.

"Chris, tell me more, what did he say? What did you say? Is he moving out? Did he threaten you?"

"Stop transmitting." I said, borrowing one of Andy's favourite terms, which means shut up and listen.

"Paul doesn't know about us; he hasn't got a clue." I assured her.

"Well, what did he want?"

"You know I had a win on Saturday, in the casino, after Cats?"

"Yes, of course, everybody's talking about it. What's that got to do with Paul?" Sarah asked.

"Well, Paul asked if he could borrow some money."

Sarah put her head in her hands and mouthed for god's sake several times.

I thought she was over-reacting.

"Listen, he said he needed to pay a solicitor's bill, so he could settle the divorce thing and see his kids. I felt quite sorry for him, Sarah." I said.

Sarah didn't move, she kept her hands over her face.

"What?" I asked.

"Nothing."

"The money's not for his solicitor's bill, is it?"

She shook her head.

"I don't understand." I said.

Sarah looked up and sighed.

"How much did you win? Someone said seven thousand?"

"Seven thousand? About half that, Christ, don't people exaggerate?"

"Paul wants a grand, doesn't he?" Sarah asked.

"Yeah, how do you know? Is that how much the bill is?"

"I've just told you, it's not for his solicitor, Chris. He asked me for it last week, but I haven't got that sort of money. And anyway, I don't want to get involved."

"Involved in what?" I asked.

"I can't tell you." She replied.

"Is it to do with the missing videos?" I asked, it was all I could think of.

"Of course not!" Sarah said, as if I was really stupid.

"For fuck's sake, Sarah, I'm trying to join the dots here, but I've only got half the picture; you're going to have to help me." I said, the frustration rising in my voice.

"I can't, Chris."

"Ok, don't tell me. But can't you use the fact he's desperate for a thousand pound as some sort of leverage to get the videos back?"

"It's not a bad idea." She replied.

"Just tell him you'll give him the money in return for the tapes." I said.

"It's a plan, but as I said, I shouldn't really get involved, and anyway, I haven't got a thousand pounds." Sarah said.

"I'll give you the money, in cash. Paul's happy, you're happy 'cos you get your tapes back, and I'm happy." I proposed.

Sarah frowned, deep in thought.

"Why are you happy? You're down a thousand pounds."

"Because you'll be so grateful, you'll let me have anal sex with you." I replied.

Sarah laughed.

"Actually, that's about how much it costs." Sarah said.

"Did he start his jury protection today?"

Again, I meant yesterday, but when I was on nights, the day before wasn't yesterday until I'd gone to bed.

"Yeah, he's working six pm to six am. Apparently, he's got some woman, that lives in an enormous house in Chigwell, to look after, up near the Sports Club." Sarah replied.

"He'll soon earn a grand on that; he said he was going to be doing over a hundred hours a month."

"But they need the money by the end of the week." Sarah explained.

"Do they?" I said, realising Sarah had probably let slip more than she wanted.

"What happens if *they* don't get it?" I asked.

"If *they* don't get ten grand together by the end of the week, Paul and half of Stoke Newington Crime Squad are going to prison for a very long time."

Chapter 16

I didn't sleep well that Tuesday morning. I had a growing concern that events were starting to control me, rather than the other way round. Apart from the ever-present threat from Paul, I don't know exactly why, but I had the feeling Sarah was unsettled and was worried she might be thinking about ending our relationship. I wasn't sure how I'd feel when, if, that happened, and, of course, there was the little matter of being under investigation by CIB for stealing the old lady's money.

Then there was the fact I'd pissed the new girl Kitty off, which shouldn't have mattered too much but, as I said, a relief is like a family and things get difficult if you can't all get along.

There was something else too, I got the distinct impression, last night, that people were talking behind my back and there were a few snide comments on the radio about the money I'd won. Ostensibly, they were humorous, but I just had a feeling, being lucky at the roulette table and shagging the stunning Sarah behind her boyfriend's back, wasn't going to get me voted man of the year by my peers on C relief.

I woke early and drove over to Dawn's Mum's house to see if she was in. After bumping into her at the grave, I'd made a decision to keep in touch, but I hadn't physically been to the house since I'd left on the morning of the bombing and, the nearer I got, the more anxious I felt.

Parked in her drive next to an unspectacular, but brand-new Mini Metro, was an impressive BMW six series coupe. Mrs M answered my knock with a warm smile and a spontaneous invitation to enter.

"How lovely to see you, Chris; do come in." She said.

I kicked my shoes off just inside the hall and followed her into the kitchen, where a white man, in his mid-thirties, was sitting at the breakfast table, reading the Daily Telegraph.

"Chris, this is Donald, Donald, this is Chris. I told you about Chris, he was with Dawn when she died."

"Oh, how terribly good to meet you old sport; a delight, an absolute delight." Donald said, with just a touch too much enthusiasm.

He jumped up and we shook hands, his grip was firm and bold.

"Good to meet you, too. Mrs M told me she'd got a new fella in her life." I said.

"Oh, we're just good friends." He said quickly, perhaps a little too quickly.

"Is that your car outside? Very nice." I said.

"Oh, that old thing, yes old sport. That's the one I drive when I don't want to look too ostentatious."

"Blimey, what do you drive when you do?" I asked.

"I've got an Aston Martin Lagonda, but it stays in the garage."

"Wow, you like your cars."

"And pretty women." He replied and threw a smile at Mrs M, who blushed with suitable humility. Donald was smooth, that was for sure.

I'd never really looked at Mrs M in a 'I wonder how attractive she is' kind of way before, but I did then. She was a couple of inches over five foot, slim but shapely, with shoulder length straight fair hair, and pointy, clean-cut features. She must have been the same age my Mum would have been, but she looked much younger.

"What do you do?" I replied, genuinely curious to learn more about this man.

"Oh, I'm retired now, but I was in property for twenty years." He replied.

"Retired?" I asked.

Donald didn't seem old enough.

"I was quite successful, Chris. Caught the property market at just the right time in the late sixties. Very lucky really." He explained.

"I gather Mrs Matthews has been helping you look for a house. Have you had any luck lately?" I asked.

"No, not yet, but Jenny's input has been invaluable; I'd be simply lost without her contribution. We're viewing a six bedroom in Alderton Hill in Loughton this evening; do you know the area?"

As a matter of fact, I did. Alderton Hill was about as desirable and as expensive as it got.

"I know Alderton Hill; very nice." I replied.

"Well, come with us old sport." Donald suggested.

"I'm nights tonight but thanks for the offer. Maybe next time." I suggested, glad to have an excuse not to go, as I couldn't think of anything worse than viewing a house I had absolutely no chance of ever being able to afford.

The kettle boiled, and Mrs M made tea, and then produced a homemade fruit cake. Donald went back to reading the Telegraph and doing the crossword. It gave me a chance to study him.

Donald was a surprise for several reasons; first, he was a good ten years younger than Mrs M, secondly, he was good looking, I mean strikingly so. As a bloke, I rarely noticed such a thing. And thirdly, he was really well spoken, almost to the point of being grating on the ear. If I'd imagined Mrs M's new bloke, he wouldn't have looked or acted anything like this man.

To cap it all this, Donald was also charming, polite and impeccably mannered.

I should have liked Donald, but I didn't. Two things in particular made me think all was not as it seemed; when I used the bathroom, I noticed a Rolex watch on the windowsill. I examined it carefully, it was quite beautiful, and really well made, it even felt solid and heavy in my hand, but I was certain it was snide. The second hand didn't glide, but ticked, which I knew to be a sure sign of a counterfeit. I speculated why a man, who retired before he was forty and who drove a top of the range BMW, would own a fake watch. I toyed with the idea of mentioning it to him but decided to keep my powder dry.

The second thing was even stranger. When Donald went into the hall to make a phone call, I glanced at his Telegraph crossword, in the hope of completing one or more of the few outstanding clues. Doing the Telegraph crossword was a bit of a hobby of mine, and had been ever since an older PC had taught me how to complete it whilst we were up north on the Miners' Strike, the previous summer. Whilst I wasn't an expert, I could usually complete over half.

Anyway, when I looked at Donald's paper, he'd just filled it in with in nonsense. At a quick glance, it looked okay but none of the answers were correct. Why would anyone want to do that?

Mrs M must have seen something in my expression.

"You alright, Chris? What's the matter?" She asked.

"Nothing, nothing at all." I lied.

"Chris, you do like Donald, don't you?"

"Seems alright, Mrs M."

"Hmm." Mrs M replied, obviously not believing me.

Mrs M invited me upstairs for a solemn visit to Dawn's old bedroom, which she'd barely touched, since that terrible day eighteen months ago. I could have done without it because I knew I'd get upset, but I just about held it together.

"It's the first time I've ever been in here." I commented, as we entered.

"I've kept it just as it was."

I smiled.

I noticed a framed picture of Barry, Dawn's married boyfriend, on the bedside table.

"That's Barry Mrs M, I'm surprised you let that stay." I commented.

"Let that stay? I found the photograph in her drawer, framed it, and put it there. It seemed the right thing to do." She replied.

"You're lovely." I said.

"Did Barry go to the funeral?" I asked after a few moments.

"I don't know, I didn't know what he looked like then and it was all muddled in my head."

"I hope so. He emigrated to Australia, you know?" I said.

"Did he?" Mrs M replied, but I could sense her mind had moved on to sadder thoughts.

"I had such a crush on Dawn." I said.

"I know. It was really obvious."

"Well, who wouldn't?" I said and smiled.

I was starting to get upset. I could feel the emotion rising from my stomach. I needed to change the subject. Donald had done the decent thing and remained in the kitchen so, whilst we were alone, I wanted to ask Mrs M a few things about her new man.

"Donald seems a nice chap." I said, not because I meant it but because I desperately needed to say something.

"He is, Chris; and I needed a distraction, if you know what I mean."

"I understand. How long have you known him?"

"Oh, about two months."

"Where did you meet?" I asked.

"At the graveyard, he was visiting his Mum's grave or something like that. We hit it off straight away."

"Where's he live?" I asked.

"He's staying in the Roebuck hotel, at the moment, but he stays here a couple of times a week."

"Good for you." I said.

I smiled and we cuddled, it made me feel warm inside.

When we got back downstairs, I said my good-byes and left. I drove off and out of the road, but then turned around and went back. From a discreet distance, I clocked the registration mark of the BMW. My antennae were indicating that something about Donald wasn't right.

Chapter 17

When I got back to the Section House I knocked for Andy. We went and bought a kebab, which we took back to the canteen to eat.

"CIB were at the nick today." He said as I took my first bite.

"Really?" I replied, immediately picturing the stolen one thousand pounds hidden in my car.

"Any idea what it's all about?" I said, casually.

"The rumour mill's working overdrive. There's some suggestion it's to do with the Crime Squad but everyone is being really tight lipped about what that could be." Andy replied.

"That's funny 'cos Sarah said something about the possibility of the Crime Squad all getting nicked, when I was having breakfast with her this morning. You've no idea what that might be about?" I asked in the hope that Andy might know whatever it was Sarah was not telling me.

"As I said, those that know are keeping mum. I have a theory but it's only that." Andy said.

"Go on." I encouraged him.

"Have you been in the Property Store, lately?" He asked.

"Probably; why?" I said.

"Haven't you noticed anything strange?" Andy said.

"No." I replied.

"It's full of fruit machines."

Andy was right, now I came to think about it, it was.

"What about it?" I asked.

"The Crime Squad are doing all the Greek and Turkish bars down Green Lane and seizing their fruit machines, 'cos none of them have got gambling licenses." Andy explained.

"Do they need one?" I asked.

"Of course, they do, they need an operating license." Andy said.

"I'll take your word for it." I replied, with mock indignity.

"Well, that's exactly the point. As policemen we really don't deal with unlawful fruit machines, do we?"

"No, but I don't get your point." I replied.

"Why is the Stoke Newington Crime Squad going round seizing fruit machines, when this Division has got the highest robbery and burglary rate in London?"

He had a point.

"I don't know, you tell me, mate."

"Word on the street is, Danny Chicago, you know, that short, dark-haired guy that always wears sunglasses?"

"Yeah,, yeah." I said.

Everyone knew Danny because he was such a stereotypical cheeky cockney.

"Well, his old man owns a company what supplies fruit machines. Danny seizes an unlawful one on Monday and, on Tuesday, Danny's Dad turns up with a 'police approved' machine. It's a right old scam and they've been at it for months."

"So, do you reckon that's what everyone is keeping quiet about?" I asked.

"Could be." Andy replied.

"That doesn't seem serious enough, does it? I mean, is it even illegal?"

I wanted to believe Andy. I hoped he'd got it just right and the presence of CIB at Stokey was nothing at all to do with me, but Andy blew my hopes away with his next statement.

"Mind you, someone else was saying it's to do with a theft, but if it was just a theft, area complaints would be dealing with it. If it's CIB, it must be a sizable theft, that's all I can say."

"Has anyone had any one six threes?" I asked.

"No, not yet; that's why there's so much speculation."

"Have they gone yet or are they still about?" I asked.

"The last thing I heard, they were in with the Chief Superintendent. They'll be long gone, now."

Despite Andy's assurance, I made a mental note to do a recce of the nick, before getting the money out of my car to give to Sarah.

"Oh, yeah, what did Paul Pollock want with you? Has he found out what you're doing to his beautiful girlfriend? You know? The one he gave up everything for." Andy said, rolling his eyes.

"He wanted to borrow some of my winnings to pay a solicitor's bill." I explained.

I knew from Sarah this wasn't the truth, but it would do for Andy, I didn't need to draw him into the pile of shit that, somehow, I now seemed, just about, to tread in.

"He's got a bit of a nerve, ain't he? Why would you want to help him out?" Andy asked.

"Well, I know the Sarah thing is dodgy, but we've always got on quite well, you know. When I joined the relief, he gave me a couple of great bodies; I was grateful then and I like to help people out, where I can."

"When he finds out, you'll never see the money again." Andy said.

"Listen, Andy, the way I see it is, if you lend someone money, then don't expect to ever see it again. If you do, well you've had a result, haven't you?"

"Are you sure you're not giving him the money 'cos you feel guilty?" Andy suggested.

"Maybe." I replied.

"How much does he want?"

"A gorilla." I replied.

"A gorilla?" Andy asked.

"You know, two monkeys? A grand? A bag of sand?"

"Don't try to come that cockney bull shit with me, you carrot cruncher." Andy said, to remind me that, although I was rapidly acquiring a credible East End twang, my roots lie in the rolling hills of Wiltshire.

"I've never trusted Paul Pollock. He's your typical macho, bull shit, fanny rat. Be wary my friend and give him a wide berth."

I liked Andy Welling and respected his opinions, but I knew this time I wouldn't be taking his advice.

The conversation with my closest friend had worried me on several levels, but I couldn't show it, so I ate the rest of my kebab, despite having lost my appetite for it.

I told Andy about Dawn's Mum and her new suitor. It took my mind off the CIB thing and helped improve my digestion.

~~~

I was getting changed for night duty when there was a gentle tap at my door, which I answered, in my pants and socks. To my surprise, I saw Sarah standing there, I ushered her in quickly. Sarah never came to my room, and I took it as a signal that something significant had happened.

"Have you got the money?" She asked eagerly.

"Yes, what's happened?" I replied.

"We've had a long chat; he's right on the edge, Chris. I think he's having a break down. At first, he denied knowing where the tapes were, even though in a previous conversation he'd admitted taking them. Then, after half a bottle of vodka, he remembered that he'd hidden them somewhere and said that, if I ever pissed him off, he'd sell them to the News of the Screws. I told him I could get him the thousand pounds, he so desperately needs, if he gives me back the tapes. They were in his car, wanker! He thinks he's going to be arrested because he got a phone call earlier that CIB were at the nick. Do you know anything about that?" Sarah asked.

"Andy told me they'd been in, but no one seems to know why. It could be to do with a theft or something to do with the Crime Squad." I replied.

"That news will send Paul into orbit." Sarah commented.

"I don't understand. Paul's never been on the Crime Squad, has he?" I asked.

"Last month, he did a few days strapping, remember?" Sarah replied.

I shook my head.

"Actually, I think you were at CTC. Anyway, he's gone to work pissed but I've got the tapes and I promised him that, when he comes home, I'll have the money. You have got it?" She asked.

"Yes, don't worry, it's here." I replied.

"Thank goodness for that. I'll pay you back when Paul pays me, if that's all right?"

"Yeah, no problem." I replied, but the truth was I didn't really care; the money from the box wasn't like real money, after all.

"Chris, I need to talk to someone about something that's happened. Are you happy if I tell you? You know, you always say, sometimes it better not knowing stuff."

"You mean the trouble Paul's in?"

Sarah nodded.

"Does it involve you?" I asked.

"No."

"Okay, but not here, walls have ears." I said.

"No, I agree, meet me tomorrow, at eight?" Sarah proposed.

"In the morning? At the café again?" I asked.

"No, eight in the evening. Meet me at the Hare and Hounds Leabridge Road, do you know it?" Sarah said.

"Of course." I replied.

"Did you two talk about your relationship?" I asked.

"Oh yes, that went really well. He said, if anything happened to us, he'd top himself!"

"Oh great, that's reassuring. We can relax now." I said, sarcastically.

I could see Sarah was really uptight; I took a deep breath.

"Listen Sarah, do you think we should, you know, have a break? I mean, this relationship is meant to be fun, but it doesn't feel like it, lately." I said.

I was surprised when the words left my mouth, it was undoubtedly the sensible thing to do but I wasn't sure it was what my heart, or cock, wanted.

Sarah sat on the bed looking at the floor; she looked sad but still lovely. I sat down by her side, put my arm around her and squeezed. Her head fell against my shoulder, and I turned towards her and sniffed her hair.

"No, Chris; I can't get through this without you." She said quietly.

"I'll be here for you, hon; I promise." I said.

There was a knock at the door.

"Nostrils?"

It was Rik.

"I'm getting changed, Rik, what do you want?" I shouted.

"Open up, I've got some post for you."

"Slip it under the door, mate; I'm having, I was trying to have, a wank."

"Do you want that dirty mag back then?" Rik asked, which was a little embarrassing in front of Sarah.

"No, it's alright, I'll just think of you in the shower, that should do it." I replied.

A white envelope slid under the door, and I heard Rik go into his room, which was across the corridor. The envelope had been downstairs in my pigeonhole for at least a week, and I'd ignored it because I knew what it was, my Barclaycard bill. I picked it up and threw it onto the desk.

"Aren't you going to open it?" Sarah asked.

"It can wait; it's only my latest Barclaycard bill." I replied.

Sarah picked it up and turned it over.

"I don't think so." She said.

She handed it to me and when I examined it more closely, I had to agree, it wasn't my Barclaycard bill, after all. I slipped my finger through a small gap in the corner and ripped it open. It was one page of typed writing and my eyes scanned quickly to pick out the relevant information; Criminal Injuries Compensation Board, claim, injuries suffered, terrorist bomb explosion, award of £15,000.

"Oh my god." I said.

"What is it, Chris? Let me see." Sarah said.

I handed the letter to Sarah and sat back down on the bed.

"Chris, CICB have awarded you fifteen grand, there's a cheque stabled to the back."

"When's the letter dated?" I asked in a state of shock.

"The twenty-third, it must have been downstairs for over a week. Don't you collect your mail?" Sarah asked.

I just sat there shaking my head as the realisation dawned that, when I'd stolen the old lady's money, this letter was in my pigeonhole waiting to be opened. What the fuck had I done?

Chapter 18

Throughout parade, I was in a bit of a daze. Fifteen thousand pounds, plus the three I'd won, plus the five left in the box, was a total of twenty-three grand, enough to buy a decent terraced house in Walthamstow without even getting a mortgage, unbelievable. Mind you, I had debts to pay off and, if I didn't count the money I'd stolen, that would leave me with about nine or ten grand. I could put that down as a deposit and get a very manageable mortgage. Of course, whilst all this was going through my head, I didn't forget, for a moment, that I might be spending the next four or five years in a prison cell.

After parade, in the canteen, everyone was talking about CIB and what they were doing at the nick. I noticed Sarah was very quiet, she clearly thought she knew why they were here and I, too, thought I had a good idea. We couldn't both be right, or so I hoped. Eventually, I asked Dave Preston, who was our Federation Rep.

"If they're investigating someone, don't they have to serve a one six three on them?"

"Normally, yes, but not if it might prejudice the enquiry." He replied.

"What does that mean?" I asked.

"It means, they think they can get more evidence if the person doesn't know they're under investigation." He explained.

"Give us an example, Dave." I asked.

"Ok. Let's say they're investigating money being stolen out of the station safe. They're not sure who it is but they think it's you. They might want to trap you into stealing some more by planting some money in there, for you to nick. Obviously, they wouldn't want to pre-warn you that you were under suspicion by serving a one six three on you beforehand."

"I get it." I replied.

The conversation moved back to speculating what it was they were investigating, and I thought through the implications of not having had a one six three, if as I suspected, they were investigating me. It seemed to suggest they didn't have enough evidence at the moment, so I thought I better be on my guard in case they tried to set me up.

During parade, and over tea, Kitty ignored me, which I found really annoying, but at least she did make the tea for everyone.

It was half ten and we were still in the nick when I was called on the radio.

"Four six six? Eighteen?"

Eighteen was Sergeant Key, he'd been on relief about a year having been promoted from the infamous Special Patrol Group, the SPG. I found him alright but some of the older PCs hated him with a passion and I didn't understand why.

"I'm in the canteen, Sarge; just clearing up the kitchen." I said.

"Stay there, I'll come and see you."

"Received." I replied.

Everyone cleared out the canteen quickly, as it was getting too late for us all still to be in the nick. Kitty said she'd wait for me in the front office. It was the first time she'd spoken to me.

I was curious to know why he was coming to me and not the other way round. I came to the conclusion that, whatever he wanted to say, needed to be said in private, and he'd assume the canteen would be empty by this time of night.

"Hi, Sarge." I said as he entered, I was washing up.

"Hi, Nostrils." He replied.

"I gather you really hit it off with Eggshells last night?" Sergeant Key said.

"Sarge, it's not my fault she fainted and fell on a corpse." I said.

"Make me a cup of tea, Nostrils; the events of last night have reminded me of an old wind up we used to do on the Group. I thought we could roll it out tonight and see if we can toughen old Eggshells up a bit. We're gonna play the mortuary joke on her, have you heard of it?" He asked.

I shook my head. When I'd been a very new probationer, I'd been the subject of a practical joke, which culminated with me trying to produce a sample of semen, which was allegedly required for testing, to see whether I'd been exposed to radiation. I was caught by the entire relief masturbating in the back of a police van, outside Casualty. I must confess, it was really cleverly done, and I took it in good spirits. Dawn had explained that being the subject of such a prank was a bit like a rite of passage, a trial that you past, if you took it well. I must confess, the thought that it was Kitty's turn to be the butt of a practical joke was more than a little appealing.

"Tell me more, Sarge?" I implored, as I poured him a brew.

"It's really quite simple and, after what happened yesterday, most appropriate. Basically, someone pretends to be a corpse and when she goes up to it, the corpse sits up, or it grabs her leg or something" He explained.

"Sarge, she'll die; this could go seriously wrong." I said.

"What could go wrong? With any luck, she'll literally shit herself and feel so embarrassed she'll have to resign and we'll have one less split arse to worry about." He said.

"Are you sure she won't like, make a formal complaint or anything? She already dislikes me."

"Listen, Nostrils; I'll take full responsibility if she does, you have my word. You don't have to worry about any repercussions." Sergeant Key assured me.

This made me feel better but only until Sarge delivered his next line.

"We'll get you to pretend to be a corpse…

"Fucking hell, Sarge, not me!" I interjected.

"Listen, we'll get you up the hospital and you'll pretend to be a corpse. She'll be told to take your fingerprints to confirm your identity, as it's believed you're a missing person. You'll have a sheet over you, so she won't recognise you. At an appropriate point, when she rolls back the sheet or starts to take your prints, you jump up and scare the life out of her."

"For fuck's sake, Sarge; this is not a good idea." I said.

"We'll use the mortuary at St Bart's, my girlfriend, Emma, is on nights." Sergeant Key said.

Suddenly this all sounded a bit too much. I know I didn't like Kitty, but I had serious doubts about taking part in such a cruel prank.

"I'm not sure." I said.

"Listen, Nostrils; everything's been arranged and everyone's relying on you. Don't let us down." Sergeant Key implored me.

"Why me, Sarge?" I asked.

"Cos everyone knows you've got the balls." He replied.

It was pathetic, the flattery, the peer pressure, if Sergeant Key thought he could persuade me so easily, he was going to be very disappointed.

Chapter 19

Shortly after midnight, Sergeant Key dropped me off by a fire escape, at the side of a brick building, as far from Casualty as you could possibly be, without leaving the hospital grounds.

Ten minutes earlier, Kitty had been called in to search a female prisoner as a ruse to separate us.

"Emma will meet you here, as soon as, she's free. She'll get you ready. When you're in place, she'll call me, and I'll dispatch Kitty on her urgent identification assignment." Sergeant Key explained.

"OK." I replied, and he drove off.

I'd expected to wait longer than I did, for only perhaps five minutes passed before Emma arrived. Sergeant Key's girlfriend was one good looking woman. She was in her mid to late twenties, with a mop of dark curly hair and a shapely, very feminine, figure. Her face was simply gorgeous with high cheek bones and natural, round pouting lips. She was smoking as she walked towards me and carried a hospital gown over her right sleeve. She smiled broadly.

"Nostrils, I presume?" She said.

"Hi, Emma." I replied.

"Do they really call you, Nostrils? I thought they were winding me up when they told me that was your name." Emma said.

"My name's Chris but everyone calls me Nostrils."

"Why?" She asked.

"I had a close encounter with a sawn-off shotgun when I first arrived at Stoke Newington." I said.

"I don't understand." Emma replied.

"Nostrils is slang for a sawn-off shotgun, because the two barrels next to each other look like the end of a nose, I suppose." I said.

"Oh, I get it." She replied.

We had walked to a dark green door and Emma searched through an enormous ring before selecting a large brass key and unlocking the door. Then she turned back to me, fluttered her eyelids, and moved closer, too close, and into my personal space. Our bodies touched, her breasts pressed firmly against my jacket and then she giggled and slipped away. It was outrageously flirtatious. I didn't know how to respond, but before the moment had completely passed, she took hold of my hand and led me through the door, as if she was leading me to her bedroom.

Instead, we entered the hospital mortuary and Emma switched on the lights. A few florescent flickers later, the whole room was illuminated like a football stadium before an evening kick off.

I'd been to mortuaries several times before; they were always cold, clinical and unfriendly but more than anything, they have a unique smell, which is a mixture of disinfectant and blood, with just a hint of decomposing bodies. The smell gets into your clothes, your hair, your lungs and stays for days. The walls and floor were tiled in clean, but ageing, white porcelain and there were two separate metal body slabs, both were empty and spotless, and, I assumed, I would be laying on one of these.

"Get undressed. Leave your pants on but give me the rest of your clothes; and put this on. Don't worry about me, I'm a nurse, I've seen it all before." Emma said.

I hesitated.

"Hurry up, now get your clothes off, big boy." Emma said teasingly, with a wink and a smile.

Emma placed my uniform in a cupboard on the other side of the room, whilst I struggled to fasten the gown.

"I'll give you a hand with that." She said, as she walked back across the room, so I gave up trying and let her assist me.

As she finished, she squeezed my right buttock hard.

"What a great arse." She said.

I felt my penis stir and had consciously to fight my growing erection because, in the flimsy gown, there was no hiding place. Naturally, I should have turned round to face Emma but I delayed momentarily to allow my hormones to settle. I heard a clunk and a swish behind me.

"Come on then hop in, Chris." She said.

Emma had opened the middle of five, square, wall doors and slid out a corpse rack. Surely, she didn't expect me to get in there?

"Why can't I just lay on one of the slabs?" I said.

"Don't be silly, we don't leave corpses out, they decompose. We haven't got much time. Kitty was already on her way when I came to meet you. She'll be here in a few minutes. Are you afraid?" She asked.

"No, no." I lied.

Whilst I didn't mind enclosed spaces, this was spooky.

"I'll get you a light." Emma said, helpfully.

She returned to the cupboard containing my clothes where she collected a white folded sheet and a small black torch which she flicked on and off to check it was working.

I wasn't very keen but wanted to impress Emma for no better reason than she was an attractive woman, and I was a horny young man. Also, I suppose, I knew I couldn't let the relief down because I'd never live it down, if I chickened out.

I climbed up and onto the rack and Emma shook the sheet out and placed it over me from head to toe. I placed the torch between my legs so it wouldn't roll off the slab and put my hands by my sides. She pushed me feet first into the hole. When I heard the door slam above and behind my head, I instantly regretted my foolishness. This was really fucking scary!

"Don't be long." I shouted.

When I waited for a reassuring reply, all I heard was the light switch being thrown and the main door slamming shut.

"It's freezing in here." I shouted.

Within five minutes my regrets were so widespread they'd grown to include ever joining the police. After ten minutes I was starting to regret being born.

With my right hand I reached between my legs and located the torch, and then with my left, I gripped the sheet just below my chin and pulled it down several inches until it cleared my eyes. I turned the torch on and arched my neck to look back and to the door.

Fuck! There was no inside handle! I couldn't get out! Panic started to grow. I turned my head to the right. Fuck! Two feet away on the next rack was a corpse under a blanket. I looked to my left, all clear. This was horrible, truly horrible and I wanted out. I didn't care whether I let everyone down, I wasn't bothered if I ruined a well-planned wind-up, I wasn't bothered if Kitty found out and ended up laughing at me. I wanted out, and I wanted out, NOW.

I turned back to look at the corpse, just in case. At that precise moment, it sat up right, the blanket fell from his face and Sergeant Key state, unequivocally:

"Cold in here, isn't it, Nostrils?"

It is said, you could hear my scream in Casualty.

Chapter 20

I'd done a vehicle check on Mrs M's boyfriend's BMW and discovered it was a hire car so, the following afternoon, I engaged the services of my two best mates and got them to come with me to Prestige Leasing in Knightsbridge.

I loved being with Andy and Rik and only wished I was on the same shift pattern as them. As it was, there were only a couple of times a month when we could all get together. Rik and I had been on the same selection day, but my entry was fast tracked because they needed me to play rugby, so he joined three months after me.

Rik was about my age and every bit a Londoner. His father had emigrated from Pakistan, in the fifties, and opened a corner shop in the East End. Rik was funny, genuinely laugh your socks off funny, but most of the time he didn't mean to be, which made it even funnier. Academically, Rik was bright, but not quite bright enough to become a doctor like his two older brothers, so when his father started to line him up to take over the family business, Rik sidestepped his plans with a move Phil Bennett would have been proud of and joined the Metropolitan Police.

I'd been friends with Andy since my arrival at Stokey, he'd helped me get through the first few difficult months, when Dawn couldn't stand me and I lurched from mistake to crisis to blunder. Andy was fit in every sense of the word; he was a qualified fitness instructor and took circuit training at the local gym. He was obsessively clean and showered more often than a dark rain cloud. All the women loved Andy, which was rather pointless because he was gay, not openly so, but discreetly and you'd never have guessed it from interacting with him. Only a few people knew about his sexuality, even Rik didn't know because, from comments he made when we first got to know him, his religion was very much against the practice.

What I liked most about the pair of them is that they just weren't like normal old bill and, more importantly, they didn't strive to be. I think neither of them had a particularly easy time on relief, especially Rik, who was just a little bit too smart, and a little bit too polite, for most of his colleagues.

One occasion he'd been on aid up the West End and was patrolling the Aldwych with a jack-the-lad PC, when an American tourist stopped them to ask directions. The other PC took his helmet off and pointed to the badge.

"What does that say?" He asked

The American looked slightly nervous and shook his head.

"It says E to R, not A to Z. Find your own fucking way!" The PC said, before walking off.

Rik was really embarrassed, apologised to the Yank, and gave him the directions.

When he caught up with the PC, Rik told him exactly what he thought of his attitude, and they almost came to blows, there and then, in the middle of the Strand. Of course, the relief took the PC's side and rumours circulated that Rik couldn't be trusted. Couldn't be trusted? Rik? Wankers, the lot of them, I'd have trusted that man with my life.

I got into a spot of bother about a year ago in a pub in Wanstead. I was meeting a girl called Tracey and, as usual, I'd arrived early. I waited patiently at an understaffed busy bar to buy a drink when a white bloke, who strolled in only moments previously, ordered before me. I made a bit of a fuss and he squared up to me. In this job I'd soon learnt that in a fight, he who strikes first, normally wins, and, as I was pretty certain he was going to lump me, I got a right hook in first and he dropped to the floor unconscious. The sort of people I arrested every day for doing the same thing, having got their opponent on the floor, would have given him a good kicking, but I'm not like that; I'm not a thug, so, while he was coming round, I shot out the pub, jumped in the XR2 and fucked off.

Later I got a phone call at the Section House from Tracey, who, technically of course, I'd stood up. She said that when she arrived at the pub, the old bill where there reporting the assault and taking descriptions of the suspect from eyewitnesses. She said everyone was describing me, but I fiercely denied it and said I'd had an afternoon nap and overslept. I kept apologising for standing her up and begged her for another chance. I think she bought my story because the next week, when we'd arranged to meet again, in retaliation, she stood me up!

If the old bill had traced me, my best course of action would have been to say it was self-defense, which it was, really. Obviously, I'd have to gild the lily to make it more convincing and I was chatting this through with Rik, when he said.

"I'll say I was with you, if it'll help. I'll say I was sitting at a table whilst you were getting the drinks and saw the whole thing. Run me over to the pub tomorrow, just so I can have a look at the lay-out."

"I can't go in." I said, rather needlessly because Rik replied.

"I know that Einstein, but it'll be useful, if you do end up getting nicked. When you're interviewed just say I was with you and suggest they speak to me. I mean, then it'll be the word of two old bill against one slag, and one of those old bill is a Paki who they've got to believe, no way you'd be charged." Rik said.

Rik was right and it was good of him to make the offer because he didn't have to. As it transpired, nothing came of it, but it was nice to know I could rely on such a good friend. In the police, true friendships are forged on such demonstrations of support.

Up until now, I would have been able to say that I could tell Andy and Rik anything but that was no longer the case. I couldn't tell them I'd stolen the old lady's money because I was too ashamed. I mean, they wouldn't turn me in or anything, but they wouldn't be able to trust me again.

We always thought we were better than the others, the thieves, and the slap happy, they were the Met's dishonorable past, and we saw ourselves as the noble future. I realised, at that moment, that whilst Andy and Rik might be better than all the others, I could no longer make that claim.

For what I wanted to do that afternoon, there had to be three of us; two to front out the manager and one to stay with the car because it was becoming impossible to park anywhere in the West End, someone would have to fend off traffic wardens with a flash of their warrant card.

En route, I relayed the mortuary story and the pair of them roared with laughter and ribbed me about my gullibility. I'd have done exactly the same to them.

I'd taken the wind up in good spirits, whatever I felt inside. I knew how important that was. Last night's joke had been terrifying, and I'd felt no inclination to laugh, but I had to. The fact was they couldn't have done it to Kitty, not even the original wind up where I just grabbed her leg, because she'd have gone mad and definitely raised a grievance. I vowed before the month was out, however, I'd have my revenge on Sergeant Key and I asked the lads for any suggestions.

"How about some sort of honey trap?" Rik suggested.

"Yeah, not bad, but I'll need more than that. And he'll be on his guard so, whatever it is; it can't look like I've got anything to do with it." I replied.

"Did Rik tell you about his little problem?" Andy asked.

"No; what's up, mate?" I said.

Rik leaned forward through the gap between the two front seats and Andy turned the radio off.

"You know my uncle?" Rik said.

"The one in East Ham?" I asked.

"Yeah, my Dad's oldest brother, Badal. You know the one we call Jimmy Saville 'cos he can make your dreams come true and get you anything?" Rik said.

"You mean Fagin the Fence?" I said.

"Yeah, that's him." Rik replied.

Rik had mentioned him several times. He was what we would call in the job, a receiver of stolen goods. His house was always full of nicked gear, TV's, videos, car radios, trainers, sunglasses and whatever else he could lay his hands on. He was the black sheep of the family, but a likeable rogue, whose company everyone delighted in.

"What's happened? Has he been nicked?" I asked.

"No, that's not it. A few months ago, I casually mentioned at a family gathering that I was thinking of taking up golf." Rik said.

"I didn't know that." I said.

"I did mention it but never mind. Anyway, last week I went to see Dad and what's Uncle Badal done? He's dropped off a complete set of brand-new Ping golf clubs, in a Ping bag, Ping balls, gloves, tees."

"Rik, why do you keep saying ping?" I asked.

"It's the make, you arse hole. It's about the best make there is. It's like four hundred pounds worth of equipment and he wants a oner for it." Rik explained.

"Can't you just say no?" I asked.

"No; I'm not on Grange Hill, Nostrils." He replied.

"You've had hooky gear off your Uncle before Rik, what you worried about?" I asked.

"This gear isn't just hot, it's steaming." Andy interjected.

"What do you mean?" I asked.

"The thing is, I was reading Police Gazette last week, have you read it?" Rik said.

"No, why? Don't tell me it's in there?" I said.

"A lorry load of golf equipment was hijacked in Kent a couple of weeks ago." Rik explained.

"Can you be sure it's the same gear?" I asked.

"Not until Sunday when they featured the very same bag on Police 5." Rik replied.

"Just tell your Uncle, no. He's not stupid Rik, surely, he'll understand?" I suggested.

"It's a family thing, Nostrils. He'll be like really insulted and my Dad will feel obliged to buy it, I know how it works. It's like a culture thing, there's a lot of pressure, I don't think you lot really understand." Rik said.

"What do you mean?" I asked.

"Our families are a lot closer than you appreciate. And he's my Dad's *older* brother so he's sort of senior. I'm going to have to buy them and never use them." Rik said.

"Be careful Rik, get caught and you could be in real trouble." Said the man who'd recently stolen six thousand pounds.

"Rik you gotta say no." Andy said.

"I agree." I added.

We were somewhere in Holborn and about to turn left on a filter, when the car in front, a dark blue Jaguar, stopped on double yellow lines, the driver got out and went to open a rear door. I sounded the horn and flashed my headlights. The driver ignored me, held the door open and a passenger alighted from the rear.

Andy opened the passenger door, got out and shouted.

"Move you wanker, you can't stop there!"

The passenger turned slightly but then walked off towards the front door of a hotel.

I thought Andy would go and give the driver some advice, but he quickly got back into the car.

"Aren't you going to tell him to move?" I said, surprised by his swift retreat.

"Nope." He replied definitively.

"Why?" I asked.

"Because the man who got out of the car was the Commissioner." Andy replied.

I maneuvered the XR2 around the offending Jaguar and we all kept our heads down. When we knew we were safe, we had a good laugh, after all it's not every day a police officer gets to call the Commissioner a wanker and keep his job.

Andy had got out a map and directed me through the back streets behind Harrods. Eventually, we turned down a wide cobbled Mews and pulled up outside Prestige Leasing. The company owned several garages which, once upon a time, had been stables. Parked inside, and in front of the garages, were a dozen really expensive cars; Mercedes, BMW's and Porsches. My XR2 looked rather cheap beside them; this was East End meeting West End.

"Listen, this is the SP. Andy come with me. We're going to be asking about a BMW six series index B555 PCS. We'll say we're trying to trace the driver who may have witnessed a serious assault in Buckhurst Hill." I said.

I was carrying a clipboard and pen to reinforce the image that we were on official police business. We walked into the garage. To the right was an office behind a glass partition and a white man in his late twenties, who was sitting at a desk, saw us and waved us over. As I entered, I produced my warrant card and flashed it quickly, Andy did the same. If I could avoid it, I didn't want the guy to be able to remember my name.

"Hi guys, is it about the overdue hire?" The man said.

"No, Sir. We're making enquires about a BMW B555..." but before I could complete the registration number the man replied.

"PCS, yes that's the overdue hire."

"Ah." I said, a little taken back, but Andy picked up the conversation.

"We're trying to trace the person who was driving that car a week ago because he may have witnessed an assault."

"It's just a coincidence then. I phoned Kensington police station this morning about it. That car was due back two weeks ago. I know the score; they won't report it as stolen until thirty days because before then it's a civil dispute, but I thought I'd try."

"Have you got the hirer's details, Sir?" I asked.

The relevant file was already on his desk, and he handed over a thin cardboard folder which I opened. It contained the vehicle registration document and a completed hire form.

"Can we have a copy of this please?" I asked.

"Of course."

I'd only glanced quickly at the name, Donald Cole, so it was the right file.

"Can you describe this Donald Cole to me please?" I asked.

"Yeah, average height, 'bout forty." He replied.

Members of the public never know how to describe people. You always have to help them. I did.

"White?"

"Yes." He replied.

"Was he taller or shorter than you, Sir?" I asked.

"About the same I think." He replied.

"And how tall are you?" I asked.

"Six two." He replied.

"About forty years old?" I said.

"Yeah." He replied.

"Build?" I asked.

"Average." He replied.

That bloody word again, I thought.

"Was he thin, slim, overweight or fat?" I asked.

"Slim." He replied.

"Hair colour and length?" I asked.

"Brown, short." He replied.

"Clean shaven?" I asked.

"Yes."

"Glasses?"

"No." He replied.

"Anything else you can remember? Did he have one arm or three legs?" I asked.

"Yes. He was really well spoken." The man said.

"Thanks for that. So, the car's overdue?" Andy asked.

"Yes, the bastard." The man replied.

"Can't you just charge his credit card?" Andy asked.

"Normally yes, but not when he pays in cash. This guy, he paid for six weeks in advance so you'd have thought we'd have been safe, wouldn't you?"

"Yeah" I replied.

"From what you've said, at least I know the car's still in the country. I expect he'll send the keys back to us and park the car up somewhere, that's what usually happens. That way he gets the car free for a month."

"Did he show you a driving licence?" Andy asked.

The man looked at the original form as he handed me a copy.

"Yeah." He said.

"Thanks for your time. If we trace him, we'll get your car back I promise." I said.

"Tell you what, you get the car back undamaged, and I'll sort you out with a drink or perhaps a Merc for a few days, what do you say?"

"Deal." I replied.

"Can you give us the spare keys? It'll save causing any damage if we trace the car but not Mr Cole." I suggested.

The man retrieved them from a locked cabinet and handed them over with his business card, I read his name, Michael Poulson, and we shook hands.

"I'll be in touch Mr Poulson." I said.

Chapter 21

It was a bit of a rush in the end, but I met Sarah as arranged at eight o'clock in the pub on Leabridge Road.

"Did you give Paul the money?" I asked.

"Yes. I didn't tell him it had come from you though."

"Is he happier?" I asked.

"A bit."

"How's the jury protection?" I asked.

"All right, I think. His partner's some guy from Holloway who he used to work with years ago. The woman they're looking after brings them out cups of tea and sandwiches, which is nice of her. It's a huge house with a swimming pool and everything. It's over near the police club in Chigwell. Apparently, the woman's husband has just upped and left her for some younger woman."

"And how are you?" I asked.

"I'm stressed, Chris. This wasn't the life I'd planned. I wanted a few years being young free and single; you know, in my own place, no one to answer to. But I've got to get on with it, there's no other option is there?"

"Yeah, there is." I replied.

"Don't start again. I know I should finish with him, but I can't, all right. Not just now, anyway."

"I hope you're as hesitant when you decide to dump me." I said, only half joking.

"You're different, Chris; you're strong, Paul isn't, which is why he's in the pile of shit he's in."

"The Crime Squad thing?" I asked.

Sarah nodded.

"Why have you decided to tell me? I mean, you seemed pretty adamant the other day that it was best if I didn't know."

"I don't know. I'm probably being selfish because I desperately want to discuss this with someone, you know, to see if I'm overreacting. And now, well, what with the thousand pounds you're sort of involved too, so, perhaps, you should know what's going on."

"Go on then, fill me in." I urged her.

"Are you sitting comfortably?"

"You can begin." I replied.

"Last month Paul did a week strapping on the Crime Squad 'cos both their drivers were off. They had some information from Crimestoppers about an address just off Sandringham Road, a small council house. Apparently, the I C 3 occupier was dealing puff and speed twenty-four hours a day and must have been pissing his neighbours off, 'cos it was pretty obvious, it was someone living nearby that put the call in.

Early one morning, they executed a drugs warrant on the address, they did the door and all piled in. There's no sign of a bloke living there, the female occupier goes ballistic, gets nicked for obstruction and is carted off to Stokey. To complicate matters, her elderly mother has a heart attack and spends a week in intensive care."

"Oh yeah, I read something about that." I commented.

Sarah looked around to make sure we weren't being overheard, so I gathered, she was getting to the interesting bit of the story.

"They searched the house, and it gradually dawns on them there's something wrong because the place is really respectable and the occupiers are honest, law abiding Christians. There's no trace of either drugs or a male living at the address.

They're all scratching their heads when someone takes a closer look at the warrant. You see, they've got the ticket on number thirty-two A, but they've gone into thirty-two, which was immediately next door."

"Fucking hell! No wonder the woman went mad!" I said.

"I know."

"Okay, it's a problem but it's not an insurmountable one." I suggested.

"What would you have done, Chris? You know if you were in charge?"

"It's a complete hands up, isn't it? Get the woman released from custody immediately, admit that you've fucked up, apologise, wait for the one six three and start saving 'cos the woman and her mother are going to be suing the arse off the Met. Get the door fixed, make sure the place is tidy, buy her some flowers. Shall I go on?" I said.

"I've got your drift." Sarah said.

"I mean it ain't good but it's a genuine mistake and not career ending."

"I agree. Do you want to know what they did?" Sarah asked.

"Go on."

"They decide to solve their problem by planting twelve bags of herbal."

"Oh, for fuck's sake! But what about the warrant?" I asked.

"I'll come to that. The woman who's been nicked for obstruction gets charged with possession with intent. She's forty-five, owns two hairdressers in Dalston and hasn't got any previous. She is Mrs

Respectable and everybody, I mean everybody, in the local community knows she is. She even had run ins with some of the local dealers because she's challenged them in the street over what they're doing."

"Sarah that's dreadful." I said.

"I know but it gets worse."

"How can it?" I asked.

"They destroyed the original Crimestoppers docket and create a new one with the woman's details and address. They make up a Collator's card with some old intelligence on it to suggest she's a dealer and slip it into the appropriate drawer. They destroy all the information on the real dealer." Sarah said.

"What role exactly did Paul play? I mean, he was only the driver, wasn't he?" I asked.

Sarah looked at me and I knew she was considering whether or not to tell me something.

"Go on." I said quietly.

"Paul supplied the twelve bags of cannabis."

"What? He's not like that is he?" I said.

"Apparently, he is. I couldn't believe it when he told me." Sarah said.

"Why on earth did he tell you?" I asked.

"He was pissed, we were arguing, you know how it goes sometimes."

"Not really, but never mind. So why do they need the money? They're not trying to buy her off, are they?" I asked.

"No, they've still got the problem of the warrant. One look at that and it's obvious what's happened. The DS on the Crime Squad got the warrant from a local Magistrate, who he's on the square with. He's had a chat with this guy, you know masonic brother to brother, and for the right money, he's agreed to give them another warrant, you know suitably back dated and for the woman's address. The bent Magistrate wants ten thousand, and there were ten of them involved, so they've each had to raise a grand. Well Paul hasn't got any money at all, so I suppose when he heard about your win, he saw his opportunity." Sarah explained.

"Oh my god Sarah! Suddenly I'm fucking involved!"

"You're not, Chris, because no one knows it was your money. And even if someone found out, you could just say, he told you it was to do with paying his solicitor's bill, which he did." Sarah said, emphasizing the last three words.

"Yeah, okay, I understand. Has he had a one six three yet?" I asked.

"No; they're expecting them any day. Meanwhile, the 'Stokey Ten' as they're calling themselves, have had several meets at a rugby club in Woodford to discuss things. They realise they're all in it together and their only hope is if they stick together like glue. The DS has allocated jobs to everyone, Paul's is to collect the money and pay the Magistrate."

"That doesn't seem right? If the Magistrate is friendly with the DS, surely, he should be doing that?" I said.

"Do you know Dave Feltham?" She asked.

"Is he the DS?" I said.

Sarah nodded.

"No, why?" I asked.

"He's pulling all the strings and, if you ask me, making sure that if it all comes on top, most of it misses him. It gets worse, though." Sarah said.

"That's impossible." I said.

"It only turns out it was the woman they nicked who gave the information about her neighbour in the first place."

"No!" I said, incredulously.

"When she was charged, her reply to caution was, you've got the wrong house you idiots, the guy you want lives next door, it was me who called Crimestoppers. As her solicitor was there, the Sergeant had to write it down."

"Jesus Christ Almighty." I said.

"It's a real mess but they've done a good job. They found and burnt every scrap of incriminating evidence before CIB could lay their hands on it."

"I'd be surprised if Paul was the only one struggling to find a grand, that's a lot of money." I said.

"I don't think that's a problem for many of them." Sarah replied.

"Really?"

"From what Paul has told me, Stoke Newington Crime Squad have been running amuck for years now. They nick money and drugs off all the dealers and recycle the drugs through a network of informants. They're making a fortune."

"I had absolutely no idea." I said, genuinely astonished.

"Why would you? They're really tight. Something big happened a while ago, you know, they came across a load of money or something and had an opportunity to nick it, which they took. Of course, once they'd done that, they were all in it together and it just kept going. Now they don't do anything without making out of it. One of them said to Paul 'I don't get out of bed in the morning unless I can make a hundred quid today'.

"What about the poor woman? And her mother? You got to feel sorry for them, haven't you?" I said.

"Yeah of course, it's terrible. The problem is, Chris, the I C 3s always say they've been fitted up and, whilst we both know it does go on, nine times out of ten it doesn't. Sandringham Road's cried wolf for too long and the Crime Squad hope now there is a fire, no one will take much notice of it." Sarah said.

For a few moments we both sat in silence. I have to admit I was quietly relieved because it was probable that, when CIB were all over the nick yesterday, it was much more likely to be about Paul's problem than mine.

"Sometimes I feel so sorry for the woman, I can't sleep." Sarah said.

"Of course, if you grassed Paul up, you'd help the innocent woman and solve your problem with him all in one go."

Sarah didn't say anything, but she looked me in the eyes and in that nanosecond, I knew she'd already thought of that.

Chapter 22

We went from the pub straight onto nights and I was posted with Kitty who seemed a bit happier. I couldn't help but think it was because of the practical joke and, maybe she thought, I'd been put well and truly in my place.

It was a quiet night which gave us an opportunity to chat and get to know one another. She'd grown up in Wembley and now lived with her musician boyfriend in Hornsey. She'd worked for Brent council as a typist before joining the job. She said she'd ended up taking her employers to an Industrial Tribunal for something or other but, when I questioned her more closely, she seemed reluctant to discuss the details. She said she'd got several thousand pounds in compensation which she put down as a deposit on her flat.

It had taken her eight months to get through Hendon because she struggled with exams. She had some reading disorder, which I'd never heard of, and kept getting back classed. Personally, I didn't think she was very bright but who was I to judge? In my day, well two years ago, if you failed more than once you got sacked. I couldn't help but think Kitty was being treated more leniently because she was coloured; or maybe, they'd just changed the policy since I was there.

Anyway, when we were talking about the job and why we'd joined, she said something which nearly made me laugh out loud.

"I just hope the Metropolitan Police knows how to make the best use of my extraordinary talents."

I wondered what extraordinary talents she thought she possessed but avoided the temptation to ask her.

Kitty was alright but I didn't think we would ever be best friends.

During the night there were two alarm calls to an off-licence in Church Street, which was on our beat, but on both occasions mobile units were nearer; and each time the result was the same.

"No trace of a break-in, can you call the keyholder?"

Alarms are the bane of every police officer's life as ninety-nine percent are a complete waste of time. They go off for a myriad of reasons; because they've been wrongly set, they're faulty, someone's left a window open, someone's pressed the panic button, a fly has landed on the sensor, and so on. Very rarely is an alarm activated by a burglar breaking in because, as a rule, a thief will avoid them, preferring to find premises less well protected. I'd learnt a long time ago, however, that a few smarter members of the criminal fraternity had discovered how to exploit our complacency.

I always watched out for two factors which set my in-built alarm bell ringing.

The first is *when* an alarm keeps going off. Alarms that go off at opening and closing times were invariably set off in error. A bank hold-up alarm might be the exception to this rule, as blaggers liked to go in at these times.

The second is *the type of goods* stored at the premises. Thieves like things that are easy to carry and quick to resell; drugs, booze, cigarettes, jewellery, so I'd ignore an alarm in a grocery store, hairdressers or butchers, and concentrate on chemists, off licences and pawn brokers.

An alarm at an off licence going off twice in the middle of the night was worth a look. So, after the second call, I thought we'd take a punt and see what was going on.

"Why are we going to that alarm?" Kitty asked, a reasonable question under the circumstances.

"It's probably nothing but sometimes a burglar will keep setting an alarm off so that the owner either deactivates it or the police become so pissed off with it going off, they don't send anyone to check it. Then burglar Bill breaks in. Get it?" I explained.

"I see. So, what are we going to do?" She asked.

"If we can, we'll hide up somewhere nearby and just wait and see what happens." I said.

"But we could be wasting our time." Kitty said.

"Well, we could be but let's just give it a try, shall we?" I suggested.

"Okay." My partner replied, without enthusiasm.

The off licence was on the main road amongst a row of shops which sat between two junctions. I knew a gravel service alley ran behind the shops linking the side streets. We walked slowly passed the front of the off licence and, whilst I pretended to take no notice of the place, I subtly studied it. It was quite conceivable that, if someone was casing the joint, they'd probably be close by. I noticed that the front window and door had heavy metal shutters which made an attempt to enter from the road unlikely.

Instead of taking the next right, which would have taken us to the far end of the service alley, I carried on and took the second right and came back by an elongated route. The alley was about one hundred and fifty yards long and, walking in the shadows, removing our helmets, and turning our radios to almost silent; we picked our way back along the rear of the shops. We entered the small back yard of the off licence through a partially open white wooden gate which sat between high brick walls.

The yard was about fifteen yards deep and eight wide, and cluttered with hundreds of discharged cardboard boxes and plastic crates, which made it difficult to walk, if one stepped off the thin pathway cutting straight through the mess. I clambered to the back right corner and found a hiding place to the side of an old wooden hut which might have once been a toilet. Searching with my torch, I found an old tin bucket and a milk crate, which I turned upside down, to make two passable stools.

If anyone did enter the yard, unless they closed the gate behind them and looked specifically in our direction, we wouldn't be very easy to detect. Whilst in an ideal world, we would watch and wait until we actually saw the person trying to break in, in reality, anyone who stepped in this yard, even if they saw us straight away and gave it legs, was going to be chased, caught and arrested for something.

When the rain started to fall heavier, I put my helmet back on my head and tried to retreat into my large police overcoat. Kitty huffed and puffed but didn't otherwise articulate her obvious displeasure. We were getting wet, but we'd survive, and I decided to give it an hour, in case my hunch was right. After a while the rain abated, so I removed my helmet and lit a cigarette which I smoked slowly, savouring each draw. Kitty didn't smoke, so I was grateful when, what wind there was, blew my smoke away from her.

"This is stupid." She whispered, just as I heard a sound from the alley behind.

"Shush, listen." I said.

A fox entered the yard through the gate and Kitty jumped, the animal bolted. We settled down again. Kitty pulled a face.

From where I was sitting, I could see the rear windows of perhaps half a dozen houses and flats and, behind opaque glass, some person of indeterminate gender showered and got ready for their day ahead. Somewhere away to our left, a dog barked, intermittently.

Just when I realised my backside was getting damp and I'd have to stand up, I heard a car coming down the alley from the nearest end, the opposite way I'd come in. Of course, it could be nothing, these access roads led to several shops which fronted the main road and, at four-thirty, it was very possible a member of staff might be arriving to set up for the day. When the car stopped right on the other side of the fence from where we were sitting, I got a lot more excited. I heard car doors open, at least two, and then male voices.

"Turn the fucking headlights off, get the boot unlocked and leave it open and keep the engine running." A rough East End voice said.

In that moment, I knew we were in business and gave Kitty the thumbs up sign, followed by the finger over the lips.

Kitty looked simply terrified.

I heard footsteps on gravel, then a thud followed by a load of cursing.

"Fucking hell, Dave, just get up; stop fucking about, we need to be in and out in ten minutes." The rough voice said.

"I think I've broken my wrist." Protested Dave, and I worried for a second that they were going to abandon their escapade.

"I don't give a fuck, just get moving."

The gate swung slowly open, and I saw two men enter the yard. They were white; the first one carried a jemmy, the second one was holding his right wrist and obviously in some discomfort. We were no more than six yards away, but they hadn't a clue we were there.

I stayed really still, I could feel my heart beating and I could hear Kitty's breathing becoming quicker. As they moved nearer to the building, they passed out of our sight and Kitty turned to me, the expression on her face asking me what we should do next.

Again, I put my finger to my mouth and, by pointing to the ground, indicated we should do nothing, just yet. Although we had enough evidence already to arrest them for being on enclosed premises and going equipped to steal with the jemmy, I wanted to arrest them up for attempted burglary, so I'd let them run for just another few seconds.

Then there was another noise from the alley, someone was walking towards us and panting heavily. Kitty and I looked at one another and then a man's voice said.

"Find him Ben, find him."

A German Shepherd came tearing into the back yard and, was heading straight for the men, until Kitty screamed, and the dog turned direction and came towards us, instead, covering the ground in seconds and stopping about a yard in front of me. Its lips were pulled back exposing enormous teeth and from its mouth came a deep and menacing guttural growl. It's heckles were up. I've never been bothered by dogs but this one was truly frightening.

We stood up in unison, but Kitty also stepped backwards and fell over, so I stepped across between her and the growling dog.

"Stand still, don't move." A dog-handler had appeared in the yard and was shouting orders, although whether he was shouting at us, the burglars, or his charge, I had no idea because I didn't want to take my eyes off the dog.

The two burglars were walking towards the dog handler and the gate, their only escape route.

"Ben, Ben, come." The dog handler called, and the dog hesitated and took several backwards steps back towards his master.

"Chris, help me, I can't get up. I think my leg is caught." Kitty said, desperately.

I didn't really want to take my eyes off the dog, but I couldn't leave Kitty struggling, and the dog was definitely retreating. What's more, a quick glance at the men suggested they were squaring up for a fight and dog or no dog, we needed to be there to help our colleague out.

I turned around quickly and held out my hand to my struggling partner, determined to get her up, so we could get over to the gate, before they overpowered the handler. Kitty grabbed my arm and as I pulled her up, I bent forward.

I heard a scrabbling noise and felt a sharp pain in my backside.

Chapter 23

In the toilets back at the nick, I examined my injuries; four puncture wounds right in the middle of my right buttock. Surprisingly there was very little blood, but it felt badly bruised, although they would probably take several days to come out. Next to me stood the dog handler, PC Brian Wilkins, who was holding an antiseptic wipe.

"You're not thinking of seeing the Divisional Surgeon or anything, are you?" He asked, tentatively.

"You should always get an injury on duty recorded, that's what I've been told, but I'm guessing you don't want me to." I replied.

"Ben's on a final warning; he could be off the books if you report this." Brian said.

"How come?"

"He's not meant to bite, unless he's bringing down a suspect who's running away." Brian explained.

"What exactly does 'off the books' mean? Will they put him down?"

"It's possible, but unlikely. But they'll certainly remove him from operational duties, which would be a shame 'cos he's a cracking dog, really brave, very reliable."

I dabbed the antiseptic wipe against my buttock. It was starting to bleed a bit now. Brian gave me another wipe.

"Will I have to have an injection or something? You know in case of infection?" I asked.

"No, you'll be fine. He hasn't got rabies you know; he's a very clean dog." Brian said.

"So, he doesn't lick his balls then?" I asked.

"Of course, he does but you know why don't you? You know why dogs lick their own balls?" Brian asked.

"No." I replied, slightly perplexed to be asked such a ridiculous question, but hoping I was going to learn some significant piece of information.

"Because they can, mate; because they can." Brian laughed, and I guessed he'd told that joke many times before.

I smiled too.

"I didn't realise you two were in there otherwise I'd have kept him on the lead. Great minds think alike, eh? It's one of my fortes, sitting up on alarms which keep going off."

"I learnt the hard way." I said.

"What do you mean?" Brian asked.

"Couple of years ago I persuaded a jeweller, Cohen's just down the High Street, to turn his alarm off when it kept going off and what happened? He got screwed." I said.

"I remember it, a load of gold sovereigns were nicked." Brian said, much to my surprise.

"How the fuck do you remember that?" I asked, absolutely amazed at this man's recall.

"I don't know, just do. It's the sort of thing that sticks." Brian replied.

"I'm impressed." I said, pulling my trousers up.

"That plonk you're with, is she okay?" Brian asked.

"Why do you ask?"

"Well, when I'd got the prisoners in the van, I took the jemmy and, you know …" Brian said.

"Did the back door?"

"Yeah." He replied.

"Did she see you?" I asked.

"Of course."

"Did she say anything?" I asked.

"Yeah, she had a right go at me, told me she wanted nothing to do with it and not to show her involved in any way." Brian replied.

"She's just off Street Duties and she's …" I hesitated

"Grief?" Suggested Brian.

"Grief." I agreed, he'd found exactly the right word to describe our Kitty.

"Shall we share the prisoners? One each?" I suggested, moving the conversation onto a more cheerful note.

"And what about reporting the bite? Look, if you insist, let me try to contact the other Ocsar unit and see if they'll take it?"

"I'll keep shtum, don't worry, but make sure you write the plonk completely out of it." I told him.

"Thanks, and I'll bring you the usual."

"Ok" I replied.

I had no idea what the usual was, but I would look forward to receiving it.

~~~

In the charge room we eventually booked in our prisoners who were a couple of cheeky cockneys, with a keen sense of humour, who had been through the same process a dozen times before. Of course, they thought it was hilarious that I'd had my arse bitten and reckoned it was worth getting arrested to witness such an amusing event. I smiled through their comments, but I'd had just about enough of being the butt of everyone's jokes that week.

When I put the first guy into a cell, a voice called out from the drunk tank at the end.

"Officer, officer?"

I wandered over and dropped the wicket. The face of a small black guy, in his fifties, appeared.

"What's the matter, mate?" I asked.

"I don't think this guy's very well, his breathing is funny." He said.

He stepped to the side so I could see beyond him into the half light of the rear of the cell, but all I could make out was a bloke, apparently asleep, lying on his side.

I looked at the small blackboard by the door, two names had been written in chalk: Smith and Perkins.

"Are you Smith or Perkins?" I asked him?"

"Smith." He replied.

"I'll go and get the keys." I said.

When I returned to the main charge room, I dug out the charge sheet for Perkins. He'd been arrested for drunk and disorderly, four hours ago, he was fifty-two years old and of no fixed abode.

"Sarge, can I have the keys? I want to check on a prisoner in the tank. The other prisoner in there says he's not breathing properly." I said.

Sergeant Felix looked up.

"I'll come with you." He said.

We headed off down the cell passage.

We quickly discovered the problem. Perkins had vomited and it was blocking his mouth, making it difficult for him to breath. Sergeant Felix pulled his head back and laid him on his side. Sergeant Felix, Smith, and I listened carefully. The man was still breathing but it was a strange rasping sound. I know this sounds terrible, but if he did stop breathing, there was no way I was giving him mouth to mouth.

"I'll stay with him, Nostrils. You get the Reserve to call an ambulance for one male prisoner with breathing difficulties." Sergeant Felix ordered.

I didn't wait to be asked twice.

When I returned a few minutes later, Sergeant Felix was thanking Smith for alerting us.

"Do you want me to go with the prisoner to hospital, Sarge?"

"No, you're alright Nostrils; I'll bail him, he's only here for drunk and dis. What you in for?" Sergeant Felix asked Smith.

"Breach of licence." Smith replied.

"Recall?" Sergeant Felix asked.

Smith nodded.

"You've done a good thing here, mate. Sorry I can't help you; I would under different circumstances." Sergeant Felix said.

"I know. Don't worry about it, Sarge, I'm alright." Smith replied pleasantly.

The ambulance came and the crew carried Perkins, wearing an oxygen mask, out on a stretcher. I went to close the cell door.

"Before you do that, officer, can I just tell you something?" Smith said.

"Of course, what is it?" I asked.

"It's probably a load of rubbish but it's been troubling me for months. When I was in Winson Green, just before my release, the bloke I was sharing a cell with told me something when he was off his head. I couldn't say anything whilst I was inside, because in prison there's no worse crime than being a grass, and now I'm on my way back, which leaves me just this moment in time, to let someone know what this bloke said to me."

For someone who was about to go back to prison, Mr Smith was very articulate.

"Before you tell me what this guy said, tell me why he told you?" I asked.

"He told me 'cos he was off his head on brown and didn't know what he was saying."

"He was in prison? How did he get heroin?" I asked.

"Officer, you are very naïve. The screws bring it in, they make a fortune smuggling drugs. Anyway, this guy, he's a Geordie and off his head, and I'm telling him to get off the gear and sort his life out. I'm older than most cons, so sometimes they take a little notice of me. Anyway, he tells me he needs the shit 'cos he needs to forget this terrible thing he's done. I'm not taking a lot of notice, when suddenly, he blurts out he's killed a young girl, a girl called Sandra something, who was on her way home from some night club years ago. I mean he's only in for taking and driving away. As I said, I couldn't say anything, but when I was released on licence last month, I went to the library and did some research. A seventeen-year-old girl called Sandra Zarzo, a Spanish student on an exchange trip, was murdered in 1979 in Gateshead. When I read the article, my blood ran cold."

"What was your cell mate's name?" I asked.

"I knew you'd ask me that." He replied.

"Don't tell me you can't remember, Mr Smith." I said.

"I can't, I'm sorry. I was only with him for a few days."

"Okay, what else can you tell me about him?" I asked.

"He was a white guy, mid-twenties, Geordie…"

"Height?" I asked.

"I've no idea, in prison you spend most of your life horizontal."

"Hair colour, build?" I said.

"Brown, average." He replied.

"Can you think of anything else, at all?" I asked.

"As I said, only that he was in for nicking cars. But whatever you do with what I've told you, I don't want it getting traced back to me. If anyone comes to speak to me about this, I'll deny this conversation ever took place. Do you get me, Officer?"

"I do, Mr Smith; thanks." I said.

"For what?" he asked.

"For saving that man's life." I replied.

"And for anything else, Officer?" He asked.

"No" I replied.

"Good." He said, content that I had understood his request.

I went to find Kitty and asked her to type Smith's information up on a report for the Collator.

"I'm not doing your typing!" She replied indignantly.

"But I'm really rubbish at typing, and you said you used to be a typist. It'll only take you a few minutes, but it'll take me half an hour." I said, gob smacked by her reaction.

"I am not your secretary." Kitty declared, before turning on her heel and walking off.

"You selfish bitch. I took a dog bite for you." I exclaimed and walked off to type the report up myself. Kitty was really starting to get on my nerves.

Chapter 24

I was posted with Kitty for another couple of nights, but I decided to avoid getting involved in anything contentious because I just couldn't trust her to back me up.

On the Friday, our last night together, we'd only been out about twenty minutes, when we turned the corner of a side street to see a large silver Nissan, stationary across and completely blocking the road. As we walked towards it, I noticed the engine was running and expected the driver, at any moment, to complete the three-point turn he or she appeared to be making. As I got closer, however, I noticed the windows, including the windscreen, were really misted up.

Kitty and I exchanged a quizzical look, and I wiped the driver's door window but to no avail, as the steam was on the inside. I tried the door which was unlocked and, as I slowly opened it, the light came on and illuminated the interior. There was only one person in the car, a large white lady, in her fifties, wearing a long black fur coat. She was asleep, so asleep in fact that she was snoring and, as I opened the door further, it became apparent she was leaning against it because, with no dignity at all, when the door had opened far enough, she fell gracelessly out and onto the road. Her eyes opened briefly and then closed. The inside of the car, and the woman herself, stunk of booze.

"Wow, someone's had a good night." I said.

I stepped over her and got into the car, put the handbrake on and turned the ignition off. On the driver's seat was the woman's handbag and I rooted through it for any details of the woman's identity.

"Call the van up, we're in Watling Avenue." I told Kitty.

"What shall I say?" She asked.

I knew Kitty was new, but she'd been puppy walked for three months and I was rather surprised she had to ask.

"Tell them who you are, where you are, and that we require transport for one prisoner. Also ask them for an authorised driver to reposition a vehicle." I instructed her.

"But we haven't arrested her yet?" She said.

"Kitty, I think that's rather academic; she's comatosed."

"Can't you just move the car? There's a space there?" Kitty suggested.

"I could, Kitty, but I'm not going to, I'm not authorised to drive someone's car. Just ask for an authorised driver, they'll know why." I said.

"Golf November, Five, five, four?" Kitty transmitted.

"Go ahead, five five four"

"Can we have transport for a prisoner and an authorised driver? Watling Road please?" Kitty asked.

"Yes, yes."

"Thank you." She replied.

"Five five four, eighteen?"

"Yes Sarge?" Kitty replied.

"What you got?" Sergeant Felix asked.

"One for drunk and incapable, Sarge." She replied.

"Received." He said.

"Kitty, I think it's a drunk in charge, not a drunk and incapable, she's in a car with the engine running." I said.

"But she might have just been trying to keep warm."

"What? Parked across the road? Kitty she was doing a three-point turn and fell asleep because she's completely pissed." I said.

I was getting exasperated.

"I never saw her driving, and neither did you." Kitty declared.

I wanted to be patient, but this was a ridiculous conversation. The woman had clearly committed the offence of being drunk in charge of a motor vehicle, or as it was more commonly called, a Section 5. After six months at training school studying the law and then three months on Street Duties, Kitty should know that, too.

I bent over the lady to check she was all right. She was breathing deeply and started to snore, once again. Her whole person smelt of alcohol. She must have been drinking heavily for hours.

"Have a look in the car, Kitty." I said.

"What for?" She asked.

"For anything valuable so we can take it back to the nick for safe keeping, for any medication she might be on, for any information which might help us to trace a next of kin, for a driving licence. I've checked her handbag but it's just full of make-up." I said.

"I'm not sure we've got the power to search her vehicle."

"She's under arrest, of course we have." I said.

"But you haven't arrested her yet, have you?" Kitty replied.

"Oh, for fuck's sake Kitty. You fucking arrest her, and arrest her for drunk in charge, and, even though she's completely dead to the world, fucking caution her if it'll make you happy. She's your prisoner anyway." I was shouting.

I knew it was unprofessional, but I couldn't put up with Kitty a second longer.

"I'm not having anything to do with this." She replied, as if I'd just fitted up Mahatma Gandhi with a flick knife and a bag of Charlie in front of the Queen and Prince Phillip.

~~~

When we got back to the nick, Kitty was conspicuous by her absence in the charge room. I gave the facts of the arrest to the Station Officer Sergeant Key, who had the woman put in a cell to sleep it off. I called the Divisional Surgeon to examine her to decide whether she was too drunk to be at the wheel of a car.

"I'm going to need her strip searched, aren't you with that new plonk?"

"I am, Sarge, but I've no idea where. She's disappeared, shall I see if anyone else is about?" I replied.

"Get Sarah, she was in the PC's Writing Room a couple of minutes ago and then do your notes; it shouldn't take you long."

I stuck my head round the door to the PC writing room. Sarah was writing up a crime sheet. I checked no one else was about.

"Hello, gorgeous." I said.

Sarah looked up and smiled. There was something about her smile.

"Can you search a prisoner?" I asked.

Sarah nodded and smiled again. Sometimes, at times just like that and for no reason I could really explain, I just loved her.

~~~

I'd just sat down in the canteen to start writing, when I got a message to go and see Golf November one, in his office. Golf November one was the call sign for the Duty Officer, Inspector Simon Portman, who was in charge of our relief. He was a nice bloke, a few months short of retirement, and a real gentleman. He was liked by all.

I knocked at his office and entered without waiting to be summoned. I had a feeling this was going to be something to do with Kitty, so I wasn't at all surprised when, having indicated I should sit, he opened by saying.

"Kitty's been in to speak to me."

"Oh, yes." I said, politely.

"You swore at her, Nostrils." Inspector Portman said.

"I beg your pardon, Sir?"

"You swore at her, you used the F word." Inspector Portman said.

"That's not quite right. I didn't use the F word towards her as part of an insult, I used it in conversation to emphasise my point."

"She very upset, Nostrils. She's been crying her eyes out." Inspector Portman said.

"Sir, I don't know what to say. I'm sorry if she's upset, but she's going to have to toughen up." I replied.

"She seems unhappy about the arrest too; have you done your notes yet?" He asked.

"No, Sir, I'd just started when you called me up. The arrest is as sound as a pound, I promise you." I asserted.

I looked Inspector Portman in the eye.

"As sound as a fucking pound." I said, making two points, at once.

"Fair enough, Nostrils; but I think we'll post Kitty out with someone less…" he hesitated

"Less what, Sir?" I said, eager to hear the next word.

"Less you."

Chapter 25

The following night I was posted Second Reserve. I didn't particularly enjoy being inside, but that night it was quite convenient because I wanted to get a name check done on Mrs M's boyfriend, Donald, and it would make things easier. The only downside was that Kitty was posted Assistant Station Officer, so the atmosphere was somewhat strained.

After a couple of hours, there was a raised male voice at the front counter and, even though I couldn't stand her, I stuck my head around the corner to see what was going on and whether Kitty needed a hand.

There was a white man in his thirties, holding a dog lead, and he was really upset about something.

"It's just not good enough. I'm fucking furious." He said, almost shouting.

"I'm really sorry. I've said I'm sorry." Kitty said defensively.

"Fucking sorry? Fucking sorry?" He said, now he was shouting.

"Excuse me, stop shouting and don't swear." I said firmly.

"What's the problem?" I asked Kitty.

"I'll tell you what the fucking problem is." The man interjected.

"Listen, Sir, if you swear again, you'll be arrested. That's it, that's your one warning." I said.

"Now, Kitty; what's the problem?"

"The gentleman's come to collect his dog but I can't find the Dog Book and the kennel is empty." She replied.

Kitty was close to tears; her face was really red and her eyes were welling up.

"Did the police tell you the dog had been found, Sir?" I asked.

"No, my neighbour did. He knew I'd lost her and overheard two kids talking, in one of the local shops, about finding her and handing her in, here."

"Are you sure you've got the right station? Because you're only getting the information third or even fourth hand, aren't you?" I said.

"That's true." He replied, a little calmer.

"Have you reported your dog lost?" I asked.

"No." He replied.

"Right, this officer will take a report of the missing dog and then phone around the local police stations to see where your dog's been handed in. I'm sure we'll find her." I assured him.

He nodded.

"How can I report the dog missing when the book's missing?" Kitty asked, really unhelpfully.

"I'll get a new one from the stationery store." I replied calmly.

As I wandered off to track down the Sergeant who has the keys to the store cupboard, I heard the man start to give a description of his dog.

"She's a Red Tibetan Mastiff, she's only a puppy …"

~~~

In the middle of the night, I asked the PNC operator to do a name check on Donald Cole. I had to be careful because you only normally did a name check on someone you'd stopped or arrested. If it transpired Donald was wanted, then I might have to ride out some difficult questions and, the more I thought about him, the more likely I thought it was that there was an arrest warrant with his name on it, somewhere in the system.

"What's the details, Nostrils?" Asked Matt, who was the PNC operator, that night.

"Cole, Donald Anthony; fourteen twelve forty-four, male, white, six two. I ain't got a place of birth."

A few taps of the keyboard later Matt looked up.

"Got him, born Buckhurst Hill, Essex. Do you want me to draw his CRO file for you?" Matt asked helpfully.

"Yes, please."

"Any warning markers or reports? I asked.

"Just the one, but it's not really one to worry about." Matt said, confidently.

"Go on?" I said.

"He's dead, Nostrils."

~~~

About five o'clock I wandered into the back yard to get some fresh air and light a cigarette. One of the panda cars was in but no one was around. I meandered absent mindedly over to the kennels, which were down a short alley to the side of the Street Duties portocabin. There were two separate kennels, and both were empty. I swung one of the doors, casually.

"Hi Chris, what you doing?" Sarah said.

She'd followed me down the alley, but I hadn't seen her.

"Nothing really, bit bored. I hate this last hour on nights, it really drags."

"Thanks for the money, Chris; I really appreciate it." She said.

"That's all right. Thanks for not telling anyone about the fifteen grand; people were off with me after my little win at the casino, they'd really hate me, if they knew about that too." I said.

"I think you've got it wrong. They weren't being off with you the other night; they were busy planning the wind-up." She explained.

That actually made sense.

"And after what you went through last year, I don't think anyone would begrudge you the money. I suppose Dawn's Mum must have received her payout, too." Sarah said.

"I've no idea, I suppose so." I replied.

"Listen, why don't we go away for a couple of nights next week, you know, after lates? I'll tell Paul I'm going to see one of my old school mates." Sarah said.

"Yeah, that'll be good. Where do you fancy?" I asked.

"Brighton?" She suggested.

"No, I had a bad experience there once and vowed I'd never go back, again. How about Bournemouth?" I replied.

"Yeah, you book it though, 'cos obviously I can't have anything coming to my home." Sarah said.

"Okay. That'll be great." I replied.

"It'll be nice to relax; I'm so stressed, Chris."

"I've noticed." I said.

I was referring to the fact we'd not slept together for ages, well nearly a week.

I flicked my cigarette and stepped forward to give Sarah a hug, but she put her hand up and stopped me. I didn't realise things were that bad between us, but I'd misunderstood what she was doing, and she pushed me back against the kennel. My backside met the slopping felted roof.

"Let me show you one of the disgusting things I got up to in those videos." She said.

She pushed her hand against my groin, unzipped my trousers and crouched down. I leant back and shut my eyes.

Chapter 26

I was really fed up when I got into work the following night and discovered I'd been posted Second Reserve for the rest of nights. To make matters worse, once again I had Kitty to keep me company, as she was Assistant Station Officer.

We'd only been in ten minutes, when she started moaning at me for smoking in the front office; Christ, the way she went on you'd have thought there was a law against it. She was fighting a losing battle though, because the Station Officer, Sergeant Key, the guy who'd orchestrated the mortuary wind up, was a smoker, too.

The first few hours on nights are usually quite busy, with the pubs turning out, but from about one, the work tapers off to nothing, by about three in the morning. At four, yesterday becomes tomorrow, and the capital starts to wake.

Sometimes, between three and four, Inspector Portman used to allow the relief to return to the nick and gather for tea and snacks in the front office. He wouldn't permit it as a matter of course, but once or twice a week, if he thought the relief were working well, he would call it on under the guise of a relief meeting.

That night, I got the nod to make the announcement.

"All Golf November units from Golf November; Golf November one invites you to a relief meeting at three-thirty; I repeat, Golf November one invites you to a relief meeting at three-thirty. Golf November, out."

"Received; Golf November four."

Golf November four was the area car, the Rover crewed by two of the most experienced officers on the relief. They were the only unit to acknowledge the call because it was a rule that the area car would stay out during these meetings and patrol the far side of the ground, in case anything urgent came in.

Someone bought a couple of loaves of bread and a tub of butter, and set up a toaster in the PC's writing room, which was next to the front office. Someone else took an order for confectionary and soft drinks, and went to the all-night garage in Stamford Hill.

On some reliefs, those that weren't driving were allowed to have a beer or two, but not on C relief, where Inspector Portman had a strict no drinking on duty policy.

If a member of the public came to the front counter, they might be mistaken for thinking there was a party going on.

The meetings were informal affairs but quite good fun, everyone took the piss out of each other and had a laugh. As I was still very young in service, I had to be careful whom I sparred with, whereas the senior PC's could say just about what they wanted to whom they wanted, with the obvious exception of the Sergeants and Inspector. Generally, though, the banter was good natured, some might be quite cutting but was rarely nasty. The meeting worked in the same way that wild animals, living in a group, play with one another to test their respective strengths, and to establish and reinforce social status. By and large I kept quiet, it was generally the safest thing to do because some of these guys were sharp. I admired the way their minds worked so quickly to produce a comment or remark that was really funny, without ever going too far.

Of course, my wind up was still the main topic of conversation and I smiled as I regaled the story for, what felt like, the hundredth time.

"If I haven't been through enough? In two years, I've been shot at, blown up, tricked into wanking in front of an entire relief, had my arse bitten by the hardest police dog this side of the Thames, and now subjected to the most frightening wind up on God's earth." I said and everyone laughed.

"Yeah, I think we'll leave you alone for a while, Nostrils; no more wind ups." Sergeant Key said, as he tucked into a chocolate bar.

Everyone was laughing.

"What?" I said realising I was missing something.

"Ain't you got anything to eat, Nostrils?" Sergeant Key asked.

I looked down; my Yorkie bar! Sergeant Key was eating my bloody Yorkie bar.

"One day, Sarge, one day…" I said.

Everyone laughed but the situation had given me an idea. Sergeant Key nodded towards the telephone console, line one was ringing.

"Can you get that, Nostrils? I've got my mouth full." He said, as he took another bite of my chocolate bar.

"Stoke Newington police station, can I help you?" I asked politely.

"Hi Stokey, its City Road here. Just to let you know the Commander's just been in, he's doing his rounds, expect him in ten."

"Are you going to let Hackney know?" I asked.

"Yes, will do, but according to his driver, he's coming to you next."

"Thanks, mate; appreciate the warning." I said.

I hung up and turned to Inspector Portman.

"That was City Road, Sir; the Commander's on his way." I said.

Inspector Portman didn't have to say a word, everyone instantly got moving, and the front office staff jumped to it to tidy up the mess; everyone, that is, except Kitty, who sat there thumbing through a magazine like she was the queen of fucking Sheba.

Within five minutes, there was no trace of anything in the front office, except an empty Yorkie packet, which Sergeant Key had left on my desk when I'd gone to the toilet.

I'd never met this Commander, but his nickname was Zebedee and he was a bit of a legend, but not in a good way. It was said, for example, he would expect you to stand when he entered the room and, that amongst many other eccentricities, he would inspect your socks to check they were the regulation colour of dark blue or black. I was moderately interested to meet the man and see if these rumours were true.

The First Reserve was a PC called Peter Foley, who was coming to the end of his service and really wasn't interested in the job anymore, but he was a likeable chap. I asked him whether we should stand when the Commander came in.

"You can do what you like, mate. I ain't standing up. Anyway, Zebedee's Upton Park, ain't he?"

"He's what?" I replied.

"Upton Park, you know two stops short of Barking?"

"Have you met him before?" I asked.

"Knew him when he was an Inspector, he lived on the ground I worked, used to slap his missus about and we got called quite regularly to sort it out. He's a bully, Nostrils; don't stand for any of his shit."

"That's easy for you to say. When do you retire?"

"Three pay days left, Nostrils; just three."

I heard the front doors swing open. I didn't think it would be the Commander because he would drive into the back yard. I looked around to find Kitty, whose role was to deal with callers at the front counter, but she'd disappeared.

I got up and walked round. A dark-skinned white man with a cab drivers licence hanging on a chain around his neck and a small bundle of papers in his right hand.

"Producer?" I asked.

"Oh, yes." He replied.

I heard a noise behind me, glanced back and caught sight of Kitty disappearing back around the corner.

"Hang on, Sir; I'll get someone to deal with you." I said.

I walked back round almost running after Kitty.

"Oi!" I called, loudly, after her.

She stopped halfway along the corridor.

"You've got a customer." I said.

"Oh, I thought you were dealing with him." She replied.

"No. It's a producer. Now get your arse, oh I'm sorry, heaven forbid I should swear in your presence, your bottom, out there and deal with it, if that's okay, if it's not too much trouble?" I said really sarcastically.

"There's no need to be like that, Nostrils." She said.

For some reason I was really offended that she called me Nostrils.

"Don't call me Nostrils or we'll all start calling you by *your* nickname." I said.

"But I haven't got one." She replied.

"Oh, you *really* have. Now go and deal with the producer, Kitty." I said firmly.

I was being really horrible and I knew it. I guess I was still smarting from what had happened earlier in the week with the drunk in charge. To compound matters she'd been either ignoring me or, when she did speak to me, it was to moan about my smoking. And now, the lazy cow wanted me to do her job for her, she hadn't offered to take over from me but slunk away hoping I hadn't seen her.

"What's my nickname?" She asked.

"Go and serve the man, Kitty; there's a good girl. Or of course you could just burst into tears and run off to the toilet? It's your call." I said.

Kitty stormed off.

"Un fucking believable!" I shouted after her.

Chapter 27

After the Commander's visit, I got myself a can of Coke from the vending machine in the canteen, and was walking back across the yard, when I saw what, could only be, a torch being shone in one of the admin offices on the second floor. I stood and watched for a few moments, it was intermittent, but someone was moving about up there. I tried to visualise the layout of the second floor to work out which room it was, my best guess was the Personnel and Sickness office.

I went inside, put my can of Coke on my desk, and said to Peter Foley:

"I'll be back in a minute, I think something's going on up on the second floor, it's probably some sort of wind up and I want to make sure I'm not the intended victim again."

I set off without waiting for his reply, but he shouted 'Nostrils' after me, so I went back to see what he wanted.

"What?" I said, impatiently.

I wanted to get upstairs before whatever was happening was over.

Peter looked around to see who could hear him.

"Sit down and I'll tell you." He said quietly.

I did.

"You know Matt is desperate to get on the Doors, Posts and Gates?" Peter said.

"No, what are you talking about?" I replied.

I assumed he was talking about Matt Richards, one of the PC's on our relief, but I had no idea about Doors, Posts and Gates.

"Matt, you know the tall ginger PC, who always gets lumbered on the PNC? He's applied, like three times, for the DPG, the Diplomatic Protection Group, but he keeps getting the brush off."

"Okay" I said, mystified what that had to do with anything.

"Well, he wanted to see if there was anything on his personnel file which was screwing his chances."

"Like what?" I asked.

"Like anything, you know, a bad report, something like that. Anyway, he found a way into the Personnel Office; the key was hidden in a drawer in the Chief Inspector's office. Then, and all credit to him, he found the keys for the filing cabinets to the Personnel files, hanging from a hook behind the Personnel Sergeant's desk, and got hold of his file." Peter explained.

"So, he's up there now looking through it?" I asked.

"No, no. That was on Monday, since then we've been taking it in turns to dig out our own files and do some weeding." Peter said.

"Weeding?" I asked.

"Yeah, you know, take out anything on there that you don't want to be on there." Peter explained.

"Have you done it?"

"I have but only out of curiosity, as I'm retiring soon, so I don't really care."

"So, who knows this is going on? Everyone?" I asked.

"God, no; the stars and stripes are in the dark but the more senior PC's are in on it." Peter said.

"Thanks for telling me." I said, rather hurt that I hadn't been entrusted with the secret.

"Listen, Nostrils, it's not personal it's just that you sprogs won't have anything on your files yet, anyway. You weren't told because you didn't need to know."

"Who's up there now?" I asked.

Before I could reply, Roger Class walked into the front office carrying a torch and I had my answer.

"I want in."

"Wait there." He replied.

Peter took Roger to one side and returned a few minutes later.

"Roger will take you up. Don't get caught, if you do, you're on your own."

I nodded and then followed Roger up to the Chief Inspector's office and then into the Personnel office.

"Be careful with the torch, I could see it from downstairs." I said.

Roger moved quickly and retrieved a set of keys from the back of a set of drawers.

"The files are alphabetical, find the drawer for P and then the colour on the cabinet there …"

He indicated a small round sticker.

"… relates to the key with the same colour indicator. When you've finished, put the cabinet keys back behind the desk, and the office door key in the Chief Inspector's office, second drawer, black tin. I'll wait for you downstairs; I'll need my torch back. Okay?" Roger asked.

I nodded and he was off.

The top drawer of the third filing cabinet was marked 'M – S' and the sticker was red. I selected the right key and, bingo, I was in. My fingers flicked quickly through the files, Portman, Potter, Puller, Ralph, Rapper. My file wasn't there or if it was, it was in the wrong place. I searched again, no luck. Then I extended my search to all the files in the drawer. It definitely wasn't there, but a piece of white paper had fallen to the bottom of the drawer. I took it out and examined it under the torch light. On it was typed a short note.

PC 466 G Christopher Pritchard. Personnel file sent to Superintendent Alec Groves, C.O. on 10th February 1985.

The 10th February was about a week after I'd stolen the old lady's money. Now I knew for certain they were on to me.

~~~

At five to six, when everyone else was setting off home to their beds, I was once again sitting in the Inspector's office getting bollocked about how I'd spoken to Kitty.

I'd told Inspector Portman exactly, and very honestly, what had happened and what I'd said.

"Nostrils, we need to tread carefully with Kitty. She made an allegation of racism against her training school instructor when she failed her final exam. They let her pass and she withdrew the allegation. The Street Duties sergeant here had been primed and was so afraid of a similar accusation, he let her do whatever she wanted. He even gave her an A on her end of Street Duties report which has made life even more difficult for us because now she thinks she's good.

When I was speaking to her earlier, she asked me why I posted her with someone who can't get on with women. I told her about what had happened to you and Dawn, but she just accused me of taking your side. She doesn't like the way you spoke to her. She says you were aggressive, and she felt frightened and intimidated.

"Are you saying Kitty is upset because I told her to get her arse in gear? You've gotta be kidding me, Sir?" I said, I could feel my emotion rising.

"I know what you're going to say, Nostrils, I know how you feel." Inspector Portman said.

"How can you, boss?" I said quietly, but not rudely.

Inspector Portman smiled submissively, almost apologetically.

I could feel myself getting upset, it was just so unfair. I fought desperately hard to fight it back.

"You're bollocking me?" I said, quietly.

I'd successfully fought back tears, but they made their way down my nose, and I searched desperately through my pockets to find a tissue. When I looked up, Inspector Portman was handing me one.

"Thanks." I said.

"I'm not bollocking you, Nostrils. I just want to talk a suggestion over with you." Inspector Portman said.

I was immediately suspicious, was I going to be moved?

"What suggestion?" I asked cautiously.

"Listen, Nostrils. The world is changing. The job goes out of its way to encourage women and minorities to join and, when they do, it wants to keep them. If she complains about you, you'll be really vulnerable. I want to protect you." Inspector Portman said.

"You're moving me, aren't you? That's so unfair."

"I'm not moving you anywhere, Nostrils, over my dead body, son. But I do want you to go and have some counseling about what happened to you. One, because it'll protect you, if Kitty puts the knife in and two …"

Inspector Portman paused forcing me to look up and meet his eye.

"…I think it'll do you good."

"Do you think I'm mad then?" I asked.

"No of course not, Nostrils, but if I'd gone through what you've gone through, I know I certainly wouldn't be over it by now; and I don't think you are. Talking things over with a trained counsellor will do you good." He said.

Inspector Portman smiled and I felt he was on my side.

"Alright, Sir." I replied.

"Now go and get some sleep, son." He said.

"Can I just ask one thing?" I said.

"Of course, Nostrils." He replied.

"Don't post Kitty and me anywhere near each other for a while."

"Oh, that won't be a problem." He replied confidently.

"Oh, good." I said.

"We won't be seeing Kitty for months, she went sick about an hour ago with work related stress, and, after what Peter Foley said to the Commander this evening, if I had any sense, so would I."

Chapter 28

Towards the end of nights, I went for tea with Andy and Rik to get an update on developments because I knew they'd been over to the Roebuck Hotel in Buckhurst Hill.

"We spoke to the Manager." Rik explained.

"Was he alright?" I asked.

"She, she was sweet. She said, he had been there a couple of months. She was under the impression that every Sunday he paid in cash for his room for the coming week. He was, she said, and I quote, 'the ideal guest'. Here's the thing though, when she went to check his account, she discovered he was two weeks behind and had run up a substantial bill at the bar and for room service." Andy said.

"That's interesting. I get the impression, you know overdue car hire, behind with his hotel bill. That Donald might be about to do a moonlight." I commented.

"I agree." Rik said.

"Did she know anything else about him?" I asked.

"He's told her he's a wealthy property developer looking to buy in the area and, guess what?" Rik said.

"What?" I asked.

"He's asked her out several times." Rik said.

"Cheeky bastard." I said, thinking of Mrs M.

"Was his car there?" I asked.

"No, but she confirmed he drove an expensive BMW." Rik replied.

"What did you tell her, you know, if we need to go back?" I asked.

"We said we couldn't say; that it was nothing for her to worry about personally but suggest she keeps an eye on his arrears." Andy said.

"Do you think she'd let you have a look through his room, without a ticket?" I asked.

"Close call." Replied Rik.

"What do you reckon, Andy?" I asked.

"I agree, difficult to call." He replied.

"Thanks, guys, I'll think things over." I said.

"How's nights?" Andy asked.

"All right, quiet, dead actually." I replied.

"No more wind ups?" Rik asked.

"No; but I've worked out what I'm going to do to old Sergeant Key. And thanks for all your help with ideas, guys." I said sarcastically.

"Go on then, what you got planned?" Andy asked.

"I haven't seen you for a couple of days, but on, I think it was Wednesday, we had you know, the old four o'clock meeting in the front office. It was cut short 'cos the Commander decided to pay us a visit but that's another story." I replied.

"Oh yeah, tell us about that. I heard one of your PC's told him to 'ef off." Andy said, interrupting me.

"I'll tell you about that in a minute. Listen. We're having the old meeting, this is before Zebedee turns up, and to everyone's amusement Sergeant Key nicked and ate my Yorkie bar. Course, I didn't realise at first and he's eating it and everyone's laughing, etcetera. Anyway, it's given me an idea. What I've done is bought a bar of dark chocolate, you know the one you get in the red wrapper? Taken the original chocolate out and carefully replaced it with a bar of laxative chocolate, that I got in the Chemist down the road. You'd never be able to tell.

Tonight, I'm Second Reserve again, and, obviously, its quick change over, so I'm going to leave the bar of chocolate on my desk and see if he nicks it. If he does, he's going to have a nasty surprise." I told them.

The chaps were laughing already.

"It said on the laxative label to take two bits, you know chunks, every four hours until, and I quote, normal motion returns. There are ten sections in all; if he eats the whole bar, he's going to have five times the recommended dose. That'll teach the thieving bastard." I said.

"Don't you think it's a bit risky, he is a Sergeant?" Rik asked.

"I know it's a bit close to the edge but, you see, he'll only come unstuck, and I mean that quite literally, if he nicks my bar of chocolate. I'm not going to offer him any or anything like that. I've thought this through, if the worst comes to the worst, I'll just say it was for me and I put it inside a normal wrapper because I didn't want everyone to know I was constipated. He might not believe me, but they'll never prove it." I said.

"Aren't you in enough shit, already?" Asked Andy, and I immediately started to worry.

"Why what have you heard?" I said, a little too eagerly.

"The Kitty thing of course, what did you think I was talking about? Bloody hell, Nostrils, is there something you're not telling us?" Asked Andy, who had clearly picked up on my rather indiscreet body language.

"Of course not!" I replied unconvincingly.

I'd dropped my guard and needed to move the conversation quickly along.

"You've heard about Kitty, then?" I asked.

"Nostrils, everyone's heard about Kitty and you." Andy replied

"Really, I didn't think it was that big a deal?" I said.

"You're kidding right?" Rik asked, raising his eyebrows.

"Why what have you two heard about Kitty?" I asked.

"That you called her a lazy black bitch." Explained Andy.

"That's fucking bollocks. Guys, you know me. Would I say that?" I replied.

Andy and Rik exchanged a smile.

"Jesus, Nostrils, you are too easy to wind up." Andy said.

"So, that's bollocks then?" I asked for clarification.

"Of course it is, but we did hear she's gone sick because you swore at her." Rik said.

"I spose that's true but, because of her, I've been doing Second Reserve *and* Station Officer on my own." I said.

"Never mind that, you'll survive. Now tell us what happened with the Commander? Is it true that Foley told him to fuck off?" Rik asked.

"Okay, here's what happened. The full story, from the only independent eyewitness. We were having the four o'clock meeting, the toaster was on, the kettle was boiling, everyone was settling down to a bit of tea and banter …

"Sergeant Key was eating your Yorkie?" Andy interjected.

"…that's right. Sergeant Key was eating my Yorkie. When I took a call from City Road to say the Commander was on his way. Everyone shot out, we tidied the place up and I had my spat with Kitty who stormed off. I'd done a producer at the front counter and just sat down, when in came Zebedee." I said.

"What is his real name?" asked Rik.

"I've no idea, and don't keep interrupting my story. Anyway, just to be on the safe side, I stand up and turn round to face him. Foley's sat reading a copy of the Job and completely ignores him. Can I get you a cup of tea, Sir, I said, all helpful like. Foley just turns a page, got a fag out and lit it. Zebedee ignores me, so an awkward few seconds pass, and then he taps Foley firmly on the shoulder and coughs. Foley ignores him, turns to me, and says if you're putting the kettle on, Nostrils, I'll have a cup. Honestly, guys, I just wanted to die, it was so rude. I went into the telex room and flicked the switch on the kettle and heard Zebedee's booming voice ask Foley, do you know who I am, Constable? I walked back into the Station Office and Foley turned to me and said Nostrils, there's some cunt here who doesn't know who he is, any idea, Nostrils?' I wanted to die, but I also didn't want to lose my job, so I ignored Foley and, again, asked the Commander, very politely, whether I could get him a tea or coffee. I was trying to disassociate myself from Foley. Stand up, shouted Zebedee to Foley; who rose to his feet really slowly and turned round to face him. Zebedee was going redder and redder in the face, I thought he might explode, but Foley looked like he didn't have a care in the world. How dare you be so impertinent he said, you can't call me a cunt, I'm a Commander. Zebedee tapped the bay leaf wreath on his shoulder with two fingers. What if I just thought it? Asked Foley. Well, you can *think* what you like, replied Zebedee. Okay said Foley: Sir? Yes, says Zebedee, I *think* you're a cunt!"

Chapter 29

That night was the last night duty and then we were quick change over to lates, which meant we finished at six on Monday morning, and had to be back at two, in the afternoon. It was a killer, and even worse for those who lived, maybe an hour's drive from the nick, as they had even less time to sleep than those of us in the Section House.

What makes it even more difficult was that, by the end of the week, your body had got used to being on nights and, at six in the morning, you were no longer tired, so it might take several hours to get to sleep. On these quick-change overs some people got as little as four hours sleep.

Occasionally, a few of the relief wouldn't go to bed at all. At six in the morning, they'd go to the Early House for a few pints, then, at about nine, they'd go for a big fry up in a café and then, at twelve, they'd be in the pub next to the nick. When they returned at two, they were ridiculously tired and pissed. I tried it once, shortly after I'd come back from sick, but it wasn't for me.

When I took my seat in the front office, I placed a sandwich I'd bought, a can of coke and my special chocolate bar on the desk, but I didn't think my plan was going to work, because we hardly saw Sergeant Key for the first few hours, as he was helping out in the charge room, which was really busy.

For a few hours the calls ticked over but, as expected, at about one, they dried up. I went into the back yard for some fresh air and a smoke. When I returned to my desk, I noticed my chocolate bar was missing. I didn't say anything but pretended I hadn't noticed.

I was chatting to Peter Foley about his retirement plans to go on a world cruise and then buy a pub in Lincolnshire with his lump sum. He was just explaining how his wife had been doing some cookery courses in preparation, when I heard someone at the front counter and went round the corner to serve them.

A dark-skinned woman, in her late forties, was standing there, her face was flushed and she was breathing quickly.

"How can I help you, madam?" I asked.

"It's my son; I want to report him missing." She replied.

"And how old is he?" I asked.

"Sixteen."

Missing persons, or mispers as they were called, were common, and they all came home eventually, so I learnt that the trick was, where ever possible, not to put pen to paper. Of course, there were times when you had no choice but, as a general rule, you tried to avoid taking a formal report.

"And how long has he been missing?" I asked.

The woman looked at her watch, so it obviously wasn't days.

"Since ten o'clock." She replied.

A sixteen-year-old, missing for three hours; it was hardly going to make the nine o'clock news.

"I'm sure he'll come home, madam. I'll tell you what, if he hasn't returned by the morning, come back, and I'll circulate his details." I said.

Of course, I knew it wouldn't be my responsibility by then, as I'd be tucked up in my bed, but she may be able to persuade someone to take the report.

"But you don't understand; we had a big argument; he was really mad. He stormed out the house." She said.

"Where do you think he might have gone?" I asked.

"Oh, he went next door, but I don't know where he is now." She replied.

I wasn't the least bit interested but, unlike some of my contemporaries in such situations, I was quite good at being polite and patient.

"So, you had an argument with your son, this evening. He got angry and stormed out and went next door. He's not there now but he's not come home yet. Is that right?" I asked.

"Yes." She replied.

"Well, he'll come home when he's cold and hungry won't he? I wouldn't worry too much, madam, really." I assured her.

The woman looked really stressed but I didn't know what else to say. I'd be a laughing stock if I took a report of a sixteen year old who'd only been missing a few hours.

"Something's happened, something's wrong, I just know it." She said.

"What makes you think that?" I asked.

"I just know, I just know." She said.

"Okay. Is your son in good health?" I asked.

"I suppose so. I mean he smokes twenty a day, but he's not been to the doctors, lately." She replied.

"Is he at school?" I asked.

"No, he officially finished last summer but he was never there anyway." She explained.

"Is there any reason to think he'd deliberately harm himself?" I asked.

"No."

"Can I ask what the argument was about tonight?" I said.

"I found an old glue bag in the outside bin. He promised me he'd stopped and, when I confronted him, he went mad." She said.

"Where do you think he is? Has he got anywhere to go, you know, an older brother or sister or a friend's house? I asked.

"I've checked, he's not anywhere."

"He'll come home, honestly. He's probably there now, where do you live?" I asked.

"Just over the road." She said.

"What, literally?" I asked.

"Yes. Down Manse Road." She replied.

"Hang on there." I said.

I popped back into the front office. For the first time that evening, Sergeant Key was sitting at his desk; he was writing something in the Occurrence Book.

"Sarge, if it's okay with you, I'm just going to pop down Manse Road with the woman at the front counter. She lives there and her sixteen-year-old son's missing. I've told her he's probably come home by now, so I'll walk her home and check." I said.

"Yeah, no problem, Nostrils, I'll cover the front counter. Take a radio." He replied.

It was only two hundred yards to her home address. When we got there her son, who on the short walk, I discovered was called Bobby, still hadn't come home. The house was clean and tidy so, when Bobby's Mum asked me if I wanted a tea, I accepted and we stood in the kitchen chatting; she was trying to convince me something awful had happened and I was trying, with little success, to reassure her.

"You said earlier that, after the argument, Bobby went next door, so if you count the time he was there, he really hasn't been missing that long, at all. Who did he go to see next door?" I asked.

"Mrs Garrett, she's a lovely old lady and Bobby's really fond of her, always has been. When he was a baby, she used to babysit him. Sometimes, when he's really stressed, Bobby goes next door and she makes him a cup of tea and they chat." She said.

"Have you spoken to Mrs Garrett, tonight?" I asked.

"No." She replied.

"How do you know he went there then?" I asked.

"I saw him go in." She replied.

"How do you know he's not there now?" I asked.

"I knocked but there was no reply." She said.

"I'll tell you what, I know it's late but let's get Mrs Garrett up and see if she can help. I mean it is possible he's asleep on her settee and you're getting yourself in a right state for nothing. Which side is it?" I asked.

"Number twenty-two, twenty-six has been empty for years." She replied.

When we went to knock next door, you could see through the glass in the front door, the lights were on downstairs. I knelt and looked through the letter box but there was a small curtain which obscured the view. I couldn't hear anything when I pressed my ear up to the opening. I knocked on the knocker and rang the doorbell. We waited, and then did the same thing, several times, before accepting that we couldn't raise Mrs Garrett from her sleep.

"That's what happened earlier. I couldn't get any reply." She said.

"Can we get around the back?" I asked.

"You can but it's a high fence covered in brambles. I suppose we could use the key?" She proposed.

"I beg your pardon?" I said.

"Mrs Garrett gave me a key years ago; she said, if she ever got locked out, it would be useful."

"Can you go and get it, please?" I asked.

I wasn't sure whether I could go into the house in these circumstances. I didn't have a warrant and there was no immediate risk to anyone's life, but it did seem the eminently sensible thing to do, as there was a missing youth, and he was last seen going into this house. I needed some advice.

"Eighteen, eighteen; receiving, four six six?" I transmitted.

"Go ahead, Nostrils." Sergeant Key replied.

"Can you come down to twenty-four Manse Road, please? I need some advice." I said.

"Yes, yes, two minutes." He replied.

In fact, Sergeant Key arrived before the woman, whose name I now knew was Mrs Kyraicou, found the key. This was handy, as it gave me time to explain what was going on, and why I needed his advice.

"You're right, Nostrils; there is a legal dilemma but we'll go in and wake up the old lady, what's her name?" Sergeant Key asked.

"Mrs Garrett." I replied.

Mrs Kyraicou arrived with the front door key and several apologies for taking so long.

"Do you think my son's in there?" She asked the Sergeant.

"Well, hopefully, we'll either find him or we'll discover where he's gone, dear." Sergeant Key replied.

After several twists and fiddles, the lock turned, and the door opened. Sergeant Key stepped inside, and I followed. To the right was the front room and, at the end of the hall, was what I suspected to be the kitchen, but the rear of the house was clouded in steam, which was hanging from the ceiling to about two foot from the floor. I sniffed, there was a definite hint of smoke in the air, something was burning.

"Someone's left the kettle on, get in there and turn it off." Sergeant Key said.

I walked quickly along the corridor and through the open door; the light was on, but it was impossible to see anything because of the steam. A few paces in, I slipped and fell on a wet tiled floor. I landed flat on my back and knocked the wind out of me. It had happened to me before playing rugby and it was quite frightening because, for a few seconds, it really feels like you can't breathe. I knew not to panic but the experience was still mightily unsettling.

I was vaguely aware that immediately after my fall, Sergeant Key had shouted something out and, just as I started to get my breath back, he came into the room. I wanted to warn him about the dicey floor but couldn't quite get the words out before he too slipped. Unlike me, however, he managed to stay on his feet but he crashed into a table and several items fell on to the floor, not far from my head.

To add to the chaos, one of the objects which came clattering to the floor was a milk bottle which smashed, sending glass everywhere and splinters into my hair.

"Where's the fucking cooker?" He said.

"I don't know!" I said through clenched teeth.

I had really landed hard.

Sergeant Key stumbled and then slipped again. The floor was like an ice rink, which must be where the steam had condensed and fallen on to the tiles.

I tried to sit up without putting my hands down because there was glass all around me. I heard Sergeant Key almost skate across the room to my left and, from his intermittent swearing and other expletives, guessed he had found the kettle, picked it up, burnt himself, dropped it and turned the heat source off. I heard a window open, and the room quickly started to clear.

I got to my feet and looked around. The scene was developing before my eyes like a Polaroid photograph. I saw that I had slipped over on, and then fallen backwards into, an enormous pool of blood. I could even see where Sergeant Key's foot had slipped in the same puddle. I looked at my hands and the back of my uniform; I was covered in blood. And then I looked further to my right, as the room cleared; sitting on the floor, clutching a knife which was driven deep into her stomach, was a very dead Mrs Garrett.

"Fucking hell, Sarge, look!"

I looked across at Sergeant Key, he was as white as a sheet and his mouth was wide open; he looked really ill.

"Are you all right, Sarge?" I asked, genuinely concerned that he was about to faint or throw up or something.

"No not really, Nostrils." He replied, nervously.

"It's all right, Sarge, it's only a dead body." I said reassuringly, a little surprised that a police officer as experienced as he, would be so bothered by such a sight.

"It's not that, Nostrils?" He replied, sheepishly.

"What is it, Sarge; what the hell's the matter then?" I asked.

"Don't know how to say this but …"

"But what, Sarge?"

"I've just shat myself!"

Chapter 30

Despite being covered in poor old lady's blood, I had to stand at the door of the address for the next six hours and log everyone who came and went.

Sergeant Key was in a right mess and made his way slowly and uncomfortably back to the nick, about an hour after we'd discovered the macabre murder scene. In that time, he'd soiled himself on several more occasions. He blamed his wife's attempt at cooking a spicy chicken curry, the previous evening, and didn't for one moment suspect me and my chocolate.

When I returned to work, after quick change over that Monday afternoon, I popped into the CID office, just before late turn, to find out what had happened. DS Cotton filled me in with the events which had unfolded, whilst I slept.

"Bobby was hiding in the empty house next door. He gave himself up to the guy from early turn who took over from you on the door." DS Cotton explained.

"That's annoying; I could have had an arrest for murder." I said, with genuine disappointment.

"Don't worry, you'll have a few of those in your time." DS Cotton replied.

"Did he say anything in interview?" I asked.

"Yeah; unusually, he answered all our questions. The Sergeant in the charge room did the right thing too and didn't let him have a brief, not that he knew to ask for one anyway. We got Judith, you know the old cleaner with the gammy leg, to sit in as his adult. The lad said that, after his argument with his Mum, he'd gone next door, where his kindly neighbour and confidante, Mrs Eleanor Garrett, did the two things she did best, she made tea and listened. After two cups and for a reason which he couldn't explain, he picked up a kitchen knife and drove it into the old girl's stomach. And that was about it."

"Unbelievable, Sarge." I said.

"The thing is, the young lad spoke about what he'd done as if it was as mundane an event as going to the shops. He seemed almost bored when we kept asking him questions about it. Both DC Falmouth and I were left with the distinct impression we were dealing with someone who was seriously evil, psychopathic even. Thinking about it now, it sends a shiver down my spine, and I've dealt with a lot of bad people in twenty years."

"What will happen to him?" I asked.

"Detained at Her Majesty's pleasure I suppose. It started out as a misper didn't it?" DS Cotton replied.

"Yes, Sarge."

"A lot of murders start as mispers. Ironically though, it's usually the murder victim that's reported missing, not the suspect." DS Cotton commented.

"I hadn't thought about that, yeah, of course." I replied.

"Listen, Nostrils; you did well last night, you really did. I'm going to have a word with your relief Inspector, is it Simon Portman?"

"Yes, Sarge." I replied.

"I'll arrange for you to have an attachment to the Crime Squad, they're working really well at the moment, really busy, lots of bodies. What do you say?" DS Cotton said.

Bearing in mind what I knew about the Stoke Newington Crime Squad, my first reaction was to run a mile.

"That would be great." I replied, what else could I say?

~~~

When I went downstairs, someone told me Sarah was sick which made me unsure as to whether we'd be going to Bournemouth, the following day, as planned. I'd booked a hotel called the Chine which looked really nice, but we'd yet to make the final arrangements, so I'd have to call her after six, when I knew Paul would be at work.

Sarah wasn't the only one who was absent. Unsurprisingly, there was no sign of Sergeant Key and, when I checked the messages, I saw he'd gone sick with stomach cramps and diarrhea.

As I was flicking through the pad, I saw a message from a Mr Toby Saunders to PC Paul Pollock; the message said; 'The item which you requested is ready for collection.'

I'd had dealings with a Toby Saunders when I was on Street Duties. He owned a factory at which he'd reported a rather dubious burglary and then later, he'd tried to bribe me, when he produced an out-of-date insurance certificate. He was a nasty piece of work, and from this message, it didn't take a genius to work out he was probably the Magistrate who the Crime Squad were paying off to obtain a back dated search warrant.

When I phoned Sarah later, I told her about the message, which I'd already destroyed and replaced it with a fictitious one. You couldn't just tear it out because the messages were numbered, and it would be obvious that one was missing.

Sarah said she was feeling a bit sick but was sure she'd be alright for tomorrow.

"I'll tell Paul I'm getting the train to Southampton to see an old modeling friend. Park in the Green Man car park at eleven, I'll come round and meet you. I really need a break, Chris. We'll have a great time, I promise." She said but her voice didn't sound as enthusiastic as her words.

"I can't wait." I replied.

We'd been seeing each other a couple of months, so the relationship with Sarah was still exciting. She was good company and, I confess, I enjoyed the fact that, wherever we went, men stared at her. It made me feel good to have her on my arm. Sarah knew men fancied her, there was no doubt about that, but I think she'd got so used to it that it was just how life was for her. She'd mentioned several times that she struggled to get on with women, and I could understand that, too. When Sarah walked into a busy canteen, it was fascinating to watch the contrast in the glances she received behind her back, lust from the men and contempt from the women.

I'd noticed, in the last few weeks or so Sarah, had become a bit moody but I put that down to the mess she was in with Paul. The only sex we'd had in two weeks was when she'd seduced me on top of the dog kennel, so I was full to bursting point.

I thought the break would also give me a chance to escape from work related stuff; the theft of the money, the CIB investigation, my fight with Kitty and the constant threat of Paul finding out what was going on and turning up. I'd just about had enough, I wasn't sure I could take much more.

Chapter 31

I got up at five, which was stupidly early, but I had a plan. Andy was less than impressed when I banged on his door but I managed to persuade him to run me over to Buckhurst Hill, so I could recover the overdue BMW and be there at Prestige Cars, when the company opened at nine.

At eight, I was sitting outside their offices, in the delightful Kensington mews. While I waited, I looked through the car for any clue as to Donald Cole's true identity. In the glove box I found three hundred pounds, in twenty-pound notes, and a piece of lined white paper with 'Donald Anthony Cole' written above two dates, one was the same date of birth as on his driving licence, fourteen, twelve, forty-four, and the other was fourteen, two, eighty. I'd wager the second date was the real Donald Cole's date of death. Then I remembered something else, Mrs M had said she'd met this chap in the cemetery, where Dawn was buried. Next time I got a chance, I'd take a punt back to the cemetery and see if I could find what I suspected to be there.

My plan with the BMW worked. When I returned it to Michael Poulson, along with the three hundred quid I'd found, he lent me a beautiful Mercedes coupe for the next week.

"One condition." Michael said.

"What's that?" I asked.

"Don't smoke in it."

"No problem." I replied.

"And, Officer?"

"Yes?" I replied.

"As I'm entrusting you with forty thousand pounds worth of car, I think I should at least know your name?" Mike said, as he handed me the keys.

"Chris Pritchard, Mr Poulson; but everyone calls me Nostrils."

"Call me, Mike. Why Nostrils, Nostrils?" He asked.

"On my first day on the beat I was shot at by an armed robber who discharged both barrels of his sawn off at my head." I replied.

"Yeah, but why Nostrils?"

"Nostrils is slang for a sawn-off shotgun. I was called it for months before I had the courage to ask why." I replied.

"Listen, Nostrils. We get these overdue hires now and again, perhaps one a month, two or three, if we're really unlucky. How about we work together? I'll give you the details of the car and the customer and you see what you can do, how does that sound?" Mike proposed.

"I'll think it over, what you offering?" I enquired.

"A century."

"Per car?" I asked.

"Obviously." He replied.

"I'll think it over and let you know when I bring the Merc back."

The Merc was an absolutely fantastic car, a V8, five litre monster and it was perfect for my little run down to Bournemouth, with the gorgeous Sarah, by my side. As I drove over to Leytonstone, I felt like a millionaire and, even though it was bloody freezing, leaned my elbow out of the open window like I was cruising down Ocean Drive in California.

It wasn't just the car, there was another reason I felt good. I was really pleased with myself that I hadn't kept Donald's three hundred pounds. Perhaps I wasn't a thief, after all.

Of course, when Sarah came into the car park where we'd arranged to meet, she was expecting to see my XR2, so she didn't spot me at first. She looked good, and I knew it must have been her T shirt or perhaps a different bra, but her tits looked fantastic. I admired her for a few seconds more and then tooted the horn and waved. As she walked towards the car, I flicked a switch on the dashboard and the boot opened. She deposited her case in the boot and climbed in the passenger's door.

"You robbed a bank? Cos your CICB payout wouldn't buy half of this." She asked, with a disapproving tone in her voice.

"Nothing illegal, Sarah; I just did someone a favour." I replied.

"Some favour!" She said incredulously.

"No, it's not mine; I've just borrowed it until the week-end." I told her.

Apparently, that was what Sarah wanted to hear because she visibly relaxed. We set off.

We stopped for lunch somewhere near Winchester. Sarah said she was pacing herself and just wanted coke, which pissed me off, because I had every intention of getting a couple of large glasses of wine down her neck and then persuading her to give me a blow job, whilst I drove the Merc.

When we arrived at the Chine Hotel, Sarah shot to the toilet, and I went to reception. I was surprised there was a queue but even more stunned when I recognised several of those waiting to check in. I didn't know any of them by name but they were all from Stokey and it dawned on me that there must be some sort of social function going on. Blind panic struck. Not only was I with someone I most definitely shouldn't be with, I was also driving forty thousand pound of car. I turned round abruptly and nearly walked into DS Cotton who, unseen, had joined the queue behind me.

"Nostrils, I didn't know you were coming. Who are you with?" He asked.

"Hi, Sarge, I'm not with anyone. I've just come away for a few days." I replied.

I was desperate to get to the ladies' toilet before Sarah emerged. I'd always got on with DS Cotton, so I took a chance and told him the truth.

"Sarge, I'm here with someone I shouldn't be, if you understand, and I need to get her out of here. I didn't realise when I booked it that half the nick would be here. I've gotta go, sorry."

DS Cotton laughed and called out good luck, as I walked quickly by him.

Probably, for the only time in my life, I walked straight into a ladies toilet. There were two cubicles, and one was occupied by someone who was being sick.

"Sarah?" I asked.

"What?" She replied.

"We've got to get out of here; it's full of old bill from Stokey. There must be some do on." I said.

Sarah didn't reply but she was sick again.

"Listen, Sarah; stay in here. I'll move the car round to the front and, when the lobby's clear, I'll come and get you." I told her.

As I was speaking, the toilet flushed.

"Sarah, did you hear me?"

The cubicle door opened and Sarah, looking deathly white and very sorry for herself, said.

"I feel dreadful, Chris; just get me out of here."

"Okay, but don't be sick in the car, remember, it's not mine." I said.

"Chris?" She said.

"Yeah?" I asked.

"Shut up."

~~~

That we got out of the hotel and into the car without being seen was quite amazing. I later learnt from DS Cotton that there was some masonic lady's night in the hotel and that at least fifteen old bill were there from Stokey, including Roger Class from our relief.

We relocated to another hotel in the town itself and, when we got to our room, all Sarah wanted to do was go to bed and sleep. I was a bit fed up, but she did look rough. I went downstairs, bought the Telegraph, and had a few pints sat in the bar, whilst I did the crossword. It wasn't quite the weekend I had planned.

As I was finishing my third pint, Sarah walked into the bar, looking slightly more human, and said the four words no one in a relationship ever wants to hear.

"We need to talk."

Chapter 32

All Sarah wanted to drink was a glass of water.

"Have you been sick again?" I asked, trying to sound sympathetic.

"No, I feel a bit better, thanks. Look, Chris. I wasn't going to say anything but clearly the matter cannot be so easily avoided."

"Look, Sarah, whatever it is, let's talk it through." I suggested.

I assumed we were discussing ending our relationship and was keen to try to persuade her not to.

"I'm so glad you've said that. I need you to be supportive, Chris." She paused.

"Go on." I said to encourage her.

Sarah looked down at the table.

"I'm pregnant."

I couldn't help it, but I laughed, I didn't find it funny so it must have been a combination of shock and tension.

"Fucking hell." I said quietly.

Then I remembered she wanted me to be supportive, so I reached across the table and held her hand, she continued to stare at the table.

"How far?" I asked.

"Six, seven weeks." She replied.

The next question was awkward, but it had to be asked.

"Sarah, is it ..." I corrected myself.

"...is the *baby* mine?"

Sarah stared at the table,

"Sarah?" I said, trying to prompt her to respond.

"I don't know." She whispered; her eyes still fixed on the table top.

The next thing I needed to know was even more sensitive, but, again, it had to be asked.

"What are your intentions?"

"I'm not having a termination." She replied, swiftly, having clearly been waiting for that question.

Supportive, she wanted me to be supportive, I reminded myself.

"Okay." I said, although I wanted to ask why not.

"Have you told Paul?"

She shook her head.

"I wasn't going to tell you either but since yesterday morning I've been as sick as a dog so I can't really pretend, like, it's not happening." She explained.

"How do you feel about it all?" I asked, pleased to have found the right question.

"Confused, frightened, scared, but since the weekend, mostly just plain sick." She replied.

"Can I ask, how come?" I said.

"I've no idea, I'm on the pill. Okay I might have forgotten it once or twice, but I thought that wasn't a problem; apparently, it is." She said.

"Do your parents know?" I asked.

"Nope." She replied.

"Does anyone else know?" I asked.

"Just my sister, and now you." She said.

I hadn't seen this coming. I thought we were going to have a lovely few days, away by the sea, with lots of alcohol and even more sex. Then I thought she was going to dump me. Now I'd discovered I'd possibly fathered a child, who I might or might not, must support for the next sixteen years. And how will I ever know whether he or she was mine or Paul's? Was there some blood test they could do? No wonder Sarah had been a bit off recently, a bit non-committal about our future together.

"Say something." She pleaded, and I realised I too had adopted the 'gazing at the tabletop' pose.

"Are you going to stay in the job?" I asked.

She shrugged her shoulders, giving me the distinct impression that wasn't what she wanted me to say.

I was sitting opposite Sarah, so I stood up and went to sit by her side. I put my arms around her.

"Thanks." She said.

"Do you fancy a stroll along the beach?" I asked.

"It's freezing out there." She replied.

"It'll do you good, a woman in your condition, in the family way, should have plenty of fresh sea air and exercise, and err, sex." I said.

"Go on, then." She replied, and for the first time that day a smile was on her face.

~~~

On the beach we held hands, as much to keep each other from blowing away as to show affection. The tide was on its way out and the damp pebbles crunched under our feet. It felt more like a stomp than a stroll and our conversation was shouted rather than spoken, to overcome the wind.

"Did you tell Paul about the message from Toby Saunders?" I asked.

"Yes, did you destroy the original?" She replied.

"Of course. I know the charming Toby Saunders, he tried to bribe me a few years ago." I said.

"Did he succeed?" She asked.

"Of course not." I replied, indignantly.

"That's what I like about you Chris, you're honest. What you see is what you get, no dark side."

I swallowed hard.

"You're so different to Paul; he's always looking at what's in it for him, you know overtime, expenses, earns." She said.

Before I'd joined the job, I'd never heard the expression, or to be more precise, the verb 'earns'. It has a very specific meaning for the criminal fraternity and the old bill alike; it means to obtain something by a dishonest act. I was surprised that Sarah used it to describe Paul, I mean, I know he'd got mixed up in that Crime Squad thing but that wasn't dishonest in the strict sense of the word, it was just a fuck up, followed by a cover up.

"Paul's not really dishonest, is he?" I asked.

"Chris, from what I can make out, everyone has their price and, since his wife has screwed him for every penny he earns and is going to earn, put it this way, his price has fallen."

"Is it really that bad at Stokey? I mean you've got longer in than me, so you ought to know." I asked.

"Yeah, but I'm a plonk; they don't trust us; they think we're more vulnerable to pressure."

"But what do you really think? Is everyone on the take?" I asked.

"Until Paul moved in, I'd have said a definite no, but since Paul's got mixed up in this trouble, I've been really hard on him, you know, having a go at him for fitting the woman up and saying how can you do that and things. Well, to make what he's done look less bad, and normally when he's pissed, he's told me loads of other stuff. Some guy's got some scam going with gaming machines, I don't understand what; another one targets illegals and lets them stay in return for sexual favours, and another is taking backhanders from a load of pimps to keep the police away from their brothels.

I was out with Paul once; we'd just started seeing each other and I was operator on the area car with him. Anyway, we visited this clothes factory off Green Lane. We went into an office at the back and Paul obviously knows the Turkish guy, you know, the manager or owner or whatever. We sit and have that strong sweet Turkish coffee. Anyway, after all the pleasantries, the guy said to Paul, thanks for sorting my friend out and hands him an envelope. Paul just smiles and pops the envelope in his pocket and, ten minutes later, we're on our way. I asked Paul what was all that about and he says that he's known Mustafa for years, as he used to go Mumping there, when he was a home beat. Mustafa had asked him if he could help to get a friend of his British citizenship. Paul takes some details and says, he'll see what he can do but he can't promise anything as his contact in the Home Office had changed jobs, recently. Of course, there wasn't a contact in the Home Office, it was all bullshit, but Paul knows he can't lose. If the guy's application is turned down, Paul will say sorry, but I told you it might be difficult, if it's successful, he takes the credit and, as it transpired, five hundred quid." Sarah explained.

I must admit, I quietly admired Paul's game because it was totally risk free.

"I didn't realise it was that bad. I must have been walking around with my eyes shut." I said, in all honesty.

"I'm sure there are a lot of honest guys, guys like you, you know, the younger generation. But the older guys, they were in the job when the money was shit and you had to do earns to get yourself a living wage, and old habits die hard." Sarah said.

"So, you don't think I've got a price then?" I asked

"Chris, everyone's got a price, but with you it won't be a desire for money that gets you into trouble."

"No?" I replied

"No, it'll be your cock."

Chapter 33

All things considered and, much to my surprise, we had a nice break in Bournemouth. It was the first time we'd spent any quality time together and, as it turned out, we got on really well.

Sarah hardly ever mentioned Paul and, I suppose because of that, I got the impression she was going to finish the relationship soon. Perhaps that was just my wishful thinking. Her flat was rented, so she could walk away and all she'd lose would be her deposit. Her parents lived in the Midlands somewhere and I could see her escaping there, until everything died down.

Sarah's sickness eased up and we spent lots of time discussing baby names, childcare arrangements and stuff like that.

If the baby was a girl, I asked Sarah to name her Dawn. She said she wasn't keen and explained that she thought it would be classified as child cruelty to name a child Dawn Starr, I saw her point. She said if, it was a boy, she had no objection to Matthew.

She asked me whether, if things were different and she wasn't with Paul, I'd help with looking after the baby, at one end of the day? You know, so she could stay at work. I was really surprised, as most plonks who got pregnant left the job. I can't say I was all that keen on assuming any childcare responsibilities, I mean I didn't even know if the baby was mine. Would I be able to get attached to a child that might be Paul's?

I was less shaken about potentially being a father than I would have anticipated. When we discussed my understated reaction, Sarah reckoned it was something to do with surviving the bomb and the fact that, compared to such a traumatic event, nothing could ever shock me again. I think there was an element of truth in that. In the months after the bombing, I really didn't care about anything and, in most respects, this was a positive thing. I didn't get annoyed with people or stressed about anything, absolutely nothing worried me. The only downside was that this laissez faire attitude extended to spending money and getting into debt. Of course, as the months passed my approach to life slowly returned to normal, but by then, financially at least, it was too late.

It was good to get away from everyone and everything but, when we set off home, I realised I was, in fact, bringing back from Bournemouth one more problem than I'd taken with me.

Of my increasing list of troubles, taking the old lady's money worried me the most and not necessarily because I might get caught. I knew I was under investigation. One day, I thought it unlikely CIB would ever be able to make anything stick, and the next, I was convinced I was about to be nicked at any moment.

When I put what Sarah said, about me being honest, alongside what Dawn's Mum had told me, about Dawn admiring my integrity, I realised what an appalling thing I'd done.

I couldn't turn back time. I had stolen six thousand pounds from a dead person, of which I'd spent two hundred pounds myself and given Sarah a thousand for Paul. Ironically, since I'd taken the money, I'd won at the casino and had the CICB cheque through, so my financial position had turned full circle but, even if I hadn't got all that other money, I wished I'd never taken it.

So, what to do now?

I couldn't put the money back because that would be ridiculous. I could leave it in the ground for ever. or I could dig it up and drop it in the Thames, actually, the more I thought about it, the latter seemed a fairly good idea.

The one thing I wasn't going to do was spend it. From that weekend on, and for the rest of my service, I wanted to be uncompromisingly honest old bill.

~~~

Our few days away were over far too quickly and, when I dropped Sarah off and watched her walk away, it crossed my mind, for the first time, that I might really love her and not just in a sexual way.

As I drove to Prestige Leasing, I chewed over the idea of taking the occasional repossession. I couldn't really find a reason not to accept Mike Poulson's offer. It was good honest work, and the pay was excellent. What could possibly go wrong?

Mike was on the phone when I arrived, but he'd seen me out of the corner of his eye and waved me into his office. When he hung up, he greeted me with a friendly handshake.

"Well, Nostrils? You gonna work with me?" He asked.

"I'll take you up on your offer Michael, but I want a pony on top if the car's recovered in a week, deal?"

"Okay, but I'll tell you what. Obviously, I'm always buying and selling cars so, it would be really useful if you could do the occasional car check for me on the old police computer. It's nothing illegal or underhand, I just want to make sure they're not stolen or owned by a finance company. If you do that, we'll call it a straight one two five for every car you recover, as long as you get it back in one piece. What do you say?" He proposed.

"Yeah, okay. As long as you're not after a PNC check every day, 'cos I can slip the odd one in amongst the legit ones. And while I think about it, don't report your overdue hires to the local old bill because I don't want lots of my checks suddenly coming up as overdue hires, people aren't stupid, and they'll soon cotton on." I said.

"That sounds fair enough. How do I get hold of you?"

"Here's my telephone number but it's a payphone in the Section House so leave a message saying, can I come and see you, so I'll know to come here, collect the keys and bits and pieces. If your message just says please call, then I'll know you want a car check." I said.

"Yeah, understood." He replied and scribbled something on a piece of paper.

"Good." I said.

"Where do you work, Nostrils? Are you at a nick or on some squad somewhere?"

"I am based at Stoke Newington." I replied.

"That's where they had the bomb last year wasn't it? In the shopping centre?" Mike said.

"It's coming up on two years ago actually, look …"

I leant forward and showed him the scar on the top of my head, where I'd had the stitches; it was still quite visible, if you looked for it.

"Gosh, was that you?" He asked, incredulously.

I nodded.

"In that case, I'm buying you a pint." He said.

So, we sealed our new business arrangement by drinking several pints in a nearby pub.

Michael was an interesting character. The son of a Walthamstow market trader; he'd made an absolute fortune working as a stockbroker and got out, before he burnt out. With the money he'd made, he bought a dozen top of the range cars, set up Prestige Leasing, and over the last three years, built the business up. He now turned over half a million pounds a year.

It was at times like these I wished I'd chosen a more profitable career than policing.

Chapter 34

That weekend my relief were early turn. Sarah was still complaining about nausea and didn't resume from sick. We spoke just the once, on the Saturday evening, she was down and said it was because she was back in the same house as Paul.

On the Monday and Tuesday, I was meant to be off but instead got warned for Snaresbrook Crown Court, which was really fortunate because it meant both my rest days were cancelled, with less than eight days' notice. I got sixteen hours at double time and two more days off, which was a right touch.

I seemed to spend half my life at court, either Old Street Magistrates or Snaresbrook Crown, with the occasional trip to Kings Cross Coroners Court.

Snaresbrook Crown Court was known to everyone at Stokey as Slagsbrook because the acquittal rate was the highest in the country at something like eighty percent. We all put it down to the fact that the juries came from the East End of London.

That Monday, when I arrived at the court, I went to the Police Room to book on and meet the other officers in the case; Sarah's Paul and another guy called Alec Shepherd. Alex had been on the relief when I'd first arrived but had soon gone on to the Crime Squad. There was also a DC who everyone called ET because, with her long slim neck and bulbous eyes, she bore an uncanny resemblance to the strange little creature from the film of that name. Although she wasn't involved in the original arrest, because she was a detective, she took charge of the case, when we got back to the nick. She would have conducted the interview, dealt with the prisoner's solicitor, done all the paperwork and charged the guy. Personally, I didn't understand why anyone would want to do that side of the job, as it seemed to involve all the shittiest bits.

I knew the case I was required for was called R –v- Noakes and I remembered it quite well because it was one of my first arrests, after I'd joined the relief.

From what I could recall, I'd been posted walking Nightingale beat and, at about three in the morning, the Area Car stopped and picked me up which I much appreciated. Paul was the driver and Alec the operator. It was almost unheard of for the Area Car to pick up a probationer; well unless the probationer was female, young and attractive when, for some reason which has always escaped me, Area Car drivers seemed especially keen to pop them in the back of their cars.

As I was very new and inexperienced, I'd kept my mouth shut and only spoke when one of them asked me a question, which wasn't very often.

We took a punt around the red-light area in Amhurst Park when Alec saw an old Mercedes which was driving really slowly, along a side road.

"There's a kerb crawler, there's a new law coming in that'll make that a specific offence." Alec declared.

"Let's give him a tug anyway." Paul said.

The driver was a Richard Noakes, a white guy, in his thirties, who vehemently denied looking for a tom and claimed to have just dropped off a friend. Paul spoke to him, Alec started to search his car and I did a car and a name check which came back showing the driver had one conviction for handling, from years ago.

"Give Alec a hand, Nostrils." Paul said, after I'd given him the result of the check.

On the back seat of the car was a tweed jacket and, in an outside pocket, I found half a dozen bags of herbal cannabis.

Paul actually arrested the guy but gave the body to me so I could show it in my record of work, which was a nice gesture.

Until ET handed me my IRB, a small booklet which contained my original notes, that was about all I could remember. After I'd read over my notes, I also remembered he'd said the jacket wasn't his and he then accused us of planting the drugs.

When we got back to the nick, apart from making my notes, I had nothing more to do with the job.

It seemed really straight forward, and I was surprised the bloke didn't cop a plea to possession, get a fifty-pound fine, and let us all get on with our lives.

As I was reading my notes over for a third time, Paul called over.

"Nostrils, Eileen wants a word, she's in the interview room." He said.

I wasn't really listening.

"Eileen?" I asked.

"ET, the DC; she's in there."

He pointed to a small room usually used by counsel. I got up and walked over.

"ET, you want to see me?" I said, still holding my IRB open on the appropriate page, in case she had a question about my evidence.

"Have you given evidence at Crown Court, before?" She asked.

"About a dozen times." I replied, exaggerating greatly.

"You found the drugs, didn't you?"

"Yes, I did."

"And you arrested him?" She asked.

I nodded.

"I'll need to check with counsel, but I suspect he'll want you to go first, then Paul and Alec, if the defence want them called, and then I'll do the drugs and interview."

"OK." I said, a little unsure whether she was asking me, telling me, or simply thinking out loud.

"Was there anyone else in the car when Noakes was stopped?" She asked.

"No, just him, why?" I asked.

"Because the defence are calling a witness; I just can't work out why."

"Definitely just him ET." I assured her.

"I've no doubt he's going to stick to what he said throughout the interview."

"What? That they were planted?" I asked.

"Yes and no. He actually said it wasn't his jacket and that the drugs had been planted in it."

"Well, if it actually wasn't his jacket, how could he know there weren't any drugs in the pocket? He can't have it both ways, can he?" I suggested.

"I know." ET replied thoughtfully.

"Were there any dabs on the drugs?" I asked.

"Yes, yours and Paul Pollock's."

"Not his?" I asked, somewhat surprised.

"No. He alleged they were …"

I interrupted her before she could complete the sentence.

"ET, let me stop you there. I didn't plant the drugs, I found them. There is absolutely no question about that. Paul must have handled them at some stage and, obviously, I touched them when I took them out of the jacket."

I said the statement resolutely. Whatever else I'd done wrong recently, I could swear before the Almighty himself, I didn't plant those drugs. In fact, I was kind of proud that I didn't go in for that sort of thing.

ET nodded.

"Ok; good. I'll go and see if we've been allocated a court yet. We were on the floating list, last time I looked."

ET went off and I left the small room, lit a cigarette, and walked over to sit down and go through my notes, again. I'd only been there a few moments when Paul joined me. I tried to ignore him because I always felt awkward around him, and I really did want to get my notes almost off pat.

"How was early turn weekend?" He asked.

"Quiet. Sarah sick then?" It was the obvious thing to say, anything else would have been a bit suspicious.

He nodded but I sensed something.

"Sorry, I had to ask you for that money the other week." He said.

I'd completely forgotten about that and was relieved he didn't have anything more sinister to say.

"No problem, mate. When I didn't hear from you again, I assumed you'd got it sorted." I lied.

"I did, no sweat." He replied.

Again, the conversation went quiet for just a moment too long and I felt uncomfortable.

"How's jury protection?" I asked, grateful to have thought of something to say which was both relevant and neutral.

"Yeah, good. The woman we're looking after is really gorgeous, Nostrils. Really nice, too. The other day, when she went out for a meal with an old school friend, she invited us to join her, you know, actually sit with them. I know that's not strictly allowed but we all agreed we'd keep quiet about it. She was telling her mate all about the case she's on and how they've got this right weary foreman who thinks the defendants are all innocent. I gave her a few tips, you know, if a defence doesn't mention that their man is of previous good character, then you can assume he's got stacks of previous."

It was reassuring that Paul was chatting to me easily. I felt myself relax.

"I think she liked the old gun." Paul continued.

"What do you mean?" I said.

"Well, when we were sat there in the restaurant, she kept talking about it and, when I lifted my jacket slightly so she could see it, I'm pretty certain she had an orgasm."

There was a mischievous smile on Paul's face.

"You are kidding?" I said, incredulously.

He shook his head.

"I ain't. I think she like, gets off on it." He said.

"Behave yourself, Paul; don't let Sarah catch you." I warned him.

A look flashed across Paul's face and any trace of humour disappeared.

"You alright?" I asked but he didn't reply.

"What is it, Paul? What's the matter?" I pressed him.

"I think Sarah is seeing someone else; I think it's someone on the relief. When I find out who, Nostrils, I'm gonna fucking kill him."

Chapter 35

We hung around all morning, and at one stage, I wandered into court one and sat at the back to watch proceedings.

It was a murder trial and a new witness, a suited gentleman in his late fifties, had taken the oath. A rotund black barrister stood, and he spoke with a strong Nigerian accent. He opened his questioning by saying to the witness.

"I put it to you, Sir, that your name is Brian James Fricks?"

The witness thought for a moment, frowned, and replied,

"No."

Somewhat taken aback he had encountered such an early and unexpected obstacle; the barrister rephrased his question.

"Is it not right that your name is Brian James Fricks?"

The witness shook his head and replied.

"No, it is not right."

The Barrister was flummoxed but the Judge quickly came to his rescue.

"Counsel, why don't you just ask the witness his name?"

"I'm obliged for your Worship's assistance." Replied the barrister; and he did just that.

"Please, tell the court your name?"

"Certainly; I am Brian James, Fellow of the Royal College of Surgeons."

It's not often a court room erupts in laughter but that was one such occasion, even the Judge had tears running down his face.

At one o'clock we were told our case had been listed for tomorrow, in court twelve and, therefore, we could go home. Snaresbrook was only a short run from Buckhurst Hill so I popped up to St John's Church, to pay a quick visit to Dawn's grave, and to check something out.

My suspicions were right. About fifty yards from her grave was the real Donald Anthony Cole's grave. He was born on the fourteenth December 1944 and died, aged thirty-six, on the fourteenth of February 1980. It wasn't a difficult jigsaw to put together, the fact he'd met Mrs M in the graveyard was the first clue and the paper in the car, the second. It was the oldest trick in the book, to steal the identity of someone who's dead. I was certain he wouldn't assume it for long, only as long as it took him to fleece Mrs M.

I drove round to her house afterwards; she was in but, thankfully, Donald was out.

"Oh, how lovely to see you, Chris." She said with genuine warmth.

"Come on Mrs M, put the kettle on." I said.

"I thought you were out, where's your car?" I commented, as we walked into the kitchen.

"Donald's had his car stolen, Chris; you know the BMW? From the hotel; and in Buckhurst Hill too."

"Always thought it was a bit rough round here." I said, jokingly.

"Thing is, he'd left three thousand pounds in the glove compartment which the insurance are refusing to cover. Anyway, I've lent him a thousand quid and my Metro for the time being."

I hadn't anticipated that turn of events when I'd repossessed the BMW.

"Don't you need it?" I asked.

"Not for a while, well six weeks to be exact." She replied.

"How come?" I asked.

"I'm going into Whipps on Friday week for an operation on my elbow. It's nothing serious."

"Whipps Cross hospital?" I asked.

"The consultant says I won't be able to drive for four weeks so Donald might as well have my car, until he's sorted one out."

I had a bad feeling about this; I could see Donald doing a disappearing trick with Mrs M's new car, but it was about to get worse.

"Chris, a few weeks ago, I received a payout from the Criminal Injuries people. It's a lot of money but I don't want it. I know they mean well but I don't need it and, well, I think I'm going to give it to charity. Luckily, Donald says his brother works with Bob Geldof on that African charity thing, you know LiveAid. His brother produced that Christmas song. I'm going to donate the money to them. Donald's going to sort it out while I'm in hospital."

At that moment I knew, with absolute certainty, that when Mrs M went into hospital, Donald was going to steal her payout money, car and, probably, anything else he could lay his hands on, such as cheque books and credit cards. Then he would disappear, and he'd have, however long she remained in hospital, to empty her bank accounts and run her credit card up to its limit.

I excused myself and went to the toilet because I needed to think things over. Was there enough to arrest him now? Probably not, as he hadn't stolen anything yet and the BMW was just overdue, not re-plated and sold on. Using someone else's name was not illegal, until you combined it with a substantial offence, when it might become part of the deception. More importantly than any of these considerations though, was the fact I had to tell Mrs M what I thought was going on; now that I really wasn't looking forward to.

When I came out of the toilet, Mrs M had put the kettle on again and produced her famous biscuit tin.

"How are you coping, Chris?" She asked.

"I'm fine, why?" I replied, surprised by the question.

"Because you weren't coping very well a couple of weeks ago when we met at the grave."

"Oh, that was a one off Mrs M, just a one off, really, I'm okay." I tried to assure her.

"So, you think you're over what happened?"

"Yeah, I was back at work within three months. My hand took ages to heal but the doctors put the rest of me back together really well. I was lucky…"

And that was all it took. I burst into tears, I sobbed like a baby, again. The thing was, when I wasn't with Mrs M, I put those dreadful events out of my mind, but in her presence, there was no escape. And whilst I cried and apologised, Mrs M handed me tissues, told me not to worry and stroked my back. I felt like a child, but I didn't care.

Slowly, eventually, I pulled myself together.

"I'm so sorry, this is ridiculous. It was ages ago." I said.

"It was yesterday." Mrs M replied.

"Sorry."

"Listen, Chris. You need to get some help; I think they call it counselling; it's nothing to be ashamed of. You did brilliantly getting back to work so soon but I am not sure all your injuries were physical."

"It's only when I'm with you, honestly, it's stupid." I said.

"It happens when you're with me because that's when you can't avoid it, it's when you're forced to face up to what happened. I suspect at other times you keep it buried."

What she said made sense. I nodded, slowly.

Mrs M took a deep breath and pursed her lips. I wondered what she was about to say.

"Chris, I've made a decision." She said.

"Go on, Mrs M."

"The money I got for Dawn, the hundred thousand pounds, I'm not giving it to Bob Geldof, I'm giving it to you."

Chapter 36

Anything that kept the money from Donald was welcome, so ostensibly I agreed to accept Mrs M's very kind offer. If I'm being honest, I did briefly flirt with the idea of buying a decent house, I'd be set up for the rest of my life. The thing was, everything had been ruined when I took the old lady's money. I saw, in declining Mrs M's offer, an opportunity for atonement.

By the time I'd driven home from Mrs M's I made a decision. I decided to decline Mrs M's proposition, replace the money I'd taken out the tin, add in the money I'd won at the casino, and donate the whole lot to Help the Aged and Victim Support. I knew it wouldn't completely compensate for what I'd done but it would be a start and at least the money would go to two good and relevant causes.

My only problem was that I'd have to wait. I'd already been told I was under investigation and my file had obviously been seized for the same reason. There was a real possibility that I was being followed so I couldn't go anywhere near the money for the time being. I'd have to be patient, but my decision was made.

I hadn't heard from Sarah but, in light of what Paul had said the previous day, I thought it was wise to steer well clear for a few days. I'd turned his words over in my mind several times to see if there was any suggestion that he knew it was me but, the more I did, the more convinced I was that he didn't. There is no way he would think she would be interested in me; so I hadn't appeared on his radar as yet.

The next day, I met Paul in the car park of the court. He was getting out of his car at the same time as me.

"Hi Paul, you alright?" I asked.

"Yes, mate." He replied.

So far, so good, I thought.

"I'm glad I bumped into you." He said.

Stay cool, Pritchard, I told myself.

"Why's that then?" I asked, as casually as I could.

"You know what I told you about Sarah, yesterday?"

"Yeah." I replied tentatively.

We were walking very slowly around the side of the building; he was by my side.

"Well last night I looked through her handbag. I found a receipt. When she said she was away with her mate, Dee, in Southampton, she was in fact in Bournemouth. Do you know if any of the relief were in Bournemouth last week? Has anyone mentioned anything?" He asked.

I pretended that I needed a few seconds to think.

"No Paul, no one's said anything about Bournemouth, nothing. Look Paul, are you sure? Sarah doesn't seem the type to be unfaithful." I said.

"I'm pretty sure, not one hundred percent, but pretty sure."

"Ok, apart from the receipt, and thinking about it, Southampton and Bournemouth aren't a hundred miles apart…"

"True." He interjected.

"…have you got any actual evidence, Paul?" I asked.

"No, she's just really distant at the moment; and she keeps going missing, you know, not for long but just the odd hour here and there."

"Doesn't sound too convincing to me." I said

"Maybe, maybe." He said.

I felt pretty rotten but what could I do?

~~~

Shortly after ten o'clock, I was called to court twelve and took my place in the witness box.

It was a modern room, devoid of character, with light pine functional furniture. His honour, the Judge, was to my right, the jury in front of me on the other side of the room and counsel to my left; prosecution counsel was nearest to me. Behind counsel in the dock was the defendant.

I was nervous; any police officer who says they're not nervous when they give evidence is either a liar, stupid or drunk. I introduced myself and took the oath, swearing on the bible to tell the truth. Although I didn't believe in God, I thought it went down well with the jury.

I was always taught there were two fundamental principles to giving evidence under oath, genuinely try not to lie but, if you absolutely have to, don't get caught.

Prosecution counsel took me through my evidence; there was really nothing to it. We stopped the car because we thought the driver was kerb crawling in an area where prostitutes were known to frequent; the car contained only one person, the defendant; we searched the vehicle; there was a jacket on the back seat of the car; I searched it and found six bags of a herbal substance which I identified to the court when shown. I recognised a little green cannabis leaf printed in the centre of each plastic bag, which was quite unusual. I told the court that the defendant had said the jacket wasn't his and then he accused us of planting the drugs. I arrested and cautioned him, and he was transported back to the police station. Whenever counsel asked me a question, I took my time to think it over and then directed my answer to the Judge, as I'd been taught.

"I have no further questions, your honour." Prosecution counsel said.

The defence barrister stood up, he was a short white man in his fifties.

"PC Pritchard. You have told the court why you stopped the vehicle; can you please also tell the court why you searched the car." He asked.

I thought the question through. I remembered that Paul had told me to do so but that seemed a pretty feeble reply, so I said.

"PC Shepherd was searching the vehicle so I helped him, your honour."

"So, what grounds did you have to conduct the search?" He asked.

This was a more difficult question. I knew there were powers under the Misuse of Drugs Act but if he was looking for grounds I was going to be a bit stuffed, as it hadn't been my decision. I'd only just joined the relief, I just did what I was told or, as was often the case, what I thought was expected of me.

"I assumed it was a search under the Drugs Act your honour, but PC Shepherd had already started the search and I was just helping him." I explained.

This wasn't a good answer, and I knew it.

"But you found the drugs, PC Pritchard?" He said.

"Yes, your honour." I replied.

"But you don't really know why you were searching or what you were looking for?" He asked.

"Well, I was assisting PC Shepherd, your honour."

"Can you look at the defendant, PC Pritchard?"

I did.

"How would you describe his build?" He asked.

"The defendant is well built your honour."

"Muscular?" He asked.

"Yes, your honour."

"Bigger build than yourself officer?"

"Yes, your honour." I replied.

I had no idea where this line of questioning was going but I was relieved we'd moved off the grounds for search.

"When you arrested the defendant, did you seize the jacket which allegedly contained the drugs?" He asked.

"No, your honour."

"Why?" Defence Counsel asked.

"I didn't think it was necessary, your honour."

"Really?" He said, sarcastically and he held up a brown jacket.

"Can you look at this jacket please, PC Pritchard? Can the court please note this as exhibit two?" He said.

He gave it to the Usher who handed it to me.

"Is that the jacket which allegedly contained the drugs?" He asked.

I examined it. I must admit it did look similar, but I couldn't possibly say for sure, not so long after the arrest.

"I don't know your honour; it was a long time ago." I replied.

"Ok PC Pritchard let me help you. Is it at least *similar* to the jacket you allegedly found the drugs in?" Defence counsel asked.

"Yes, your honour."

"Is it very similar?"

"Yes, your honour." I confirmed.

"And, assuming for a moment that it was the jacket, which pocket did you allegedly find the drugs in?" Defence Counsel asked.

I held the jacket up and put my hand in the front outside right pocket.

"Thank you, Officer. Officer, what size chest are you?"

"Forty-two, I think your honour." I replied.

"Can you look at the label in that jacket and tell me what size that jacket is?" He said.

"Thirty-eight, your honour."

"So that jacket would be much too small for you, PC Pritchard?" Defence counsel asked.

"Yes, your honour."

"And even smaller for the defendant?"

Prosecution counsel stood up, I assumed to object to the question, but Defence counsel said quickly.

"Don't worry officer; you don't have to answer that question."

And my counsel sat down again.

"Only a few more questions, officer. Do you know what the expression to plant evidence means?" He asked.

"Yes, your honour." I replied.

"Please explain it to the court."

"It means to put evidence on someone that they didn't actually have." I replied.

"An excellent definition, officer. Do the police at Stoke Newington do a lot of planting evidence on innocent people?"

I had to word my reply carefully. A 'yes' would obviously be disastrous but a simple 'no' would suggest we did it sometimes.

"I have never planted any evidence on anyone." I replied, decisively.

"But you've heard of the expression officer, and you gave us an excellent explanation, so the subject of planting is obviously quite commonly discussed, it is not?" He asked.

"No, Sir; it is not. I've heard the expression because prisoners always allege it, not because I've ever done it or seen it done." I replied, quite satisfied with my answer.

I suddenly realised I was no longer addressing my answers to the Judge but, instead, to counsel for the defence

"So, lots of prisoners, who are arrested by police officers from Stoke Newington, allege they had evidence planted, that's what you're telling the court?" Defence Counsel asked.

I walked right into that one and didn't know what to say, I started to think of an answer, but Defence Counsel then asked another question.

"Did you plant the drugs on the defendant, PC Pritchard?"

"No, your honour."

"I have no further questions for this witness." Defence Counsel said.

"I have no questions." Prosecution Counsel said.

"Very well." The Judge said.

Defence counsel, who had just sat down, stood up again.

"If I might request, your honour? Can this officer not be released and, can I respectfully ask you to consider reminding him, not to discuss his evidence with his colleagues."

The Judge nodded and looked at me.

"Officer, you are suitably reminded. Please remain in the court for now, sit at the back."

I'd thought I'd done okay but I was starting to get a bad feeling about this, which was ironic really, as this was one of the most straight-forward arrests I'd ever been involved in.

Chapter 37

Paul was the next officer in the box, and he was called into the court. As he came through the doors, he looked at me and I saw a strange look on his face. For a second, I thought that in the short time I'd been giving my evidence, he'd discovered it was me who was seeing Sarah.

Paul was taken through his evidence in chief by Prosecution Counsel.

Defence Counsel stood up; his first question was the same as I'd had.

"PC Pollock. You have told the court why you stopped the vehicle; can you please also tell the court why you searched the car?"

Paul looked through his IRB, but we all knew the answer wasn't there, otherwise he'd have covered the point in his evidence in chief, perhaps, I thought, he was giving himself some thinking time.

"I haven't made a note of the reason, Sir, but I'm fairly certain PC Pritchard said he smelt cannabis in the vehicle." He replied.

I was flabbergasted, the reply was complete and utter bollocks and it made me look like a liar, but it got worse.

"I would like to point out, Sir, that as I said earlier, I took no part in the search of the vehicle, I was talking to the defendant." Paul said.

"Did you observe the search?" Defence counsel asked.

"Yes, Sir." Paul replied.

"Can you tell the court which officer searched what?" Defence Counsel asked.

"Yes Sir, PC Shepherd searched the front of the car and the boot, PC Pritchard the back."

That was sort of true, but it didn't reflect what really happened. For one thing, PC Shepherd started the search well before me because I was doing the name check and had wandered off a short distance to do so. If you can help it, you never do a name check within earshot of the person you've stopped because you don't want them to overhear what you're being told. By the time I joined in, PC Shepherd could have done the whole car twice.

"So, when did you first see the drugs? May I ask the Usher to show exhibit one to the witness?"

Paul took the drugs and examined them.

"PC Pritchard showed them to me when he got out of the back of the car." Paul said.

"And can you just confirm that from the moment PC Pritchard produced the drugs from the back of the car, the defendant has protested his innocence?"

"I can." Paul replied, I thought he could've added something else, but he didn't.

"May I ask the court if the witness can be shown the jacket, exhibit two? Is this the jacket which PC Pritchard allegedly found the drugs in?" Defence counsel asked.

"I don't know Sir, I never saw it, PC Pritchard didn't take it out the car." Paul replied.

That was a big fat lie too; I did take it out of the car, and I did show it to Paul and Alec. Why was he saying that? It didn't make sense. And suddenly the questions ended, and Paul was released. Why wasn't he asked about planting evidence? At this rate it was beginning to look like I really had planted the evidence!

Paul and Alec had obviously got their heads together because under cross examination, Alec also said that I'd said I smelt cannabis and that he'd never seen the jacket before, but he went even further, and said that I'd started searching the vehicle before him. Again, there were no questions for Alec about the practice of planting. It was quite clever really because it meant the Jury's focus was entirely on me as the guilty party.

We broke for lunch after Alec's evidence and the two of them shot off before I could speak to them. ET, as the officer in the case, had been allowed to sit at the back of the court so she, like I, knew this was looking really bad.

"What's going on ET? I'm being fitted up here, it looks like I planted the drugs, but I didn't, honestly."

"I confess it hasn't been a great morning, but I think we'll be alright." She said.

"They were lying ET, I never smelt any cannabis in the car, why are they saying that?" I asked.

"Be careful what you say, Chris." She admonished me and I realised I'd overstepped the mark.

"Okay, I take it back; but what's going on?" I asked.

"See that guy there?" She said.

We were in the waiting area outside the courts and ET nodded towards a small black man with grey hair. He was sitting down reading a book and wearing a dog collar and red shirt.

"The priest?" I asked.

ET nodded.

"Is he here to give my career the last rites?" I asked.

"No, he's the defence's witness. I think he'll say he's the owner of the jacket." She said.

"Oh fuck!" Was all I could mutter.

~~~

It was a painful experience, but I sat through the afternoon session. The defendant said he'd just dropped his friend, the Right Reverend Christopher Umande, off at his home when, within thirty

143

seconds of driving off, he realised his passenger had left his jacket on the back seat. He was just completing a three-point turn, when he was stopped by police. His vehicle was searched, and drugs found in the Right Reverend's jacket. As he didn't think for one moment that his friend smoked cannabis, he immediately realised they'd been planted and that he was being fitted up. From the lackluster cross examination from our counsel, I got the impression he'd already given up on the case.

The Right Reverend was about the most credible witness I'd ever seen. He confirmed the defendant's account, put the jacket on to show it fitted perfectly and declared, before God, that he had never purchased, possessed or used cannabis. Even I believed him, and I'd been the one that had found the drugs.

The Jury took just twenty minutes to acquit. The Judge summoned the Court Inspector and directed that a formal investigation be conducted into an allegation of perverting the course of justice and perjury.

Of course, there was only one explanation. Alec had put the drugs in the jacket pocket so that I would find them and, when the going had got tough, they'd both conspired to drop me in the shit.

When I talked it through with ET, she may have been bullshitting me, but I got the impression she believed me. Before I finished for the day, I had to mention one thing to her, which was completely unrelated to the case.

"Don't you mind being called ET?" I asked.

It had been troubling me for two days, every time I heard someone address her.

"Not really, why?" She replied.

"Well, it's a bit derogatory, ET; Extra Terrestrial, I mean it's hardly a compliment, is it? Not that *I* think you look like him." I added.

"Chris; I'm called ET because my name is Eileen Tweet."

And that, I thought, just summed up my day.

Chapter 38

Over the next few days my priority was to sort out the Donald issue before Mrs M went into hospital. I considered various options, which included giving him a good hiding and sending him on his way, but I kept coming back to the only really viable one. I had to tell Mrs M what was going on and then arrest Donald. What could I arrest him for? I decided I did in fact have enough to arrest him for obtaining the BMW by deception, that would do to start, after all he'd provided false details to Prestige Leasing.

I was late turn on Wednesday so I got up early and drove over to Buckhurst Hill. I got no reply at Mrs M's but I took a chance that I knew where she might be and went to the cemetery where I found her tidying up Dawn's grave.

"Hi Mrs M." I said.

"Hi Chris, I'm surprised to see you again so soon." She said.

I sat on the bench and waited for her to finish.

"You ok?"

"Not really."

"Still upset?" She asked.

"Not today, I've got something else on my mind today. Something that's really troubling me." I said.

"Oh Chris, what is it?"

Mrs M sat down beside me.

And then I had a thought. I stood up.

"Come with me Mrs M, please."

"What's going on, Chris; you're scaring me?"

I walked the short distance across the grass and stood before the real Donald Cole's headstone. Mrs M was a few steps behind me. When she drew next to me her eyes followed my gaze.

"What?" She said quietly.

I didn't reply.

"Is this a coincidence?" She asked.

I shook my head slowly from side to side.

"I don't think so." I said.

"I don't understand, Chris?" She said, slowly.

"I'm sorry Mrs M but I think Donald is a conman." I said.

"But he can't be, Chris; he can't be." She said.

"He's a wealthy businessman, he..." her voice petered off.

"Mrs M; apart from your car and the thousand pounds, what else have you given him?" I asked.

"Nothing." She replied.

"Are you sure?" I asked.

She shook her head.

"When did you last see him?" I asked.

"Yesterday, just after you'd left." She said.

"And did you tell him you'd changed your mind about donating the money to that charity thing?" I asked.

"Yes. He suggested I donate half to the charity and give half to you. I said I'd think it over. Oh Chris have I been really stupid?" She asked.

"No, you haven't Mrs M. I think he's quite a sophisticated fraudster. I'm sure you're not the first but I am certain of one thing." I said.

"What's that?" Mrs M asked.

"I'm going to make sure you're the last." I replied.

We stood in silence for a few moments.

"Are you sure, Chris?"

I nodded.

"He had The BMW on hire, but he hadn't returned it. It wasn't stolen the other day, it was repossessed by the leasing company." I told her.

"I'm such an idiot Chris." She said.

"No, you're not, you're lovely Mrs M. Almost as lovely as your daughter but not quite." I said.

"When are you seeing him again?" I asked.

"Tonight, he's coming round about seven for dinner." She replied.

"Has he still got your Metro?" I asked.

"Yes. Well, he had it last night. I don't want to see him again Chris. Can you help me? Please?" She asked.

"Of course, Mrs M. Leave it with me, I'll get your car back and you'll never see him again. I promise you." I said.

She turned into me, and we hugged.

When I left, Mrs M went back to talk to her daughter.

I could have actually walked to the Roebuck Hotel from St John's church but I drove. Mrs M's Metro was parked outside so I knew Donald would be about. When I went in I showed the receptionist my warrant card, asked to speak to the manager and she lifted up the counter hatch and invited me into a rear office. An attractive young black lady soon appeared and asked immediately if it was about Donald Cole.

"Yes madam; I understand you spoke to some colleagues of mine recently about him?"

"Yes I did. A good looking black officer, now you don't get many of those do you?" She said.

"What, good looking police officers, they're everywhere." I replied.

"Not from where I'm standing." She said smiling.

I liked this woman; she had a good sense of humour.

"I meant black police officers, as well you know." She said.

"Why are you interested in joining?" I asked.

"Might be, perhaps we could discuss it later?" She replied.

"Yeah, of course."

Had I just been asked out on a date? How did that happen? Would going out with her be being unfaithful to Sarah?

"Officer?" The woman said impatiently.

"Sorry, I was miles away. Yes, Mr Cole, what's he been up to lately?" I asked.

"He's still behind with his bill but when I spoke to him about it, he said he'd pay up and be out by Saturday. Oh, he had the BMW stolen but has hired a Metro which you probably passed on the way in." She explained.

"Is he here?" I asked.

"Yeah, I think so; in his room. After your colleague had gone the other day, you know the really good looking one..."

"All right don't rub it in." I said.

"...when Donald was out, I had a nosey around his room."

"Did you have a warrant?" I asked with a smile.

"Sorry?" She replied, my remark going completely over her head.

"Nothing; did you find anything of interest?" I asked.

"Our Mr Cole sure likes cutting things up."

"What do you mean?" I asked.

"Photographs, passports, driving licenses, letters, letter heads, cheques, bank statements, you name it and he's cut it up. He keeps all the documents and cuttings and sellotape and scissors in a suitcase in the wardrobe." She explained.

The woman put her finger to her mouth to indicate I should be quiet, and she turned her head to one side, apparently, listening to something.

"He's at Reception." She whispered.

At that moment the joining door swung open, and the receptionist said to the manager.

"Corrine? Mr Cole wants to settle his account with a cheque, but he hasn't got a cheque guarantee card. He says as he's not leaving until Saturday, we should have time to clear it. Is it alright to take it as payment?" The receptionist asked.

"Give me two minutes please, I'll come and see him." Corrine replied.

The door closed.

"I'll take over from here, shall I?" I said quietly.

Corrine nodded.

I stepped through the door and came out behind the counter. Donald was looking down writing out a cheque.

"Hello Donald." I said and smiled.

He looked up and, as cool as a cucumber, replied.

"Oh, hi Chris."

As if I was exactly who he expected to see at that very moment; he looked back down and continued to write out the cheque. With an impressive flourish of activity, he signed his signature, tore it from the stub and handed it to the receptionist.

"Don't tell me you lot have found my BMW?" He asked.

"Oh, we found the BMW Donald." I said as I lifted the counter flap to walk through to the lobby.

"Oh great." He replied

I smiled and for the first time the slightest hint of concern flashed across his face.

"Is it here?" He asked.

"Oh, good god no; let's just say the vehicle has been returned to its rightful owner." I replied.

"I don't understand?"

"Prestige Leasing Donald. I think you still owe them a few hundred quid." I said.

"Chris, you're acting as if I've done something wrong. So, I had a lease car and I might have pretended it was mine, so what? That's not a crime is it?" He replied.

"Donald, let's not fuck about, shall we?" I said.

"Don't talk to me like that, who the hell do you think you are young man?" He said, with almost an air of authority.

"Who do I think I am? I'm Chris Pritchard. Who the fuck are you 'cos you ain't Donald Cole. And don't think I don't know what you're up to with Mrs M, trying to get your hands on her pay-out. Whoever the fuck you are, you're under arrest for deception and forgery."

I turned to Corrine who'd been watching the unfolding drama.

"Can you dial nine, nine, nine please and request transport for one prisoner for an off duty PC?" I said.

"Of course." She replied and turned to the receptionist.

"Make the call from my office Debbie." Corrine said.

"You can't be serious, Chris?" Donald pleaded.

"I am obliged to tell you that you do not have to say anything unless you wish to do so but what you say may be given in evidence." I said.

"I am Donald Cole and I have no idea what this is about or what I've done wrong." He protested.

"Turn your pockets out. Put everything you have on the counter."

He didn't have much; a cheque book, a wallet containing some cash, documents in the name of Cole and some receipts, and the keys to the Metro which I popped into my pocket. When I did my own search I found another piece of paper which he hadn't produced, on it was written 'David George Fortune, born two/nine/forty six, died two/two/forty seven.'

"What's this?" I asked.

"I've had that for ages." He replied.

"That's not what I asked. What is it?"

"It's nothing." He replied.

"Is that your hand-writing?"

"Yes." He replied.

"What is it? Why did you write that information down?" I asked.

"I can't remember, it was ages ago." He said.

"Where is the gravestone from which you copied it?" I asked.

He didn't reply.

"Because the real Donald Cole, who died in 1980, is buried just up the road at St Johns. And you'd written his details down in a similar fashion on a piece of paper which was recovered from the BMW." I said.

He didn't say anything but he was suddenly looking grey so I thought I'd keep the pressure on.

"I've done a thorough investigation. Been to Prestige Leasing, spoken to LiveAid about your brother, run some checks on your alleged bank account, photographed the real Donald Cole's grave and obtained details of his death. I've spent some time with Mrs Matthews getting her account and working out exactly what you were up to. Oh and I've had you under surveillance too." I said.

I hadn't done half of these things but he didn't know that.

"Well? What have you got to say?" I asked.

He didn't say a word.

"You've been lucky Donald, really fucking lucky today. Do you know why?" I said.

He shook his head slowly.

"Because for what you've done to a beautiful person who has suffered enough already, I should break your fucking neck and bury you in the forest. In fact, if you ever, *ever* go within ten miles of Mrs M, that is exactly what I'll do you CUNT."

I was aggressive. If he'd given me the slightest excuse, I'd have punched him unconscious.

I glanced across to Corrine who looked shocked, apparently, she wasn't all that keen on my choice of vocabulary, and I knew I'd lost any chance I had of taking her out on a date. But I didn't care because I was protecting Dawn's Mum and wanted this cock sucking bastard to know what would happen to him if he went near her again.

Chapter 39

I missed my late turn completely. I phoned in to explain that I was dealing with an off-duty arrest at Chingford. The search of Donald's room was interesting; as I suspected, he was obviously preparing to disappear when Mrs M had gone into hospital, and he'd got control of her money from the payout.

The work he'd put into the identity, he was about to assume was impressive. He'd created a driver's licence, a passport, and a pile of business cards all in the name of David Fortune. He had loads of other stuff too, like library tickets, a cheque book and even bank statements.

After I'd booked him in, I handed him over to the CID to deal with. They were a bit reluctant until I explained that his victim was a murdered WPC's Mum. A nice guy called Simon took the case.

When I finished it was half eight. From the CID office I called Sarah who told me to come round to her flat that evening as Paul was working all night. I was reluctant in case he came home unexpectedly but she explained she was being sick so frequently that leaving the flat was not an option. I agreed and told her I'd be round after I called in to see Mrs Matthews.

Mrs Matthews looked like she'd been crying all day. I took her through everything that had happened since I'd left her that morning.

"But who is he really? And has he done it to anyone else?" She asked.

"We don't know yet; they're running his fingerprints up the Yard to see if they can get a match. I'll go back tomorrow morning by which time the results will be back and I'll pop in and tell you. The CID at Chingford are dealing with it now and they'll need a statement from you. Do you want me to take it or are you happy for them to come round?" I asked.

"They can come round, Chris.. I'd rather not trouble you anymore; you've done enough already. If it wasn't for you, I don't like to think what I'd have lost. Oh, while you're here I'll give you a cheque, you know? That pay-out thing."

"Mrs M I'm not going to take it." I said.

"Why ever not? You said you would the other day?"

"I only said that because I didn't want you giving it to Donald, or whoever he is. I think it's a lovely thing for you to do but I can't accept it. I just can't Mrs M and please don't push me. I've made my decision." I said.

"But what shall I do with it? I don't want it either?"

"Why don't you stick it in a bank account and forget about it? You don't have to spend it but you never know when you might need it. Or you could give it to that Bob Geldof thing but make sure you know who you're giving it to this time." I said.

She smiled.

"I will." She said.

"Good, now give me a hug, I've got a hot date to go to." I said.

As I drove over to Leytonstone, I felt a weight lift off my shoulders and knew I'd done absolutely the right thing. The truth was that if I hadn't stolen the old lady's money, I would have accepted Mrs M's offer but because of what I'd done, I couldn't. It was difficult to articulate why but I think it was something to do with punishing myself; I was effectively fining myself a huge sum of money for the crime.

I wanted to be an honest cop not a thief. I mean I didn't mind telling the odd lie or verballing someone up if it was required to make sure they went down for what they'd done but I wouldn't fit anyone up or steal. I'd made a mistake, a bad mistake. I couldn't turn back time so I'd atone, learn a really good lesson, and get on with my life.

Such was the nature of our relationship, I'd never seen Sarah dressed in slops, with her hair unwashed and no make-up on so when she opened the door looking like death, it was quite a shock.

"Drink?" She asked.

"Tea?" I replied.

"I'm not cooking, Chris; beer or coke?"

"Beer please." I said.

I didn't like being there, but I had a cover story ready; if Paul came home I'd say I'd come round to see him about what had happened at court yesterday.

"Can't say pregnancy's making you glow." I commented, as she handed me a can of Fosters.

"I know. I've puked about twenty times today; I can't keep anything down. I thought I was through the worst of it." She said.

"Sorry." I said.

"What's happening at work?" She asked.

"I don't know I haven't been at work today, but I'll come to that later. I need to talk to you about your boyfriend." I said.

I told Sarah what had happened at court and how it had dawned on me that I'd been fitted up by Paul and Alec. Sarah sat and listened nodding and shaking her head as the tale unfolded.

"What are you going to do?" She asked.

"I'm fucked Sarah. If I go to Complaints my career will be over, no one will talk to me let alone work with me ever again. But I'm not happy, I mean, really not happy."

"How do you think the poor cow from Sandringham Road feels? I mean, it's awful. They're out of control, Chris." Sarah said.

"I must admit I'd not thought about her but let's face it, she's only looking at a con dis, I mean six bags of weed in your own house. It's hardly the great train robbery is it? But if I get done for perverting, I'm looking at five to seven." I said.

"You won't go down, Chris; they'll never prove it. It'll go to Area Complaints and they're notoriously ineffective, just a bunch of old has-beens waiting to retire; anyway, that's what everyone says." She said.

Sarah stood up.

"Come here." She said.

She led me into the bedroom but I knew it wasn't for sex. She moved a chair from in front of a dresser and placed it under a loft hatch.

"Just hold my hand please." She said.

She stood on the chair, lifted the hatch clear, reached inside and removed a shoebox.

"Hand it down." I said helpfully.

"No no; you don't want to touch this. Just hold my hand again." She said.

Sarah climbed down, put the box on the bed and took the lid off.

"Look." She said, taking the lid off.

The box was stuffed with hundreds of small clear plastic bags, each containing a fiver's worth of herbal cannabis. Tellingly, on each of the plastic bags was printed a small green cannabis leaf.

"Where did this come from?" I asked.

"Paul calls it his First Aid box, I don't really know why. Anyway, he usually keeps it in his locker at work but there have been loads of rumours flying round the nick about what CIB are up to so he thought it was safer here. Of course he didn't tell me. I found it and challenged him. I don't know what to do, Chris." Sarah said.

"Well at least he's hidden it well, no one would ever think of looking there." I said sarcastically.

"He's lost it, Chris."

"Is he still drinking?" I asked.

"It's a bit better now he's working these twelve-hour night shifts but he's still doing half a bottle when he gets in."

"Does he know about the baby yet?" I asked.

"No."

"What about you being sick all the time?" I said.

"I've told him it's a bug."

"What happened with the other thing, you know? The dodgy warrant, did they get it?" I asked.

"Sorted. The geezer from the lodge did the business. They've even made up a collator's card for the woman showing a couple of pieces of information saying she's a dealer which pre-dates the warrant. Then they've got someone else to phone up anonymously and claim to be a neighbour. This 'neighbour' says she's still dealing." Sarah explained.

"Talk about fitting someone up!" I said.

"I know, they've done a thorough job. They've planned it all with military precision. They have regular meetings at a rugby club somewhere in South Woodford."

Sarah put the box back.

"Aren't you going to wipe your prints off?" I asked.

"No, I can just say I put something into the loft and moved it out of the way without opening it, which is nearly what happened when I found it anyway." She said.

We sat back down in the lounge and Sarah got me another beer.

"I need to ask a favour, Chris." She said.

"Go on." I said.

"Wednesday week, you're early turn but I'll still be sick." She said

"You might be okay by then." I said hopefully.

"No, you don't understand, I *will* still be sick. Can you take the day off and drive me to and from a medical appointment in Buckhurst Hill?" She asked.

"Of course, but why?" I replied.

"Because I'm having a termination."

Chapter 40

If I'm being honest, Sarah having a termination was a weight off my shoulders and I slept better that night than I had done for ages.

Late turn the following day was even busier than usual. I reported three burglaries, two thefts from and one theft of motor vehicle, did two bail enquiries, a please allow, and a domestic, where the woman's boyfriend had attacked her with an axe. I arrived after the ambulance crew who were taking her to hospital to have a nasty wound in her right forearm stitched. She didn't want to know of course, which made my life easier as it was one less report to complete when I got back to the nick. Amazingly I was off on time.

When I was getting changed, Ben, the chap who tipped me off about being under investigation gave me a tug.

"You got a second Nostrils?" He asked and my heart jumped but I tried to act calm.

"Of course, mate, what is it?"

"Not here." He said and pointed up the stairs towards the back yard.

Two minutes later we were standing in a corner of the back yard talking in hushed tones.

"What is it, mate?" I asked, my demeanour untroubled and carefree but my heart pounding.

"You know what I told you before?"

Were my worst fears about to come true? Was he going to tell me that I was going to be arrested?

"Yeah? Why? Have you heard some more?" I said eagerly.

"No, it's nothing to do with that." He said and after a tension mounting pause, he laughed out loud. I could have killed him.

"Very funny, you wanker." I said, perhaps with a little bit too much relief in my voice.

"Blimey Nostrils, you're obviously worried about something. What have you been up to? I thought you were whiter than white."

"I've done nothing Ben but I don't like the idea of being looked at by the Rubber Heelers, no one would." I said.

"Perhaps?" He replied.

"Look, about that theft thing and to put your mind at rest, I haven't heard anymore, well not about you specifically. The Rubber Heelers are definitely looking at a theft here and you've somehow crossed into their sights but why and in what way I really don't know." He said.

"A theft of what though? You got any idea?" I asked.

"Blind Rudolph, mate." He said.

"What?" I asked.

"Blind Rudolph, you know? No idea, no eye deer." He replied.

"Hilarious Ben, did you used to be a stand-up comic?" I asked.

"I've been known to tell a joke or two."

"Look, Ben; much as I love standing here chatting to you, when all I want to do is go next door and sink a nice cold lager after the busiest late turn ever, did you really want to see me or were you just winding me up?" I asked impatiently.

"Steady, tiger; I'm getting there. Listen, mate; after this you'll owe me a pint." He said.

"Go on, then." I encouraged him.

"Well, I know this sounds strange, but have you upset old Keyhole, lately?" He asked.

"What do you mean?" I said.

"He's blaming you for a severe dose of the shits. You know, he was off, all last week?" Ben said.

I shook my head.

"Well, he thought he had food poisoning and, when he kept going back to the doctors they did some checks, you know, a stool sample and a blood test. Well, the results came back that he'd had an overdose of laxative. He did a bit of thinking and came up with the idea you gave it to him. Perhaps, in retaliation for the mortuary wind up thing?" Ben explained.

I didn't want to admit anything until I knew where this was going.

"Nothing to do with me, Ben." I said.

"You're a shrewd boy, Nostrils. I wouldn't expect you to admit it for one moment. Just listen then. He's got a plan to get his own back." Ben said.

"Go on." I said.

"He's got a powerful laxative from his girlfriend, you know, the nurse. It's in a little black bottle and he's going to slip it in your drink or food or something. It's like the most powerful one you can get." Ben explained.

I was suspicious. I could see some sort of double bluff, like with the mortuary wind-up. Fool me once, shame on you, fool me twice, shame on me, I thought.

"Why are you warning me?" I asked cautiously.

"Why? Cos Keyhole is a wanker, and I wouldn't cross the road to piss on him if he was on fire."

I'd never heard Ben talk that way; he wasn't like that, he was a cut above the rest of us.

"Christ, Ben; what did he do to you?" I asked.

"Couple of years ago, a group of us went on a stag weekend to Amsterdam. I got pissed and ended up paying twenty guilders for ten minutes of passionless sex with a Brazilian prostitute. No problem, or so you'd have thought; you know the principle; what happens on tour, stays on tour. Anyway, we get back and some bastard writes to the wife a nice letter telling her what I got up to. The coward typed the letter, but he hand-wrote the envelope. I checked the handwriting, carefully, against everyone who'd been on the stag weekend and, what did I discover?" Ben said.

"Sergeant Key?" I said.

"What a coward! Who would do a thing like that but a complete tosser?" Ben said.

"But why would he do that?" I asked.

"I don't know for sure but, over the weekend I'd taken the piss out of him, occasionally, and, all I can put it down to is that he didn't appreciate it. But whatever I'd done, you just don't do that. I mean he involved the wife and kids in whatever dispute he had with me because he didn't have the bollocks to front me out."

"Does he know that you know?" I asked.

"Oh no, Nostrils; and I want it to stay that way please."

"No sweat." I assured him.

"Anyway, since then, I've taken every opportunity to get my own back. I am careful and clever. I don't go over the top, just every now and again, I stitch him up." Ben explained.

"His tyres last Christmas?" I asked.

"All four." He replied, with a satisfied smile.

I remembered the fuss Sergeant Key had made. It was Christmas Eve, and we were late turn. He had it all planned out. He was going to drive home, pack his case and drive up overnight to his parents in Scotland. When he went to his car, he discovered all four tyres had been slashed and his plans, and his Christmas, were completely scuppered.

I decided Ben was telling me the truth.

"Thanks for tipping me off, Ben, I'll buy you a pint." I said.

"No problem, but please remember, keep your mouth shut." He said.

"Will do, I promise." I assured him.

Chapter 41

The following week I got my first assignment from Prestige Leasing, to recover an overdue VW Golf GTI, from a guy called Gary Hardman, who'd given an address in Theydon Bois. Mike got the keys couriered over to me.

When I did a PNC check and Gary Hardman came back as a thirty-two-year-old man born in Hoxton who had four previous convictions for varying degrees of assault, I had my first pangs of doubt, about my chosen sideline.

On my next day off, which was a Saturday, I did a recce of his address. The house was an impressive, detached property, guarded by tall, wrought iron gates, which operated on some sort of remote-control entry system. I wouldn't be able to get to the car once he'd parked it on his drive, so I started to form some vague plan of following him, until he parked it up, somewhere.

Flashing my warrant card and purporting to be on official police business, I made some enquiries with the neighbours. I learnt my man and his wife were renting the house from a retired couple, who were going round the world, for six months. The couple were due back in a few weeks, so Gary Hardman would soon be moving on. I also learnt that he was picked up by a scaffolding lorry, early most mornings, and returned mid-afternoon and, yes, he had been driving a white VW Golf, for some months.

"Do you know where he might be, now?" I asked, each person in turn.

I was getting nowhere until a man, living in the house opposite, which was my last call, looked up at the sky and said.

"Possibly, playing golf; he plays the public course in Chingford. I've seen him there several times and it's the first decent day in weeks."

Chingford Golf Course was only a few miles down the road, so I took a punt and there was the Golf GTI, stationary and unattended, in the car park

I parked my own car up nearby and decided I'd just reposition the Golf, in the back streets of Chingford, and tomorrow, I'd get Andy or Rik to run me back and pick it up. What could possibly go wrong?

The car park was behind the clubhouse, on the opposite side of a road to the first tee and eighteenth green. I carefully watched the eighteenth green to see who was just finishing their round of golf and, therefore, most likely to be going back to their car. Four men were putting out, and another two, waiting to play up. The four on the green were in their sixties, or maybe even older, but the two waiting to play up, were much younger and, therefore, potentially, one of them was Gary Hardman. I calculated they wouldn't be back in the car park for a good six or seven minutes and, although, as I drove onto the road, if they were looking, they would see the Golf driving away, they'd have to cover a good deal of ground to get anywhere near me. I decided I was fairly safe.

I moved quickly towards the Golf, all the time looking around to see who else was about. As I put the key in the lock, a black cab pulled into the car park and then stopped, completely blocking the exit, whilst the driver chatted to someone, who was just outside my line of sight. This caused me considerable anxiety. I decided not to get into the Golf until I knew my escape route was clear. Leaving the car unlocked, I walked away because, I was sure, I was starting to look suspicious. A couple of cars away from the Golf, was one of the most unusual cars I'd ever seen. It looked like a cross between a Rolls-Royce and something you'd see in Thunderbirds. I wandered around the rear of the vehicle and read the manufacturer's name, Bristol. I'd vaguely heard of the car company but never seen one of their cars, before. Looking at such an unusual car had the advantage of being quite a natural thing to do, so I made a big thing of looking through the door window at the interior.

When another car tried to pull into the car park, the black cab pulled forward to allow it to pass and my window of opportunity opened.

I moved back to the Golf and got straight inside. I fiddled nervously getting the key in the ignition and, when I started the car, it lurched forward against the handbrake and stalled, as it had been left in gear, and I'd not put the clutch in. As I knocked it in to neutral and restarted the engine, I noticed my hands were shaking. Because of the delay caused by the cab, the two men on the eighteenth might well, by now, be shaking hands and strolling back towards the car park. I shouldn't have taken this risk, but it was too late now. I turned right out of the parking space and the car bounced across the bumpy gravel and sand terrain.

Bang, bang, bang.

I nearly died of shock, when I looked in the mirror, someone, obviously Gary Hardman, was banging with a clenched fist on the rear window, although, I can honestly say, I didn't actually see him, at all. God knows from where he'd appeared.

"Oi, you cunt!" He shouted, but I put my foot down.

The front wheels momentarily span, and then gripped, and the Golf shot forward. I turned left and then right, onto the main road, without looking to see if it was clear. I waited for a collision or a screech of brakes, but none came, I knew I'd been extremely lucky.

In my panic I'd turned the wrong way. I'd meant to go left and towards the houses and the residential back streets, with which I was vaguely familiar, this way took me towards the forest and unknown territory.

When I accelerated, I selected the wrong gear and the car hopped down the road, like a kangaroo. I stopped, put the car in neutral and started again.

I drove for a hundred yards in first, before I risked changing into second. Should I turn round? No, don't be an idiot! I'd have to go this way and see where it took me.

I checked my offside door mirror. The silver Bristol was tearing out of the car park and turning right, in that second, I knew it contained Gary Hardman and, because I was both driving like a complete learner and dithering, it was now only three hundred yards behind me.

I was in real trouble.

Chapter 42

The Golf GTI was quick, noticeably quicker than my XR2, and, when I managed to find the right gears in the correct order, I started to really go. The road went slightly uphill and then started to twist and turn through the forest. About half a mile later, I hit the brow of a small, humped bridge and all four wheels left the road. On the other side of the bridge, the road turned quite sharply left, but I had no steerage until my tyres were once again in contact with the surface, it was a slow and agonising second, but I just managed to turn in time and avoided a tree and a ditch, by inches. How I stayed on the road, I'll never know, but I did. It was a testament to the Golf's handling.

I checked my mirror to see the Bristol come charging over the same bridge. It never left the road surface, the car was far too heavy, but as it turned left the rear lost grip and the offside slammed into a tree with an audible thud.

I didn't wait to see whether that was the end of the chase but put my foot down and drove for my life. I can honestly say, I didn't look back for another minute but concentrated on driving as fast, as I possibly could.

The road straightened out and I saw a T junction ahead. I glanced in my rear-view mirror. The Bristol was still chasing me, but I'd put a little distance between us. At the junction I turned left and caught sight of a sign which said Chingford and Edmonton.

The road I was on twisted and turned through open countryside and had several, really tight, bends. I noticed that, when the road straightened out, the Bristol closed on me but when it was bendy, the Golf was the better car to be in.

Shops, garages and houses began to appear, and I realised I must be coming back into Chingford. There were traffic lights ahead, which presented the obvious danger that I might be blocked, but they were green, and a steady flow of traffic was moving slowly through the junction. I checked my mirror, because I was slowing down, the Bristol was closing. The lights went amber and the car in front went through, perfect. I slowed, as if to stop, and looked right. My light went red. I wanted to time this, precisely. The cars from the right started to move across the junction and I could have turned left well ahead of them, but I had a plan. I checked my mirror; the Bristol was hurtling towards me and, for a second, I thought the driver might be intent on ramming me. I held my nerve and then, at the last moment, accelerated through the red light and turned left, cutting up the lead vehicle of a long line of traffic, which braked hard, to avoid hitting my side. Perfect. The Bristol wouldn't be able to come through, without hitting something.

I put my foot down hard. The road went steeply uphill, and I knew I was heading towards the police station, which was at the top, and on the left. I looked in my mirror, nothing.

If there was still no sign of the Bristol when I got to the top, I'd turn left, and left again, into the back yard of the nick. They'd never look for me there, and I'd lay low for an hour or four.

I did just that. The back yard at Chingford nick was quite large and, from the selection of cars already parked up, I guessed that, unlike at Stokey, police officers working here could park their own vehicles. I selected a parking slot which would be out of sight from outside the back entrance.

I opened the windows, turned the engine off, and mentally collapsed. When I looked at my hands, they were still shaking and my legs had that feeling you get when you've just been in a car accident, all shaky behind the knees.

I got out and lit a cigarette. When I finished, I lit another one.

As I stood there, I watched two officers come jogging out of the back of the nick, jump into the Area Car, hit the blue lights and two tones, and speed off, on some urgent business. A minute later the Duty officer came out in a hurry and jumped into an unmarked Astra and drove swiftly out of the yard. I hadn't realised it was so busy on these outer Divisions.

After my second cigarette, I found my way to the CID office and spoke to Simon, who was the CID officer dealing with the Donald Cole case. I was interested as to how the case was progressing and it gave me a legitimate excuse to be there.

"Donald Cole is Sergio Valentine, or at least that's the name he gave when he was first arrested back in sixty-seven, but he's got about twelve aliases. His first few convictions were for forgery and fraud but in the seventies, he did a stretch for counterfeiting five-pound notes. Since then, he's preyed on lonely, middle-aged women. He searches the obituaries in local papers to identify possible victims, but the meeting with Mrs Matthews seems to have been by chance. I've identified three different victims but there's bound to have been more who are too ashamed or embarrassed to come forward."

"What did he actually do to them?" I asked.

"He befriended them and gained their trust. He usually took them round looking at expensive houses and cars and said that he was considering buying them and needed a lady's opinion. Curiously, he doesn't normally sleep with them, and even turns down their advances, which reinforces his image as an honorable, trustworthy man. Then he bides his time until he sees an opportunity. One woman I spoke to went to the library one morning, only to return to no boyfriend, no car, and no jewellery, and, when she opened her credit card bill, she saw that he'd been spending on it, in the month up to his disappearance."

"Did he put his hands up?" I asked.

"No, he no commented but his brief has indicated, he'll cop a plea." Simon said.

"Good, Dawn's Mum won't have to give evidence then." I said.

"Well, he might change his mind but, probably, not. I took her statement, she's nice, isn't she?" Simon said.

"Mrs M? She's lovely." I replied.

Simon looked around and then leaned forward.

"Look, I'm not sure I should be telling you this, but he's made an allegation against you." Simon said.

"What about what I said when I arrested him?" I asked.

"No, not that. He said you're trying to fiddle Mrs Matthews out of her CICB payment, you know, for her daughter's death. I had to tell the governor, you know what with you working at Stoke Newington and everything."

"Bastard." I said with real menace.

"Not you." I added, quickly.

"Listen, the DI wanted to see for himself whether there was any truth in what the guy was alleging so he, you know, paid Mrs Matthews a visit and she told him that she'd offered you the money and that you'd categorically turned it down." Simon said.

"I have." I said quietly.

"The DI was very impressed; last thing I heard, he was contacting his counterpart at Stoke Newington, so you can expect a tug in the next few days." Simon said.

"Thanks for the heads up." I replied.

Throughout our conversation a telephone on a nearby desk had been ringing. The DC didn't take any notice of it and neither did I. It was still ringing, when an older uniformed officer walked into the office and asked.

"Why don't you lazy fuckers ever answer the phone?"

Before Simon could reply, a vehicle came into the back yard of the police station with its siren on and pulled up right under a nearby open window. The sound filled the room making normal conversation impossible. It was unheard of for a police vehicle to enter a police station on blues and twos. They often left in a hurry but always returned at leisure; it was the nature of the business. I stood up, and took a few paces over to the window, to see what was happening. The vehicle with its siren on wasn't a police vehicle but an ambulance and, at that moment, fortunately, because the noise was quite deafening, the siren was turned off.

"What's the problem, mate?" Simon asked the uniformed guy.

Simon checked his watch, which made me suspect he was about to go off duty, and wasn't too keen on picking up a job.

"There's been a serious assault in the charge room. One prisoner's bitten off another prisoner's nose." The PC said.

Chapter 43

Simon stood up slowly and shook his head.

"Bloody typical." He said.

"What's the matter?" I asked.

"I've got a ticket for the Irons this afternoon; great seats in the chicken run."

"Who're they playing?" I asked, feigning a polite interest I didn't really possess.

"Villa." He replied.

"Are you coming down before he goes off to hospital?" The PC asked with growing frustration.

"All right mate, I'm on my way."

Simon picked up a clipboard, on which were fixed several blank crime sheets.

"Do you wanna take a look?" He asked.

I was somewhat taken back, as I'd seen this as my cue to leave.

"Unless I'm mistaken, from the conversation I overheard between my governor and the DI at Stoke Newington, you'll soon be pursuing a career in the CID." Simon said.

Simon walked off and I followed, in bit of a state of shock; I mean, how did that work? I hadn't even applied for the Crime Squad boards, and, why would anyone do that for me anyway? Just because I'd refused Mrs M's money? It didn't make any sense. I wasn't sure I even wanted a career in the CID, spending my life doing paperwork and dealing with prisoners.

In the charge room two LAS crew were attending to a young white male who was lying on the floor, in great distress. A young PC was holding a bag of frozen peas in a tea towel which, I assumed, contained a severed nose. There was blood everywhere.

The Sergeant mistook me for a CID officer because, as we entered, he said.

"I've bailed the injured prisoner; he's wanted on warrant for a minor failing to appear and it saves having to keep him under guard at the hospital. Do you still want someone to go with him?"

I looked at Simon who replied.

"No, no; he'll be going into surgery when he gets there, so there's no point, and we know who he is, don't we?"

"Yeah, yeah." The Sergeant replied, pointing at the charge sheet on the desk before him.

The ambulance crew put the injured guy onto a stretcher and the Sergeant handed his cell keys to me; he still assumed I was meant to be there and told me.

"Open the door for them lad, it's the key with the yellow triangle."

I did as I was told and unlocked the charge room door, which I held open, whilst the injured guy was carried out, followed by the PC and his bag of frozen peas.

"What's happened then, Skip?" Asked Simon.

"I can tell you what's happened, but I'm absolutely lost as to why. Take a seat."

The Sergeant nodded towards the prisoners' bench and we both sat down. I felt a bit of a fraud as the Sergeant clearly thought I was a CID officer, or at least, a scaly aid.

"Two prisoners were brought in for threatening behavior and breach: right hard nuts. They're handcuffed but they're okay. I'm just finishing booking in the young lad who's here on a completely unrelated matter."

"What's he here for, Skip?" Simon asked.

"Failing to appear for a minor TDA, from last year. Anyway, he's moaning like mad about being nicked on a Saturday because he's got to get to a family wedding and he's running out of time. I told him, well, he shouldn't go round nicking people's cars then, should he?

Anyway, I didn't take any notice of it at the time but one of the new prisoners starts swearing and cursing and the arresting officer tells him to settle down or they won't take the handcuffs off. When I'd finished booking the young lad in, I told him to sit on the bench, because the warrant's backed for bail and his old man's on his way to act as surety. It's not worth putting him in a cell, as he's only going to be here twenty minutes, and he's hardly likely to run away as he's going to be out, anyway.

I start to book in the other two herberts. The arresting officer explains they've been involved in some sort of fracas down the bottom of Kings Head Hill. I authorised detention and they seemed fine, so I got their handcuffs taken off. As soon as they're off, the first one goes mental and attacks the young lad, trapping him in the corner. The poor guy's screaming, I mean really screaming. The arresting officer tried to stop him, but the second guy blocks his way. Eventually, everyone piles in, and we get them apart but not before the fucking animal has bitten the poor bloke's nose off."

"But why?" Simon asked.

"I've absolutely no idea. We've thrown them in separate cells." The Sergeant said.

"They obviously knew him." Simon suggested.

"I suppose so, but they hid it well when they came in."

"Can we go and have a word with them?" Simon asked.

"Of course."

The Sergeant stood up and walked down the cell corridor and we followed.

"You want to speak to the guy that bit him or his mate?" The Sergeant asked.

"The biter please Skip; what's his name?" Simon said.

"Gary Hardman." The Sergeant replied.

Chapter 44

We walked along the cell passage. I was confused. This was obviously something to do with me, but I couldn't figure out the young lad's connection to it all?

"I've got tickets for Upton Park, Sarge, so I'll probably hand this over to late turn, but it'll be good if I can let them know what it's all about." Commented Simon, as we approached the first cell.

The Sergeant dropped the wicket and spoke to the prisoner.

"The CID want a word. Alright?"

He got the reply he wanted because the Sergeant unlocked the door and stepped aside. I followed Simon in. Gary Hardman was sitting on the bench. He was a muscular white man, with a shaved head and chiseled features; he looked very intimidating.

"Gary?"

"Yes." He replied.

"I'm Simon, I'm a Detective Constable here, this is my colleague. You're a fellow Iron, I see." He said, pointing to a tattoo on his bulging right arm.

The man nodded, suspiciously.

"I've got tickets for the Villa game this afternoon." Simon said.

He dipped into his back pocket and produced two tickets which he held up, as if he was showing them at the gate.

The man nodded, approvingly.

"ICF?" Asked the CID officer but he was smiling.

"No comment." Gary replied.

The pair of them laughed. I knew the ICF stood for the Inter City Firm and was a gang of football hooligans who travelled the country, by Inter City trains, to fight other supporters. They were closely associated with West Ham but, allegedly, they all had respectable occupations. It was rumored, although I didn't believe it, that several of their members were serving police officers.

"Listen pal, off the record, 'cos you'll be interviewed later, what was that all about, in the charge room?" Simon asked.

The bloke just shook his head.

"You obviously knew the guy. Was it football related? Was he a Yido, or Millwall, or something?" Simon asked.

Again, he shook his head.

"Come on, mate. From one Hammer to another, I promise you, whatever you tell me is off the record." Simon said.

The man looked the CID officer up and down.

"Listen mate; I ain't sorry about what I did; I'd do it again, but you fucked up here, and you ain't getting out of it by putting it down to the ICF or any shit like that. The Metropolitan Police made a balls up and some thieving cunt loses a nose, so what, no big deal to me. But don't you start covering up what's happened." Gary said.

"Gary, you're not making any sense, pal. What you talking about a cover up, for? Am I missing something?" Simon said.

Simon turned towards me, to see if I had any suggestions. I didn't, so I just shrugged my shoulders.

"Under the circumstances, it's hardly surprising I had a bit of a go at that cunt, is it?" Gary said.

"All right; I'll ask the obvious question. *Why* did you assault him?" Simon said.

"Because he's just nicked my fucking car." Gary replied.

"What?" Simon said.

"What?" I said.

"And because of that little cunt, my best mate's just written off eighty-thousand-pound worth of motor." He added.

Simon was continuing to question the man, but I wasn't listening because my mind was racing. His 'stolen car' was obviously the VW Golf GTI, and his mate's eighty-thousand-pound car was the Bristol.

"Because we saw the stolen GTI in the back yard when we came in, and the Sergeant said, the man had nicked it." Gary explained.

"But the young lad you assaulted; you're saying he stole your car?" Simon asked.

"I'm not saying it, the Sergeant said it. I didn't see who stole my car, for all I know, it could have been him."

He pointed at me; I shuffled uneasily.

"I've absolutely no idea what you're talking about. The lad you assaulted was here on a warrant for failing to appear at court. He nicked a van last year, not a GTI, today." Simon explained.

"Well, how come my stolen Golf is in your back yard, then?" Gary asked.

"I've no idea but the lad had nothing to do with any motor what's in the back yard." Simon replied.

Gary looked confused, so did Simon. I decided the best thing to do would be to look confused, too.

Twenty minutes later, and after I relocated the GTI two hundred yards down the road, I found Simon in the canteen.

"Did you sort it out?" I asked innocently.

"Yeah, I think so. The victim was arrested on warrant this morning because he failed to appear last November at Redbridge Magistrates. He nicked, stroke, borrowed, his neighbour's old van and he got stopped by police and done for section twelve.

The other two herberts had an RTA this morning down the bottom of the hill, you know the lights before the Ressies. They'd been playing golf this morning up at Chingford and had gone for a drink in the nineteenth. When they came out, Gary, who works for the other one, whose got his own scaffolding company, saw his Golf GTI being nicked. They jumped in the boss's Bristol and gave chase, which ended with the GTI getting away and them doing a red ATS and ploughing into two cars.

A panda car was, literally, just around the corner and came across the two men going ballistic with the drivers of the cars they've just hit. He nicks them and puts up an urgent assistance. When they arrive here, they see a similar GTI in the yard, and assume the driver whose nicked it, had been nicked. When they get into the charge room and think that they hear the other guys been nicked for TDA, they put two and two together, and make five."

"I've checked the yard, there's no sign of a white Golf GTI." I said helpfully.

"It probably belonged to some guy off early turn. The thing is, I've just come off the phone to a company called Prestige something, who are the registered keepers of the GTI, which the herbert says has been nicked, they say the car is an overdue hire and they've contracted someone to snatch the vehicle back, so it was probably being repossessed and not stolen, anyway." Simon explained.

I was a little unsettled about enquiries being made with Prestige Leasing and hoped the man there, Michael Poulson, hadn't dropped me in it, but nothing in Simon's demeanour suggested he had.

"Any news about the victim?" I asked.

"No, not yet." Simon replied.

I checked my watch; it was ten past two.

"You're going to miss your match." I said.

"I know but I'm dealing with this, now. It's a bit complicated and I've got a rapport with the prisoners, so I'll stay on. Do you want to give me a hand?" Simon asked.

"Umm. No if that's okay. I only popped in to see about Mrs M's case." I said.

I was mindful of the fact that I wanted to get the GTI back to Knightsbridge and then come back to Chingford on the train, if I couldn't get a lift, and pick up the XR2.

"Listen. I've got a load of stuff to do but I'll be back about seven. If you're still here, perhaps I could buy you a drink to say thank you for tipping me off about the allegation." I said.

"Alright, mate." He replied.

"What's your name?" I asked.

"Simon Pollock." He replied.

"You're not related to Paul, are you? He's a PC at Stokey." I said.

"Yeah, he's my brother." He replied.

Before I left Chingford nick, I phoned the Section House and spoke to Andy. He told me Michael, from some company, was desperately trying to get hold of me and had been calling, all day. He gave me a telephone number which was the one for Prestige Leasing.

"You're exaggerating Welling, he hasn't been calling, all day." I said.

"He has, Nostrils; every half an hour, since ten. Is everything ok?" Andy asked.

"Andy, do me a favour, call Michael back on that number and tell him, I'm on my way." I said.

It didn't really make sense that he'd been trying to get hold of me all day. I could understand him trying to get hold of me after he got the phone call from the CID officer but not before. Perhaps, he had another car for me to repossess? If he did, he was going to be disappointed because I wasn't going through all that again.

The drive to Knightsbridge was a nightmare; there was some demonstration in the West End, which I had to circumnavigate, and when I arrived, it was half five and Michael Poulson was waiting for me, so he could go home.

"There you go, one Golf GTI." I said, throwing him the keys.

"What the devil happened? I had a call from some CID officer about a GBH, I thought you'd been hurt, but obviously couldn't ask too many questions, 'cos I didn't want to drop you in it." Michael said.

"Let's just say, recovering the car cost the write off of a Bristol …"

"A Bristol?" Michael asked.

"You know, those hand made cars. Wasn't there one in a Bond film once? And, it also cost two blokes their liberty and one poor guy his nose." I said.

"Oh my god, Chris. Are you alright?" Michael asked.

"Me? I'm fine, piece of cake Michael."

I told him the whole story, over a pint, and then I remembered, he'd been trying to get hold of me all day.

"If you've got another car for me, I'm afraid you're going to be disappointed, Michael. I've decided to retire from this business." I said.

"I'm sorry to hear that, Chris; but don't make that decision, just yet, I'll give you a call when another job comes in, there's nothing on the horizon, at present; all my customers are paying their way."

"You haven't got anymore?" I asked.

"No, why?" He replied.

"Because you've been trying to get hold of me all day." I said.

Michael shuffled uncomfortably in his seat.

"Michael Poulson, what is it?" I asked.

"Look, Chris; I didn't know whether to say anything, after all the trouble you've obviously been through, but …"

"What?" I said.

"…when I opened the post, I had a backdated cheque from the scaffolding company, on behalf of Gary Hardman, for another six months lease of the GTI. Obviously, that would cover the month that's outstanding. I didn't mention it to the DC that phoned and, if anyone asks, I'll say it arrived on Monday." Michael said.

I didn't know what to say; just put my head in my hands.

Chapter 45

I declined to take the money which Michael owed me for the repossession, told him I definitely wouldn't be doing it again, and apologised for mucking him around.

I'm not quite sure why I turned the money down, but something inside was starting to associate money with dishonesty. You see, if I avoided taking money, I felt better about myself and what I'd done, or was doing. I had a job, a well-paid job, and that was what I accepted money for doing. If I avoided taking money from anywhere else, perhaps, I could be the honest cop, I strived to be? I know it sounds a ridiculous thing to say, but I'd started to think money equaled corruption.

I got the underground and then the over ground back to Chingford and collected my XR2. I took a punt along the route from the golf course to the nick, which I driven earlier in the day, and parked up at the junction, where I'd done the red light to escape my pursuers. There was the Bristol. It was a poor imitation of the car I'd admired in the golf club car park, with dents and scratches all along one side, and a smashed headlight cluster.

I popped into the CID office, to be told Simon Pollock was next door in the Kings Head. I bought him a pint and he gave me an update on the two herberts, as he called them. They'd been interviewed, no commented and both had been charged with grievous bodily harm. They were being kept in custody for court on Monday. The victim's nose had been sewn back on, but they had to wait to see if the operation was successful. Listening to Simon talk, for the first time, I started to think a career in the CID might be more interesting than I had previously considered, and I mentioned this to him.

"Listen, Chris; what you got in? Three, four?"

"Two." I replied.

"Do you want to spend your next twenty-eight years tearing round the ground, from one call to another, rolling round the floor, fighting drunken prisoners, and nicking people for off wep and bags of weed? Seriously, get in the CID and the world opens up. The Bomb Squad, the Regie, the Sweeney, Drugs Squads, Crime Squads, even the Fraud Squad, is better than pounding the beat all day, every day, and in all weather."

"I've missed this year's Crime Squad boards, they had them last week. Besides, with two years in, I wouldn't have stood a chance."

"Listen, Nostrils; in this job it's not what you know, but who you know, that counts. I told you earlier, my DI has spoken to someone he knows at Stokey about you turning down that money from that WPC's Mum. That was a good thing to do, you've no idea. And you've got a good reputation anyway, you know, it always helps if you've been blown up, once or twice, by an IRA bomb; does your credibility no harm, if you know what I mean.

If you get offered an attachment to the Crime Squad or the main office, grab it, with both hands, it may never come again. My brother's been strapping for years and always regrets not pursuing a career in the CID. He had a board once, years ago, but he wore brown shoes with his suit and, as soon as he walked in, the DCI told him to fuck off, without asking him a single CID related question."

"Are you serious?" I said, incredulously.

"That was fifteen years ago, but even today, some DCIs and DIs are really funny about looking the part. Another mate of mine had a board. It was going like shit, and he knew he'd failed. Anyway, right at the end, he's asked what particular skill he could bring to the CID. He knew he'd failed, so he thought, damn it, I've got nothing to lose, and said, I can sing 'How Much is that Doggy in the Window', backwards. The DCI said, go on then, and he did, all three verses, and got the job."

I laughed out loud; it seemed so ridiculous, it had to be true.

"Do you know my brother, then?" Simon asked.

The question took me a little by surprise.

"Yeah, we're on the same relief but he's on jury protection, at the moment."

"Is he?" Simon replied.

"Haven't you spoken to him, lately; he's been doing it for weeks, maybe even a month."

"We're not particularly close." Simon said.

"I'm sorry, he's a nice bloke." I said.

"Yeah." Simon said, without enthusiasm.

I didn't know what to say really, so I finished my pint and started to get ready to leave, standing up and putting my coat on. Simon didn't respond, he looked deep in thought, as if he was turning something important, over in his mind.

"Well, thanks again for sorting Mrs Matthews out." I said.

"Before you go, Nostrils; sit down, shut up and listen." There was a change in his voice, a cut.

"When you get on the Crime Squad, be very careful."

He looked me straight in the eye, assessing my reaction, waiting to see if I would say anything. I didn't.

"Don't get dragged down. They need people like you; people with honesty and integrity, even the governors are getting worried. There are rumours it's all coming on top. If it does ..."

He corrected himself.

"...when it does, don't end up getting caught up in it. I know it's hard, you'll want to fit in, you don't like to be the one to say no, particularly, if you're as young in service as you are; particularly, if you're the new boy. Your next six months are either going to be hard, but safe, or easy, and very dangerous. Be careful. Chris. The house of cards is about to collapse. It's too late for many, Paul included, but not for you. They've all gone over to the dark side. Something happened a few years ago, something big. They saw a chance and took it."

"Who?"

"The Stoke Newington Crime Squad. It was probably a big haul of drugs or cash, you know, they came across it during a search or something, and decided to have it off."

Throughout his lecture, I held his stare. Not long ago, I genuinely wouldn't have had a clue as to what he was talking about, but after the conversations with Sarah, I knew, only too well, the kind of things to which he was referring. I stood up and put my coat on, but Simon didn't move a muscle.

"Thanks." I said and turned to leave but, as I did, Simon started singing quietly and I turned back.

"Window the in doggie, that is much how? Tail waggly the with one the. Window the in doggie, that is much how? Sale for is dog that hope do I!"

I smiled broadly and left.

Chapter 46

The more I turned the strange conversation with Simon Pollock over, the more it sounded like my going into the CID was some sort of 'done deal'. All because I'd turned down Mrs M's money? It didn't add up, there was a piece of the jigsaw missing, somewhere.

Chingford nick wasn't far from Mrs M's place. I checked my watch, ten past nine, I thought she'd probably still be up. She was. By half past, my legs were curled up under me, on her settee, and I had a mug of tea in my hand.

"I gather a senior officer came round to ask you about the CICB payout?" I asked.

It wasn't the reason I'd come round but I wanted to get the matter out in the open.

"And jolly annoyed I was, too." She replied.

"I'm so sorry that happened. I didn't know they were …"

"I'm not cross with you, Chris; I'm cross with Donald. How dare he accuse you of such a thing!"

"Oh, don't worry about him. I suspect, he's so used to his way of life, you know, conning people out of money, that he just can't imagine someone who's not that way inclined. Was the DI alright with you?" I asked.

"Yeah, he was fine, but I have to tell you, I told him what I did with the money was my business and not his."

"I know, but he, sort of, had to ask, you know, just in case there was any truth in what Donald was alleging." I said.

"Surely by now they know you're honest, Chris?"

"It doesn't work like that."

"Well, it should." She said sternly.

"They had to check up, really, they were protecting you, honestly." I assured her.

"I suppose so, but I don't expect to be troubled about it, again. If I want to give you the money, which I do, I really do, there's only one person who can stop me."

"Me?"

"Right."

"I respect your decision, Chris; but I still think you're mad. It would set you up for the rest of your life."

I didn't reply, intending that she should take my silence to mean that the issue was closed. Just to make sure, I changed the subject.

"How are you about the Donald thing? And can I remind both of us, that Donald is not his real name?"

"I don't know if I'm kidding myself or not, but I'm ok, I really am. I liked Donald, or whatever his name was, but do you know what, he wasn't right for me, and I knew that."

"Good, glad to hear it Mrs M, glad to hear it, you were way too good for that ..."

I struggled to find the right word because I was speaking to Mrs M, usually I wouldn't have had any difficulty.

Mrs M smiled, I think she knew why I was in difficulty.

"Go on, Chris; say it, I don't mind." She urged me and, just for a second, I detected a real glint in her eye.

Now my chosen word for Donald, particularly after he'd accused me of being a conman, would have begun with C but, despite granting me permission, I couldn't bring myself to say it in front of Mrs M.

"Wanker." I said finally and laughed.

Mrs M laughed too, which was nice to see.

"I could have said worse." I said.

"I'm sure you could." She replied, and we laughed again.

When she laughed, she reminded me so much of Dawn.

"Listen, Chris. How do you fancy a glass of wine? It's nice to have some good, honest company, from a man who's not trying to fleece me out of everything I own. What do you say?"

"That would be great but just the one, I'm driving." I replied.

I'd moved in with Dawn and her Mum about a month before the bombing and, I can honestly say, it was the happiest time of my life. Mrs M would go to bed quite early, deliberately to leave Dawn and me alone, and we would chat, late into the night. I think it was during these late-night chats that I fell in love with Dawn, although it's difficult to remember because of what happened, so soon afterwards. I fancied Dawn so much, it was difficult not to fall for her, but nothing ever happened between us because Dawn never felt the same way about me.

"How old are you, now?" Asked Mrs M, as she handed me the glass.

"Twenty-one, why?"

"I just wondered."

"Still a baby." I said.

"Hardly, Chris; not after two years walking the streets of Stoke Newington. If you're anything like Dawn, you've grown up very quickly, working for the Metropolitan Police."

"Did Dawn talk about her work much?" I asked.

"Yeah, sometimes but because I used to worry so much, I think she was very careful what she told me."

Two glasses of wine later, it was agreed that I could sleep in my old room. I confess to being a little spooked by the whole idea, but Mrs M assured me, it had been redecorated and the furniture re-arranged, so I wouldn't feel like I'd just travelled back in time. I'd had a long and tense day and I could feel my body relaxing with every sip of red wine. The chat was easy, and the hours ticked by, effortlessly. Sometime around midnight, the second bottle of wine was opened, and the conversation rolled on unabated.

"Mrs M, can I ask you, how old you are?"

She smiled again.

"I'm forty-two. Chris, I was pregnant with Dawn, at sixteen. Why do you ask?"

"I just wondered, really. Are you keen to find someone else, or has Donald put you off men, for life?"

"Now you're sounding like Dawn; she was always telling me to find someone."

"Well? Don't avoid answering the question." I said.

"Seeing as you asked, oh I don't know whether I should tell you …"

"Tell me what, do go on." I urged her.

"No, really, I've had too much to drink; if I tell you I'll be embarrassed, in the morning."

"Listen, tell me, then give me another large glass of wine and I won't even remember, in the morning."

She laughed.

I learnt from my interview training never to fill a silence in these circumstances, but to leave it hanging, to encourage the other person to speak into it.

"I err, well, occasionally I see someone, a gentleman, you know …"

"You mean you're seeing someone, not Donald, so you were two timing Donald? Oh, I wish I could tell him."

"It wasn't like that, Chris. Not long after my David left me for his secretary, his best friend came round; you know, to see how I was doing and well, you know …"

"But that was like ten years ago." I said.

"Fifteen, actually." She corrected me.

"And you've been seeing him all this time?" I asked.

"I'm not sure seeing is the right word, Chris. And after what happened to Dawn, well you know …"

"Haven't you seen him since? Is he married?"

"One question at a time please; yes, he's married, but well separated now, and yes, I saw him just before Donald appeared on the scene."

I must have looked shocked, which I was, because Mrs M said.

"Don't look like that, Chris; just because I'm older doesn't mean I don't need …"

This time it was her turn to struggle to find the right word.

"Go on, say it, I don't mind." I said repeating her earlier encouragement to me.

"Stuff."

I laughed at her choice of word.

"I could have said a lot worse" she said.

Then, just for a moment, our eyes touched.

"So, what about you, Chris; I bet you're a right smoothie."

"Not really, Mrs M, you see …"

"What, Chris? What?"

"It's really embarrassing."

"No need for secrets here, Chris. I promise you."

"Since the bombing, I haven't been able to have sex."

Chapter 47

I didn't spend the night in my old room, I spent the night with Mrs M. When I woke, I should have felt like shit, but I didn't, I felt okay. The truth was she was an attractive woman, and I was a little drunk, and very horny, as I hadn't had proper sex with Sarah in about a month. She wanted to have sex and so did I and, as we were two consenting adults, I didn't care.

I wondered how Mrs M would react, but I think, from the easy interaction between us the following morning, everything was fine.

My first sexual experience had been with the wife of, and consent of, a PC on Street Duties, who'd replaced Dawn, when she was off for a week with a broken nose. It was all a bit peculiar, but the sex was dirty and coarse. The only other person I'd slept with was Sarah and the sex with her was quick, because we were always stealing the time, and erotic, because she was really attractive. The sex with Mrs M was different. It was slow, and kind, and gentle, and meaningful, and intimate, and I'd never experienced anything like it. It blew my mind, and turned on its head, everything I'd thought I liked about being with a woman.

As we hugged in the hall before I left, she whispered.

"Thank you."

I couldn't figure out why.

Of course, it crossed my mind what Dawn would have thought but the way I saw it, if Dawn had still been with us, it would never have happened, so it was a moot point. I didn't want it to corrupt our relationship.

When I got back to the Section House, I phoned Sarah. It was risky, but we had this thing worked out, where, if she answered, I would ask for Paul. If he was in, she'd say hang on and pass the phone over, at which point, I would hang up. If Paul was suspicious, Sarah would just say it was a woman asking for you, I'm the one who should be annoyed. If he wasn't there, she'd just say, hi, and we'd chat. Obviously, you couldn't do it too often, but the ploy could certainly be used in an emergency. As Paul was on nights, I thought it would probably be safe to call.

"Paul's not come home; I've no idea where he is." Sarah explained.

"What time was he due in?" I asked.

"Seven." She replied.

"Did you get up to much, yesterday?" She asked and images of the car chase, a nose-less prisoner and a naked Mrs M flashed through my mind.

"Nope, you?" I replied.

"Remember Wednesday, have you got it off?" She asked

"I don't need to, I'm floating rest day Wednesday."

"Oh, that's handy. Pick me up by the pub, about eight thirty, it'll give us an hour."

"Where we going?" I asked.

"A clinic in Russell Road, Buckhurst Hill. Do you know how to get there?"

Did I know how to get there? It was practically opposite the church where Dawn was buried and half a mile from Mrs M's house.

"Yeah, I know it, we'll have plenty of time 'cos we'll be going against the traffic. What you doing today? Want to meet up?" I asked.

"I don't fancy it, Chris; I'm still being sick." Sarah replied.

At that moment, I suspected our relationship was over, because Sarah had never missed an opportunity for us to be together, but I was okay, it was time to move on.

Chapter 48

The day before Termination Wednesday, as I had named the big day, I was early turn.

I didn't mind early turn, and could just about survive getting up at five, if I promised myself an afternoon nap. The first two hours were always quiet, and most people found somewhere on the ground to have breakfast. Several of the relief had the procurement of the first meal of the day, off to a fine art, and had cultivated several old ladies who, in return for an hour of their company, would gladly cook them a full fry up.

From nine onwards, there'd always be a stream of central station alarms, as banks, building societies and other businesses set them off by accident, when opening up. Refs was at either nine or ten and, by the time you got out and about again, and took the odd bail enquiry or please allow, it was time to book off and get into the pub for a couple or three pints, before closing.

There was never much crime to report on an early turn and, if you were keen or in your probation, it was a good time to do process and get a couple of entries in your record of work. All probationers had to keep a record of work book, which was a small, yellow diary. Every time you did someone for a traffic offence, made an arrest, went to court, reported a crime, or whatever, you made an entry, which a Sergeant countersigned. A full record of work book meant that, provided you passed your final probationer's exam, you would be made up to a substantive constable, at the end of two years. My reporting officer, the Sergeant who oversaw my development, was Sergeant Felix, a genuinely nice man, with whom I got on well. I was fairly confident I wouldn't have a problem.

I was called in at nine to relieve the Assistant Station Officer whilst he had his refs. It was probably my least favourite thing to do, as you ended up filling in the same old forms, over and over again; although, just occasionally, something interesting might come in.

At parade, someone else had been posted to relieve the ASO, so I was surprised to be called in, but didn't think much about it, until I saw Sergeant Key was the Station Officer. In view of what Ben had told me the previous week, my suspicions were immediately ignited. They were on fire when Sarge put the kettle on and asked who wanted tea.

My first customer was a lady with a foreign accent who'd found a dog. A few weeks ago, I'd got a spate of sudden deaths to report, recently, it seemed that every time I came on duty, somebody lost or found a bloody dog.

When I tried to take the woman's details, she said it was unnecessary, as she was on her way to Heathrow and would be leaving the country and not coming back. She handed me the end of the lead and walked off. I was left holding the most peculiar looking dog I'd ever seen. She, I looked closer, no, he, was small and fluffy and, quite frankly, ridiculous. When I walked him to the kennel in the yard, everyone who saw me had something witty to say but I had to laugh when Roger Class commented.

"You look absolutely ridiculous with such a pathetic excuse for one of god's finest creatures."

"Leave the poor thing alone, he can't help it." I replied.

"I was talking to the dog." Roger Class replied.

I'd walked right into that one.

"Ha fucking ha." I replied, sarcastically.

"Did you get the Crime Squad board?" I asked, remembering that he'd had the interview yesterday.

"It's not official until Friday but …"

He tapped his finger to his nose.

"…it's in the bag, Nostrils. I told you, it's not what you know, it's who you know."

I remembered his claim of having a masonic connection to a senior officer at the nick.

"Oh, that's right, you're relying on the square, aren't you?" I said.

He smiled.

I admit I was curious to know more. Dawn had mentioned the Freemasonry thing, but Roger was the first person I knew who'd actually admitted being a member of this secret society. I decided to take a chance.

"Roger, if I buy you a pint after early turn, would you tell me a bit more about Freemasonry? It kind of intrigues me." I said.

"Yeah, alright Nostrils. The Hart?" He replied, seemingly genuinely pleased that I showed an interest.

I nodded.

Back in the Station Office, I served my next customer, some bloke who was signing on as a condition of his bail.

"Tea's up, Nostrils." Sergeant Key announced, as I finished.

Sergeant Key making the tea? I don't think so. Sergeants never made the tea, that's why they had Constables. I watched, as he added one sugar to his own and, even though I didn't take sugar, I copied him. There was no way I was going to drink the tea he'd given me.

An urgent voice over the radio suddenly caught everybody's attention.

"Golf November, chasing suspects, chasing suspects, one five six."

The First Reserve responded.

"All received one five six, location first, and then keep the commentary going, please."

I didn't know who one five six was, he wasn't on our relief.

"Craven Walk, towards the River Lea."

"Description please?"

Above the Reserve desk was a large street map of the ground which had been hand drawn by the Plan Drawer. Sergeant Key was running his finger across the surface to find Craven Walk.

"Its north of Clapton Common, Sarge." The First Reserve said, helpfully.

I'd noticed that Sergeants didn't know the ground as well as us PC's, probably because they never walked it. Whilst Sergeant Key squinted to read the road names, I took my opportunity and swapped my tea for his.

"One five six, please keep the commentary going." The First Reserve said.

There was no reply, and the sirens and bells of several police cars left the back yard and headed north. It would take them a good six or seven minutes to get there because the location of the chase was right at the top of the ground.

"Urgent assistance; I require urgent assistance." The PC cried.

Nothing got the adrenalin going like hearing those two words. It was the shout that officers only made when they were in real trouble.

"One five six, you have unit's running …"

A loud, dominant female voice came over the radio.

"Golf November, this is MP. I understand you have a unit requiring urgent assistance. The link is in, channel one."

"Yes MP, we have a foot unit, one five six, requiring urgent assistance. Last location was Craven Walk N16 toward the River Lea."

"Thank you, Golf November; you have Yankee Tango units very close to that location, MP over."

MP was the call sign of the control centre at Scotland Yard and by putting the 'link in', the surrounding Divisions could hear what was going on, and come to assist, if they were nearby.

"I've been shot, I've been fucking shot." Screamed a terrified voice across the airwaves.

Chapter 49

One five six was one lucky son of a bitch. The shot had been heading straight for his heart but had been stopped by the two-inch layer of the eight different notes books he carried, in his left breast pocket, and a metal comb. In fact, the bullet hadn't penetrated his chest at all, but the force of the shot had knocked him backwards, and he'd fallen to the ground, where the Tottenham unit found him, within seconds of his last transmission. There was no sign of the suspect, despite the area being saturated with police, within minutes.

The PC was taken to hospital for a checkup and the search continued. He was a Home Beat officer, which explained why I didn't know him.

I was vaguely aware that, for the last few minutes, two people had been waiting at the front counter, a male and female, both white and very respectable. They carried briefcases and, if I'd seen them knocking at the front door of a house, I would have assumed them to be Jehovah Witnesses.

"Thank you for waiting so patiently; we've had a serious incident going on. How can I help you?" I said, politely, as soon as it started to calm down again.

They both took my question as a cue to produce identification cards, with their photographs on, and I got the distinct impression that they expected me to recognise them and do something. I smiled and repeated my question.

"How can I help you?"

"We're lay visitors, please admit us, immediately." The female said, as if she was giving me a direct order.

The term lay visitors was vaguely familiar, where had I heard it before?

"I'm sorry?" I said, quite obviously a little confused.

"Officer, we are lay visitors. Last week your Chief Superintendent signed up to the Lay Visitor Scheme, which allows us immediate and unrestricted access to your charge room and cells. I thought you would have been informed..."

"Yes, sorry, I have read something about the scheme; I'll come round and let you in." I replied.

I'd remembered just in time. I read about it in the Parade Book, last week. Everyone was a little surprised, to say the least, that the old Chief Super had agreed to let do-gooders in to the charge room. I mean, what if someone was getting a good hiding? They told us it was all about greater accountability and openness. Personally, I thought the bosses were asking for trouble.

In order to let them in, I had to walk back round the Station Office and past the Charge Room door, I glanced inside. Sergeant Felix was sitting at the desk reading a newspaper. The white board on the wall was completely blank, meaning there were no prisoners in the cells, which was unusual, but not unheard of at that time of day, because those who had been in overnight, would have gone to court, a short while ago.

Just then, the door from the back yard opened and a white prisoner entered, he was handcuffed, and Ben was holding him just above the elbow, but it looked peaceful, and Ben wasn't the punchy type, so I took the view, it was safe to bring the lay visitors in, unannounced, as per the new policy.

I opened the door to the public section of the Front Office and smiled.

"Come this way please."

"Thank you." The woman replied, politely.

The door into the Charge Room was directly behind Sergeant Felix, so, whilst he'd have probably been aware that someone had entered, he'd have to turn right around to see us. He'd just started booking Ben's prisoner in and, whilst under other circumstances, I would never have interrupted him, I thought he should know he had lay visitors watching his every move.

"Sarge, sorry to trouble you but …" I said, a little tentatively.

Without looking up, Sergeant Felix replied.

"Button it; Nostrils I'm busy; come back later."

What could I do? My eyes met Ben's and he frowned and looked at the two people standing next to me but, feeling them looking at me, I had to resist the temptation to mouth the words 'lay visitors', and just smiled.

Ben's prisoner, a white man in his early twenties, who seemed compliant, was sitting quietly on the bench. Sergeant Felix was fiddling with the large charge sheet, three copies of which had to be slotted one on top of the other, onto a large black plastic template. I thought about having another try at introducing the lay visitor, but before I said anything, Ben asked Sergeant Felix.

"Can I take the cuffs off, Sarge?"

"One moment, I'm just helping out in here today, I need to consult the Custody Sergeant."

With that, Sergeant Felix opened the top drawer of his desk, put his right hand inside and took it out, a few seconds later, wearing Sooty the glove puppet, who was suitably adorned in the uniform of a police sergeant.

Although I'd never seen it before, I'd heard that Sergeant Felix, very occasionally, did this with prisoners, usually those worse for wear through drink. It was said to be very amusing, but I wasn't sure the lay visitors would find it so.

Sergeant Felix spoke to Sooty, who obediently turned to face him.

"Good morning, Sooty." He said.

Sooty nodded.

"Do you think we should take the prisoner's handcuffs off, Sergeant Sooty?"

Sooty turned to face the prisoner and in an exaggerated fashion looked the prisoner up and down, slowly. Then he turned quickly back to Sergeant Felix and nodded. Sergeant Felix, in turn, nodded to Ben, who removed the handcuffs.

I looked at the lay visitors; both their mouths were open, as if in complete shock.

When the handcuffs were removed, Sergeant Felix instructed Ben:

"Can you please give the circumstances of arrest to Sergeant Sooty?"

"Sergeant Sooty, this is David McDonald, he's wanted for an ABH on his ex. DS Cotton is dealing and asked me to see if I could pick him up this morning. He was arrested at his home address; he says he knows all about it and just wants to get it sorted out."

"What do you think, Sergeant Sooty?" Sergeant Felix asked.

Sooty whispered in Sergeant Felix's ear. The puppet had decided the arrest was lawful and detention was authorised. Throughout the whole bizarre episode, the prisoner smiled, obviously finding the whole charade quite amusing. Ben acted as if the whole thing was completely normal, and I just looked back and forwards, between the lay visitors and the Stoke Newington Police Station 'Sooty and Sweep' Show.

"Um, any chance of bail, boss. I don't want to be in overnight." The prisoner asked, as the booking in process concluded.

Sergeant Felix took a sharp audible intake of breath, shook his head slowly from side to side, and opened the other drawer.

"Sergeant Sweep decides whether you get bail and, I'm sorry to say, it's not looking good, 'cos he's in a foul mood this morning and I haven't even shoved my hand up his arse, yet."

I'd heard enough and was going to have to put a stop to this, genuinely amusing though it was, but as I stepped forward, the door from the main office swung open violently and struck the back of the male lay visitor, with considerable force. He cried out in pain. Sergeant Key marched in, grabbed me around the throat and pushed me firmly up against the wall. I thought for a moment he was going to punch me. In his anger he'd trodden on the lady lay visitor's foot and she jumped, squealed, and started hopping up and down. Sergeant Felix turned round, Sergeant Sooty still on his right hand, to see what was causing the commotion.

"Nostrils, you are fucking dead, fucking dead, you cunt." Shouted Sergeant Key, as his hands tightened around my throat.

There was a waft of shit and then the sound of a slow, but wet fart, as Sergeant Key's bowels completely opened.

Chapter 50

After early turn, I went for a drink with Roger Class. As he was one of the older PCs on the relief I hadn't previously had much to do with him, but I was genuinely intrigued to know more about this freemasonry thing.

We went to the White Hart which was just along the High Street from the nick. The landlord was a small Irish guy called Murphy, who was in his sixties, and very pro police. Everybody drank there and, as we took our seats in one corner, I noticed the DCI and the two DI's in another. We nodded, respectfully, and the DCI waved Roger over. After a short conversation, which I couldn't hear, Roger went back to the bar, purchased three large malt whiskies, which he delivered to the three senior Detectives, before, eventually, joining me. He was all smiles.

"I gather you got your board, then?" I said.

"Yeah, I've just been told. I'm really happy, actually. I want to get off relief, it's driving me mad." He said.

"Why?" I asked.

"I did fifteen years at SB, Nostrils; after that it's very difficult to settle back into earlies, lates and nights and all the bull shit that goes with it."

"So, your freemasonry connection swung it for you then?" I said.

"Yeah and no. He didn't order them to take me, it doesn't work like that, but he got me the questions I was going to be asked and helped me to prepare the answers. Obviously, that gave me a distinct advantage. One of the questions was about the correct procedure if you seize a load of cannabis plants which is pretty obscure. Nobody would have known the answer, but I did. Another was about pace which, of course, no one knows anything about yet, unless, like me, you've had time to do a bit of research."

"Pace?" I asked.

"See." He said, proving his point that no one would know anything about it.

"What is it?" I asked.

"It's the Police and Criminal Evidence Act. It's a new piece of legislation that has been passed which is going to change the way we do just about everything. For example, when someone's in custody, you're going to have to like, write everything down that happens to them. You know like, he ate a meal, he had a piss, he phoned his wife, everything. And they're going to start what they call a dry run later this year. See, I even know that."

"Sounds like a nightmare." I commented.

"It will be." Roger replied.

"More importantly though, what you gonna do about Sergeant Key? The whole nick's talking about you tricking him again, into taking another load of laxative."

"Listen, Roger; he slipped it in my drink, all I did was swap the drinks around." I explained.

"That wasn't smart, Nostrils." Roger said.

"What was I meant to do, drink it?" I asked.

"No, Nostrils; what you should've done is pretend to drink it and act out getting the shits. That would have been smart. You've made an enemy of a nasty, vindictive man."

"Fucking hell, Roger; do you really think it's a problem?" I said.

"Do I?"

"What should I do?" I asked.

"Get off relief and get off, quickly." Roger suggested.

"Great advice! How am I going to do that? I'm still in my probation."

Roger thought for a few moments and then said.

"Ok. First thing you do, is buy Sergeant Key a very expensive bottle of Scotch, I mean, spend like a score. Then go and see old Inspector Portman and ask for a move on the grounds that you're shagging Sarah and it's all coming on top. 'Cos you've been blown up, everyone's quite keen to help you, well you know that ..."

"I didn't, but go on..." I said.

"...you'll be on A relief before you know it." Roger forecast.

It seemed a little drastic, but I had to admit, it was good advice which by myself, I'd have never thought of. And then I realised exactly what he'd said.

"What do you mean, I'm shagging Sarah?" I said, with as much incredulity as I could muster.

"Listen Nostrils, I'm not stupid; I see how you two look at each other sometimes, when you think no one else is watching."

"Does everyone think that?" I asked.

"No, just me, maybe Ben, he's a shrewd cookie."

I didn't deny it, but I didn't admit it, either.

"So that's what you recommend is it?" I said, steering the conversation away from Sarah.

"I do." He replied firmly.

"Scotch and then transfer request?"

Roger nodded.

"OK, I'll think it over. I mean, I'll definitely do the Scotch thing, obviously. What do you mean when you say, everyone's keen to help me 'cos of the bombing?"

"Nostrils you're a nice guy but if you hadn't been blown up, you'd have had a harder time than you have. I mean people are nice to you, probationers usually get a rough time, particularly ones like you."

"What do you mean? Ones like me?" I asked.

"One's who are best mates with a Paki and a coon, and a queer coon at that. And you're so honest, Nostrils, you need to loosen up."

I was really taken aback but my first reaction was to protect Andy.

"Andy's not homosexual. He can pull stunning women, I tell you."

"He could but he doesn't because he's queer." Replied Roger, unequivocally.

"He's not." I replied.

"He is; and you know it and you're sticking up for him, which is fine. Listen, Nostrils; I haven't got a problem with it. My brother was one of them. You know, bent as a nine-bob note."

"What do you mean was? Is he straight now?" I asked.

"No mate, the poor sod's dead." Roger replied.

"How come?" I asked.

"He got myeloma; you know bone cancer. He went down, really quickly." Roger explained.

"I'm sorry mate, were you close?"

"So, so. I didn't really agree you know, with his turd burgling. Anyway, you wanted to speak to me about the Masons?"

"I'm just intrigued really, what is it?" I asked.

"It's an ancient institution, men only, dedicated to doing work for charity and based on a set of principles which include an oath to assist one another, wherever possible. We meet five or six times a year, have a meal and a few drinks, it's quite formal but good fun. In my lodge are several senior police officers, a Colonel, a very senior civil servant and even a couple of celebrities. There's talk about setting up an all-police lodge and, if they do, I'm keen to be a founder member." Roger said.

"How do you join? I mean presumably you've got to be invited?" I asked.

"Well, young Nostrils; you've just taken the first step, *you* have to ask. People think it's the other way round but it's not. The first thing a person has to do, if they're interested in becoming a Freemason, is to ask."

"I am interested." I replied.

"In that case, I'll get you an application form. You might have to wait a while because we have a candidate for this year. When there's a slot, you'll be interviewed but that's easy, it's a bit like a board for the Crime Squad."

"What do you mean? They'll ask me about police things?"

Roger laughed.

"No, you idiot. I mean you'll know all the questions, and all the right answers, before you go in."

Chapter 51

I was lucky. The Sergeant Key incident was eclipsed by the shooting of PC one five six; or, to be more accurate, the non-shooting of PC one five six.

PC one five six was a Home Beat officer who'd recently transferred, under a cloud, from Hounslow. No one knew very much about him, until that fateful morning when he made up a fictitious chase and shooting for reasons which can only be guessed. His sham soon unraveled. The Tottenham unit was much nearer to him than he'd anticipated and saw him seconds after, he'd put up that he'd been shot. They should have seen something of the suspect as he fled and, when they didn't, became immediately suspicious that all was not what it purported to be.

Then the doctor, who conducted the medical examination of the PC's chest, could find no trace of, even the slightest, injury beneath where the bullet allegedly struck. As it turned out, the doctor was an ex-military guy, who'd done service in Northern Ireland, so he'd seen his fair share of bullet wounds. He told the DS it wasn't right, that there should be impact bruising, especially if, as the PC claimed, the force of the shot had knocked him off his feet.

With his suspicions aroused; the DS spoke to the Tottenham unit, who shared their own concerns. When they spun the PC's locker, on a screwed-up piece of paper, they found the PC had written out his radio transmissions, almost word for word, ending with the words 'urgent assistance, I've been shot, I've been fucking shot' and a sketch of the exact location of the incident.

By six o'clock that evening, the PC was suspended, and a press statement issued. it was all rather embarrassing, but it overshadowed what had happened to Sergeant Key.

I gave Andy a tug to let him know what Roger Class had said, well not about him being a coon, but about him being homosexual. He looked a little uncomfortable.

"Did he say how he knew?" He asked me.

"No, but I didn't ask. I just kept denying it." I said.

"Yeah, I think you might have been on a loser there, mate." Andy said.

"Why?" I asked.

"'Cos I saw his brother, for a while, last year." Andy explained.

"Did you hear about him? He died."

"Fucking hell, what of?"

"Some type of cancer." I said.

"Bloody hell. What cancer was it? Do you know?"

"I can't remember, now."

"Well, bugger me. I hadn't seen him for, like, a year. Poor sod, he was a nice guy, really fit. Definitely cancer, was it?"

"That's what he said, leukemia or something." I replied.

"Oh, have you heard Rik's news?" Andy asked.

"No, I haven't seen him for days; don't tell me he's found himself a white girlfriend, at last?"

"No, and he's never going to, either?" Andy replied.

"What? Why?" I said.

"His parents have found him a nice Pakistani woman; you know an arranged marriage. He went over last night to meet her. He's really, really, really pissed off."

"Can't he just say no?" I asked.

"It's a culture thing, isn't it?" Andy explained.

"I don't get it Andy, do you? I mean he's an adult; he's a police officer, for fuck's sake. Why can't he just say no?"

Andy shrugged his shoulders.

"I can't criticize, can I?" Andy said.

"What do you mean?" I asked.

"Well, my parents don't know about my sexuality, do they?"

"Ah, I see what you mean. Do you think you'll ever be able to tell, them?" I asked.

"No mate. It would kill them. My old man was a professional boxer, you know, a real hard bastard, and Mum's a good Evangelist, who thinks such behaviour is a one-way ticket to hell fire and damnation. They're lovely people, who are very proud of their eldest son, you know, 'cos he's a police officer and doing really well. I can't tell them. It would really, really, hurt them."

"Why is life so bloody complicated?" I asked.

Andy smiled.

"I've got no one to answer to." I said, almost to myself.

"What do you mean?" Andy asked.

"Well, you're worried about your parents finding out that you prefer sausage to fish. Rik's always stressing about his family. Most blokes here are worried about their wives finding out what they're up to, but me, I have no one to answer to. No parents, no wife, no responsibilities, at all. I can do just exactly what I like." I explained.

"Do you think that's why you are, you know, like you are?" Asked Andy, and for a moment I thought he was taking the piss but, one glance at his face, and I knew he wasn't.

What did he mean when he said, you are like you are? It was very similar to what Roger had said to me in the pub, a few hours ago. I needed to get to the bottom of this, I needed to know what Andy meant.

"What the fuck do you mean by that?" I asked.

"Steady, tiger." He said, and I realised my question might have been a little too aggressive.

"What do you mean when you say, 'is that why you're like you are'?" I said, lowering my voice and speaking in a much more controlled manner.

Andy laughed.

"You're just …" he hesitated, searching for the right word.

"Just what?" I asked.

"Just you!" He replied, leaving me none the wiser.

Chapter 52

The following day was Termination Wednesday, so it was hardly surprising I only slept for a few hours that night. When I woke it was still dark, but I showered, dressed, and went downstairs to mump a cup of tea off Sergeant Bellamy, who was always in early.

"Hi, Sarge."

"You done it in?" He asked, assuming I was late for early turn.

"No, floating today. Can I have a cup of your excellent tea, Sarge?"

"Sure. You up to much, today?" He asked.

I thought about the day ahead; taking Sarah to the abortion clinic, digging the money up, a trip to the bank to top up what I'd spent and won, packaging and posting it to the charities, popping in to see Mrs M, and then collecting Sarah and taking her home.

"Nothing planned." I replied.

"Have you heard what's happened?" Sergeant Bellamy asked.

"What? With that Home Beat? Yesterday?" I replied, assuming he meant the fake shooting.

"No, the other thing, with Paul Pollock?"

"No." I replied.

"You know he's on jury protection?" Sergeant Bellamy said.

"Yeah, he's on my relief, Sarge."

"Well, he's only been caught shagging the person he's meant to be protecting!"

"No?" I said.

"Oh yes, bang to rights. The skipper was doing the rounds. When he came across Paul's car, there was only his partner in there. He questioned the partner, who tried to cover up by saying Paul was using the toilet in the house, which is a big no, no, anyway. The skipper takes a look around the house, some massive drum in Chigwell, and peers in through the windows, only to see Paul and the woman naked on her settee. To make matters worse, if they could get any worse, Paul is doing something with his gun which it wasn't designed for! The trial will have to be stopped this morning, the jury discharged, and then there'll be a retrial. It will cost like thousands and thousands of pounds."

"What will happen to Paul?" I asked.

Sergeant Bellamy swept his finger across his throat.

"Sacked?" I asked.

"At the very least, there may be criminal charges for contempt of court, as well."

"Fuck me." I said.

"The thing is, he's disappeared."

"What do you mean? Disappeared?" I asked.

"He was caught and told to report to wherever, you know, to hand in his firearm and get suspended, but he's sodded off."

I didn't feel sorry for Paul, not after what he'd done to me at court.

"He's always been a nightmare; I've known him for years. His brain is in his pants. He left his wife last year for that ex-model, didn't he?" Sergeant Bellamy said.

"Sarah? Yeah." I replied.

I waited for Sergeant Bellamy to make some comment which suggested he knew I was shagging her, but he didn't, so I assumed he didn't, in fact, know.

"Mind you, she is crumpet." He added, a few seconds later.

"Yeah, she's lovely." I agreed, but not too enthusiastically, just in case.

"Not as lovely as Dawn, though." He said, and he smiled sadly.

"I agree." I said.

I had always known Sergeant Bellamy had a soft spot for my old instructor and friend.

I smiled back and, suddenly, Sergeant Bellamy looked really sad. It was nice to know I wasn't the only old bill that missed her.

~~~

As I waited for Sarah, I wondered whether she knew anything about Paul's indiscretion with the juror. If she didn't, should I say something? On the one hand, she had enough to deal with today, but I was pretty certain this news would be just the excuse she needed to end their relationship.

When she arrived, she was carrying a small suitcase and I jumped up and popped it in the boot for her.

"You're not in overnight, are you?" I asked, as we fastened our seat belts.

"No, they said about four hours, depending on the bleeding." She replied.

"Why you got the bag then?" I asked.

"You know, pyjamas, dressing gown, a towel, a bit of slap."

"How are you feeling?" I asked.

"Shit."

"Sorry." I said, sympathetically.

"It's not your fault."

"You don't have to go through with this, you know?" I said, delivering a line I'd rehearsed for several days.

"I know but I just can't cope with everything, and this is something I can deal with and, when I do, I'll have one less thing to worry about." She replied.

"Okay; do you want to get some breakfast? We've got time." I suggested.

"I'm not allowed to eat, Chris; not after ten o'clock last night, but you can if you want, I really don't mind but let's get over to Buckhurst Hill, first, so I know I'll be on time."

"Is Paul in? Where did you say you were going?" I asked.

"He's not back yet; he never comes straight home. I think he finds an early house, somewhere."

So, Sarah didn't know what had happened.

I drove past Snaresbrook Crown Court where Paul and Alec had tried to fit me up.

"I'm still waiting on my one six three for the drugs your boyfriend planted." I commented.

"Sorry." Sarah said.

"It's not your fault. I'm just so fucking annoyed. Is the box still in your loft?"

"Yeah, but not for much longer." She said.

I detected a steely determination in her voice.

"Why? What you going to do?" I asked.

Sarah didn't respond. I got the feeling that the termination would mark some sort of watershed in her life. We drove in silence for the rest of the journey. Sarah was really quiet, understandably so, and when I did glance across at her, she was just staring out of the window.

The clinic was a large old house, within sight of the cemetery where Dawn was buried. I went into the reception with Sarah, and we sat thumbing through some old magazines, as the room filled with other nervous women, all obviously there for the same reason. We were early, and had to wait nearly forty minutes, before a nurse with a clipboard called out several names, one of which was Sarah Starr. I hugged her goodbye and left. It was nine o'clock. I had to pick her up at three thirty.

Chapter 53

My first job was to go to the forest and dig up the money box. This was easier said than done because, every time I went anywhere near it, someone came along walking a bloody dog. I must have looked very suspicious, standing there without a dog, but holding a spade. I wished I'd brought a dog lead, possession of which would have instantly dispelled the fears of passers-by, as it would have given me a reason to be there. Come to think about it, a metal detector would have been an even better cover story, as it would have explained the spade, as well.

I'm sure one poor woman, with a Dalmatian, was convinced I was going to attack, rape, bludgeon her to death and then bury her, six feet under. Having already dug one hole in Epping Forest, I knew just how difficult that would be, so she was quite safe.

Eventually, I got the money box up and took it back to the car and, just in time too, because, no sooner had I sat in my car, than a police car pulled up and two officers went off towards the very spot where I'd been loitering. It was obvious that someone had gone home and called nine nine nine about a bloke acting suspiciously in the forest. All they'd find now would be a hole but, if they'd got there just a few minutes earlier, I'd have had to explain what I was doing digging up a metal box containing six thousand pounds.

I drove to the shops, which were in a one-way street called Queens Road, that ran down the hill to the underground station. I parked up outside the library, almost opposite my bank, Barclays.

I calculated what I needed to take out of my account by adding the hundred I first took, to the thousand I'd given to Sarah, and then to the amount I'd won at the casino. I had plenty of money because I'd paid in the cheque from the Criminal Injuries Compensation Board.

I withdrew the money, five thousand, nine hundred and fifty pounds and added it to what was already in the tin.

I'd visited the small library opposite the bank and looked up the registered addresses for the two charities I'd chosen.

I bought stamps and two jiffy bags from the Post Office, split the money roughly in half, addressed each envelope and posted them by recorded delivery to Help the Aged and Victim Support.

The money was gone, once and for all, no longer was it a millstone around my neck. And it was going to charities, not the government, as would have happened if I hadn't diverted it. I can honestly say, nothing I'd ever done had made me feel better, but I think it was an overwhelming sense of relief rather than happiness. I put the car seat back and shut my eyes. I turned the radio on and tuned into Capital. I found myself singing along to *'Things can only get better'* and I knew I never wanted to do anything as stupid as taking the old lady's money, ever again. That senseless act of greed had cost me a hundred thousand pounds but, more than that, it had cost me my identity. For the last month, I'd not been who I wanted to be. But I was back now. I was Chris Pritchard, an honest cop again and it felt great.

A firm knock on the window, immediately next to my head, made me, quite literally, jump and I opened my eyes to see two uniformed officers beckoning me to speak to them. My first reaction was one of 'thank fuck' I've just got rid of the money, so I wound down the window to see what they wanted.

"Excuse me, Sir; can you step on to the pavement, please?" The older PC said.

I did as I was told. The other PC walked back to their police car which was parked on the other side of the road, further down the hill towards the florists, opened the rear door and a woman got out. It was the poor lady who was walking the Dalmatian and, although I couldn't hear what she was saying, from her body language I could tell she was making a positive identification.

The PC who was with her nodded to his colleague who was standing by my side.

"Have you been in Epping Forest, today?" The PC asked, politely.

"I have, yes, officer. Is there a problem?" I replied.

I didn't really want to show out if I could help it and I knew, from being on the opposite side of an interaction such as this, the right attitude should bring me through.

"A lady called police to say you were acting suspiciously." The PC explained.

"I can understand that completely. It must have looked peculiar, but I can assure you I was doing nothing wrong. Would you like to search my car, officer?" I offered.

"That won't be necessary yet." The PC replied slightly defensively, and I suddenly sensed weakness, or perhaps inexperience.

I thought it was possible that officers on these outer divisions, these nice law-abiding suburbs, didn't do stop and search as often as we did at places like Stokey.

"I saw the lady that was concerned. She was walking a Dalmatian. The thing was officer …"

I lowered my voice as if I was to impart a great secret. The PC leaned slightly in towards me.

"…I wasn't walking a dog."

"Sorry?" The PC said, confusion written on his face.

"Officer, if I'd been walking a dog, she wouldn't have been concerned and we, well, we wouldn't be having this conversation. It's always the same but this is the first time anyone's called the police." I said.

"Oh, well, I'm sorry, but she, well, you know …"

This was easier than I thought it would be. He'd just apologised to me! Christ he wouldn't last a second on the streets of Stokey.

"Officer, don't worry, I understand. She did the right thing." I assured him.

The PC looked slightly confused and, for a second, I thought he was going to let me go.

"What were you doing in the forest? The woman said something about a spade?"

It was strange to be on the other side of a stop and I couldn't help but analyse this guy's performance. Personally, I wouldn't have mentioned the spade to me, not at that stage of the questioning.

"I was carrying a spade, officer. Entomology is a hobby of mine."

"Entomology?"

"The study of insects. I dig up a small area of the forest floor and study the insects."

A while ago, one Saturday, I'd failed to complete the Telegraph prize crossword by just one clue, the answer to which was entomology. When I looked up the word the following week, I'd discovered what it meant and, for some reason, the word had stuck.

"Oh." The PC said and he seemed genuinely relieved to have got to the solution, so quickly.

"As I said, officer; I can understand the woman's concerns, I really can but she had nothing to worry about."

I thought I'd prompt the PC's next action, so I fed him the line.

"I've never been arrested before, never even had a parking ticket."

My trigger worked perfectly.

"Look, I'll just do a name check on you and then you can be on your way. Have you got anything with your name on it? A driving licence or something?"

"I've got a cheque book and Barclaycard; I've just been to the bank, so they'll be able to confirm who I am."

I reached into the glove box and handed my cheque book to the officer, which he examined.

"Can you give me your date and place of birth, please?" The PC asked.

I did and the officer did the check on his radio, but no sooner had he given my details, and before the PNC operator would have had time to complete the check, another unit came in on the radio, addressing the officer by his first name.

"Dave, regarding the name check you've just done. Is the male you've stopped in the job?"

The PC looked at me and I nodded.

"Yes, yes." The PC said into his radio.

"Christopher Pritchard is the name of the PC who was blown up last year in that IRA bomb in Stoke Newington."

"Is that right?" The PC asked me.

I nodded again.

"Juliet Bravo, Juliet Bravo. You can cancel that name check."

"Why didn't you show out, mate?" The PC asked.

"I didn't like to. I mean the woman was right to call you. It seemed a bit inappropriate just to flop out the old brief and assume that everything would be alright." I replied.

"You could have done, mate. I wouldn't have minded but I respect that you didn't. It's nice to know there's at least one decent officer at Stoke Newington."

"It's not that bad really, there are hundreds of us, well dozens, well at least three." I replied.

He laughed.

"It's got such a dreadful reputation." The PC said.

"I gather but it's really not that bad."

The PC looked sceptical.

"I won't keep you, Chris. Thanks for being so cooperative and I really appreciate the not showing out thing. Take care my friend." He said, warmly.

He walked over to the panda car where his colleague, who would have overheard the radio conversation, and the woman were waiting for him. I saw him speaking to them, explaining the situation and the woman frowned. Clearly, she wasn't entirely satisfied. She was of course right; I was, indeed, up to no good in the forest.

I got back into my car and set off to see Mrs M.

As I drove, I reflected on what had just happened. Everyone I worked with said a week working at Stokey was like a year working in the sticks, the implication being that, even some of the longer serving PC's there, were useless thief takers. On what I'd just experienced, they might be right. On the other hand, the PC who'd stopped me obviously thought that anyone working at Stoke Newington was corrupt. The irony was that both our stereotypes had been proved pretty accurate.

Chapter 54

As I stopped outside Mrs M's, I saw a Ford Granada pull away with two white males inside. I was curious to know who they were. When Mrs M opened the door, she looked ashen.

"What on earth's the matter?" I asked, entering without waiting for an invitation.

"Oh, thank god it's you, Chris." She said.

I put my arm around her, as I was convinced, she looked on the verge of passing out, and led her through to the lounge and onto the safety of the settee.

"Cuppa tea?"

"Please, Chris." She replied and I disappeared to the kitchen.

By the time I'd returned, Mrs M looked a little better. I put the tray on the table and sat at the opposite end of the settee.

"Right, Mrs M. Who were the two men I just saw driving away? I assume that whatever has happened, it is something to do with them."

Mrs M looked momentarily confused.

"You mean you don't know?" She asked.

"Don't know what?" I replied.

"You don't know who they were and what's happened." Mrs M asked.

"Mrs M I've got no idea what you're talking about, honestly. I've never seen those men before. Is this to do with Donald?" I asked.

"So, they didn't send you to smooth things over with me then?" Mrs M said.

"Who?" I asked.

"The men who've just left."

"What? No." I replied.

I was getting frustrated, as the conversation was going nowhere. I took a deep breath.

"Mrs M, who were the two men who've just driven off in the Ford Granada?"

"Detective Superintendent Collins or Collinwood or something and a Detective Sergeant."

"And where are they from, Chingford?"

"No, the Bomb Squad."

"So, this is to do with Dawn, then?" I asked.

About three months after the bombing and about the same time that I went back to work, the Bomb Squad arrested five Irish guys who they thought were going to blow up a pub in Winchester. They linked them to the bombing in Stoke Newington and charged them. I was told the evidence against them was very strong, but because I was a witness and would be required to give evidence at the Old Bailey, I wasn't told the specifics about the job. The Bomb Squad DI explained to me, at the time, the less I knew, the better would be my evidence. As a result, I knew none of the evidential details, all I was told was they were one hundred percent certain that they had caught those responsible. When I discussed the matter with Andy, he said it sounded like they'd, or at least one of them, had confessed.

"Yes, it's about the bombing and the trial." Mrs M continued.

"Oh, so there's a date then?" I asked.

I started to feel butterflies in my stomach. The thought of giving evidence in this case really frightened me because I knew I would break down and look such an idiot in front of the whole world.

"No, Chris; there's not going to be a trial. They've just dropped all the charges."

"Fucking hell." I said, momentarily forgetting who I was with.

"Sorry, Mrs M."

"So, they haven't told you yet?" Mrs M asked.

"No. But I was up and out early this morning, so if they've been to the Section House, they've probably missed me. Did they tell you why they dropped the charges?" I asked, the news slowly sinking in.

"Yes, they explained it. They're furious themselves but it's not their decision."

"I don't understand, I thought the case against them was really strong,"

"It is, Chris, but the Judge has excluded the most important piece of evidence." Mrs M explained.

"What do you mean? Has the trial started?" I asked.

"Yes, it started several weeks ago but there's been a reporting ban on it, so none of the newspapers could say anything. They haven't sworn in a jury yet, because it was anticipated that the first few months would be legal argument about what could be admitted and what couldn't."

"I understand that's quite common. I was once told by DS Cotton that at the start of a criminal trial everyone knows the truth and it's the prosecution's role to make sure the jury hear as much of the truth as possible, and it's the defense's role to try to exclude as much of the truth as they can, so the jury can acquit."

"The Detective Superintendent called it a *voir dire*, or something like that." Mrs M added.

"Yes, I remember now; that's what it's called. It means a trial within a trial." I said.

"A long time ago, one of the detectives told me not to discuss the case with you, Chris. He explained that they were able to tell me things that you weren't allowed to know because you were a witness."

"Yes, that's right. I was told that too." I said.

"Anyway, it didn't matter because we weren't in touch then. Chris, they told me what the evidence was, you know against the men."

"Go on." I said.

"Well, when they arrested them for planning the Winchester bombing, they took them to Paddington Green police station and put them into cells in which they'd hidden recording devices. They recorded them discussing the Stoke Newington bombing. That's how they know for certain it was them."

"So, what's the problem then?" I asked.

"Well, the Judge has ruled that the recordings cannot be used in evidence." She explained.

"That's ridiculous." I said.

"I know. But it's something to do with him thinking the evidence was unfairly gathered."

"How can that be?" I asked, incredulously.

"I don't really understand, but because they weren't told the recording equipment was there, the Judge says, they were effectively tricked into confessing and, also, it was to do with the timing of the conversations."

"What do you mean?" I asked.

"Well, they'd asked for their solicitors, but they hadn't spoken to them at the time the conversations were recorded and that's relevant."

"That's ridiculous. So, they effectively admitted to the bombings, and that is recorded, and everyone knows they did it, but the Judge has decided it's unfair. It was unfair on Dawn and me, too!"

"I know."

"So, what's going to happen now?" I asked.

"Well, there's still the case against them for planning the Winchester bombing but apparently that's weak on its own. They've been released on bail and the matter is being referred to an Attorney something."

"The Attorney General?" I said.

"Yes, that's right, the matters being referred to the Attorney General, but the Detective Superintendent said he thought all the charges would be dropped. It's even possible they'll be in line for a big pay-out, you know, compensation."

I didn't know what to say. I was absolutely astounded. I think I'd have been less shocked if I'd known the trial had started. Then I realised it must be much worse for Mrs M.

"I'm so sorry, Mrs M. I really am."

"Bastards." She said in a whisper.

"I'm sorry." I said.

"No justice for my beautiful daughter, Chris. I've let her down. I wasn't there when she needed me at the end, and now, the men who did it have walked free."

"It's not your fault, Mrs M. None of it, you know that." I assured her.

"When you have a child, Chris. Whether you're there or not doesn't matter, because you're responsible for everything. One day you'll understand, when you have a baby of your own."

Her words hit me like a train. I thought about a baby whose life was, at any moment, now, being terminated.

"I have to go Mrs M. I've got something very important to do." I said, as I got up and sprinted out of the room.

Chapter 55

I had to stop Sarah having the abortion. As I drove away, I checked the clock on the dashboard, it was half eleven. I had no idea if I'd be in time; that would depend on whether she was first or last on their list.

I drove quickly, and it was only perhaps half a mile between Mrs M's and the clinic. When I pulled up, I paused briefly to reconsider my actions. Was I bothered that the baby might be Paul's? I didn't think for long, there just wasn't time. I took the stairs leading up to the front door two at a time and marched up to the reception, where a young nurse was speaking to someone on the phone. I shuffled impatiently and she hung up.

"Can I help you?" She said pleasantly.

"Yes, I bought my girlfriend in this morning, Sarah Starr. Can I see her, please?"

I detected a flash of confusion spread across her face, but it disappeared in an instant.

"Can I ask you to take a seat? I'll get someone to come and talk to you."

I couldn't really argue, I mean, for all I knew Sarah could have been in the middle of the operation or just had it. I sat down in the, now deserted, waiting room and flicked through a car magazine, looking up, regularly, to see whether anyone was coming to speak to me. A good twenty minutes past and nothing happened. I stood up to speak to the nurse again when a man, in a white coat, whom I assumed to be a doctor, came down a flight of stairs and walked towards me.

"Are you the gentlemen who's come to collect Miss Starr?" He asked.

"Yes, but I need to speak to her, urgently. I think this is a mistake." I said.

The doctor smiled.

"Can you just step into my office, please?"

He opened a nearby door and ushered me in. I assumed he was going to tell me I was too late, and that Sarah had had the operation.

"Please take a seat."

I did.

"Mr?"

"Pritchard, but please call me, Chris."

"Chris, it's always a little awkward when this happens." The doctor said.

"I'm too bloody late, aren't I?"

"Chris, Miss Starr is not here."

"She is. I dropped her off at eight-thirty. A nurse called her name out and took her and several other women off. They went upstairs." I explained.

"No, Chris; you don't understand. She was here but she checked herself out a short while later. I'm afraid, I'm not allowed to tell you anymore."

"Did she have the abortion?" I asked.

"I'm afraid you must ask her."

"Okay, let me put it this way. What time did she leave?" I asked.

He checked his watch.

"One moment."

He got up and walked out of the office. He was only gone a few moments.

"We called a cab for her at nine thirty." He said.

"So, she didn't have the operation?" I asked.

"I've told you all I can."

"Thank you." I said.

I sat in the car contemplating my next move. I was really pleased that Sarah had obviously changed her mind at the last moment and decided to keep the baby. She'd got a cab back to her flat in Leytonstone. My first reaction was to get round there and see how she was getting on, but I had a problem, because Paul was probably there, too. And he wouldn't be going out later either, as he now had no job to go to. I also knew I'd left Mrs M's place in indecent haste and should really get back round to support her on such a difficult day.

I found a phone box and called Sarah's flat, but Paul answered so I hung up. I then called the Section House just in case Sarah had left a message for me. Sergeant Bellamy answered.

"Hi Sarge, Nostrils, here." I said.

"Oh good, I've been trying to get hold of you. A suit from the Bomb Squad is looking for you. He called about two hours ago. I've got a telephone number for him; he says can you give him a call? I think it's quite important, so I'm guessing you've got to give evidence."

"I haven't got a pen Sarge and I know what it's about anyway. I'll call him later when I get back."

"Okay." Sergeant Bellamy replied.

"Are there any more messages for me?" I asked, hoping Sarah had left a coded message.

"Nope, that's it." He replied.

"Can you check, Sarge, I'm expecting someone to have called. It's really important. Thanks Sarge."

"Nostrils, I've been here all day. No one else has called. Are you alright?" He asked."

"Yes Sarge?"

"Are you sure?"

"Yea fine, why?" I asked.

"It's just …" He hesitated.

"What Sarge?"

"There are some strange stories circulating, I'm sure it's all rubbish but …"

There was that disconcerting hesitation again.

"What, Sarge? Come on tell me."

"Look its nothing, and anyway, I don't like talking on the phone. I'll see you when you get back. Pop in the office and we'll have a chat."

I really didn't like the sound of that, at all.

~~~

I paid a quick visit to Mrs M's to apologise. She wasn't in, but I knew where she'd be, and met her at Dawn's grave. We sat on the bench and cried together. I didn't try to fight my emotions this time and just let it all come out. I'd managed to keep my feelings in check for so long by not thinking about Dawn, or anything to do with that terrible day, but my plan, which had had worked really well for over eighteen months, fell apart when I was with Mrs M. I left Mrs M there an hour later when it began to rain really heavily.

I drove over to Sarah's to see if her car was outside the flat. The flat was in darkness and, as it was really overcast and miserable, I would have expected at least some of the lights to have been on. There was no sign of her car so she must have come home and gone out.

I grabbed a sandwich and coffee down the High Street and sat up with a long eye on the car park to wait for her return. After an hour, it struck me that she was probably at the Section House waiting for me, so I abandoned my vigil and set off home.

I spent the rest of the day waiting for Sarah to appear, but she didn't. In the early evening, I again drove over to her flat but it was still in darkness. When I got back, I knocked for Andy who should have been going on to nights, but he said through his door that he was feeling like shit and asked not to be disturbed.

I didn't get to speak to Sergeant Bellamy because he'd gone home by the time I got back; he always started early and was usually gone by mid-afternoon. For a while, I stayed rather pathetically by the communal phone in case Sarah called but it was to no avail.

I was early turn the next day, so I went up to my room at about ten and tried to sleep. I didn't. I tossed and turned for hours wondering where Sarah was until, at last, a little after two, I heard footsteps coming towards my room and I felt elated.

I threw the light switch on and unlocked the door before she'd even knocked. I was wearing a pair of pants and as the door opened, I quickly kicked some discarded clothes under the bed to make the room look at bit tidier. Sarah was always moaning that Paul left her flat in a mess and I didn't want her to think I lived like that, too.

But it wasn't Sarah who entered my room, it was Paul. And it wasn't just Paul, it was Paul and a handgun which he leveled at my head, as he rounded the door.

Chapter 56

Paul was breathing rapidly; his hand was shaking, and his clothes were disheveled, as if he had been up for days, and hadn't changed or washed. He smelt of alcohol, stale tobacco and sweat.

"You fucking cunt." He said.

"What you doing, Paul?" I said, putting both my hands up, palms open, in a gesture of surrender, and stepping slowly backwards, away from the muzzle.

"I'm going to blow your fucking brains out, you lying, cheating, good for fuck all, fucking scum."

His face was red like he was about to explode.

"Paul, I don't know what's going on." I said, my voice the epitome of calm.

"Don't fucking lie to me. Where is she?" He asked, aggressively.

"Who?" I replied.

"Trying to be smart are you, you fucking cunt. You always think you're so fucking superior, well your fucking dead, fucking dead."

His eyes narrowed and his grip tightened on the gun. He stepped forward, lowering the gun so it was pointing directly at the middle of my chest. This is it, I thought, this is where I die.

I stepped backwards again but came up against the window. There was nowhere else to go. My window didn't open more than a few inches.

"Please don't kill me, Paul." I said.

I was prepared to beg for my life, if that would help. There and then I would have done anything to live.

"Please don't kill me, Paul." I repeated.

"Where is she?" He asked.

"If you're asking me where Sarah is, I have absolutely no idea." I replied.

He looked around the room, as if he expected Sarah to be hiding somewhere. He opened the cupboard and even glanced under the bed.

"Sarah's not here, Paul; she's never been here, ever." I assured him.

It was nearly the truth, she'd only been there once, a few weeks ago, and that was about the thousand pounds.

"She's not here but you know where she is?" Paul said.

"I've no idea where Sarah is, Paul." I replied, calmly.

"Liar!" He spat.

"I have absolutely no idea where Sarah is, Paul, why would I?"

"You fucking cunt, you know why." He spat.

He stepped forwards until the gun tip was only a few inches from my chest. I knew from our self defence training that, if I was going to try to fight my way out of this situation, this was the best time, for the gun was within my immediate reach. We'd been taught some sort of manoeuvre, where you swing both arms and twist the gun away from yourself, but I really didn't fancy it.

I saw Paul's finger gripping and then coming off the trigger. I didn't know much about guns, but he was carrying the only one in the world I would recognise, a police issue Smith & Wesson revolver, half a dozen of which were always kept in the Station Officer's safe.

"Listen, Paul. I'll tell you what. Let's talk about this and then, if you want to, if you're not happy, you can kill me. But let's talk first."

I saw something in his eyes which suggested he was completely against this idea.

"I mean it, Paul. You can ask me anything you like; I will be completely honest. If you don't believe me, or you still want to kill me, you can. What do you say?"

Paul considered my proposal for a slow ten seconds and, when ordered me to sit down on the bed, I knew I had a chance of getting out of this alive.

Paul went back and locked the door. I was relieved to see that his right arm had relaxed a little and he was now holding the gun lower down and, less obviously, in a position to shoot me.

He went to pick the chair up and reposition it just inside the door, so he could sit facing me. For a moment, I considered letting him do so, in the certain knowledge that the broken leg would collapse under his weight and he would fall to the floor. He was pissed, so in a fight with him, already on the floor, I had a chance of getting my hands on the gun.

"Don't sit down, the leg's broken; it won't take your weight." I said.

Why did I tell him? Probably because deep down I knew the idea of fighting someone with a loaded gun wasn't the best plan I'd ever come up with. Besides, I calculated that I just might get a few brownie points from him for the warning.

He lifted the chair higher, looked more closely and kicked the leg, which was obviously at a wrong angle, it fell off.

"Thanks." He said, as he swung it back under the desk.

He sat down on the floor and leant against the wall adjoining Andy's room. The gun remained in his right hand, but it was now pointing only in my general direction.

"Where is she?" He repeated, the anger in his voice suddenly replaced by a tired desperation.

"I've no idea, Paul; honestly, no idea. When did you last see her?"

"Yesterday. I can't remember. Did you phone the house today? And then hang up on me?" He said, angrily.

I had to decide how I was going to play this. My biggest disadvantage, at that moment, was that I didn't know how much he knew. I needed to change that quickly, if I was to survive his interrogation.

"No, of course not." I replied, that was a fairly easy question because, under the circumstances, it might just as well have been Sarah who called and then hung up.

"What makes you think, I would know where she is?" I asked.

Paul looked at me and a flash of undiluted hatred returned to his face. He raised the gun again, closed his left eye, and pointed it directly at my head. I closed my eyes and waited.

"How long have you been seeing her?" He said.

I breathed out and opened my eyes, the gun was still pointed at my head.

"I'm not seeing Sarah, Paul." I replied, looking past the end of the gun and straight in the eyes.

"If you don't tell me the truth, I'll pull the trigger and blow your fucking brains all over the wall." He said.

I was fucked. If I denied it again, I was fairly certain, he'd kill me; if I admitted it, I was fairly certain he'd kill me.

"Listen Paul, we're good friends and I won't deny that things *might* have happened between us but I'm not seeing her. She's *your* girlfriend, everyone knows that."

The gun lowered again, and I breathed a quiet sigh of relief.

"What exactly has happened between you two? I want to know everything." He asked.

"Nothing yet but, Paul, if I'm honest, wanted it to."

"You cunt." He spat.

"Oh, for fuck's sake Paul, she's stunning and I'm a twenty-one-year-old bloke. Of course, I wanted something to happen. I'm only human." I explained.

"But you knew she was living with me, how fucking dare you?" He asked.

"Paul, my cock just doesn't think like that!" I replied.

Paul laughed, just slightly and I knew I'd said the right thing.

"But you said something had happened?"

"No, I didn't Paul, I said something *might* have happened, you know, if we'd have got any closer. We are good friends, Paul. I talk to her about Dawn, you know, and stuff like that."

"Yea, she is a good listener." He said.

"And, of course, I fancied her, she stars in every wank. But nothing has ever happened."

Paul looked me hard in the eye, trying to assess my honesty.

"My mate tells me, he reckons something was definitely going on?" Paul said.

"Tell me who told you? For fucks sake Paul, we're on the same relief, you two live together. How could anything be going on and you not notice?" I said.

Paul didn't reply, so I assumed my words must have made some sense. I decided to push on with this theme.

"I've been on this relief over a year. And practically every day, I've worked with you and Sarah. In god's name, when would I, we, have had any opportunity to do anything?"

I knew this was a fairly strong argument because we'd only actually been having a relationship for about eight weeks, so if I could get Paul to start thinking over the whole year, he might be convinced.

"Did you take her to Bournemouth?" He asked.

"No, I didn't, I've never been to Bournemouth in my life." I replied, although sitting on my desk not two feet from Paul's head, was a hotel receipt that would prove otherwise.

"Paul? Are you sure that she's seeing someone else? It just doesn't sound like something Sarah would do." I said.

I actually thought I sounded quite convincing.

"Well, where the fuck is she? When she didn't come home today, I knew something was up. I thought she was early turn and then I find out she's taken the day off. I checked the duties binder and what did I discover?"

I shrugged my shoulders, innocently.

"That you're fucking floating today, too." He said, accusingly.

"Paul you've put two and two together and made five." I said.

"Then I started asking around, really asking around, and I hear that you're shagging her."

"From who?" I asked.

"That doesn't matter but it was a reliable source."

"Paul, she's never been here. I assure you."

Again, he held my eyes with a stare.

"Have you had sex with her?" He asked.

"No, of course not!" I replied, unequivocally.

"Have you kissed her?" He asked.

"No. For fuck's sake Paul, look at me, handsome I ain't. Why, oh why, would she be interested in me?"

"Well, where the fuck is she?" He demanded.

"I've no idea." I replied, for once I was telling the truth.

"Have you had an argument or anything?" I asked.

"No, but she's been really moody, lately." He replied.

"In what way?"

"Just distant. I started to think she didn't want me living there anymore." He explained.

"Really?" I said, with as much incredulity, as I could muster.

"She never mentioned anything to me. In fact, she talked about you all the time." I said.

"I really love her." He said.

We sat in silence. Then I remembered there was something I wanted to discuss with Paul.

"Yes, you bastard. What was all that about at Slagsbrook? You dropped me right in it." I said, perhaps attack was the best form of defence?

I knew it was a bit of a risky strategy to take the argument to a drunken man holding a loaded firearm, but I calculated anything that took the conversation away from Sarah, was good.

"You were grateful enough for the body." He said.

"You didn't just fit him up Paul, you fitted me up, too. I'm certain to get a complaint out of it, the Judge summoned the Court Inspector. That was really out of order, Paul."

"Shit happens." He said.

"That was a nasty thing to do, Paul." I said.

He didn't reply but he did look awkward. I sensed an opportunity.

"Listen mate; do you want a drink?" I said, lowering my voice.

"What?" He asked.

"Open the cupboard and look on the top shelf. There's a bottle of malt whisky, up there. A dog handler bought it for me, but I don't drink the stuff."

"A dog handler got it for you? Oh, that's right, you were bitten, weren't you?" He asked.

"Yes, in my arse!" I replied.

"That's the going rate for a dog bite. Did you agree not to report it?" Paul asked.

"I did; apparently his dog would have been decommissioned." I replied.

"Decommissioned? It's a dog not a battleship, Nostrils. It's bollocks anyway, they always say that, so you feel bad and don't say anything. What Scotch is it?

I pulled a face indicating that I had no idea.

"Just help yourself, Paul, and it would be good if you'd put the gun down."

He uncocked the gun but kept hold of it. I still didn't fancy rolling around the floor trying to get him to let go of it, instead, I had another plan. He was already pretty tanked up, how much more would it take before he would become incapacitated?

He opened the cupboard, reached up, took out the bottle and nodded, approvingly.

"Laphroig. You were lucky; all I got was a bottle of Bells. Glasses?"

I nodded towards the sink. I was going to have to join him, which would be a problem because I'd probably be drunk before him, notwithstanding his head start.

"I love Sarah, you know?" He said.

I didn't reply.

"I've lost her, Nostrils"

He handed me a tumbler containing the largest, neat Scotch I'd ever seen.

"Thanks." I said.

"Are you sure, maybe she needed to get away for a few days for some reason? Maybe she's gone to her Mums? Has she taken stuff; you know, packed a case?" I asked.

Paul took greedy gulps of Scotch, I smelt it, god, it was strong and smelt really disgusting, like something you gargle with, if you had a sore throat.

"Yea, she's packed a few things but I'm worried, Nostrils. She's taken something of mine, and I just can't figure out why." Paul said.

"What's she taken?" I asked, although I thought I already knew.

"It doesn't matter but I think it's significant and could drop both of us in deep shit."

~~~

My plan worked; well sort of, because Paul didn't shoot me. In fact, we chatted all night or, to be more precise, he talked, then he slurred, and I listened and agreed with whatever he said. I deliberately avoided making any conversation myself because I was worried that I might let something slip which would reveal I knew more about his girlfriend, and their lives together, than I should.

When he wasn't looking, I poured my Scotch away but I still ended up drinking two or three large glasses. I was very conscious that I was early turn in a few hours. The obvious thing to do would be to go sick, but sometimes with those of us who lived in the Section House, the Inspector or Sergeant would come to your room to check and, if that happened, I'd be in big trouble 'cos my room and I would stink of scotch.

Paul got drunker and drunker, and my bottle of expensive whisky steadily emptied until there was only a smidgen left in the bottom. I didn't care about the whisky; it was a small price to pay if it helped to persuade him not to blow my brains out.

He bemoaned his life, said that he regretted leaving his wife and kids and, repeatedly, wished he could turn the clock back a year. He lectured me throughout the small hours, imploring me not to make the same mistake as him, when I was older. He said the same things over and over again, like only a drunken bore can. I felt like screaming but played the part of his best mate and subtly kept looking at my watch.

He said, when someone had told him I was shagging Sarah, he knew it was a lie.

"She wouldn't be interested in someone like you, I mean, Nostrils, you, *you*? No offence, mate, but, but, but you're so ..."

Of course, I agreed. Then he'd say the same statement six or seven times and, each time, I'd agree again, just as if it was the first time he'd told me.

"She is shagging someone, though, I know, I do 'cos she's a very sexual being, she's a very sexual being, and we have had, haven't had, haven't had sex for weeks, months." He slurred.

"Haven't you?" I replied, realising that if what he was saying was true, Sarah's baby was mine.

"And she's been 'stracted, really 'dis, distracted lately. Some cunt is screwing her, I know, I really know ..."

"Thing is mate, Nostrils, mate. Thing is ..."

"What's the thing, Paul?" I said, as if I was hanging on his every word.

"Thing is, mate, I really love her. Really, really, love her. Couldn't believe my luck, you know, you know don't you, you do know?"

I assured him I did.

"Thing is. She's gorgeous, isn't she?" He asked.

"She is, mate." I replied.

And so, the conversation went on, hour upon hour. As the longest short night drew on, several times Paul closed his eyes, but then a few seconds later, he'd wake up with a start, and begin his declarations, protestations and lectures over again.

I managed to pretend I was matching him glass for glass but, in reality, had about a quarter of the bottle.

When it got to five-thirty and I stood to get dressed for early turn, I realised I was pissed.

I left Paul so he could get a few hours kip in my bed and then go to his home, where I assured him, his lovely Sarah would be waiting.

I had hoped Paul would fall asleep before I went to work, and I'd have the opportunity to remove the gun from him, but it was not to be.

I cleaned my teeth very thoroughly and bought a packet of mints from the vending machine in the canteen. On parade, I stood as far away from the Inspector and Sergeant, as was possible, and tried to only breathe in.

After the postings, and the parade book entries, Inspector Portman addressed us.

"I am aware the Sergeant's exam is next week, but if you want to study for it, please do so in your own time. I do not want to catch you hiding in some quiet corner of the nick with your head in General Orders when you should be on your beat. Do I make myself clear?"

I didn't feel obliged to acknowledge the warning personally, as I wasn't studying the Sergeant's exam, but a few of the PC mumbled a begrudging, 'yes, sir'.

My attempts to only inhale were unsuccessful because, after we'd been dismissed, Ben turned to me and said.

"Bloody hell, Nostrils, you had a good night!"

I grimaced, apologetically.

"Sorry." I said meekly.

"Don't apologise to me mate, just get straight out the nick before anyone else notices and get some food inside you." Ben suggested.

I had every intention of doing just that but, as we were forming a small queue to leave the Collator's office, Sergeant Felix came back in.

"As you were, guys. I've just been told to mention one more thing." He said.

Those who had already left filed back in, and those of us still in the room, resumed our former positions.

"PC Paul Pollock is missing. Has anyone seen him?" Sergeant Felix asked.

Nobody, including me, said a word.

Chapter 57

As soon as I could find a café open, I had a big breakfast. I felt absolutely shattered. I decided that, after early turn, and assuming that Paul had in fact vacated my bed by then, I would have the mother of all afternoon naps.

I took a few alarm calls and reported a theft from motor vehicle, before coming back at nine to relieve Harry, the Second Reserve, for grub. Harry was on restricted duties, which meant he couldn't do anything which involved interacting directly with the public. He had been the Divisional Immigration Officer, but several African ladies had alleged he'd made an indecent proposal to them which suggested that, in return for sexual favours, he would grant them indefinite leave to remain in the country. It was a ridiculous allegation, but he was confined to the station, while it was being investigated.

As I took over from him, Harry had some hot gossip for me.

"You know CIB are here?" He asked.

"Again?" I replied, casually.

"Yea, they've nicked a PC off night duty."

"Really, why didn't we hear about that on parade?" I asked.

"The PC was dealing with an RTA up Stamford Hill and didn't get back to the nick until eight. When he walked in, they were waiting for him and felt his collar."

"Who was it?" I asked.

"Dave Grant." Harry replied.

"I don't know him. What's he done?" I asked.

"Apparently, he's been nicking pedigree dogs."

"What?" I said.

"If a pedigree dog got handed in, he'd get it out the kennel and sell it. He's been doing it for years."

"You gotta be kidding me. Nicking pedigree dogs! There can't be much money in that, can there?" I asked.

"You'd be surprised, Nostrils; they can be worth a thousand squid." Harry replied.

"Really? How did they catch him?" I asked.

"They put a hidden camera on the kennels."

I'd had loads of dealings with bloody lost dogs recently and Ben had said that my name had been mentioned in connection with a theft. I'd obviously been an innocent party. And then I remembered the foreign lady who'd handed in that ridiculous looking dog. Had that been a set up? To see if I, or someone else, stole the dog? If the 'theft' they were investigating at Stokey was this, then I had nothing to worry about in respect of the old lady's money. I'd never given a thought to the fact that dogs were regularly escaping or rather going missing. It was so ridiculously trivial compared to everything else that was going on here. A sense of relief came over me, but at the back of my mind, something was still troubling me, nothing too serious, but something was nagging away. I turned over every recent interaction I'd had with a dog. I acted correctly. I'd always booked them in, put them in the kennel and fed them, when they'd needed to be fed. No, I couldn't decipher what was troubling me.

"They reckon he's not just done it here but at some of the other nicks, as well." Harry was still chatting to me, although I confess, my mind had wandered.

"A thousand pounds? Are dogs really that expensive?" I asked, pretending I was listening to him.

"Some of the rare breeds are worth a fortune."

"Oh." I said.

"Anyway, I'll be back in an hour, mate. The canteen's bound to be buzzing about this latest bit of news." Harry said.

He shot off and I spent the next hour answering the phone and allocating units to calls. One call was from a journalist for the Sun Newspaper who wanted confirmation that a PC had been arrested for stealing pedigree dogs. I was amazed that news of this insignificant event had already made its way to Fleet Street and I politely referred the caller to the Press Office at the Yard.

When Harry returned, he had more disturbing gossip.

"Listen, Nostrils; this is great, word on the street is that CIB had a hidden camera on the kennels in the yard. You know, to see who was nicking the dogs. Anyway, the camera caught two officers having sex. Speculation is rife as to who, but my bet's on that mad couple from B relief, you know, Sweaty Betty and Fishcake. Apparently, they're at it all the time. Last week the Section Sergeant caught them shagging in the back of Golf November Two."

~~~

I had to find Ben. He might know exactly what the hidden camera had caught. I called him up on the radio.

"Four hundred, four six six?"

"Go ahead." He shouted back from the PC's Writing Room, next door.

I walked in to find him just finishing a crime report.

"Ben, can I have a word?" I urged.

"Of course, Nostrils, is your cough better?"

"What? In the back yard?" I suggested.

"Of course; give me two, I've got to put this in the Major Crime Book. Wait for me by the kennels. You know where they are, don't you?" Ben said, with a knowing smile.

As I wandered across the back yard, I looked up at the window to my room to detect any evidence that my visitor had departed. I saw Paul standing at the window starring down at me. I looked around quickly to see if anyone else was, either in the vicinity, or also looking up at my window. I was alone, so I risked a friendly thumbs up.

I assumed he was getting up and ready to leave my humble abode, once and for all. Was I right to have kept quiet about him being in my room? Probably, but it would be hard to justify in the unlikely event that anyone found out.

Whilst I was waiting for Ben, I lit a cigarette and tried to work out where they'd hidden the camera. There were several possibilities, but my favourite was in the Chief Superintendent's office, which afforded an excellent view down onto the area. Whilst I was a little concerned what the job would think of Sarah and I participating in a sexual act on the Commissioner's property, I felt genuinely relieved that it was highly likely the 'theft' they were investigating had nothing to do with an old lady in Roundhouse Avenue. I mean, apart from the old lady's money thing, I genuinely didn't think I'd done anything wrong. Then I remembered the court thing, where Paul and Alec fitted me up, which was really ironic, because I was completely innocent of any wrong-doing, there.

Ben joined me, just as I was finishing my cigarette.

"Shouldn't you be giving that up? How you doing, now?" He asked.

"I'm alright mate, I think. You know why I wanted a quick word?"

"Of course, but as I told you earlier, it's sorted." He said.

I was confused. The only thing we'd spoken about all day was the fact I'd stunk of booze.

"What are you talking about? Has anyone said anything about, you know?" I said, assuming, perhaps, that Sarge had said something to him about the fact that the parade room smelt like the saloon bar of the White Hart.

"As I told you upstairs, it's sorted." He repeated.

Upstairs? What was he talking about upstairs?

"Ben, I know I'm stupid but just explain what you mean by, I told you upstairs? Exactly what did you tell me? And when?" I asked.

He looked as confused as I was.

"Nostrils, are you being deliberately stupid or are you in fact still pissed?"

"I'm probably still pissed, Ben, so just humour me, please. When did we speak upstairs? I haven't been upstairs in the nick, today."

"Not the nick you wanker, in the Section House. About an hour ago." He said.

"I haven't been in the Section House since I got up this morning, Ben."

"Oh." He replied.

"Oh what?" I asked.

"About an hour ago, I went back to my room to get my overcoat 'cos it looks like it's going to piss down." Ben explained.

We both looked up as if the weather was the whole point of the conversation. There was hardly a cloud in the sky.

"It came over all dark." He replied, by way of explanation.

"Forget the fucking weather, Ben. Just tell me what happened upstairs." I implored him.

"Well, I heard you in your room; you were coughing your guts up."

Of course, I wasn't, it was Paul Pollock, but I didn't want to inform him of that, yet, until I knew what had happened.

"Go on." I said.

"Well, I told you about the CIB video of Sarah giving you a blow job, and that my mate had *lost* it for you. You said, thanks. Now, did I dream that? Or did it just happen? Not an hour and a half ago?"

He looked at his watch, as if the exact timing here was important.

"Did I say anything else or just 'thanks'?" I asked.

"No, you went back to coughing your guts up. If you haven't been in your room at all this morning, then who was I talking to?" He asked.

I looked down, uncertain whether to tell him or not. I thought I'd try to buy myself some more thinking time, so I asked.

"How long have you known about the CIB video?"

"My mate told me a couple of weeks ago, but he swore me to secrecy because, obviously, they still had the hidden camera in and wanted to catch whoever was nicking the pedigree pooches. The SIO had a good laugh and isn't bothered about it from a disciplinary point of view. In fact, he asked to borrow it so he could study it more carefully, at home. Well, they all knew what that meant."

"So, I'm not going to get in trouble for that then?" I asked.

"Not at all, mate." He assured me.

"There's only one small problem…" I added.

"What's that then, Nostrils?"

"The person you told about this, earlier, wasn't me."

"Oh god, Nostrils. That was a bloke in your room. You're not queer, are you?"

"Obviously not, Ben, as I think the hidden camera will testify, but I had a visitor last night. An angry drunken man with a gun, who wanted to blow my brains out, because he'd heard a rumour that I was shagging his girlfriend."

"Nooooo." Ben said, who was clearly ahead of the story.

"Yes. Having calmed him down and convinced him that I was not shagging his girlfriend, when I came to early turn, I left Paul Pollock in my room sleeping off his hangover."

"Oh my god, Nostrils; what have I done?"

"Listen, I've just seen Paul at my window, he's still in my room but he's got a handgun. I assume it's the firearm they issued him with on Jury Protection." I said.

"Did you hear about that?" Ben asked.

"What? That he got caught shagging the person he was meant to be protecting? Yea, Sergeant Bellamy told me."

"Did Paul mention it last night?" Ben asked.

"No, and no I didn't bring it up, either. But let's face it, Paul has lost his wife, kids, job and now his girlfriend. I wouldn't be surprised if he locks himself in my room and we end up with an armed siege." I said.

There was a loud bang. It was the unmistakable sound of a single gunshot. It came from the nick not the Section House.

"I think that's highly unlikely, now." Ben said.

Chapter 58

As I'd set off to see what had happened, Ben had grabbed my arm.

"Be smart, Nostrils; stay here, wait and see." He said, calmly.

He looked me straight in the eye and I knew he was giving me good advice.

"Let's go to your Section House room; see if he's left anything there." Ben suggested.

"Like what?" I said, a little perplexed as to what exactly we were going to be looking for.

"Like a suicide note, like anything which could link you and me to what's happened."

"But we don't know for sure what's happened, yet." I said.

Ben didn't answer me; he just gave me a look which said I was a fucking idiot. I didn't feel inclined to argue.

I don't know if anyone noticed, but Ben and I were the only people walking away from the nick. Everyone else was making their way from the canteen and portacabin to see what was going on. One of those making his way was Sergeant Bellamy and, I was probably being paranoid, but I thought, for a moment, he threw me a questioning glance, as we passed.

I also noticed that a unit was repeatedly calling Golf November but not getting a response, which was absolutely unheard of. As we got to my room, someone in the Station Office transmitted.

"All units, from Golf November. Only urgent transmissions please, until further notice. I repeat, all units from Golf November; only urgent transmissions please, until further notice."

"What's going on?" A unit asked.

"We've got a problem." Was the unusually informal response.

My room stunk of alcohol and cigarette smoke, so I opened the window. I noticed, what little there had been left in the bottle of Laphroaig when I'd left, had been drunk. Everything looked okay, and a thorough, if rapid, search suggested Paul hadn't left anything in my room.

"Let's just watch proceedings from here." Ben suggested, standing at the window.

"Won't it look suspicious, if we don't go and see what's happened? I asked.

"No one will remember who was where. It'll be mayhem down there, let's just sit it out for ten and decide what we're going to say, you know, get our stories straight. Sit down and shut up."

"We could just tell the truth. This is fucking serious, Ben." I said.

"Okay, let's just talk that one through." His eyes looked skyward, as he considered the various options.

"Nothing we've done is career terminal, is it?" I asked hopefully.

"I'm not sure. What *have* we done wrong? When asked directly if you knew where he was, you know, this morning on parade, you said nothing. Because you said nothing, Paul is now dead."

"I ..."

"Don't argue, I'm just saying what they'll say. You know, playing the Devil's Advocate. You ignored the fact that he was illegally in possession of a loaded firearm, pissed and, clearly, mentally unstable. You know, all things considered, he could have killed several people. We've had a bit of a touch here. There's an ambulance pulling into the yard."

I got up and glanced out the window.

"Sit down." He ordered me, abruptly.

"What have *I* done wrong? I leaked sensitive information about a secret internal enquiry and, as a result, a man took his own life. My mate who told me, he'll definitely be out of a job. The Superintendent who took the video home for a wank will have some awkward questions to answer, too." Ben said.

I was impressed by his clinical analysis of the situation. His experience was shining through. I was glad he was here.

I know I should have been feeling sorry for Paul, but I wasn't. I was thinking about me and the new pile of shit that had landed directly on top of me. This time, unlike when I stole the money, I didn't feel I'd contributed to what had happened. It wasn't my fault Paul had left his wife and kids for a much younger woman, or got in trouble because he'd shagged the juror, or that his girlfriend had done a disappearing act. All I'd done was try to do the bloke a favour and not rat him out.

"Does anyone know Paul came to your room last night?" Ben asked.

"No, but of course I don't know whether anyone saw him leave this morning."

"How did he get here, Nostrils?" He asked.

"No idea." I replied.

"So, probably, at this moment only you and I actually know what happened, and why."

"Right." I agreed.

"I think we should keep it that way. But you have to agree, and agree forever, you know the score, Nostrils."

"I know, when you lie you lie forever." I said.

"It's more than that, Nostrils. When you lie, it becomes the truth." He said.

I thought it over, quickly.

"I agree Ben." I said.

"Stand up, Nostrils."

We shook hands.

"Now, we know what we're doing, it's time to go and see what's happened." Ben said.

We went downstairs separately, and I wandered over to a crowd of people who were standing, as a group, in the back yard.

"What's happening?" I asked, innocently.

"Paul Pollock, the area car driver on early turn, he's killed himself. He took a gun out the Station Safe. We heard the gunshot." said Bernadette, a young, pretty girl, who worked in the Admin department.

I stood and listened for several minutes whilst everyone speculated as to why. Some theories were more accurate than others, although I was pleased to note that, even these, were still far from the truth. I lit a cigarette and stepped away from the group. A hand took hold of my elbow. It was Sergeant Bellamy and he guided me away from the others.

"Listen, Nostrils. About two minutes before he blew his brains out, Paul was in the Section House and, I'm guessing, he was looking for you."

"What makes you think that, Sarge?" I asked.

Sergeant Bellamy raised his eyebrows, so I moved the conversation quickly on.

"You saw him then?" I asked.

"Only briefly. I must have missed him coming in, I was probably in the loo, but I saw him strolling out, he looked like a defeated man; his head was down, and he never even acknowledged me, when I called out to him. Two minutes later, bang. I bet it's not just about you, though, I'm sure being about to lose his job didn't help. I've known him for years; his brain was always in his pants, which is ironic really because some of it, literally is, now."

"Sarge!" I said, reproachfully.

"You know what they say, Nostrils; if you can't take a joke, you shouldn't have joined."

"But still, Sarge."

"There's a lesson there, Nostrils."

"What, about tasteless jokes?" I commented.

"No, you wanker; about your cock getting you into shit. You could go the same way, you nearly did, if my suspicions are right."

"Received, Sarge. What happens now?"

"They've just shut the nick and there's a big argument about who's going to deal with it?"

"What do you mean?"

"Well, technically, it's just a suicide but it's bound to attract a load of media attention. Someone said CIB were coming but I can't see it's anything to do with them. The DCI says, he'll deal, but some Assistant Commissioner's coming to take charge. It's a right old mess."

Another PC joined us; it was Roger Class, the guy with whom I'd discussed freemasonry.

"He's been shagging the juror he was protecting, and Sarah has found out and left him. That's what this is all about. It's gonna cause me a problem, that's for sure. See Nostrils, the trouble your dick can get you into, be warned."

"Oh, fuck off Roger." I said and walked off.

~~~

Paul had put the revolver into his mouth and pulled the trigger. The bullet parted his skull and splattered his brains over the walls of trap one in the Gents toilet. These were adjacent to the male locker room.

Harry was the first person to find him, followed, moments later, by Sergeant Felix and Inspector Portman. They didn't attempt to resuscitate him, there was no point.

The DCI ordered the body to be photographed in situ and a cursory forensic examination. Then he called the undertakers and Paul left Stoke Newington nick for the last time. When he arrived, the Assistant Commissioner, apparently, went ballistic that a more thorough scene examination hadn't been undertaken and the DCI retaliated by questioning the Senior Officer's jurisdiction in 'his' police station.

And all the time this battle was raging, the nick remained closed. The distrusting local population feared the worst and assumed that one of their own had died, because of police brutality, and suspected that a full scale cover up was in swing. When no one moved to allay their fears, that afternoon, the streets of Stoke Newington erupted in violence and disorder and police were bussed in from all over London.

Those of us that knew Paul were excused from getting involved, so I retreated to my room and watched the petrol bombs and looting.

Eventually, some very senior officer had a brainwave and gave a statement to the press saying that the person who had died was a police officer. Strangely, the local population didn't have their suspicions completely quelled until all the shops in the High Street and High Road had been looted, at which point, they all went home.

Chapter 59

The weekend after the riot, I was off duty. The atmosphere on the streets of Stoke Newington was really weird an, for the first time, I regretted living at the Section House, as I couldn't escape.

For several days, TV news broadcasters lived out of their aerial covered vans, which were parked in the side street by the nick, and they tried to speak to us, at every opportunity. We were ordered not to visit the local pubs, an instruction which we all decided to ignore.

I really didn't see what all the fuss was about. I mean, people killed themselves every day, as I knew only too well, doing the job I did. A few weeks previously, I'd called on a middle aged woman to inform her, her husband had jumped under a train at Bethnal Green and died. She invited me to have his dinner which she was in the process of cooking otherwise, she explained, it would just go to waste. I'd politely declined. It transpired she and the rest of the family thought him a miserable old sod who no one would miss.

The Assistant Commissioner had taken over the investigation into Paul's suicide and a small enquiry team was set up in the Street Duties office. I expected them to call on me at any minute but, by Sunday, it was becoming clear that no one knew Paul had spent his last night in my room.

Several times that Saturday, I drove over to Sarah's to see if she had returned. On the second visit I made some enquiries with the flat next door which was rented by a couple of nurses. Some plain clothes police officer had already spoken to them about Paul. They told me they had no idea where Sarah might be.

When I turned the conversation with them over in my head later, something they'd said suggested to me that whoever had spoken to them about Paul, must have known where Sarah was, or they would have been questioned closely as to where she might be.

I had a drink with Rik and Andy that night. We went to the White Hart, in a deliberate act of defiance, that went completely unnoticed. The big news of the night was that Rik had met the girl his parents had set up, as a potential wife, and to everybody's amazement, most of all Rik's, she was absolutely stunning and he'd completely fallen for her.

"I thought you only fancied white women?" Andy said.

"So did I, mate; so did I."

"Well, what happened?" Andy asked.

"She's just gorgeous man; she looks just like Hema Malini"

"Emma, who?" I asked.

"Not Emma, you ignorant idiot, Hema, Hema Malini. She's, like, the most famous Indian actress ever, and she's gorgeous. My wife to be, Esha, looks just like her man."

I'd never seen Rik so happy about anything. It was nice.

"What happened about those Ping golf clubs?" I asked, remembering his dilemma as to whether to take them off his uncle, knowing that they were stolen.

"I said no, my father was furious. But I don't care, and do you know why?" He smiled from ear to ear.

I had to laugh; his happiness was infectious.

"Why's that then?" I asked.

"Because I, me, the only non-doctor, the one who refused to take over the family business, who took up a crappy job with the Metropolitan Police, is marrying the most gorgeous creature that ever walked this planet."

Andy and I laughed.

We'd avoided talking about the suicide or the Stoke Newington One, as our irreverent colleagues had started to refer to the incident. We'd probably have one more before closing, and I was keen to discover what was being said, so I steered the conversation.

"Any interesting rumours circulating about poor old Paul Pollock, then?" I asked my friends.

"Did you see that bollocks on the news, lunchtime?" Rik asked.

"No." Andy and I replied, in unison.

"They were linking it to the guy that was nicked for stealing the dogs, insinuating, though they didn't actually say, that the suicide was connected to that investigation. I mean, the only pedigree dog Paul was interested in was that blonde girl on your relief, Nostrils."

Although Andy knew everything, well most things about my life, I kept some things back from Rik. Not because I didn't trust him with my secrets, far from it, but because he was sometimes a little bit moral about such things. It was the same reason Andy didn't confide in him that he was homosexual.

"Rumour on the streets is that the blonde had left him and that's the reason. That's all I've heard." Rik said.

"That's possible. Sarah hasn't been at work for some weeks, she's been sick." I replied.

"Old Skinny was telling me he'd been caught shagging the Juror he was meant to be protecting." Andy said.

"That's right, I heard something about that too." Rik said, who stood up and wandered off to the loo.

"Don't you know any more?" Andy asked, seizing the opportunity which Rik's temporary absence afforded for him to be more candid.

"Andy, I haven't seen Sarah since Wednesday. She's disappeared off the face of the Earth. I suspect she's done a runner to her Mum's place." I replied.

"Haven't you had any contact with her at all?" He asked.

"Nothing mate, not a word since Wednesday." I said.

"Are you okay with that?" Andy asked.

"As it's turned out, yes. I mean I can honestly say, I don't think the Paul thing is anything to do with me."

I held Andy's stare just long enough to see whether I could detect anything in his eyes which suggested he knew I was lying. There wasn't a trace of suspicion. I was relieved because, if he hadn't joined the dots yet, and worked it all out, perhaps no one else would, either.

As usual, the evening ended in the curry house where a chicken madras was washed down with several more pints of lager. There was no more mention of Paul Pollock but several times I wished there had been because Rik was driving us both mad going on and on about his fiancée.

Halfway through his curry, Andy suddenly, and quite rudely, interrupted Rik in full flow, his face was deadly.

"I've just realised something?" Andy said.

"What?" I said.

"I've worked out why Paul killed himself."

Rik and I sat there in silence. I hoped Andy thought carefully before he said anymore.

"Why?" Asked Rik, speaking into the tense silence.

I could feel my heart pounding in my chest and my palms growing sweaty.

"It's 'cos Paul bumped into you Rik and you were talking about bloody Esha naan bread!"

Chapter 60

I hate Sundays, I've always hated Sundays, even when I was a little kid. They were so boring.

Today, I was even more bored than usual, as Andy had retired to his bed and Rik was doing a less than eight on some demonstration up the West End.

I drove for, what I decided was, the last time over to Sarah's flat and then I visited Dawn's grave and had a chat with her. I popped in to see Mrs M, but she was out, and I ended up at a cinema in Walthamstow watching Police Academy 2, I think I only laughed once, but the popcorn was good.

It was three days since Paul's death. There had been some house-to-house enquiries which had been made at every Section House room, but they were just routine. Apart from these, I hadn't been asked any questions. If someone was going to tell the enquiry, about any suspicions they had that I was seeing Sarah, I thought they probably would have done so, by now.

I think it was more likely, because of the timing, that the suicide was being directly linked to the incident with the juror and Sarah's disappearance, which weren't really anything to do with me.

~~~

On Monday morning, I stayed in bed as late as possible, as I was on nights. When I eventually went downstairs, it was lunchtime. I chatted to Sergeant Bellamy, who told me the small team set up by the Assistant Commissioner had concluded their enquires and moved back to the Yard. I took that as a very positive piece of news.

"And there's a message in the book for you and a letter in your pigeon hole."

The message asked me to call Roger Class and quoted a telephone number. I used Sergeant Bellamy's desk phone and spoke to Roger, who invited me to an interview to join the Masons on Wednesday, someone who was scheduled to be interviewed had dropped out, at the last moment, and they were ringing round to see if there were any candidates free, at such short notice.

"But we're nights." I reminded him.

"It's no problem; the interview is at three-thirty in St James's. You'll be back by six. We'll have a chat tonight about your answers but it's quite informal. No one's trying to catch you out. What shall I tell them, Nostrils?" He asked, putting me directly on the spot.

I know I'd chatted with him a few days ago but this had happened more quickly than expected so I wasn't entirely sure. Damn it, I thought, I'll take a chance.

"Go on then Roger, we'll chat more tonight but tell them, I'm free on Wednesday."

"You won't regret it, Nostrils." He assured me.

When I hung up, I realised Sergeant Bellamy had been listening. If I remembered correctly, he was on the square, as they called it. He smiled at me, I smiled back.

When I picked up the letter from my pigeon hole, my heart missed a beat. The address was handwritten, and I immediately recognised Sarah's distinctive writing. I looked at the post mark for some hint of where and when the letter had been posted. Thursday, it was posted the day of Paul's suicide, and the postmark was stamped 'Bristol'. I searched my memory, but I couldn't recall Sarah ever mentioning knowing anyone in the West Country.

"You alright, Nostrils? You look like you've seen a ghost." Sergeant Bellamy asked.

"I'm fine Sarge." I replied and went back to my room.

I opened the letter, with shaking hands, using a flick knife I'd found in the top drawer of my desk, when I'd moved into my Section House room. I sat on the bed.

My dearest, Chris,

I've been told to have no contact with anyone from Stoke Newington police station so please destroy this letter as soon as you have read it. As you read o,n you will understand why. I am trusting you to do this, please don't let me down.

It is three o'clock in the morning, Thursday morning, and I can't sleep. I have a thousand thoughts going around my head and they are slowly driving me mad. I hope it will help to write this letter.

When you left me at the clinic, the doctor asked me to sign a consent form. I hesitated, so he gave me time to think it over. When he returned, I told him I'd changed my mind and asked him to get someone to call me a taxi because I knew I wouldn't be able to get hold of you. I didn't want to wait around at the clinic all day until you came back to pick me up. Then I'd have to explain to you that I hadn't had the termination and, I know and really appreciate what you said about was I sure I was doing the right thing, but I didn't know how you'd actually react.

You have a right to know, Chris, this is your baby. I lied when I said I didn't know who the father was because there is absolutely no doubt in my mind. Paul and I haven't had proper sex in two months.

When I got home, I was surprised that Paul hadn't come back from Jury Protection. I sat on the bed and cried. I just couldn't understand how my life had become such a mess. I've never felt more unhappy in my life.

I knew I had to get myself out, somehow, but I couldn't just walk away because of something I'd overheard last week. I haven't told you this and, when I do, I hope you'll understand why I've done what I've done.

It was in the middle of the afternoon, and I'd gone to bed feeling sick (we both know why). I heard Paul on the phone to someone, I don't know who, but when I heard the words Snaresbrook Crown Court, I realised they were discussing that case you told me about, so I listened carefully. If I'm being honest, when you said Paul was making it look like you'd planted drugs on someone, I'd thought you were being paranoid. You weren't. I know that from what I heard. Paul said he was relieved that they'd dug themselves out of a dangerous hole. The other bloke must have said something because I heard Paul say, 'fuck him' and I guessed he was talking about you. Then, for a good ten minutes, they discussed hiding drugs in the boot of your car and then putting in a call to Crimestoppers. You'd be stopped by the police and, when the drugs were found, Paul said it would corroborate the fact that it was you, and not them, that had planted them on that bloke and they'd be in the clear. Especiall,y as the drugs they'd plant would be the same one's he'd planted in the Vicar's jacket.

I knew I couldn't walk away and leave you to be fitted up. I also knew that I wanted out of the police. I think it is a great job, but not at Stoke Newington. I've got mates from training school that went to other nicks and when we talk, I realise things are really mucked up where we work.

I still didn't know why Paul was so late home, but I made my mind up and left. I knew as I closed the front door, I would never come back.

I drove to Tintagel House, it's a building in Vauxhall where CIB are based. I walked in and asked to speak to a senior officer. I told this Superintendent I wanted to tell him what was going on at Stoke Newington but that I wanted immunity from prosecution for anything I might have done wrong. He asked me exactly what I wanted to talk about. I told him about the overheard conversation, and he was quite dismissive until I produced Paul's box of cannabis. I'd taken it from the loft when I left.

He went very quiet, and I knew he'd have to take what I was saying seriously. He disappeared for ages, it felt like hours. Some young girl kept bringing me cups of tea. I think it was worse than waiting for the termination.

Just when I was thinking about getting up to leave, another bloke came back who introduced himself as a DS and told me to come with him.

They drove me to this hotel in Bristol and got me a local solicitor to represent me. I spoke to him for hours and told him everything I know. It felt like I was the guilty one. All day yesterday, this solicitor and another Superintendent were negotiating a deal for me, some form of limited immunity. Basically, if I'm completely honest with them, at all times, and in respect of all matters, they'll use me as a witness but if they find out I've lied, then my immunity will be withdrawn.

Tomorrow I will be interviewed by the Superintendent. They want to discuss three things; the case you were at court with and fitting you up; the woman Paul planted the drugs on in Sandringham Road and something about stolen dogs. I've told my solicitor I don't know anything about stolen dogs but, apparently, they still want to ask me some questions.

I'll have to tell them about the thousand pounds, but I'll say I gave it to him, I won't mention that you gave it to me. I also won't say anything about the message you destroyed. I won't let you down, Chris, I promise.

If they ask, I will tell them we were very close, I'll perhaps say we were on the brink of an affair. If you get questioned, make sure you say the same.

I know Paul will be arrested and I'm guessing it'll be over the weekend. It might be a good time to go away for a few days.

They've told me not to speak to or contact anyone, but I had to let you know what's going on. I'll try and get out and post this letter later before they come back.

Finally, Chri,s I need to let you know about the decision I've come to about us. When this is over, I'm going to Mum and Dads. I'm determined to have my baby and start my life over. I don't want to see you again but will always remember you as a true and loyal friend. So please don't contact me but know that you will always be in my heart.

I am aware this means I am asking you not to have anything to do with your child, but I believe this is for the best. I hope you will understand.

I know this will hurt Chris. I will miss you terribly, but I don't want to be in a relationship with someone who is completely in love with someone else. Yes, Chris, I am talking about Dawn. No woman will ever compare with her in your eyes.

You are so strong; I know you will survive.

I love you, I love you, I love you.

Sarah

xxxxxxxxxx

PS PLEASE DESTROY THIS LETTER

I re-read the letter three times and then I sat on my bed in silence, barely moving. I felt completely numb, and tired too, so very tired. After some considerable time, and with a gargantuan effort, I snapped myself out of my contemplation and picked up the flick knife. I carefully cut out the three penultimate lines and soaked the rest of the letter in water until it turned to pulp and disintegrated.

Chapter 61

I felt lonely and confused. The biggest thing was that I would miss Sarah, terribly. And then, I wasn't sure it was entirely fair for her to decide that I could have nothing to do with my own child. On the other hand, I'd always imagined that, when I was a father, it would be a full-time role, within a proper and committed relationship, so the idea of being allowed an hour or two, every couple of weeks, really did seem pointless. What's more, if I was entirely honest, at least this way I wouldn't have to pay hundreds of pounds a month in maintenance.

I thought her comment about me still being in love with Dawn was interesting. Was I still in love with her? I'm not sure I ever had been, not in the proper sense. Nonetheless, I made a mental note not to mention Dawn too often if I ever got into another relationship.

I was grateful that Sarah had done the decent thing and not let Paul and Alec fit me up by planting cannabis in my boot. I was distraught enough about the trouble I might get in by my own volition regarding the old lady's money, I don't think that, mentally, I could have coped with being sent to prison for something I didn't do.

No, Sarah had done the right thing in the end, by me, and probably by herself and her baby. I hoped it all worked out for her, I really did.

I decided the best thing to do would be to try to forget about her, to put her completely out of my mind and not think about her again. That way, I figured it wouldn't hurt.

When I went into the nick, later that evening, for night duty, I was amazed at how different the place felt to me. I know Sarah hadn't been there for several weeks but knowing she was never coming back made everything feel very ordinary again.

The atmosphere on parade that Monday night duty was really strained. Paul's death hung heavily in the air and, standing as we always did, in a loose semi-circle, it felt like we were around his grave, as his coffin was lowered slowly into the ground. It crossed my mind that, at least, he didn't live long enough to see his girlfriend, the person he undoubtedly loved more than anyone else in the world, betray him by going to CIB. Then I thought of his three kids and how they must be feeling. For just a second, I started to feel guilty about my own part in this whole miserable affair, but I quickly stopped myself straying into that nightmare, my capacity for guilt was already at overload.

From my experience, police officers made a joke out of everything, no matter how sad or macabre the situation but, that day, there was no banter or black humour. In fact, there wasn't even any idle chatter. Several PCs smoked in silence, as we waited the arrival of the Sergeant and Inspector.

Inspector Porter entered and we stood as one. He gave us out various postings. Roger had obviously had a word with one of the Sergeants because I was posted with him on one of the panda cars. It would give me an opportunity to chat through the interview on Wednesday but, more importantly, it would help to take my mind off Sarah and he would tell me what everyone was saying about Paul.

As the parade ended, Inspector Portman asked me to see him afterwards in his office, which was directly opposite the Collator's, where we paraded. This was unusual and I assumed it was bad news, so I was immediately worried. Was this about Paul, Sarah, what Sarah was telling CIB, the old lady's money or the court case? Quite frankly, I was getting to saturation point with worry, as well as guilt.

"What have I done, Sir?" I asked defensively, as I entered his office.

"Sit down, Chris."

From the conciliatory tone of his voice and his use of my proper first name, I knew this was not going to be good news. I sat down. I felt sick.

"I need to advise you that …" he hesitated, and my heart sank.

"Go on, Sir." I implored him, I just wanted him to get it over with.

"It's Kitty." He said.

Was that all? Kitty?

"What about her Sir?" I asked.

"Kitty is alleging racial and sexual discrimination against you."

"Don't do that to me, Sir; you looked so serious I was, I was worried for a moment."

I started to laugh.

"This is serious, Nostrils." He said, sternly.

"How can it be, Sir?" I asked, incredulously.

"She's got a top firm of solicitors representing her. I suspect the job will try to settle before this goes to court to avoid the bad publicity. Nostrils, stop laughing. She's suing the job for two hundred thousand pounds for stress, harassment, and loss of future earnings."

I couldn't help it; I got the right giggles. Tears were rolling down my face and my sides hurt, I was laughing so much. I was so relieved.

"Nostrils." Inspector Portman barked.

"Sorry, Sir." I said through gritted teeth.

It took me a minute to settle down.

"What's so funny?" Inspector Portman asked.

"What's so funny? Kitty stressed? I've been shot at, blown up, had my best friend die in my arms and my arse bitten by a police dog and Kitty is the one who is stressed and harassed? Well fuck my old boots, boss!"

"I can see what you mean, son; I really can, but you've got to see it from the job's point of view."

"And what point of view is that?" I asked, genuinely interested to see what he would say.

"The Metropolitan Police is always accused of being racist. It's not, you know that and so do I, but the public perception is that we are, particularly in this part of the world. The best way we can address that allegation is to employ black officers. The last thing the job needs is for one of their black officers to accuse it of being racist. This is a lot more serious than you think."

"But Kitty is not even black, Sir. She's more white than black, I go darker than her after a week in the sun." I said.

"She is half-caste, Chris; which makes this even more serious and gives credibility to her allegation." Inspector Portman explained.

"But I've never been racist towards her, Sir. For god's sake, my best mate is black! You know, Andy Wellings." I explained."

"I know, Andy, he's a good guy." Inspector Portman replied.

"Listen, Sir. I only worked with Kitty for a couple of days. She was lazy and stroppy. She didn't even like making the tea for everyone. I did have a go at her, a couple of times, but it was never because of her colour or race, or whatever, it was because she was a lazy bitch. And can you believe she wouldn't even do my typing for me, even though she used to be a typist?" I said.

I could feel myself starting to get angry, not with Inspector Portman but with the sheer unfairness of the situation.

"Listen, Chris. Be smart here. Go and get that counselling I suggested for you, a few weeks ago."

"Alright." I replied, reluctantly.

I'd no intention of getting bloody counselling, I wasn't mad.

"And at some stage tonight find yourself a quiet corner somewhere, sit down and write out everything you can remember about every interaction you've ever had with Kitty. When you've done that, bring it to me and let me read it over. Do you understand?"

"Yes, Sir." I replied.

"Off the record, Kitty was probably looking for every opportunity she could find to make this allegation, but I'll deny saying that if you ever quote me." Inspector Portman said.

"I won't say anything, you know that. But I appreciate the comment." I said.

Inspector Portman nodded.

"Heaven forbid you should be allowed to be honest." I said with a wry smile.

"Haven't you learnt anything, Nostrils?"

"Sorry, Sir?" I said.

"There's a time and a place for honesty." Inspector Portman said.

It was his turn to return my wry smile.

He nodded towards the door, indicating our conversation was at an end. I stood up and turned to leave. As I took my first step towards the door, Inspector Portman spoke again.

"You? You Nostrils? You're alright. No, actually, you're better than that; you're good, good old bill, son."

I stopped in my tracks. To be described as 'good old bill' by another officer was about as high a compliment, as one could get.

"Thank you, Sir." I said without looking round and only momentarily breaking stride.

It was the nicest thing anyone had said to me since before Dawn died.

"Oh, I nearly forgot." Inspector Portman said suddenly.

I turned, half in and half out of the room.

"The Chief Superintendent wants to see you, two o'clock, Thursday, in his office."

"What's it about, Sir?" I asked.

"No idea."

Fuck me here we go again, I thought.

Chapter 62

Roger filled me in on the format for tomorrow. I had to go to Mark Mason's Hall in St James's. The nearest tube was Green Park. I should wear a dark suit and tie. I would be interviewed by the committee. It sounded more like the Wheeltappers and Shunters Social Club than a secret society. The committee would ask me obvious questions like, why did I want to join, what had I heard about Freemasonry, and things like that.

Roger explained there was only one question which required a specific answer, which was, 'do you believe in a supreme being?'

"A supreme being? What you mean the Commissioner?" I asked, innocently.

"No, you spastic. A supreme being means god, do you believe in god?" Roger explained.

"No." I replied.

"Don't you? Why ever not?"

"If you'd seen how my Mum suffered before she died, you'd know. No decent god would allow her to suffer so terribly and, if there is a god and he did, well damn him, I don't want anything to do with such a sadistic bastard. And another thing, if he does exist, why does he insist on people worshipping him? Is he like, really insecure, or what?"

"Well, let me put it this way. If you want to join the freemasons, you need to believe in him for at least one day, Wednesday. When you're asked the question, you must say yes, otherwise you cannot be admitted. Do you understand?"

"I do." I replied.

"In that case, you'll sail through. Honestly, you'll enjoy the whole thing."

"Golf November four five; Golf November?"

"Go ahead." I responded.

"Return to Golf November please. Report to the front office, Sergeant Key has a short assignment for you. Golf November over."

"All received by four five." I responded.

We were at the top of Stamford Hill, so Roger headed down the A10 towards the nick. Before we got stuck into whatever work was awaiting us, I wanted to get Roger's take on the Paul situation, to see if there was anything it might be useful to know.

"What do you reckon the SP was with Paul Pollock, then?" I asked.

As he drove, I studied him carefully for any telltale sign that he thought I might be in some way connected to it.

"Lots of rumours, Nostrils; most of them are bollocks."

I wanted to ask 'any of them involve me' but I resisted the temptation.

"What's your theory?" I asked, instead.

"He got caught shagging, didn't he? I'm guessing Sarah chucked him out. Paul is, was, a very heavy drinker and, once or twice, I saw him get really morose when he was pissed. Tox showed him four times over the drink drive limit. He was a nice bloke, though, I, I ..." Roger hesitated.

"What?" I asked, sensing that he had been about to impart some highly sensitive information but had suddenly thought better of it.

"Nothing, it doesn't matter now." He said.

"Go on, Roger; you can trust me." I urged him.

"It doesn't matter, really." He replied, and glanced across at me, momentarily, taking his eyes off the road.

"Does it involve me?" I asked, somewhat tactlessly.

"Yes and no. But let it go, Nostrils; you'll only fret." Roger said.

That made me *really* concerned, but short of pressing him further, which would have been desperate and undignified, I had no option other than to let the matter rest.

Instead of going into the back yard, Roger pulled up outside the front of the nick next to a Sussex police van.

"I wonder what they're doing here?" Roger commented.

"Probably picking up a prisoner that's wanted." I suggested.

"No, that's not right. If they were doing that, they'd have parked in the back yard."

"Perhaps they're lost and asking for directions." I said, half-jokingly.

"That's more likely. Anyway, pop in and see what old keyhole wants with us, I'll wait here." Roger said.

I did as instructed. On the bench in the public waiting area was a drunk, sleeping off the effects of a good night out. I ignored him, if the Station Officer wasn't bothered by his presence, why should I be?

I jumped over the front counter or rather jumped up, slid over and dropped down the other side. Sergeant Key was talking to two Sussex officers, so I waited politely and quietly until he was ready to speak to me.

Since the second laxative incident, I was really wary of Sergeant Key and tried to avoid him at all cost. I'd done what Roger suggested and given him the bottle of really expensive malt whisky, the same make as the one the dog handler had given me, and which was Paul Pollock's last supper, but Sergeant

Key had given it straight back to me with one word 'Grimsby'. It took me a while to work out what he meant and, when I eventually did, I went out and bought him a really expensive bottle of port, instead, which he grudgingly accepted. I still didn't trust him or think for one moment that our feud was settled. He looked up and saw me waiting.

"Nostrils, these officers have assisted a Met DCI they found outside the railway station in Brighton. He was a little worse for wear and, when they searched him, they found his warrant card, no wallet or keys or money, just his warrant card. When they asked him where he lives, he kept saying Stoke Newington, so they bought him here.

"Is he the guy on the bench?" I asked.

"That's him." Replied the taller of the two officers, as he handed me the guy's brief.

"Find out where he lives and take him home." Sergeant Key instructed.

"Will do, Sarge." I replied obediently.

Sergeant Key now spoke to the Sussex officers.

"Thanks for bringing him up, lads. I'm sure he'll appreciate your pragmatic approach. Let me take your details, so I can let him know who helped him."

I looked at the brief. Detective Chief Inspector Tony Hyland. I felt in and around the thin blue plastic warrant card container, there was nothing else, which was quite unusual, as normally officers kept a few quid or credit cards in there.

I left Sergeant Key chatting to the Sussex officers, about an old friend of his who'd transferred to their force last year, and went outside to tell Roger what we'd got. Roger got out and came into the front office with me.

DCI Hyland was fast asleep. I shook him gently, and said his name several times, until his eyes flicked opened.

"Hello, Sir. You're at Stoke Newington police station. Can you please tell us where you live, so we can take you home?"

His eyes shut and he shuffled as if to make himself more comfortable.

I shook him again.

"Please wake up, Sir; we need to know where you live."

And so, the process went on until about ten minutes later, when we'd solicited the information we needed, but it was bloody hard work.

The address he'd given was one of the nicer roads in Upper Clapton. We carried him to our panda, put him in the back, and set off. He almost immediately began to snore.

"Roger?" I asked.

"Yes, Nostrils?"

"This couldn't be a wind up, could it?"

Roger contemplated my question for a few moments.

"You're right to be suspicious but I doubt it. It's too elaborate, and to involve another force; but you're right to be thinking along those lines. We'll bear it in mind."

Ten minutes later, I was standing outside a semi-detached house in Cleveleys Road, propping up the DCI, whilst Roger knocked at the door and rang the alarm bell. Eventually, an upstairs light went on and, a minute later, the front door was opened by a white woman, in her mid-forties, wearing a pink dressing gown.

"Can I help you, officers?" She asked, wiping sleep from her eyes.

"I believe this is your husband." Roger said, stepping aside and holding an open palm towards the DCI.

"I gather he got on the wrong train home and somehow ended up in Brighton. I'm afraid he's a little drunk." Roger explained.

Right on cue, the DCI belched.

The woman looked momentarily confused and then she stepped outside, past Roger, to examine my charge, more closely.

"He's not my husband, officer." She said.

"Okay your boyfriend, then. He gave this address to us only ten minutes ago."

"Officer, my boyfriend is asleep upstairs. And my husband…"

The woman looked around conspiratorially.

"…is on a North Sea oil rig. But I do recognise that gentleman."

"Oh, thank heavens." Roger said.

"We bought this house off him and his old girl, last year. His name's Hyland and he's one of your lot."

Chapter 63

We placed the DCI back into the rear of the police car and Roger called up for advice. Ten minutes later, we were on our way to Scotland Yard to meet the Back Hall Inspector who, when he was satisfied that we had the right man, would look up his details in some personnel records and tell us his proper home address.

The DCI slept all the way and Roger put his foot down and, as it was now the middle of the night, we were there in twenty minutes.

It was the first time I'd been to the Yard, and I was curious to see what it was really like.

"Who's this Back Hall chap, Roger?" I asked, as we turned into The Broadway and the famous revolving triangle came into sight.

"He's like the Duty Officer for the Yard." Roger replied.

"You used to work here, didn't you?" I said, remembering that he was at Special Branch before he came to Stokey.

"Yea, fifteen years. It's a great place to work. It's the only operational Metropolitan Police building with its own bar; the bar's called the Tank. It's a bit of a hovel but I've been pissed in there more times than I've eaten in the canteen."

"Fifteen years! How long did you have in when you went to Special Branch?"

"Three years. You take an exam to get into SB and they like to recruit young so they can mould you. SB was great, Nostrils. It's just a shame that lesbian with no sense of humour put an end to it all. Never mind, I'll be on the Crime Squad in a few weeks, and I can lose this ridiculous uniform once and for all."

"I gather you don't enjoy this work?" I said.

"Nostrils, uniform work is a mug's game, believe me. You do all the work whilst the suits have an easy time and earn all the money. Do yourself a favour, get your arse onto the Crime Squad and into the CID, as soon as possible. You're a good thief taker, it shouldn't be too hard and the fact you'll be on the Square will help, no end."

Roger had pulled up outside the yard, he turned to face me.

"Uniform is a mug's game; the Sovereigns is the way forward." His right hand dropped down and he opened his door and went to get out.

"Wait a second, Roger. What do you mean, the Sovereigns is the way forward?" I asked, there must have been something in my voice because Roger closed the door again.

"The Sovereigns is what the Crime Squad call themselves, like a nickname. It's nothing to get stressed about, Nostrils."

"How come I've never heard the name, before?" I asked.

"I don't know." He replied and shrugged his shoulders.

"Is there a problem, Nostrils? You look really shocked."

I shook my head.

"No, of course not." I said.

"Stay here, I'll go in and see if I can find out where our man here lives." Roger said and he got out of the car.

He set off towards the Yard but turned round, came back, opened the back door, and removed the DCI's warrant card, to take with him.

When he was gone, I sat there thinking.

I had a very good idea I knew why the Stoke Newington Crime Squad were called the Sovereigns. When I was on Street Duties, I'd dealt with a burglary at Cohen's Jewellers in the High Street. The safe was blown and two hundred brand new gold sovereigns were stolen. The burglar, who Dawn and I later arrested, was an Irish guy who had his drum turned over by the Crime Squad but, allegedly, they only recovered about a dozen coins. Dawn always thought they'd had a load of them off. If I remember rightly, about seventy were unaccounted for. The burglar said the Crime Squad had stolen them and made an official complaint, but it was his word, the word of a thief, against that of ten of Her Majesty's finest. I think his allegation was NFA'd almost immediately.

Was it possible that the Crime Squad's nickname was something to do with that? Or was I getting completely paranoid about corruption and seeing ghosts where there were only shadows?

Roger was gone for what seemed like ages. The DCI snored away in the back, and I opened the window and smoked several cigarettes in the time I was waiting. When he eventually returned to the car, he was carrying a piece of paper which he dumped on my lap as he got in.

"That's his address, Croydon, he's moved to bloody Croydon." Roger said.

"That's south, isn't it?" I asked, my knowledge of London outside Stoke Newington still wasn't great.

"It's miles away. That's obviously why he was on the Brighton train, he should have got off at East Croydon, but he must have fallen asleep and woken up in Brighton. I phoned Keyhole and he told us to take him home, you'll have to look it up in the A to Z." Roger said, nodding towards the glove compartment.

Roger was right, it was a long way.

"Our man works at Obscene Publications. The Back Hall Inspector ended up having to get into their office to dig out their book one."

"I thought you were gone a long time?" I said.

"Keyhole's got the right arse but I told him, he gave us the bloody assignment." Roger said.

As we drove over to Croydon, I toyed with the idea of discussing with Roger the Crime Squad and their reputation for corruption, and I would have done, had it not been for the fact, I knew, or suspected after getting Sarah's letter, most of them would be nicked in the next few days. So, I kept my thoughts to myself and listened as Roger talked about the Masons and how they'd changed his life.

It was nearly four by the time we pulled up outside a nice, four-bedroom, detached house on the outskirts of Croydon, in a place called Shirley. Our passenger had slept all the way and he mumbled, incoherently, as I carried him to the second front door of the night. Once again, I stood back, and Roger knocked. There was no reply, no bloody reply despite Roger nearly knocking the door down. There was definitely no one in.

"According to the book one, he lives here with his wife and three kids. I can't understand it." Roger said.

With that, the upstairs window of the house next door opened and a middle-aged lady leaned out.

"Can I help you?" She said, politely.

"Yes, madam. Can you confirm that this gentleman, who's had a bit too much to drink, lives here?" Roger asked.

I turned the DCI around slightly to give the lady a better view in the half light of a nearby street lamp.

"Yes, officer; that's Tony. He lives there with his wife Sue and their three kids." She replied, helpfully.

"I can't get anyone to answer the door." Roger said.

"Well, you won't officer. They've all gone on holiday to Brighton for the week."

Chapter 64

The following afternoon I met Roger in a small pub in a passage running parallel to St James. The bar was thick with cigarette smoke and full of middle-aged men in suits, all wearing white shirts and black ties and carrying briefcases. Roger bought me drink and then, as a small table in the corner became vacant, we moved quickly in.

"So, you don't think they'll give me a hard time then?" I asked.

"The committee? No of course not, Nostrils. I mean we desperately need new members. The last thing any lodge can afford to do is to start rejecting good candidates."

That Roger thought I was a good candidate was encouraging.

"How many people are in the lodge?" I asked, keen both to show interest and to learn a little more about what I was getting into.

"I think there are about fifty of us on paper, but we only have one initiation a year." Roger replied.

"Initiation?" I asked.

"Joining ceremony."

"So only one person can join every year?" I asked.

"Fundamentally, yes. Masons from other lodges can become members but we can only get one new member a year. And as we lose at least one, but anything up to three a year, well do the maths."

"What do you mean lose?" I asked.

"The older members either die or become so old they can't travel up to London anymore so we have to get new people in. Because of unforeseen circumstances, the person that was to join this year dropped out which is, of course, very fortunate for you."

"If I pass the interview what happens next?" I asked.

"You will pass, Nostrils; don't worry. We have the lodge meeting immediately after the committee meeting and, during that meeting, we'll vote on whether to let you join. They pass a wooden box around and you get given two small balls, one white and one black. Everyone drops one of their two balls into the box. A white ball is a yes, the black ball, a no. Then they empty the box and, if there are any black balls, then the candidate is rejected." Roger explained.

"How often does that happen?" I asked.

"I've been a member fourteen years and no one has ever been rejected."

"Let's hope I'm not the first." I said.

Roger smiled.

"Dawn Matthews predicted that I would join one day, she said it was my destiny. But what exactly is it, Roger? I still don't really get it."

"I can't tell you much and, even if I could, I wouldn't, because it would spoil it. It's a secret society where like-minded men come together every couple of months to share good company, good conversation and have a decent meal and a few drinks."

"Why are so many people funny about it? You know, they say you look after each other and stuff like that." I asked.

"We help each other if we can, that's true, but most of what you read in the papers and the like is rubbish. My lodge is an honourable one with a few old bill but most of the members are businessmen, we've got two lawyers, one who is just about to become a Judge, a Magistrate and we even have a doctor." Roger said.

I was quite impressed. It would also give me an opportunity to meet people who weren't old bill which would be quite healthy.

"When you say help each other out, give me an example?" I asked.

Roger thought for a few moments.

"This isn't exactly what happened, but it'll give you a good idea. Last year one of our members forgot to MOT his car. He got stopped and given a producer and didn't even realise his MOT had expired until the PC behind the jump spotted it. He tried to talk his way out of it, but the young PC was having none of it and stuck him on. He called me later that day because he knew I work at that nick. I was, actually, off duty, but I drove in, looked through the process tray in the Station Office, you know the one they come and collect every morning."

I nodded.

"I found the relevant HORT two page and popped it in my pocket."

"But wouldn't the carbon copy of that page still be in the pad?" I asked.

"Yea, of course. But it's the process department that initiates the court proceedings and, if they don't get the front page, then they won't know to do anything and my friend's problem disappears." Roger explained.

"But if anyone investigated that, they'd find the copy."

"Yes, I know, but who's going to investigate it? There's nothing to investigate unless someone makes a fuss, is there? And my mate's hardly going to phone up and complain that he didn't receive a summons, is he?"

"No." I replied.

"See, easy peasey, lemon squeezy."

"And what did he do in return? Nice bottle of malt?" I asked.

"No, you're missing the point. He didn't have to do anything but, you know, in the future, if I need a favour, you know, he'll help me out."

"But what if he'd done something more serious? Would you still help him out?" I asked, seeking clarification as to exactly what joining this society was going to lead me into.

"Give me an example?" Roger asked.

"Mugged an old lady?" I said.

"No, of course not. But he's in the lodge, in fact, he's the Worshipful Master this year. People in the lodge just aren't the sort of people that do that sort of thing, Nostrils; so you don't find yourself having to say no when someone asks you for help. Do you see what I mean? They might get done for drink drive but who doesn't do that?"

I nodded.

"True." I agreed.

"Now drink up, we need to get going." Roger urged me.

~~~

From the outside, the building we entered in St James looked like an ordinary terraced house. Inside however it was very impressive and much bigger than one would have anticipated. On the second floor was a bar, where Roger told me to wait, until summoned.

If I did join the lodge, this would be my club. I would be a member of a club in the West End. I could tell people I'll be at my club, and I'd sound really impressive.

Several times over the next hour I checked my watch and the clock on the wall, whilst I sat patiently waiting to be called. I wandered over to the window which overlooked the junction between Pall Mall and St James. Over to the right was the palace where the Queen Mum lived.

"Are you the candidate?" A voice said behind me, and I turned and shook the outstretched hand of an old man with grey hair and large thick round glasses.

"Yes, Sir." I replied.

"Come this way." He said.

I followed him up one flight of uneven stairs and through two large wooden doors into what was about the strangest room I'd ever been in. The room was dominated by a carpet of black and white squares, on three sides of which were substantial wooden chairs, thrones almost. On the walls hung old paintings of men dressed in, what I could only assume to be, masonic clothing. I noticed immediately they all wore white gloves and a small apron.

Around the outside of the room were more chairs, some of which had been placed in a semi-circle and were occupied by about ten men, whom I gathered were the committee. In the middle of the room was a single chair which I assumed was for me.

I looked quickly around the semi-circle. Roger was not amongst them, but I recognised two of them, obviously from the nick. I had half expected to see DS Cotton, but he wasn't there.

The gentleman who collected me told me to sit down and, one of the men sitting roughly in the middle of the semi-circle, spoke. As he did, I noticed he was holding what appeared to be my application form.

"Hello. I am Simon De la Rue. I am the Treasurer of this lodge. The Worshipful Master is delayed so we shall start without him and, hopefully, he'll join us, shortly." The man explained, his voice was warm and friendly.

I smiled and nodded, politely.

"Now, I understand you're recently divorced? Will that affect your ability to pay your fees?" Mr De la Rue asked.

"I'm sorry?" I replied, confused by the question.

"I don't wish to intrude too deeply into your financial position but one of the responsibilities of this committee is to ensure that potential candidates are able to meet their financial commitments. The joining fee and annual subscription will come to two hundred and fifty pounds which you will be expected to pay on the day of your initiation. Bearing in mind your recent divorce..."

"I'm not divorced." I interjected.

"Oh, you managed to reconcile with your wife, I'm so pleased." A man to his right said.

"I've never been married." I replied.

Mr De la Rue looked at the application form.

"You are Brother Class's candidate, are you not? You are Paul Pollock?"

Chapter 65

The committee sent for Roger, but he was nowhere to be found. I politely suggested they look in the Red Lion, the pub we'd been in earlier, and a search party was despatched.

Meanwhile, I was sent back to the bar to wait but was only there a few minutes before I was summoned again.

This time I was more relaxed as I entered the room which, by then, I'd learnt was called a temple. I sat down and looked up. The Treasurer had moved to the right and, sitting in his place, was a face I recognised. Or rather, I knew that I knew him but couldn't quite remember exactly where from. Just as I was figuring it out, he started talking to me.

"Good afternoon, Christopher. I'm sorry about the little misunderstanding, earlier. I am the Worshipful Master; my name is Toby Saunders."

Toby bloody Saunders, of course it was. I'd met Toby Saunders twice; on the first occasion I was with Dawn, and we reported a burglary at his clothing business, he tried to give me a suit and I politely declined his offer. It was an act of honesty which went down well with Dawn and solicited from her the first ever compliment she gave me. The second time I met him was later that day when he produced his driving documents to me, when I was Assistant Station Officer. The insurance was out of date and, when I stuck him on, he'd tried to bribe me. When I turned the bribe down, he got quite nasty, so I told him to sod off, or words to that effect.

"So, Christopher, why would you like to become a freemason?" He asked, his face a broad smile.

I answered; well, I said something which I'd vaguely rehearsed but my mind was elsewhere.

I'd stuck Toby Saunders on for no insurance; I'd bet that was the thing to which Roger had alluded to in the pub. I made a mental note to check the records to see whether he'd ever been convicted for no insurance. Then, immediately, I changed my mind, reminding myself that, more often than not, in circumstances like these, it's so much better not to know.

"Will you be able to fit in your masonic duties around your work commitments?" He asked.

Again, I replied, but my thoughts were on another track.

If Sarah was at this very moment coughing her guts up to CIB, then it wouldn't be long before Toby Saunders was arrested, and the last thing I wanted, was to be connected with him through masonic membership. I had to think of a way to extricate myself from this situation.

"Christopher, I understand the Treasurer may have already asked you this but, in the confusion about who exactly you were, your answer may have become lost. Will you be able to afford the joining fee and annual subscription?" Mr Saunders asked.

I wondered whether Roger Class had any idea about the Crime Squad paying off Toby Saunders. What would Roger think if I just stood up and walked out?

"And, finally, Christopher, do you believe in a supreme being?" Mr Saunders asked, and from the tone in his voice, I knew this was the last question.

"Do you mean God?" I asked, quickly realising that a door had just been opened through which I could escape.

"Well, yes. In masonry, he is referred to, as the Great Architect of the Universe. It is essential for you to believe in a god. It doesn't have to be a particular god or religion, you must just satisfy the committee that you do believe in the existence of a superior being."

"Oh." I replied.

"Is there a problem?" Mr Saunders asked.

I knew what I was about to do would piss Roger off, but when Toby Saunders and half the Crime Squad got nicked, I thought he'd understand.

"I'm afraid so. You see, I'm a committed atheist. I do not believe god exists, he is a completely man made phenomenon."

I looked around the committee; there were more than a few shocked faces. I felt like I'd committed, what in freemasonry terms, amounted to a mortal sin.

"In that case, Christopher, can I thank you for coming but, unfortunately, the committee will be unable to support your application. I hope you are not too disappointed."

"Of course, not; I understand, completely." I replied, standing up and holding out my hand.

~~~

When I got back to the Section House, I met Andy in the corridor. He'd just had a shower.

"How're you feeling, mate?" I asked, aware that he had been rough, lately.

"Going to the doctors again, today, Nostrils. I am having lots of tests. Last time I saw him, he said he doesn't think it's too serious. He said something about being anaemic. I must admit, I feel a bit better today."

"I can hear you coughing sometimes, is there more to it than that?" I asked, genuinely concerned.

"I am really tired, all the time; and in the middle of the night, I wake up in a cold sweat. I mean the bed is soaking with sweat but I'm not especially hot." Andy explained.

"I'm sorry, mate. At least you've seen a doctor now, so you should be able get it sorted."

"Talking about hearing through these paper-thin walls …"

Andy lowered his voice.

"...was Paul Pollock in your room the other night? The night before he, you know..."

"Come on in." I said, not wanting to have that conversation where we might be overheard.

Andy made himself comfortable on the end of the bed. I stood looking out of the window at the comings and goings in the back yard.

"He was here, yes. He'd come to front me out about Sarah and still had his gun from jury protection." I said.

"I guessed as much. Well, I guessed he'd come about Sarah. Where is she anyway? There are wild rumours circulating that she's gone to CIB." Andy said.

"Listen, Andy. No one knows Paul was in this room, that night. Please keep it to yourself." I implored him.

I didn't want to complicate matters by telling him Ben also knew; besides, that might be a step too close to the truth.

"Of course, you wanker. I didn't mention it until now because it all seems to be dying down. What do you take me for, anyway? What about what they're saying about Sarah? If anyone knows where she's gone, then you must Nostrils?" Andy asked me.

I really didn't know what to say. I hated lying to Andy, but I wasn't sure I should tell him all that I knew. I changed the subject hoping he wouldn't notice.

"I've got to see the Chief Superintendent, tomorrow." I said and pulled a mock grimace.

"What's that about then?" Andy asked.

"No idea." I replied.

"Nostrils, do me a favour?"

The change in tone in Andy's voice made me turn to look him in the face.

"What?" I said.

"Sit down. I've got something to tell you. I think it might be something to do with you meeting the Chief Superintendent tomorrow. Don't over react, will you?"

"What is it?" I asked, feeling suddenly nervous.

I sat down.

"Right, listen, carefully. I was in trap three yesterday. Two guys come in chatting; now I recognise one of them as DS Cotton, but I can't say who the other one was, but I'm guessing he's a suit. I'm not really listening until your name's mentioned."

"Go on" I said, cautiously.

"The other guy says the DCI's not very happy about Pritchard. DS Cotton says, Pritchard? And the guy says, you know the kid on C relief that was blown up, and Cotton says, oh, Nostrils, yeah; I know who you mean. What's wrong with him? I've always found him alright."

I was pleased to hear someone saying something, well almost nice, about me.

"The guy says, the DCI's got no choice, it's come from right up high. Cotton asks, is it because of, you know what? The other guy doesn't say anything so I'm guessing he's nodded. Cotton asks, how many people know? And the guy says top secret. Cotton says, how long will he do? The guy says two years, but it obviously depends on his behaviour."

I felt sick, not just a little sick, nauseous.

"You alright, Nostrils? You look really ill?"

I took three paces across the small Section House room and threw up in my sink.

Chapter 66

I went sick. I couldn't face night duty.

It was the longest night of my life. Longer than the night after my Mum died, longer than my first night in hospital after the bombing, longer even than the other night spent with a drunken, armed, and suicidal, Paul Pollock.

I thought I'd got away with it, I really did. I'd buried the money, hadn't told a soul, and kept my head down but, apparently, somehow, someone had discovered what I'd done. I was going to do two years, which would mean I would be sentenced to four and released after I'd served half, unless I misbehaved. It wasn't going to be easy inside, there were horrendous stories about what happens to police officers, when they're sent down.

I'd heard an account about one ex old bill who went to prison and had his anus cut with a razor. He was then buggered every day, so that, on each occasion, the wound would open up again. I'd heard another story about a police officer being jugged, that's where a prisoner gets a jug of boiling water and adds a load of sugar to it to make it into syrup, which is thrown into someone's face. The skin burns so badly, it peels off.

These stories were apocryphal but nonetheless scary. I'd have to go on Rule 43. This would mean I would be separated from the normal prisoners and living with all the nonces and rapists.

I didn't sleep at all, not for one minute. I kept turning over in my mind the following day's likely sequence of events. I guessed I was seeing the Chief Superintendent, so I could be formally suspended from duty and my warrant card taken from me. Then a senior officer from CIB would arrest and caution me. My Section House and car would be searched, and I would be transported to another nick, probably one in the West End, like Paddington or Charing Cross.

There I would be booked in and allowed to contact a Federation Rep who would arrange for me to have a solicitor. Probably the next day, I'd be in a police cell overnight, I would be interviewed under caution. Sometime later, probably in the early evening, I would be charged with theft and kept in custody to go to Bow Street Magistrates Court the next day.

Particularly in light of Sarah's cooperation, I wondered whether they would try to turn me. That is, try to persuade me to make a statement about other officers at Stoke Newington and what they'd done wrong. I probably knew enough about the fitting up of the innocent woman and Mr, or should I say Worshipful Master, Toby Saunders, to fill in a few gaps for them. I also knew a lot of other stuff, but it went against the grain to start dropping other people in the shit, just because I'd been caught doing something stupid.

I couldn't imagine I'd be remanded in custody awaiting trial. I mean, living as I do in police accommodation, if I did try to do a bunk, it's going to be pretty obvious, very quickly. And what with my CICB payout I could put down quite a significant surety.

I tried to estimate what sentence I'd get. If I could prove I'd given all the money to charity, showed a good portion of remorse, played on the fact I'd been blown up and pleaded guilty, I reckoned I could possibly get it down to three years. So, what DS Cotton had said about two years, wasn't far from my own estimate. With remission, I'd be out in eighteen months. It was not what I wanted to do but I knew I could manage eighteen months. The hardest bit would be picking my life up afterwards. I'd never get a job with a previous conviction for theft. I formed some vague notion about going abroad to work, perhaps in a bar in Spain, or something like that.

I was glad my Mum wasn't alive to see this pathetic tragedy unfold; it would have broken her heart. She was always ridiculously proud of everything I did.

By the time the sun rose on a damp and miserable March morning in Stoke Newington, I'd sort of reconciled myself to my fate. The only small query in my mind was what exactly was I going to be arrested for? My money was on the theft but, there was an outside chance, it would be something to do with Paul's suicide or, even perhaps, destroying the message from Toby Saunders to Paul. The *timing* of the arrest suggested it was more likely to be something to do with that.

I packed a small suitcase with some clothing, toiletries and several books, in the hope they'd let me take it with me, when they arrested me. I hid two packets of cigarettes and a box of matches in a pair of socks.

I looked at my watch in the forlorn hope that time had somehow raced magically forward. It hadn't. I still had six hours to wait, so I took a long shower and shaved. I would make sure I got a good lunch because the food you got in police cells was rubbish and always cold, as it had to come across from the canteen, where it had probably waited for ages to be collected.

As I got in the shower, Andy was getting out.

"Fuck me, mate; you spend more time in the shower than you do in bed. Are you queer or what?" I said, with all the cheerfulness I could muster.

Andy laughed.

"How you feeling this morning, Nostrils?"

"Yea fine. I didn't know what came over me last night. I just felt really sick, all of a sudden. Perhaps I'm getting what you've got." I lied.

"Perhaps." Andy replied, disbelievingly.

I smiled weakly.

"When you've had your shower, come and see me. We'll talk it over, you know, whatever is worrying you, I've always been a good listener, you know that." Andy said.

I nodded and, ten minutes later, I was sitting in his room, a mug of piping hot tea in my hand and several chocolate biscuits melting in the other. I didn't know how I was going to play this. I knew it was unwise to tell anyone what I'd done but there was a huge part of me that wanted to talk about it and there was no one I'd rather talk to than Andy.

"Nostrils, what's up, mate? You haven't been yourself, lately; and then, yesterday, your reaction to what I told you was ..."

"I know." I replied, before he'd finished his sentence.

"Why are you so worried?" He asked.

"Wouldn't you be worried if you found out you might be going to prison for two years?" I replied.

"Nostrils, my old friend; I wouldn't be worried unless I'd actually done something which was capable of getting me sent down, and I haven't, so I'm not." Andy said, his logic was of course unarguable.

I sipped my tea and dunked a biscuit.

"Well?" Andy asked.

"Well, what?" I replied.

"Don't be a wanker, Nostrils. What are you so worried about? Is it to do with what happened to Paul?"

I shook my head.

There was a sharp knock at the door.

"Yes." Andy shouted, an element of frustration was detectable in his voice.

"Sergeant Bellamy here; you looked out the window?"

Andy and I looked at each other and got up.

Andy walked over and opened the door, and I looked out the window. The rear yard was swarming with suits, and I didn't recognise any of them. I'd never seen it so busy.

Sergeant Bellamy came in.

"What the fuck is going on?" I asked.

"CIB are raiding the nick, they're everywhere." Sergeant Bellamy explained.

The three of us vied to look out of the window.

"Listen boys, have a think. If you've got anything in your rooms you shouldn't have, now might be a good time to lose it." Sergeant Bellamy suggested.

Andy and I shook our heads.

"I'm clean." Andy said.

"Me, too." I replied.

"Nostrils, the Chief Superintendent wants to see you, now." Sergeant Bellamy said.

"But I'm seeing him at two o'clock, Sarge." I replied.

"No, you're not, you're seeing him, now. I suspect something else might have cropped up, don't you?"

"Like fifty rubber healers stomping all over his nick." Andy said.

"Precisely, Andy. Now put your uniform on and get over and see him."

~~~

I dressed quickly but carefully and with pride. I wanted to look good, if this was the last time I would wear the uniform. Before I set off, I took one final glance in the full-length mirror on the wall by the door. I was only twenty-one but the eyes of the image that stared back had seen a great deal of life. I'd come a long way too. I remembered my disastrous first few months but, under Dawn's patient tutelage, I'd got there in the end. I missed Dawn, I missed my Mum, too, but I was glad neither of them were here on this dreadful morning.

I left my door unlocked, as it would make it easier if they were coming in to search, and I stepped outside. Andy was standing there in the corridor. He looked serious, as if he sensed all my fears.

"Hello, mate." I said, quietly.

I held out my hand, but he shook his head dismissing such a formal gesture.

"Come here, my friend." He said and drew me into the warmest embrace.

When he let go, I felt tears running down my cheeks but I wasn't embarrassed because this was Andy, the only male police officer in London, who would not judge me for such an open show of emotion.

~~~

By the time I passed Sergeant Bellamy in his office, I had wiped all trace of the tears away and smiled as he wished me a cheerful 'good luck'.

I walked across a back yard full of unfamiliar faces and vehicles. Several of the suits were carrying lockers, up from the basement to a large white van, which was obviously on hire.

The Chief Superintendent's office was up in the gods on the third floor of the nick in, what had once been, the attic. As I got to the first floor, I noticed that the Crime Squad office had been sealed off with police tape and another CIB officer was standing guard, presumably to stop anyone entering. I kept walking.

As I neared the Chief Superintendent's outer office, I checked my back trouser pocket and felt my warrant card for the last time.

The Chief Superintendent's secretary was a kind older black lady called Beverley who everyone loved. She smiled at me as I entered, she obviously felt sorry for me.

"Hello, Christopher, my darling. Can you just wait a few moments? The boss is with someone." She said.

I nodded and tried to smile back but this time it was one false gesture too far. I slumped into one of two chairs in a very small waiting area, squashed in a corner, under an eve. From inside the Chief Superintendent's office, I could hear muffled voices and I imagined that I could be in for a long wait.

I was wrong. No sooner had I settled down than the door opened, and two men walked out. The Chief Superintendent himself didn't emerge but Beverley darted into his office, presumably, to tell him I was outside. She came back out a few seconds later.

"You can go in Christopher." She said.

I stood up, brushed myself down, straightened up my jacket and tie, took a deep breath and walked in.

The Chief Superintendent was looking down at something on his desk, and didn't even look up, when I entered. As I hadn't been invited to do otherwise, I remained standing. As the seconds ticked by, I assumed the at ease position, with my legs slightly apart and my hands behind my back.

I looked more closely at what was on his desk. It was an IRB, an Incident Report Book, and from the handwriting, it looked like one of mine.

Still staring down, the Chief Superintendent spoke.

"PC Pritchard?"

"Sir?"

"When you make notes at an incident, should those notes accurately reflect what you've done?" The Chief Superintendent asked.

Obviously, mine hadn't but the question only invited one response.

"Yes, Sir." I replied.

"I have a note book in front of me, dated the 3rd February 1985, it is completed by you."

My mind raced quickly to that date, yes that was it, I was pretty certain that was the day I searched the old lady's house. I said nothing.

"It is significantly lacking in detail." The Chief Superintendent commented.

I didn't know what to say. What did he mean, by lacking in detail? I was hardly going to record the fact that I'd stolen six thousand pounds, was I?

"Well?" He barked, his temper clearly rising.

"I'm sorry, Sir." Was all I could reply.

"You see your notes say…I assisted the man to leave the premises."

"Sorry?" I asked, generally confused.

"Your notes say, I assisted the man to leave the premises but I have another version of events."

The Chief Superintendent looked up, for the first time, during our conversation. He looked really stern.

"Sorry?" I said.

The Chief Superintendent put my notes to one side and picked up a hand-written letter which had been lying underneath them.

"It was an act of bravery at least equal to, if not surpassing, anything I have ever seen. I trust Her Majesty will see that this officer receives the recognition he deserves." The Chief Superintendent said, reading from the letter.

"Sorry?" I repeated.

"Pritchard. The blind man you saved when his house was on fire, he, or rather his daughter, on his behalf, wrote a letter. In his letter, a copy of which I have here, he describes how you fought your way through a burning building, filled with choking smoke, to carry him to safety. The letter says, it was an act of bravery at least equal to, if not surpassing, anything he had ever seen."

"The blind man, his name was Wheatley, he was really nice." I said, recalling the incident, which seemed to have happen a lifetime ago.

"His full name Police Constable Christopher Pritchard, is Major Retired James Archibald Wheatley Veceey."

I frowned; it seemed a strange surname and I thought, perhaps, it might have overtones of the Indian sub-continent.

"When such an opinion about your courage is proffered by a veteran of the last war, it holds some credibility. When it is proffered by a recipient of the Victoria Cross, it is likely to carry considerable influence. Well, Her Majesty certainly thought so because she, or rather her Principal Private Secretary, wrote, on Her behalf, to the Commissioner with Her recommendation that you be awarded the QGM, son."

"Sorry?" I said.

"The Queens Gallantry Medal, son. It's just one below the George Medal."

"Sorry?"

My legs started to shake, and then my whole body started to tremble.

"Well done." The Chief Superintendent said.

"Thank you, Sir." I replied, meekly.

Veceey wasn't Mr Wheatley's surname, Veceey meant VC, Victoria Cross.

"We need young men like you in this job, now perhaps, more than ever before. From Monday you will start a two-year posting on the new Crime Squad which will be based down at Dalston. As you may have gathered, we've had one or two issues with the old one."

"Issues, Sir?" I asked.

"Yes Pritchard, about an hour ago, twelve of them were arrested for an assortment of serious criminal offences. It's reassuring to know that I can be proud of at least one officer at this police station."

He came around the side of his desk and held out his hand.

I shook it. What else could I do?

Chapter 67

As I turned to leave the Chief Superintendent's office, my trembling intensified so, rather than go straight through his secretary's office and out, I sat back down on the seat I had only, a minute or two ago, vacated. I looked at my hand, it was really shaking.

"Are you alright?" Beverley asked, momentarily pausing her typing.

"I'm fine, I just feel a bit shaky, I think I must be coming down with something. My next-door neighbour in the Section House has had the flu and I think I must have caught it from him."

I replied.

The Chief Superintendent called from his office.

"Beverley, get Pritchard back. I forgot to tell him about that other matter."

I stood up and held out an open palm to Beverly to indicate that I had heard the boss.

"I'm still here, Sir." I said and walked back into his office.

"It's nothing to worry about, son, but PC Young has made an allegation of racial harassment against you." He said.

"Who?" I replied, although as soon as the word left my lips, I realised, of course, that he was talking about Kitty.

"Kitty Young, the half-caste WPC, on your relief." He replied.

"I know, Sir, Inspector Portman mentioned it." I replied, suddenly grasping what he was talking about but still in a state of shock about the award.

"It's nothing to worry about, sonny. It's not just you, it's her Sergeant at Training School, the Street Duties Sergeant and yourself. According to the letter I've just read from her solicitor, you've all been treating her differently because she's not white."

"That's bollocks, Sir. She's a lazy bitch, I'd have treated anyone, who acted like she did, just the same." I said.

"I know, son. Listen, you'll have to make a statement at some point to our solicitors, and you may have to give evidence at a tribunal, if it goes that far, but that'll be a long time in the future. Now, get on with yourself, and congratulations again about your gong."

When I walked down the stairs and across the back yard, I was in something of a daze. The suits from CIB were still going about their business. Twelve arrests I thought, hell, that's over half the Crime Squad.

I had so many things going round in my mind. I was desperately trying to put everything into context. My missing file was explained by the bravery award thing, presumably they'd drawn it in respect of that. The conversation Andy had overheard, in which DS Cotton said I'd do a minimum two years, wasn't prison, it was a posting on the Crime Squad; which, of course, reconciled with what I'd heard from Paul's brother Simon, who worked at Chingford. As I'd already kind of figured out, the theft which Ben had mentioned hearing my name in connection with, wasn't the old lady's money, but the theft of the pedigree dogs from the kennels. I was probably an early suspect as, by coincidence, I'd dealt with several of the mutts that had been stolen. Slowly, but surely, the picture was coming into focus in my mind's eye and, what was becoming ever clearer, was that none of the events of the last month had anything to do with my theft of the old lady's money. I was in the clear.

Was I still glad that I'd done what I'd done to make amends? Absolutely and unequivocally, yes. I hated being a thief, being like all the other dishonest cops. I had done everything in my power to atone for my mistake, even fined myself, one hundred thousand pounds. Now, I could move on with the rest of my career, safe in the knowledge, that never again, under any circumstances, whatsoever, would I steal so much as a paperclip.

Instead of going back to my room straight away, I wandered into the canteen and bought myself a full fat fry up. I'd hardly had anything to eat, lately, and now, all of a sudden, my appetite had returned with a vengeance.

The atmosphere in the canteen was subdued and I noticed there wasn't a single CID officer anywhere. If my best guess was right, they would be meeting somewhere in private to try to establish how far the corruption investigation would reach and to take all possible steps to extricate themselves from its implications.

As I walked into the Section House, I popped my head round old Bellamy's door; his head was down, and he was writing in the Occurrence Book.

"Bloody hell, Sarge; don't tell me you've got some work to do?" I said, cheerfully.

Sergeant Bellamy looked up, and he looked serious.

"What is it, Skip?" I asked, my voice now lower, serious.

"Go and see your mate, Andy."

"What's happened, Sarge?" I asked.

"Go and see him; he's in his room."

I took the stairs two at a time and rounded the landing corner so quickly I nearly collided with a pretty woman who I'd never seen before. She was obviously sneaking out of some PC's room, having spent the night with him.

I went to go into my room with the intention of dumping my helmet, jacket, and tie on the bed before knocking next door but as I turned my key, what I saw written in red spray paint on Andy's door, stopped me in my tracks.

Chapter 68

I knocked quietly on Andy's door, and he answered so quickly that he must have been waiting for me.

"Is it true?" I asked.

Andy closed his eyes and nodded, slowly.

"Fucking hell, fucking hell, mate; no!" I said.

I slumped onto Andy's unmade bed, and he sat down beside me.

"Who knows?" I asked.

Andy looked at his watch.

"Well, because of our friendly graffiti artist, any second now..." he waited, as if allowing a second to pass.

"...about everyone, I would think. I was going to tell you, my friend, but recently you seem to have the weight of the world on your shoulders."

"How long have you known?" I asked.

"Just over a week. I'm HIV positive at the moment; it hasn't developed into the full-blown disease yet. I had some more results through yesterday and saw the Consultant, again."

"Oh, Andy; I'm so sorry." I said.

Of course, I'd heard of HIV and AIDS, it was in the news virtually every day, but I never thought I'd know anyone who would get it; especially not my best friend. It seemed impossible.

"Are the doctors sure. They do make mistakes, you know?" I said.

Andy didn't reply, he just smiled, gently.

"So, what's going to happen? How long have you got?" I asked.

"Listen, the consultant's really upbeat. He reckons you can survive for years, even up to a decade. The treatment's much more effective these days and there's loads of research going on, all the time."

That was so typically Andy, always upbeat, always so positive.

"Who the fuck has done that on your door, if no one else knew?" I asked, suddenly remembering the four words *WARNING AIDS INFESTED QUEER,* which were written on his door.

"I had to tell the Job. The Consultant insisted because of the risk of infection. I told my relief Inspector and he contacted the CMO to make an appointment. Obviously, someone somewhere has got to hear about it."

"If, when I find out who wrote that on your door, I'll fucking ..."

I squeezed my right hand into a fist. I could feel the temper rising up inside me.

"I'll punch their fucking, lights out; mother fucking bastards."

I was shaking with rage.

"Calm down, Nostrils. Whoever has written that, is just a sad bitter individual. What good would it do to punch his lights out? Except perhaps lose you your job?"

He was right of course. It would do no good at all, but it would make me feel a lot better.

I shook my head, my temper subsiding.

"But when did they write it? An hour ago, there was nothing there. You know, when you'd just got out the shower."

"I know. I got dressed and popped down to the Chemist to pick up a load of drugs..."

Andy pointed to a carrier bag full of medicines on his sink.

"...and when I got back, there it was. Just as I was about to wash it off, old skinny came along and read it. He was furious and wants me to report it but I'm not sure that's for the best."

"Oh, Andy, I'm so sorry."

"I'll be alright, Nostrils. I'm coming to terms with it." Andy said, defiantly.

I looked at him, really looked at him to try to ascertain whether he could possibly be as calm about it as he seemed.

"Well, what did the Chief Superintendent want?" Andy asked.

"Oh nothing, it was just about Kitty. You now the lazy bitch, the probationer that fell on that dead body? She's alleging racial abuse or something against me and a couple of skippers."

I didn't want to mention the bravery award, not at that moment anyway.

"Is that all? You looked so worried, you thought it was about something else, didn't you?

"Andy, that's not important. Tell me what I can do to help you with this AIDS thing?" I asked.

"That's the thing." He replied.

"I don't get you?"

"You haven't thought it through, like I have. You're going to have to distance yourself from me, now. You can't be my best mate, if you want to survive the pit of hellfire that's about to erupt."

Andy was right. The wider implications of what had happened were starting to sink in on me. If it was common knowledge, he was homosexual, which it would be, shortly, some people would be reticent about working with him. If it was common knowledge that he was HIV positive, no one would work with him, and some would even refuse to live in the same Section House.

"How infectious is it?" I asked.

"You're safe, Nostrils." He replied, defensively, and I knew I'd said the wrong thing.

"I didn't mean that Andy. I meant, will you be allowed to keep working? You know dealing with the public and everything?"

"That's why I've got to see the CMO. He'll make that decision. As far as I'm aware, I'm the first police officer to get it. For the time being, I've gone sick with flu but that's a bit pointless, now, because the whole nicks going to know the truth."

"Jesus, Andy. You got one pile of shit to deal with." I said.

"And to cap it all, I gotta tell my parents." He said.

I didn't know what to say, I really didn't. In the last week, whilst I'd been so wrapped up in my own impending arrest and imprisonment, my best friend had learnt that he had an incurable disease, the revelation of which, would effectively cost him his job and his home and, potentially, rupture his relationship with his family.

"Oh, I nearly forgot. I've also got to track down everyone I've had sex with and tell them the good news." Andy added.

"Do you know how you got it?" I asked.

"I think so. You know Dominic?"

"No." I replied.

"You do, Dominic Class, Roger's brother." Andy explained.

"The one that died from cancer. I didn't know his first name."

"That's him. I've discovered that he didn't die from cancer. He died from AIDS but his family didn't tell anyone, you know, they were too ashamed, so they told everyone he died from cancer."

"How did you find that out?" I asked.

"I spoke to a mutual friend who eventually admitted it to me."

We sat in silence for too long. We never had nothing to say, but we had nothing to say, then.

"Fancy a pint?" I said, breaking the eternal silence.

"I can't drink, with the medication I'm on, I can't even bloody drink."

The silence returned.

"What you going to do about the door?" I asked.

"Leave it." He replied, and for the first time I felt him crack.

I turned to face him and looked directly into his eyes. A single tear ran down his right cheek. I put my hand across and rubbed his right thigh. His own hand reached down and took my own. I squeezed.

I was on the point of tears, but I wanted to be strong, to be there for Andy, just like he'd been there for me, after the bombing. I don't know how I'd have got through it, without his help. Now it was time for me to return the favour.

"I'm so sorry." I whispered.

He looked down and slowly shook his head. He grimaced, as if in deep pain.

"I'll be here for you, my friend." I assured him.

"You can't be; everyone will turn against you. I understand, Nostrils, I really do. You must walk away; it's the only path open to you."

Andy was right. AIDS was really easy to catch, everyone knew that. If the others knew I was seeing Andy, every day, looking after him through his illness, they would treat me as if I had the disease, too. No one would work with me. What's more everyone knew we were the very best of friends. The best thing for me to do, would be to distance myself from him, pretend like it was news to me, too. Supporting Andy, now, would almost certainly be the end of my career, and, after all I'd been through, too. I didn't really have a choice, if I stuck by my friend my career would come crashing down. I didn't consider my options for long.

"My friend. Whatever happens, however long this lasts, I will be by your side. I promise, you will never have to deal with any of this, alone." I said.

"But what about everyone else, what will they think?" Andy asked.

"Fuck 'em." I said quietly, defiantly.

Tears were rolling down Andy's face, but he smiled.

"Fuck 'em all." I said.

If you've enjoyed From Black to Blue, then you must read the final book in the trilogy...

Blue to Brown

It is two years later, and Chris Pritchard is a Detective Sergeant working at the Complaints Investigation Bureau.

The poacher turned gamekeeper quickly settles into the Bureau's unique work investigating allegations that serving police officers have committed some of the most serious criminal offences.

Christopher enquiries include an allegation of burglary, a blackmailer targeting London's Asian community and the theft of twenty-four thousand pounds from a police savings fund, but he becomes obsessed with the case of an old colleague, who appears to have vanished into the secret world of freemasonry.

Please go to **Amazon.co.uk** to download and *please* don't forget to post a review on this book.

Printed in Great Britain
by Amazon